DEEP DOWN

THE NEW

DEEP DOWN

SENSUAL WRITING BY WOMEN

Edited by

LAURA CHESTER

Faber and Faber

Boston and London

to the memory of Anaïs Nin

This paperback edition first published in 1989.

Copyright © 1988 by Laura Chester
The acknowledgments on pp. 325-30 constitute an extension of this copyright notice

Library of Congress Cataloging-in-Publication Data
Deep down.
1. Erotic literature, American—Women authors.
2. Erotic literature—Women authors. 3. Women—
Sexual behavior—Literary collections. 4. American
literature—20th century. I. Chester, Laura.
PS509.E7D44 1988   810'.8'03538   87-33202
ISBN 0-571-12968-4 (pabk.)

Printed in the United States of America

"Those pleasures so lightly called physical."

—Colette: *Mélanges*

○○ ○○ ○○

PREFACE

I would like to thank my editor, Betsy Uhrig, my cousin, Isabelle Chester, and several friends: Francine Segan, Larry and Nancy Goldstone, Jill Johnson, Christine Schutt, and Mildred Elman, who have helped me with this manuscript in its various stages.

oo oo oo

CONTENTS

Introduction — 1

TO GIVE AND HAZARD ALL

SHE FLUVIAL

DEAR ENEMIES

PURE SEX

THE YIELD

oo oo oo

INTRODUCTION

Is it possible that women's writing has undergone a sex change? I am tempted to say yes, for I feel that the poetry and prose written by women in the past decade has become more truly *female*, and by that I mean more vitalized, self-affirming, and whole. Not only has the writing of women become a greater part of the literary dynamic as new forms have pushed new limits, but the writing has blossomed inward, into the realm of the feminine—how wonderful not to have to "admit" that, but to applaud it.

In the mid-seventies, John Updike proclaimed Erica Jong's *Fear of Flying*, "the most uninhibited, delicious, erotic novel a woman ever wrote," and though this novel almost looks tame today, I think that it was a pivotal book. Certainly since that time there has been a remarkable freeing-up within the work of women writers, who have gone on to explore this theme of sensuality with an almost gleeful daring, extending the dialogue between the sexes, vocalizing a once submerged desire.

Aphrodite may well be springing forth again to dazzle the world anew, rising from the depths after having been immersed. But anything newly emerging can be perceived as a threat to that which is familiar. It is particularly threatening when the primal image of constancy and security is involved, especially when she is loosening her garments, not for the sake of nourishment, but so that she can better breathe, so that she can really sing. She is no longer the "angel artist with celestially muted lower parts," as Hortense Calisher put it, for the new woman artist is writing stronger, more compelling work as she draws from her feminized sexual energy.

It was not to encourage separatism, but only a further unveiling that I decided to propose this anthology. It became quickly apparent that I was merely initiating something which had been simmering across the continent, on the minds and in the work of many different women. The response I received from an ever-expanding network of writers was charged with enthusiasm, and the support I received inspiring.

I didn't approach this project with a preconceived format, but I did know that I only wanted to include serious, literary work, and I believe that the import of this particular collection will be the artistic level it maintains. These writers are not kitchen beginners. They aren't being paid to glamorize or titillate, nor are they writing work specifically for my purpose. These works exist beyond posture, cleverness, wit, or mere skill; they exhibit a knowledge and understanding that can only be earned through art and nerve. I do think that it is through literature that we can best begin to understand the emerging self, rising "from the genital wave," as Charles Olson wrote, and to enjoy its gradual unfolding. The writing here gives access.

The focus of this anthology goes way beyond localized desire, leading us to a more diaphanous enticement, where sensuality penetrates every aspect of the world. As Lydia Davis writes in *This Condition:*

> anything round and freely hanging, as tassels on a
> curtain, as chestnut burrs on a twig in spring. . . .
> anything sliding back and forth; anything sliding in and
> out with an oiled surface, as certain machine parts;
> anything of a certain shape, like the state of Florida;
> anything pounding, anything stroking, anything bolt
> upright . . .

I wanted this collection to be inclusive, open, not boxed in by one genre. Both prose and poetry offer valuable, yet different kinds of perception, moving from the more direct look to the subtler glance. Some of the most exciting new work I found lay somewhere between poetry and prose, but I mainly wanted to include the best work I could find and show the vitality and variety of our *jouissance*.

As material began to pour in, it naturally fell into various sections. It seemed logical to begin with "Early On," for it is in childhood that the core sensual self takes form. Those earliest experiences—how the little girl relates to her father, brothers, and boyfriends; how her mother deals with her as a sensual female being; whether she is rejected, tolerated, accepted, or loved—can set a pattern for life. Many of these opening pieces are written with a gentle lifting of the curtain, moving on to the racier energy of the teenage years. Some of the harsher realities, such as sexual abuse, are included as well. Given our protective stance, this theme is a particularly difficult, yet important area for women to expose. This anthology is not presented as provocation, it does not align itself with the maltreatment of anyone, but it is also a literary document, whose purpose is to show, not to condemn.

Hopefully this collection will help dispel some of the clichés that have attached themselves to the female body. I think of some of the demeaning names commonly used—piece of ass, slut, ballbreaker— and realize that women's sexuality has been labelled like this primarily because of its magnitude. There has been a shadow cast over that part of our beings, as if our sex dwelt in the cave-sucking underearth, relating to darkness and to death, the devouring dark side of nature. But all of these images are gradually changing, and this collection is part of a greater impulse to redeem the physicality of women, to bring the female body back into the light.

Still, this is a slow process, and there is much justifiable anger coming in response to the physical and emotional abuse many women have suffered, often from those they love most. The section entitled "Dear Enemies" takes a hard look at this area, where the tension between the sexes can come close to intolerable. Women often do seem to suffer in sexual-emotional relationships that are off balance, possibly because they are more apt to "Give and Hazard All." In this section we see how love and relationship can take on such significance that the hazards seem slight compared to the thrill of making that leap into the arms of uncertain love.

But our world is still a pretty hard, time-obsessed, materialistic place, and though a woman's response to that can be an excess of highly charged romantic feeling, as if in an effort to fire up, keep molten, the hardening processes of our times, it can also become correspondingly cooler. In the section "Looking at Him," the love object becomes the sex object, and the pursuer becomes the perceived. Taking it one step further, women have also begun to reflect the traditionally male perspective in regards to "Pure Sex," enjoying a physicality which is devoid of emotional trappings, choosing the health club over the honeymoon. But, as Sharon Olds questions, "How do they do it, the ones who make love/ without love?"

Sex without love was in the past usually associated with the male urge, and those incidents were graciously overlooked because they didn't mean anything. But even *that* tells us something, that something is missing, and I believe that most women, most people, ultimately want more. This collection shows more as it takes us deeper down.

How do women really feel, *deep down*. Long submerged images surface; old feelings of rage and ecstasy rise. Women's writing has dealt keenly with emotional life, our forte, but the writing here wants to dive deeper still, taking us down to gut level, to the level of the sexual chakra, unembarrassed enough to dare honesty, to see and tell it all. I believe this book will kindly topple the pedestal mounted for that honored, sexless image of the revered woman, who is really a kind of untouchable, out of physical reach. In "Pedestal Madonna" Lyn Lifshin writes:

> He puts her up
> on a pedestal
> and she goes
> down on it.

Meanwhile, some women jump down, turn around, and say, What's the big deal, who needs all this phallic imagery? "She Fluvial" focuses on how women perceive each other in this sensual mode. I found a great deal of relief and rejoicing here, where women admitted to their own desire and appreciation for each other, and this was true within heterosexual as well as lesbian lifestyles. This section seems to reflect the process of self-love, at times relating back to the bond with the mother, trying to find the right mirror. Or, in some cases, it is clearly a sexual preference, a choice apart from the tensions of male-female interaction; or again, simply a place of shelter, where the feminine qualities can come together, as if in a braid, made stronger.

I did not receive a great deal of sensual writing that dealt with the marriage bed, but there seems to be a new trend back toward monogamy, and hopefully books like this one will help keep couples pleasuring each other. The excerpt from Lynne Sharon Schwartz's *Disturbances in the Field* was a difficult inclusion, but for me it dramatized the greatest possible tragedy within a marriage—the loss of children—and how such a devastating occurrence can alter the marriage bed. The numbness, comfort, the failed efforts and new attempts in bed show what many marriages go through on a more casual level. Long-term relationships often ultimately face tragedy of one sort or another, and having that partner there, in the bed, to hang on to, "as a last wrap against the snow," is as necessary as eroticism at other times in our lives.

When I was first married, an older woman on a long plane trip surprised me by saying that she had to use her imagination to keep the sexual relationship alive in her marriage. She implied that she enjoyed it, the dressing up, the ambiance created, and she appeared to be quite a satisfied woman, but I didn't understand why she felt she needed anything beyond her own generous body. Now I've come to understand how imagination can add to the experience, and how writing about the experience with imagination can be an experience of its own, a pleasurable one for others to partake in, for that is ultimately what I hope this book brings to both men and women: pleasure, enjoyment, and delight.

This anthology does cover quite a range of subject and style. It takes on the positive aspects of sexuality as well as the darker side. Even if it is just on the fantasy level, I think the dark side is a very important element to confront, to explore and express. Why are certain disturbing or even humiliating scenes exciting to conjure? How can a woman fantasize about being overpowered by a group of men when she's a feminist? How does a sexual fantasy actually stand apart from a belief system or set of laws? What is it in the primal brain that hits the penny? A lot of this is still a mystery, but it is only through penetrating the darker aspects of the personal and archetypal self that "The Yield" will be made accessible, like the mature, golden harvest it is. That is the reward we are already welcoming, in our lives and through new language.

EARLY ON

JAYNE ANNE PHILLIPS

Sweethearts _____

We went to the movies every Friday and Sunday. On Friday nights the Colonial filled with an oily fragrance of teen-agers while we hid in the back row of the balcony. An aura of light from the projection booth curved across our shoulders, round under cotton sweaters. Sacred grunts rose in black corners. The screen was far away and spilling color—big men sweating on their horses and women with powdered breasts floating under satin. Near the end the film smelled hot and twisted as boys shuddered and girls sank down in their seats. We ran to the lobby before the lights came up to stand by the big ash can and watch them walk slowly downstairs. Mouths swollen and ripe, they drifted down like a sigh of steam. The boys held their arms tense and shuffled from one foot to the other while the girls sniffed and combed their hair in the big mirror. Outside the neon lights on Main Street flashed stripes across asphalt in the rain. They tossed their heads and shivered like ponies.

On Sunday afternoons the theater was deserted, a church that smelled of something frying. Mrs. Causton stood at the door to tear tickets with her fat buttered fingers. During the movie she stood watching the traffic light change in the empty street, pushing her glasses up over her nose and squeezing a damp Kleenex. Mr. Penny was her skinny yellow father. He stood by the office door with his big push broom, smoking cigarettes and coughing.

Walking down the slanted floor to our seats we heard the swish of her thighs behind the candy counter and our shoes sliding on the worn carpet. The heavy velvet curtain moved its folds. We waited, and a cavernous dark pressed close around us, its breath pulling at our faces.

After the last blast of sound it was Sunday afternoon, and Mr. Penny stood jingling his keys by the office door while we asked to use the phone. Before he turned the key he bent over and pulled us close with his bony arms. Stained fingers kneading our chests, he wrapped us in old tobacco and called us his little girls. I felt his wrinkled heart wheeze like a dog on a leash. Sweethearts, he whispered.

SUMMER BRENNER

from: *The Soft Room* _____

Someone had a dream about me last night
we were in a boat in the desert
marooned for several hours
it's not clear to me now
my only certainty is that I came to this person in a dream
and our bodies made light in a soft room

BUTTONS AND KNIVES

Lying back beside her, Martin slipped off his pants. Martin's feet had gone aquatic, giving themselves to the air like an ocean polyp. There was no resistance. Annie slid over the spread and put her mouth firmly over Martin's lounging sex. She held onto it lightly and strongly, like a snake with a very small pig.

Salad talk from the summer before and the summer before that. Especially in New Mexico where the zucchini came to be enormous, so big that they grew out of their flavor and left only an arctic interior for disappointed faces. By then we'd run out of any new ways to cook the things. Laura's recipe of shredding and sautéing was the best. And everyone could eat this without too many complaints in full view of the mesa, late August lightning storms, violent and very far off.

Martin was a man whose sex was sweetly compatible with her face. Annie began to ride. She pinched her buttocks together, pressing the bell between her legs against the bed. It was a hammock swing held tight and blown from side to side.

Really she didn't think of it as pleasure. That was such a weak expression. Pleasure was just an idea about experience. Her love for the sexual part of her being was as familiar and surprising as watching her random fingers move up and down. Now she let those fingers slip over the smooth insides of Martin's thighs. Find their way back under his well-used sit bones and knead the soft-pressed behind. Everything was working harder and faster. Her fingers digging under and around, stretching the two cheeks apart. Annie's mouth strangled his sex. Her whole body in long motion and her fingers at it too. A small stream of that early melon juice ran down him and over her lips.

Let's get up.
Let's get dressed.
Let's wait til later.
Let's get something to eat.
Let's go visit Jack.
Let's smoke a joint.
Let's make up the bed.
Let's water the plants.
Let's get in the car and drive.
Let's go have a beer.
Let's fuck.

In the room her mother had decorated for her, there were small cherubs printed all over the blue paper and cloth. Annie would search between their legs to get an idea of what it was like. Years before, she had showered with her father, had loved standing under that elaborate jungle. The water would fall over his distorted protrusions onto her small shoulders. There was so much hair. The man was a centaur.

I want to know the dick of an angel.

It didn't make any difference when her mother told her because the words were so awful and the reasons undisclosed. What she really wanted to know was why people fucked. She wanted to know why it felt so good. Why it felt better than anything. Why it was called love making. That was the mystery to her.

The buttons were round. They were smooth. They came in all colors, sizes, shapes. Metal, bone, wood, shell. It was the red cherry buttons that she loved most about the dress. How things fastened. How parts connected. How people undressed. How buttons slipped through the carefully stitched holes. Her legs buttoned the mystery of the smooth good feeling. Buttons. Buttocks. Butter. Bum. Bun. Butt. Ivory. Tusks. Bone needles. Clutch the lips and slip the beating rod wing through the 4 holes in a cross-stitch. Fasten tightly.

That's what she wanted to know. If she could. If she was supposed to. If it was all right. The way it felt so good when she was wearing skirts and standing over floor heaters. And a certain pair of pants whose seams perfectly matched hers, and she could drive and ride at the same time.

In school they'd ask about how it would feel to slide down a razor blade, and everyone hated to hear that said. Everyone would say, Please don't say that again. But then someone would say it again. And Annie would imagine it and twist to get out of the idea. Still the intensity thrilled her, and the rush to get away thrilled her.

Annie transported her button secretly. It was a big secret even to her. And she was a big truck. And her bed had a big post. And when her mother took her to shop, and when her father looked at the choices with smiling interest, she fingered the buttons. And always said that was the part she liked the best.

oo oo oo

SALLY CROFT

Blue

Ocean, its waves tumbling me.
Arms of loving fathers.
My eyes, and Daddy's eyes.

Mother's eyes are brown, her skin
Is fair as new snow. She hates sun,
Hates our vacations on Aunt Belle's farm.

Daddy and me picking corn in the green
Twilight, racing to the raft. Mother
Watches from the shore in her skirts.

Blue laws. June plums.

Waves bully me to shore. My lips
Blue I run home where Daddy is
Carving the evening roast.

                    In the next room, Mother
Shapes the starched napkins into tulips.
Her steps rap against the floor.

Daddy tickles me.
I punch fists he catches
In cupped hands, stalking me, singing

            "Fee Fie Fo Fum
            I smell the blood of an Englishman."

August huckleberries.
A robin's egg.
Bluebeard's forbidden room.

JOAN CHASE

from: *During the Reign*
of the Queen of Persia _____

One early spring evening when Celia was fourteen and the rest of us girls thirteen or nearly so, Uncle Dan came home, carrying the sack of groceries Aunt Libby had ordered over the phone, and saw a troop of boys sprawled around on the porch or hanging from the railings and balustrades. He stopped and asked them if there was some problem, had their mothers forgotten something at the market. They slunk off sideways and kicked the porch steps. But when Celia walked through the front door they came alive and in a fevered sprint backed away, running and hollering, to the far road, their speeding eyes in retreat still fastened on Celia, who smiled vaguely with a certain regal privilege. For a moment Uncle Dan's face was strange to us, unshielded by his bright mocking ironies. Then he recovered. Knew what was what. He appraised her long bare legs, asked if she had taken to going about half naked because of internal or external heat. She huffed, "Oh, Daddy! Don't be so old-fashioned," her face golden-lighted in the sun's reflection off her apricot hair, and she went inside tossing that mane, her legs slightly rigid at the knee, like a leggy colt. Uncle Dan flicked his gray, dust-colored eyes over the rest of us, who were dark-haired, with sallow complexions, or altogether too high-colored; he smiled outright, also an expression rare for him, and he seemed newly primed for the changed direction life was taking.

And after that we knew too that there was something different in Celia. It wasn't just that she was older. It was a confidence that came upon her, suddenly and entirely, so that it didn't matter that summer after summer her hair had swung out with more sun-riffled gleam or that her body had swelled here and tightened there into a figure that was at the same time voluptuous and lissome. Effortlessly she appealed to boys, boys who ever after seemed to wander our place with the innocent milling confusion of lambs for the slaughter. That was what Aunt Libby called them, gazing out. "Those poor souls. They don't know what's hit them." She shook her head and sometimes found fault with Celia as if she were too provocative. "Just look at that butt": she'd frown out toward where Celia was talking fifty miles an hour to some boy, leaning on a car window, her body swiveling, her hair swooping in dips, her smiles tossed like fanciful flowers. We couldn't tell for certain whether Aunt Libby was angry or proud.

Celia's change separated her from the rest of us. She seemed indifferent, didn't need us anymore. We fell back, a little in awe. Where she was bold we were unsure, wondering what Aunt Libby would say. Anxiously we tried for Celia's attention, wanted fiercely to be included. But it was no use, that desire; we could not reach her, or be content without her. So we watched her life ravenously while waiting for her to make some slip. . . .

Everything was changed. At the swimming pool Celia no longer entered the water unless she was thrown in by some boisterous youths, and then she let them, as eagerly, assist her in getting out, their hands now lingering and gentle on her. We peered out onto the front porch, the pack of boys more distant, even as we desired them more. It was seeing the way they waited, with a patient wistfulness for any attention Celia might chance to offer, boys who before had not wanted anything from a girl, that defeated us finally: Celia, in impartial imperious command, standing among them, her hands fixed like delicate fan clasps upon her jutting hips, her mouth small and yet full and piquant, like two sections of an orange. It seemed then that we were the intruders on our front porch, that everything belonged to Celia. We went into town, leaving her the porch while we sneaked into the swimming pool at night, or waited at the "Y" for the arrival of a few boys so that then we could walk the two miles home with our girl friends shadowed by the boys, who circled round us, calling out of the dark, fresh whoops coming nearer then moving further into the dark. Sometimes when we got home we'd stand behind the parlor drapes, up against the climbing roses of the wallpaper, and peek out onto the porch to watch Celia. Then we didn't laugh even to ourselves and there would be the run of saliva inside us, as though we were watching her eating steak.

○○ ○○ ○○

AMY GERSTLER

The Unforeseen _____

In bible times heavenly messengers, disguised as beggars, were everywhere. Divine communiques arrive nowadays via strange mediums. Meanings profuse and profound are inscribed in everyday life's most minor designs: the way glasses and plates rearranged themselves when our backs were turned, how my sisters and I seemed to read each other's minds, and times when something in the attic groaned at such appropriate moments ... these were glimmers, little inklings, of what we longed for. At times, from our window, we'd watch homeless men skulk around our yard, exhibiting big discrepancies between their teeth. Father would send them away. But those poor, prevented messengers! How could Father have known the effects his protections would have on four daughters, stuck in this small town few people ever leave? High hopes erode here, like houseboats sunk into the mud at the bottom of ancient Chinese waterways. We offer God strict, intimate prayers, but perhaps it would be better to simply admit our helplessness and send up waves of that agony instead. The homeless men paced under our windows at dusk, sometimes singing a little: ". . . river Jordan is deep and wide/milk and honey on the other side . . ." Those lyrics, in earthy baritones, sung by shirtless, sweating men, seemed to beckon us toward unchristian vistas. Something in the thirsty way they mouthed the word "milk" made me want to jump down from the window, into their midst, though it was some distance. These were sooty, threatening men, wearing huge weathered boots—whom Father had turned away from our door. Men with cabbage or worse on their breaths. Men on whom all clothing looked baggy and unnatural. Men who washed by sloshing trough-water on their chests and upper arms. We girls pined to be pinned down by something heavy and gruff. One of us would sometimes rub her cheek against a tree trunk, scraping her skin on its bark. There was one man in particular, less well-built than the others. At noon I caught sight of him bending down, across a meadow. When he lifted his head, sunlight shone through his ears, giving them a red glow, and I remembered the blood in him. I could almost see his delicate, hairlike capillaries, and I thought about my downfall.

LYN LIFSHIN

Fitzi in the Yearbook _____

grin muffled but
sneaky slithering
out like his penis
did in the Drive In
a June before I could
imagine anything so
slippery sliding up,
let alone inside
me after months of
Saturdays in my
mother's grey apartment
my sister Joy giggling
behind the couch,
a tongue pressing between
lips should have been
a warning in the
blue Chevy I felt
he was all whale
crashing with his
"now you've done
this to me, you have
to" everything in
me sand he
collapsed on

oo oo oo

DAPHNE MARLATT

from: *Ana Historic* ———————————————————

trying. a trying child. trying it on for size. the role. all that she had been told would make her a woman. (knock, knock.) would she ever be one?

she was walking down the back steps, self-consciously, slowly. it wasn't where she was going but what she was walking, her body, out into the world. not wanting to get anywhere fast (not that headlong rush, two steps at a time, that simple intent where she was one with the going which she identified now as childish.) now she was walking her body as if it were different from her, her body with its new look. (o the luck, to be looked at. o the lack, if you weren't. o the look. looking as if it all depended on it.) peach, she looks a peach in her sweater with its collar at the open and curving neck her neck curves up from, above, now, two mounds, small, but two (too?) peach-coloured lobes (she would almost hide) held, up to the world in her new bra like two hands relentlessly cupping her breasts to view. and her whole body is different now, walks slowly with a certain held-in (she is held, by elastic) grace, hand trailing down the familiar rail of the back steps she no longer wants to jump, her feet turn at the bottom and head slowly toward the carport, to the rockery beyond. she knows where he is, gardening on Saturday as usual in his baggy garden khakis, old hat on to keep the sun off his sensitive face. she will think of something to say (it's lunchtime, Dad), she will stand there self-consciously waiting, idle, smelling the earth his hands turn over as they uproot the last of the autumn dahlias, waiting until he turns to look at her with that quizzical smile, accepting in its affection (hand ruffling her hair when she was younger)—and I suppose you've only just had breakfast, Princess? and she will blush as he looks at her and turn away, sure that he noticed, that he sees how she has become a woman (almost), even another (the other) woman in the house.

yes i tried to efface you, trace myself over you, wanting to be the one looked at, approved by male eyes. "liked" was the word we used. "i think he likes you!" the signal of attention in the intricate game of the look during class, down the hall, on the field, or, finely-timed, the walking home from school on opposite sides of the street.

16

now i'm remembering. not dis- but re-membering. putting things back together again, the things that have been split off, set aside. what did it mean to leave behind that body aroused by the feel of hot wind, ecstatic with the smell of sage, so excited i could barely contain myself as we left pines and high-blue eagle sky, and broke into the arid insect country of the Okanagan with its jumping butterflies, its smell, familiar as apricots, our mouths full of sweet pulp, bare legs sticky with it, hot and itchy against each other, against the pelt of the dog, his rank dog-day smell as we rode the turns of the road down into summer, real summer on our skin—do you remember? how could you not?

we had endless photographs to remind us, you in baggy shorts and blouse, dumping spoonfuls of canned mixed veg on our plates ("Russian Salad for lunch!"), or you in peasant (there's your word again) skirt and blouse, bandanna and hoop earrings, like the gypsies you said we were, camping out. (you wanted a caravan but all we had was the old blue Pontiac and tents. you wanted a son but all you had were three daughters.) the three of us in swimsuits, different ones each year, different shapes and sizes of our growing bodies you presided over, our father invisible behind the camera imaging moments of this female world: eyes glowering with resentment, pudgy arms crossed sullen in front, or else draped around each other, lithe and smiling into tanned apparitions of ourselves. it's not *that* i want to remember, how we looked or thought we ought to look, learning so fast this other looked-at image of ourselves. but how it felt to be alone unseen in the bushes of the canyon, pursuing those strange butterflies that folded themselves into grasshoppers whenever they stopped still. or lying face down in the dank smell of sand, unable to swim, hearing Jan and Marta's shouts splash into thin air, hearing wind rustle high in the cottonwood trees which did not bleed but, rooted to one spot, streamed into sky as i streamed too, feeling my dark insides, liquid now and leaving me, trickle into the sand—and i jumped up, scared, had i left a stain? would it show? the new worries being a woman meant.

i was slimming into another shape, finding a waist, gaining curves, attaining the sort of grace i was meant to have as a body marked *woman*'s. as if it were a brand name. as if there were a standard shape (as remote as the stars') to trim my individual lamp to, gain the stamp of approval for: feminine translated a score of different ways: doll, chick, baby, kitten. diminished to the tyranny of eyes: "was he looking at me?" "did you see how he looked at you?"

boy-crazy you said, shaking your head as we drove, walked, rode obsessed past street corners, sauntered past certain spots on the beach, our heads full of advertising images, converting all action into the passive: to be seen.

oo oo oo

ANN DARR

At Sixteen ───────────────────────────

We come now to the space which is boy-shaped.
It has always been there, filled or unfilled.
Come ride with me on my motor-cycle, we'll do
the whole mile-square by moonlight and we rode,
I clinging to that boy shape with all the girl
shape I was, and the moon made shadows of us
on the corn rows, and we scared ourselves on
the corners, and laughed as loud as we dared
and swung on home before the night could get us.
In the wane of that same moon, he raced the mile alone
and struck an old car parked without its lights
and the night got him, and the moon had to shine
a great many nights before I was sure it wouldn't
get me too. We had been little kids together,
sitting flat out in my sand box, making pies.
We practised kissing in the alley behind his house
and mine. I can still hear the little lights
in his voice that made my nipples stand out straight.

SUSAN MINOT

Lust _____

Leo was from a long time ago, the first one I ever saw nude. In the spring before the Hellmans filled their pool, we'd go down there in the deep end, with baby oil, and like that. I met him the first month away at boarding school. He had a halo from the campus light behind him. I flipped.

Roger was fast. In his illegal car, we drove to the reservoir, the radio blaring, talking fast, fast, fast. He was always going for my zipper. He got kicked out sophomore year.

By the time the band got around to playing "Wild Horses," I had tasted Bruce's tongue. We were clicking in the shadows on the other side of the amplifier, out of Mrs. Donovan's line of vision. It tasted like salt, with my neck bent back, because we had been dancing so hard before.

Tim's line: "I'd like to see you in a bathing suit." I knew it was his line when he said the exact same thing to Annie Hines.

You'd go on walks to get off campus. It was raining like hell, my sweater as sopped as a wet sheep. Tim pinned me to a tree, the woods light brown and dark brown, a white house half-hidden with the lights already on. The water was as loud as a crowd hissing. He made certain comments about my forehead, about my cheeks.

We started off sitting at one end of the couch and then our feet were squished against the armrest and then he went over to turn off the TV and came back after he had taken off his shirt and then we slid onto the floor and he got up again to close the door, then came back to me, a body waiting on the rug.

You'd try to wipe off the table or to do the dishes and Willie would untuck your shirt and get his hands up under in front, standing behind you, making puffy noises in your ear.

He likes it when I wash my hair. He covers his face with it and if I start to say something, he goes, "Shush."

For a long time, I had Philip on the brain. The less they noticed you, the more you got them on the brain.

My parents had no idea. Parents never really know what's going on, especially when you're away at school most of the time. If she met them, my mother might say, "Oliver seems nice" or "I like that one" without much of an opinion. If she didn't like them, "He's a funny fellow, isn't he?" or "Johnny's perfectly nice but a drink of water." My father was too shy to talk to them at all, unless they played sports and he'd ask them about that.

The sand was almost cold underneath because the sun was long gone. Eben piled a mound over my feet, patting around my ankles, the ghostly surf rumbling behind him in the dark. He was the first person I ever knew who died, later that summer, in a car crash. I thought about it for a long time.

"Come here," he says on the porch.

I go over to the hammock and he takes my wrist with two fingers. "What?"

He kisses my palm then directs my hand to his fly.

Songs went with whichever boy it was. "Sugar Magnolia" was Tim, with the line "Rolling in the rushes/down by the riverside." With "Darkness Darkness," I'd picture Philip with his long hair. Hearing "Under my Thumb" there'd be the smell of Jamie's suede jacket.

We hid in the listening rooms during study hall. With a record cover over the door's window, the teacher on duty couldn't look in. I came out flushed and heady and back at the dorm was surprised how red my lips were in the mirror.

One weekend at Simon's brother's, we stayed inside all day with the shades down, in bed, then went out to Store 24 to get some ice cream. He stood at the magazine rack and read through *MAD* while I got butterscotch sauce, craving something sweet.

I could do some things well. Some things I was good at, like math or painting or even sports, but the second a boy put his arm around me, I forgot about wanting to do anything else, which felt like a relief at first until it became like sinking into a muck.

It was different for a girl.

When we were little, the brothers next door tied up our ankles. They held the door of the goat house and wouldn't let us out till we showed them our underpants. Then they'd forget about being after us and when we played whiffle ball, I'd be just as good as them.

Then it got to be different. Just because you have on a short skirt, they yell from the cars, slowing down for a while and if you don't look, they screech off and call you a bitch.

"What's the matter with me?" they say, point-blank.

Or else, "Why won't you go out with me? I'm not asking you to get married," about to get mad.

Or it'd be, trying to be reasonable, in a regular voice, "Listen, I just want to have a good time."

So I'd go because I couldn't think of something to say back that wouldn't be obvious, and if you go out with them, you sort of have to do something.

I sat between Mack and Eddie in the front seat of the pickup. They were having a fight about something. I've a feeling about me.

Certain nights you'd feel a certain surrender, maybe if you'd had wine. The surrender would be forgetting yourself and you'd put your nose to his neck and feel like a squirrel, safe, at rest, in a restful dream. But then you'd start to slip from that and the dark would come in and there'd be a cave. You make out the dim shape of the windows and feel yourself become a cave, filled absolutely with air, or with a sadness that wouldn't stop.

Teenage years. You know just what you're doing and don't see the things that start to get in the way.

Lots of boys, but never two at the same time. One was plenty to keep you in a state. You'd start to see a boy and something would rush over you like a fast storm cloud and you couldn't possibly think of anyone else. Boys took it differently. Their eyes perked up at any little number that walked by. You'd act like you weren't noticing.

The joke was that the school doctor gave out the pill like aspirin. He didn't ask you anything. I was fifteen. We had a picture of him in assembly, holding up an IUD shaped like a T. Most girls were on the pill, if anything, because they couldn't handle a diaphragm. I kept the dial in my top drawer like my mother and thought of her each time I tipped out the yellow tablets in the morning before chapel.

If they were too shy, I'd be more so. Andrew was nervous. We stayed up with his family album, sharing a pack of Old Golds. Before it got light, we turned on the TV. A man was explaining how to plant seedlings. His mouth jerked to the side in a tic. Andrew thought it was a riot and kept imitating him. I laughed to be polite. When we finally dozed off, he dared to put his arm around me but that was it.

You wait till they come to you. With half fright, half swagger, they stand one step down. They dare to touch the button on your coat then lose their nerve and quickly drop their hand so you—you'd do anything for them. You touch their cheek.

The girls sit around in the common room and talk about boys, smoking their heads off.

"What are you complaining about?" says Jill to me when we talk about problems.

"Yeah," says Giddy. "You always have a boyfriend."

I look at them and think, As if.

I thought the worst thing anyone could call you was a cockteaser. So, if you flirted, you had to be prepared to go through with it. Sleeping with someone was perfectly normal once you had done it. You didn't really worry about it. But there were other problems. The problems had to do with something else entirely.

Mack was during the hottest summer ever recorded. We were renting a house on an island with all sorts of other people. No one slept during the heat wave, walking around the house with nothing on which we were used to because of the nude beach. In the living room, Eddie lay on top of a coffee table to cool off. Mack and I, with the bedroom door open for air, sweated and sweated all night.

"I can't take this," he said at 3 A.M. "I'm going for a swim." He and some guys down the hall went to the beach. The heat put me on edge. I sat on a cracked chest by the open window and smoked and smoked till I felt even worse, waiting for something—I guess for him to get back.

One was on a camping trip in Colorado. We zipped our sleeping bags together, the coyotes' hysterical chatter far away. Other couples murmured in other tents. Paul was up before sunrise, starting a fire for breakfast. He wasn't much of a talker in the daytime. At night, his hand leafed about in the hair at my neck.

There'd be times when you overdid it. You'd get carried away. All the next day, you'd be in a total fog, delirious, absent-minded, crossing the street and nearly getting run over.

The more girls a boy has, the better. He has a bright look, having reaped fruits, blooming. He stalks around, sure-shouldered, and you have the feeling he's got more in him, a fatter heart, more stories to tell. For a girl, with each boy it's like a petal gets plucked each time.

Then you start to get tired. You begin to feel diluted, like watered-down stew.

Oliver came skiing with us. We lolled by the fire after everyone had gone to bed. Each creak you'd think was someone coming downstairs. The silver-loop bracelet he gave me had been a present from his girl-friend before.

On vacations, we went skiing, or you'd go south if someone invited you. Some people had apartments in New York that their families hardly ever used. Or summer houses, or older sisters. We always managed to find someplace to go.

We made the plan at coffee hour. Simon snuck out and met me at Main Gate after lights-out. We crept to the chapel and spent the night in the balcony. He tasted like onions from a submarine sandwich.

The boys are one of two ways: either they can't sit still or they don't move. In front of the TV, they won't budge. On weekends they play touch football while we sit on the sidelines, picking blades of grass to chew on, and watch. We're always watching them run around. We shiver in the stands, knocking our boots together to keep our toes warm and they whizz across the ice, chopping their sticks around the puck. When they're in the rink, they refuse to look at you, only eyeing each other beneath low helmets. You cheer for them but they don't look up, even if it's a face-off when nothing's happening, even if they're doing drills before any game has started at all.

Dancing under the pink tent, he bent down and whispered in my ear. We slipped away to the lawn on the other side of the hedge. Much later, as he was leaving the buffet with two plates of eggs and sausage, I saw the grass stains on the knees of his white pants.

Tim's was shaped like a banana, with a graceful curve to it. They're all different. Willie's like a bunch of walnuts when nothing was happening, another's as thin as a thin hot dog. But it's like faces; you're never really surprised.

Still, you're not sure what to expect.

I look into his face and he looks back. I look into his eyes and they look back at mine. Then they look down at my mouth so I look at his mouth, then back to his eyes then, backing up, at his whole face. I think, Who? Who are you? His head tilts to one side.

I say, "Who are you?"

"What do you mean?"

"Nothing."

I look at his eyes again, deeper. Can't tell who he is, what he thinks.

"What?" he says. I look at his mouth.

"I'm just wondering," I say and go wandering across his face. Study the chin line. It's shaped like a persimmon.

"Who are you? What are you thinking?"

He says, "What the hell are you talking about?"

Then they get mad after when you say enough is enough. After, when it's easier to explain that you don't want to. You wouldn't dream of saying that maybe you weren't really ready to in the first place.

Gentle Eddie. We waded into the sea, the waves round and plowing in, buffalo-headed, slapping our thighs. I put my arms around his freckled shoulders and he held me up, buoyed by the water, and rocked me like a seashell.

I had no idea whose party it was, the apartment jam-packed, stepping over people in the hallway. The room with the music was practically empty, the bare floor, me in red shoes. This fellow slides onto one knee and takes me around the waist and we rock to jazzy tunes, with my toes pointing heavenward, and waltz and spin and dip to "Smoke Gets in Your Eyes" or "I'll Love You Just for Now." He puts his head to my chest, runs a sweeping hand down my inside thigh and we go loose-limbed and sultry and as smooth as silk and I stamp my red heels and he takes me into a swoon. I never saw him again after that but I thought, I could have loved that one.

You wonder how long you can keep it up. You begin to feel like you're showing through, like a bathroom window that only lets in gray light, the kind you can't see out of.

They keep coming around. Johnny drives up at Easter vacation from Baltimore and I let him in the kitchen with everyone sound asleep. He has friends waiting in the car.

"What are you crazy? It's pouring out there," I say.

"It's okay," he says. "They understand."

So he gets some long kisses from me, against the refrigerator, before he goes because I hate those girls who push away a boy's face as if she were made out of Ivory soap, as if she's that much greater than he is.

The note on my cubby told me to see the headmaster. I had no idea for what. He had received complaints about my amorous displays on the town green. It was Willie that spring. The headmaster told me he didn't care what I did but that Casey Academy had a reputation to uphold in the town. He lowered his glasses on his nose. "We've got twenty acres of woods on this campus," he said. "If you want to smooch with your boyfriend, there are twenty acres for you to do it out of the public eye. You read me?"

Everybody'd get weekend permissions for different places then we'd all go to someone's house whose parents were away. Usually there'd be more boys than girls. We raided the liquor closet and smoked pot at the kitchen table and you'd never know who would end up where, or with whom. There were always disasters. Ceci got bombed and cracked her head open on the banister and needed stitches. Then there was the time Wendel Blair walked through the picture window at the Lowe's and got slashed to ribbons.

He scared me. In bed, I didn't dare look at him. I lay back with my eyes closed, luxuriating because he knew all sorts of expert angles, his hands never fumbling, going over my whole body, pressing the hair up and off the back of my head, giving an extra hip shove, as if to say *There*. I parted my eyes slightly, keeping the screen of my lashes low because it was too much to look at him, his mouth loose and pink and parted, his eyes looking through my forehead, or kneeling up, looking through my throat. I was ashamed but couldn't look him in the eye.

You wonder about things feeling a little off-kilter. You begin to feel like a piece of pounded veal.

At boarding school, everyone gets depressed. We go in and see the housemother, Mrs. Gunther. She got married when she was eighteen. Mr. Gunther was her high-school sweetheart, the only boyfriend she ever had.

"And you knew you wanted to marry him right off?" we ask her.

She smiles and says, "Yes."

"They always want something from you," says Jill, complaining about her boyfriend.

"Yeah," says Giddy. "You always feel like you have to deliver something."

"You do," says Mrs. Gunther. "Babies."

After sex, you curl up like a shrimp, something deep inside you ruined, slammed in a place that sickens at slamming, and slowly you fill up with an overwhelming sadness, an elusive gaping worry. You don't try to explain it, filled with the knowledge that it's nothing after all, everything filling up finally and absolutely with death. After the briskness of loving, loving stops. And you roll over with death stretched out alongside you like a feather boa, or a snake, light as air, and you . . . you don't even ask for anything or try to say something to him because it's obviously your own damn fault. You haven't been able to—to what? To open your heart. You open your legs but can't, or don't dare anymore, to open your heart.

It starts this way:

You stare into their eyes. They flash like all the stars are out. They look at you seriously, their eyes at a low burn and their hands no matter what starting off shy and with such a gentle touch that the only thing you can do is take that tenderness and let yourself be swept away. When, with one attentive finger they tuck the hair behind your ear, you—

You do everything they want.

Then comes after. After when they don't look at you. They scratch their balls, stare at the ceiling. Or if they do turn, their gaze is altogether changed. They are surprised. They turn casually to look at you, distracted, and get a mild distracted surprise. You're gone. Their blank look tells you that the girl they were fucking is not there anymore. You seem to have disappeared.

○○ ○○ ○○

BOBBIE LOUISE HAWKINS

Running Set of Lies _____

There was a running set of lies that got handed to me all the time I was growing up. Whenever Issue-Number-One came up all the women's faces changed and all the girls were lied to.

I realize it was a *conservative* ... as in *protective* ... device, but at my end of it it added up to a lot of confusion.

For instance, on my fourteenth birthday a boy who was maybe sixteen was going to come to the apartment and formally ask my parents if he could take me on my first official date. They had agreed that he could ask so it seemed likely the answer was yes.

I went to the corner drugstore to hang out with my friends and my mother showed my father some presents I had got that morning one of which was the classic Five Year Diary which, when she laid it down, fell open to what I had immediately written in on receiving it, so as not to forget. The week before in a movie house with my friends I had kissed the boy who was due to arrive around four this afternoon. It was there in black and white with exclamation marks for ecstasy.

That entry proved to be the first and last of that 'diary.' One thousand eight hundred and twenty-four days down the drain, precluded by stupidity.

I had taken the abstraction of *My Diary* as an allowance, proof against getting hoisted on the hook because you wrote it down. The power of a defined occasion. And I learned the way it really was when I got home and faced those two faces. There was no doubt that I had made a mistake.

My mother took me into the kitchen to talk to me.

Kissing in the movies is vulgar.

But worse than that ... and she rang the shift on me ... no girl should kiss a boy until they're engaged.

I couldn't believe it ... that she was saying it. I looked at her and she looked as solemnly back as if she meant to stand by that statement against come what may. I couldn't believe it. I mean ... she came off a *farm*.

And when Aunt Ethel's baby came seven months after she was married it was because she had got tired of carrying it and swallowed a bottle of castor oil.

I mean to say the girls and women were falling left and right and if there wasn't a good cover-up story to preserve the myth ... a bottle of castor oil to produce a fully developed eight pound premature baby . . . of course there was acceptable leeway because she *was* married . . . then you became an example of life's other side. And the sin was to be that example.

Given some proposal of *winning* you looked around and just saw the losers. I don't doubt it had to do with . . . I came from a rockbottom *poor* family that *aspired* to the lower middle class, and most of them made it. Some of them did better. But the time I'm talking about was when they were still talking it up and learning the gestures at the movies and learning what their desires were by window shopping.

It was hopeless. It was truly intellectual. The *ideal* occurred in conversation as the *real*, and what was really happening was shameful, not to be mentioned.

The fear of going lower was the real motive power. And the only *lower* was to be in the same place but disgraced as well. Just a step away. But it loomed downward like something you could avoid and the imagination of it was a misstep would do it.

Or you could jump. You could be finally desperate and jump.

Louella was my mother's youngest half-sister, Grandmama's last baby. 'This is my baby,' she'd say introducing her, even when she was grown. She was about four years older than me so when I was fourteen she was eighteen. We made a summer visit to Abilene that year and I felt awkward and pleased to walk on the street with her, the soldiers whistling and she being so cool, paying no attention.

She was a soft full-bodied beauty with blonde hair pulled up in a '40s Betty Grable pompadour and platform ankle-strap shoes. She was proud of her hands and I thought she was right to be. She had curvaceous fingers with exact long nails. She changed her nail polish every time she changed her lipstick so they would match.

Abilene was packed full of soldiers. There was a rumour for awhile that a black regiment was going to be stationed there and the old man, Louella's father, swore that he was going to buy an acre of land and a shotgun and he meant to shoot any nigger that set foot on his property. He had no notion of patriotism.

It was his usual kind of bad-mouthing. He was on relief and didn't have the hard cash to buy a shotgun shell, much less a shotgun, much less an acre of land.

Louella fell in love with a handsome and sweet-natured Italian from Detroit. They married. Ten months later Louella had twins, a boy and a girl. The boy was dark and larger with black straight hair and (after they changed colour) black eyes. The girl was tiny and blue-eyed with blonde curls. All by the book.

But there was a curve. A month before the babies were born Louella applied for the army's family allotment and learned that it was already being paid out to a wife and two children back in Detroit.

The Italian really loved her, too. He begged her to stay with him and cried. He kept crying and swearing that he'd get a divorce and that all he wanted was Louella.

But her heart was broken.

She had the babies and went on the town. That open. Within two months she was pregnant again and married to a man who turned out to be a forger and went to prison.

It seemed to me then and it seems to me now that I had about as much chance in that economy as a snowball in hell. I had a glamoured mind and I sure did want to be close to somebody.

When I was just turned seventeen I was knocked up by Blacky James in a small town near Lubbock while I was on a visit to my Aunt Hannah. He was a prize-winning diver, a cheer-leader at Texas Tech, and he wanted to be an FBI agent. He wore fancy hand-tooled boots and rode in local rodeos. He was really flashy.

It was like the sky fell in. It was a dimensional change. It was my turn. And I fought it with the slimmest, most ignorant resources. I became a living breathing salvage project. I walked around in a daze with my ears ringing from quinine and my skin parboiled from hot baths. I jumped off every table in sight.

I'd gone back to Albuquerque and it was a coincidence that my mother decided just then to go to Texas for a visit.

I called Blacky's house as soon as I could, but he was back at school.

And the self-preservation scheme went on. On a blazing hot day I went out with a pick-axe to dig a trench in the hard clay back of the garage. It seemed more to the point somehow to make a useless trench than to just dig at random. It gave me a chance to see where I'd been.

As a trench it was pathetic; a foot wide, a foot deep, and as long as it had to be. The clay was as hard as stone. Every inch counted.

At one moment my mother and aunt stood watching me, their eyes like tabulators.

'I'm getting some exercise,' I gasped.

'You better get in the house,' Aunt Hannah said drily, 'you look green.'

Mrs James was an invalid. She spent her time in bed. When she got up it was to clamber creep into a nearby wheelchair. She had dyed red hair and was fat. Her skin was gray white. The small bedroom stank with her smell.

'She knows a good thing when she sees it,' she spat at us, meaning me. 'She had to mess around and now she's got what's coming to her and she thinks she's going to get herself a college boy for its daddy.'

Mr James stood near the head of the bed watching us. He was quiet. It was clear that his wife was the master of the moment.

We had been quiet too. Shamed. We were shamed. But my mother has never passed up an opponent in her life.

'You filthy mouthed old woman. You turn your talk around or I'll haul you out of that bed and climb all over you! I don't care if you are a cripple!'

The upshot was that Blacky was telegraphed to come home.

But of course it amounted to nothing. There was nothing in it to begin with . . . not like a place to be.

The three of us drove around in a car to 'talk about it.'

Blacky explained how this would all be a large problem to him. And it was true.

'If you don't want him honey you don't have to have him,' my mother said. 'You know I'd love any baby of yours no matter where it came from.'

To make a long story short I had an abortion. One way out. One way to get on with it.

Almost home free.

I can't think why it's so much like people walking along the highway with their backs to the traffic and high odds against them. And it's the only highway.

oo oo oo

SHARON OLDS

First Boyfriend

(for D.R.)

We would park on any quiet street,
gliding over to the curb as if by accident,
the houses dark, the families sealed into them,
we'd park away from the street-light, just the
faint waves of its amber grit
reached your car, you'd switch off the motor and
turn and reach for me, and I would
slide into your arms as if I had been born for it,
the ochre corduroy of your sports jacket
pressing the inside of my wrist,
making its pattern of rivulets,
water rippling out like sound waves from a source.
Your front seat had an overpowering
male smell, as if the chrome had been
rubbed with jism, a sharp stale
delirious odor like the sour plated
taste of the patina on an old watch, the
fragrance of your sex polished till it shone in the night, the
jewel of Channing Street, of Benvenue Avenue, of
Panoramic, of Dwight Way, I
returned to you as if to the breast of my father,
grain of the beard on your umber cheeks,
delicate line of tartar on the edge of your teeth,
the odor of use, the stained brass
air in the car as if I had come
back to a pawnshop to claim what was mine—
and as your tongue went down my throat,
right down the central nerve of my body, the
gilt balls of the street-light gleamed like a
pawnbroker's over your second-hand Chevy and
all the toasters popped up and
all the saxophones began to play
hot riffs of scat for the return of their rightful owners.

JOAN CHASE

from: *During the Reign of the Queen of Persia* _____

It was beginning to storm; the oak trees up by the road tossed to silver foam, fell back green again. There had been a lover once. An Italian boy with ardent glowing eyes. We imagined him for ourselves. The purple clouds were plowing in on the wind from the darker distance, weaving into garlands that hung over us like terraces as though we dwelt in Babylon. All at once, moving as one spirit, we did what we had not done for years: we dropped our clothes on the floor, on the stairs, as we ran down, and then on the porch, so that we were fully naked by the time we leapt onto the grass. The rain chilled, stung against our skin, turned to hail. Then Celia came out too, with us again after long years, flying over the grass, prancing, flowing with rain, her golden-red hair streaked dark with rain, streaming out. She was like a separate force quickening us, urging us further by her possibilities. Over the grass we ran and slid until it churned, spattered and oozed with mud; we painted ourselves, each other, immersed in the driveway ditch of foaming brown for a rinsing, before we took the mud slide again. We formed a whip, flung ourselves over the grass. Until Celia stopped and looked up the drive, sideways, hiding herself. A car passed on the highway, silent and distant as though driven by a phantom. Celia stood covered with her crossed arms and like that, suddenly, we all ran onto the porch and grabbed for towels or rags from the shelf, shivering gooseflesh like a disease.

Celia had him in the parlor. We stayed in the living room across the hall and were quiet, listening for any sounds they might make. We never heard any talking. This night Aunt Libby and Uncle Dan had gone out and Corley had come later, so we were the only ones who saw him go into the parlor with Celia and close the door.

The hall light was out. Across the darkness we could see the slight border of light under the double panel doors and between them where they pulled together. There was no hurry. We waited.

Going out of the room, Celia left the door open so we could see Corley waiting there while she was in the kitchen. She didn't even glance at us. Corley was her new boyfriend and already she was different with him. The other boys didn't come to the house now and she saw him every night Aunt Libby would allow it. Celia arguing nonstop all afternoon, then over supper. Corley wore his wavy hair in a slick ducktail, which he was constantly combing; we watched the muscles in his arms quivering even from that little bit of movement. When he smiled, his full lips barely lifted and there was no change in the expression of his thick-lidded eyes. Aunt Libby said he was lazy as the day is long, you could tell that by looking at him, and he wouldn't ever get out of bed once he'd got Celia into one. She said he dripped sex. To us that seemed to go along with his wet-looking hair.

Still we thought he was cute and Celia was lucky. He grinned now, combing his hair. "How you all doing?" His family had come up from Kentucky and he still talked that way, with a voice mushy and thick like his lips.

"Fine." We shrugged.

"Here's some money," he said. "You want to get some ice cream?" He must have thought we were still kids. There was a Dairy Delight now on the far lot beside the gas station; Gram spoke of her fields and meadows as lots now.

Sure, we said, knowing he wanted to get rid of us, knowing too what we'd do when we got back. We took our time walking there because there were a lot of cars driving in and out of the parking lot on a Saturday night and we knew some of the guys. Walking back, we felt the connection with the rest of the world sever as we left the high lamps and passed beyond the cedar hedge onto the dark gravel, the house shadowy too now, with only one small glow of light in the front hall.

We needed no words. We moved to the grass to quiet our walking. Through the gap in the honeysuckle we sneaked and climbed over the railing and stood to one side of the window, where we could see at an angle past the half-drawn drapes. At first we could scarcely make them out where they were on the floor, bound in one shape. We licked our ice cream and carefully, silently dissolved the cones, tasting nothing as it melted away down inside us. Tasting instead Corley's mouth on ours, its burning wild lathering sweetness. In the shaft of light we saw them pressed together, rolling in each other's arms, Celia's flowery skirt pulled up around her thighs. His hand moving there. Then she pushed him away, very tenderly, went to sit back on the couch while Corley turned his back and combed his hair. He turned and started toward her, tucking his shirt in. We stared at the unsearchable smile that lifted from Celia's face like a veil and revealed another self, as she began to unbutton her blouse, undressing herself until she sat there in the half-dark, bare to the waist, bare to the moon which had come up over the trees behind us. She drew Corley to her, his face after he'd turned around never losing its calm, kissed him forever, it seemed, as long as she wanted to. Then she guided his mouth to press into first one and then the other cone-crested breast, her own face lake-calm under the moon. Then she dressed again. Our hearts plunged and thudded. At that moment we were freed from Aunt Libby. We didn't care what it was called or the price to be paid; someday we would have it.

LYNNE TILLMAN

from: *Weird Fucks* _____

NO/YES

I threw caution to the wind and never used any contraception. Nancy finally convinced me I might get pregnant this way and made me an appointment at Planned Parenthood. It was a Saturday appointment and that night I had a date with John, a painter from the midwest, a minimalist. So the doctor put the diaphragm in me and I kept it in, in anticipation of that meeting. Besides I had lied to the woman doctor when I said I knew how to do it—I was afraid to put it in or take it out. Let it stay there I thought, easier this way.

We met at the Bleecker Street Cinema and watched a double feature. Godard. Walked back to his place below Canal. We made love on his bed and he said, "I'm sorry. This must be one of my hair trigger days." "What does that mean," I asked. He looked at me skeptically. It was difficult, very difficult, for men to understand and appreciate how someone could fling herself around sexually and not know the terms, the ground, on which she lay. He said, "It means to come too quickly." "Oh," I said, "that's all right." I kept comforting men. He fell asleep fast.

I awoke at 3 A.M. with just one thought. I had to get the diaphragm out. If it were possible and not already melted into my womb or so far up as to be near my heart or wherever diaphragms go when you're ignorant of where they can go.

I pulled a rough wool blanket around me and headed for the toilet in the hall. John awoke slightly and asked where I was headed. "For a piss," I lied.

The heavy door opened into a dark hall. The toilet door opened, just a toilet and no light. I stood in the dark and threw my leg up on the toilet seat as shown in various catalogues not unknown to the wearer. Begin searching for that piece of rubber. Think about Margaret Sanger and other reassuring ideas. Can't reach the rim. Reach the rim; finger slips off. Reach it, get it and pull. Can't get it out. It snaps back into place as if alive. Go into a cold sweat. Squat and try. Finger all the way up. Pull. Then try kneeling. I'm on my knees with my finger up me, the blanket scratching my skin. It seems to be in forever. This is a Herculean task never before recorded. An adventure with my body. In forever. I pull the blanket up around me and stand, deciding to leave it in for now and have it removed surgically if necessary. In a colder sweat I leave the dark toilet to return to the reason for all this bother. I can't pull the loft door open. It seems to be locked or blocked. Begin banging heavily against the metal door. Hot sweat now. When John finally opens the door he finds me lying flat out on the blanket, a fallen angel, naked at his feet. I'd fainted.

He revives me and we are both stunned. "The door," he says, "was open." That's what they all say. He gives me a glass of water and we go back to bed.

The next morning, even though he says our signs are right, my fainting has indicated other signs. Signs and more signs. I walk toward Canal Street and a sign on the wall reads Noyes Electrical Company which I read No/Yes Electrical Company. No/Yes, I think, that's a strange name for a business.

oo oo oo

SHARON OLDS

For My Daughter _____

That night will come. Somewhere someone will be
entering you, his body riding
under your white body, dividing
your blood from your skin, your dark, liquid
eyes open or closed, the slipping
silken hair of your head fine
as water poured at night, the delicate
threads between your legs curled
like stitches broken. The center of your body
will tear open, as a woman will rip the
seam of her skirt so she can run. It will happen,
and when it happens I will be right here
in bed with your father, as when you learned to read
you would go off and read in your room
as I read in mine, versions of the story
that changes in the telling, the story of the river.

MONA SIMPSON

Lawns _____

I steal. I've stolen books and money and even letters. Letters are great. I can't tell you the feeling walking down the street with twenty dollars in my purse, stolen earrings in my pocket. I don't get caught. That's the amazing thing. You're out on the sidewalk, other people all around, shopping, walking, and you've got it. You're out of the store, you've done this thing you're not supposed to do, but no one stops you. At first it's a rush. Like you're even for everything you didn't get before. But then you're left alone, no one even notices you. Nothing changes.

I work in the mailroom of my dormitory, Saturday mornings. I sort mail, put the letters in these long narrow cubbyholes. The insides of mailboxes. It's cool there when I stick in my arm.

I've stolen cash—these crisp, crackling, brand-new twenty-dollar bills the fathers and grandmothers send, sealed up in sheets of wax paper. Once I got a fifty. I've stolen presents, too. I got a sweater and a football. I didn't want the football, but after the package was messed up on the mail table, I had no choice, I had to take the whole thing in my day pack and throw it out on the other side of campus. I found a covered garbage can. It was miles away. Brand new football.

Mostly, what I take are cookies. No evidence. They're edible. I can spot the coffee cans of chocolate chip. You can smell it right through the wrapping. A cool smell, like the inside of a pantry. Sometimes I eat straight through the can during my shift.

Tampering with the United States mail is a federal crime, I know. Listen, let me tell you, I know. I got a summons in my mailbox to go to the Employment Office next Wednesday. Sure I'm scared.

The university cops want to talk to me. Great. They think, "suspect" is the word they use, that one of us is throwing out mail instead of sorting it. Wonder who? Us is the others, I'm not the only sorter. I just work Saturdays, mail comes, you know, six days a week in this country. They'll never guess it's me.

They say this in the letter, they think it's out of *laziness*. Wanting to hurry up and get done, not spend the time. But I don't hurry. I'm really patient on Saturday mornings. I leave my dorm early, while Lauren's still asleep, I open the mailroom—it's this heavy door and I have my own key. When I get there, two bags are already on the table, sagging, waiting for me. Two old ladies. One's packages, one's mail. There's a small key opens the bank of doors, the little boxes from the inside. Through the glass part of every mail slot, I can see. The Astroturf field across the street over the parking lot, it's this light green. I watch the sky go from black to gray to blue while I'm there. Some days just stay foggy. Those are the best. I bring a cup of coffee in with me from the vending machine—don't want to wake Lauren up—and I get there at like seven-thirty or eight o'clock. I don't mind it then, my whole dorm's asleep. When I walk out it's as quiet as a football game day. It's eleven or twelve when you know everyone's up and walking that it gets bad being down there. That's why I start early. But I don't rush.

Once you open a letter, you can't just put it in a mailbox. The person's gonna say something. So I stash them in my pack and throw them out. Just people I know. Susan Brown I open, Annie Larsen, Larry Helprin. All the popular kids from my high school. These are kids who drove places together, took vacations, they all ski, they went to the prom in one big group. At morning nutrition—nutrition, it's your break at ten o'clock for donuts and stuff. California state law, you have to have it.

They used to meet outside on the far end of the math patio, all in one group. Some of them smoked. I've seen them look at each other, concerned at ten in the morning. One touched the inside of another's wrist, like grown-ups in trouble.

And now I know. Everything I thought those three years, worst years of my life, turns out to be true. The ones here get letters. Keri's at Santa Cruz, Lilly's in San Diego, Kevin's at Harvard, and Beth's at Stanford. And like from families, their letters talk about problems. They're each other's main lives. You always knew, looking at them in high school, they weren't just kids who had fun. They cared. They cared about things.

They're all worried about Lilly now. Larry and Annie are flying down to talk her into staying at school.

I saw Glenn the day I came to Berkeley. I was all unpacked and I was standing there leaning into the window of my father's car, saying, "Smile, Dad, jeez, at least try, would you?" He was crying because he was leaving. I'm thinking oh, my god, some of these other kids carrying in their trunks and backpacks are gonna see him, and then finally, he drives away and I was sad. That was the moment I was waiting for, him gone and me alone and there it was and I was sad. I took a walk through campus and I'd been walking for almost an hour and then I see Glenn, coming down on a little hill by the infirmary, riding one of those lawn mowers you sit on, with grass flying out of the side and he's smiling. Not at me but just smiling. Clouds and sky behind his hair, half of Tamalpais gone in fog. He was wearing this bright orange vest and I thought, fall's coming.

I saw him that night again in our dorm cafeteria. This's the first time I've been in love. I worry. I'm a bad person, but Glenn's the perfect guy, I mean for me at least, and he thinks he loves me and I've got to keep him from finding out about me. I'll die before I'll tell him. Glenn, OK, Glenn. He looks like Mick Jagger, but sweet, ten times sweeter. He looks like he's about ten years old. His father's a doctor over at UC Med. Gynecological surgeon.

First time we got together, a whole bunch of us were in Glenn's room drinking beer, Glenn and his roommate collect beer cans, they have them stacked up, we're watching TV and finally everybody else leaves. There's nothing on but those gray lines and Glenn turns over on his bed and asks me if I'd rub his back.

I couldn't believe this was happening to me. In high school, I was always ending up with the wrong guys, never the one I wanted. But I wanted it to be Glenn and I knew it was going to happen, I knew I didn't have to do anything. I just had to stay there. It would happen. I was sitting on his rear end, rubbing his back, going under his shirt with my hands.

All of a sudden, I was worried about my breath and what I smelled like. When I turned fourteen or fifteen, my father told me once that I didn't smell good. I slugged him when he said that and didn't talk to him for days, not that I cared about what I smelled like with my father. He was happy, though, kind of, that he could hurt me. That was the last time, though, I'll tell you.

Glenn's face was down in the pillow. I tried to sniff myself but I couldn't tell anything. And it went all right anyway.

I don't open Glenn's letters but I touch them. I hold them and smell them—none of his mail has any smell.

He doesn't get many letters. His parents live across the Bay in Marin County, they don't write. He gets letters from his grandmother in Michigan, plain, even handwriting on regular envelopes, a sticker with her return address printed on it, Rural Route #3, Guns Street, see, I got it memorized.

And he gets letters from Diane, Di, they call her. High school girlfriend. Has a pushy mother, wants her to be a scientist, but she already got a C in Chem 1A. I got an A+, not to brag. He never slept with her, though, she wouldn't, she's still a virgin down in San Diego. With Lilly. Maybe they even know each other.

Glenn and Di were popular kids in their high school. Redwood High.

Now I'm one because of Glenn, popular. Because I'm his girlfriend, I know that's why. Not 'cause of me. I just know, OK, I'm not going to start fooling myself now. Please.

Her letters I hold up to the light, they've got fluorescent lights in there. She's supposed to be blond, you know, and pretty. Quiet. The soft type. And the envelopes. She writes on these sheer cream-colored envelopes and they get transparent and I can see her writing underneath, but not enough to read what it says, it's like those hockey lines painted under layers of ice.

I run my tongue along the place where his grandmother sealed the letter. A sharp, sweet gummy taste. Once I cut my tongue. That's what keeps me going to the bottom of the bag, I'm always wondering if there'll be a letter for Glenn. He doesn't get one every week. It's like a treasure. Cracker Jack prize. But I'd never open Glenn's mail. I kiss all four corners where his fingers will touch, opening it, before I put it in his box.

I brought home cookies for Lauren and me. Just a present. We'll eat 'em or Glenn'll eat 'em. I'll throw them out for all I care. They're chocolate chip with pecans. This was one good mother. A lucky can. I brought us coffee, too. I *bought* it.

Yeah, OK, so I'm in trouble. Wednesday, at ten-thirty, I got this notice I was supposed to appear. I had a class, Chem 1C, pre-med staple. Your critical thing. I never missed it before. I told Glenn I had a doctor's appointment.

OK, so I skip it anyway and I walk into this room and there's these two other guys, all work in the mailroom doing what I do, sorting. And we all sit there on chairs on this green carpet. I was staring at everybody's shoes. And there's a cop. University cop, I don't know what's the difference. He had this sagging, pear-shaped body. Like what my dad would have if he were fat, but he's not, he's thin. He walks slowly on the carpeting, his fingers hooked in his belt loops. I was watching his hips.

Anyway, he's accusing us all and he's trying to get one of us to admit we did it. No way.

"I hope one of you will come to me and tell the truth. Not a one of you knows anything about this? Come on, now."

I shake my head no and stare down at the three pairs of shoes. He says they're not going to do anything to the person who did it, right, wanna make a bet, they say they just want to know, but they'll take it back as soon as you tell them.

I don't care why I don't believe him. I know one thing for sure and that's they're not going to do anything to me as long as I say no, I didn't do it. That's what I said, no, I didn't do it, I don't know a thing about it. I just can't imagine where those missing packages could have gone, how letters got into garbage cans. Awful. I just don't know.

The cop had a map with X's on it every place they found mail. The garbage cans. He said there was a group of students trying to get an investigation. People's girlfriends sent cookies that never got here. Letters are missing. Money. These students put up Xeroxed posters on bulletin boards showing a garbage can stuffed with letters.

Why should I tell them, so they can throw me in jail? And kick me out of school? Four-point-oh average and I'm going to let them kick me out of school? They're sitting there telling us it's a felony. A federal crime. No way, I'm gonna go to medical school.

This tall, skinny guy with a blond mustache, Wallabees, looks kind of like a rabbit, he defended us. He's another sorter, works Monday/Wednesdays.

"We all do our jobs," he says. "None of us would do that." The rabbity guy looks at me and the other girl for support. So we're going to stick together. The other girl, a dark blonde chewing her lip, nodded. I loved that rabbity guy that second. I nodded too.

The cop looked down. Wide hips in the coffee-with-milk-colored pants. He sighed. I looked up at the rabbity guy. They let us all go.

I'm just going to keep saying no, not me, didn't do it and I just won't do it again. That's all. Won't do it anymore. So, this is Glenn's last chance for homemade cookies. I'm sure as hell not going to bake any.

I signed the form, said I didn't do it, I'm OK now. I'm safe. It turned out OK after all, it always does. I always think something terrible's going to happen and it doesn't. I'm lucky.

I'm afraid of cops. I was walking, just a little while ago, today, down Telegraph with Glenn, and these two policemen, not the one I'd met, other policemen, were coming in our direction. I started sweating a lot. I was sure until they passed us, I was sure it was all over, they were there for me. I always think that. But at the same time, I know it's just my imagination. I mean, I'm a four-point-oh student, I'm a nice girl just walking down the street with my boyfriend.

We were on our way to get Happy Burgers. When we turned the corner, about a block past the cops, I looked at Glenn and I was flooded with this feeling. It was raining a little and we were by People's Park. The trees were blowing and I was looking at all those little gardens coming up, held together with stakes and white string.

I wanted to say something to Glenn, give him something. I wanted to tell him something about me.

"I'm bad in bed," that's what I said, I just blurted it out like that. He just kind of looked at me, he was nervous, he just giggled. He didn't know what to say, I guess, but he sort of slung his arm around me and I was so grateful and then we went in. He paid for my Happy Burger, I usually don't let him pay for me, but I did and it was the best god-damn hamburger I've ever eaten.

I want to tell him things.

I lie all the time, always have, but I keep track of each lie I've ever told Glenn and I'm always thinking of the things I can't tell him.

Glenn was a screwed up kid, kind of. He used to go in his backyard, his parents were inside the house I guess, and he'd find this big stick and start twirling around with it. He'd dance, he called it dancing, until if you came up and clapped in front of him, he wouldn't see you. He'd spin around with that stick until he fell down dead on the grass, un-conscious, he said he did it to see the sky break up in pieces and spin. He did it sometimes with a tire swing, too. He told me when he was spinning like that, it felt like he was just hearing the earth spinning, that it really went that fast all the time but we just don't feel it. When he was twelve years old his parents took him in the city to a clinic to see a psychologist. And then he stopped. See, maybe I should go to a psychologist. I'd get better, too. He told me about that in bed one night. The ground feels so good when you fall, he said to me. I loved him for that.

"Does anything feel that good now?" I said.

"Sex sometimes. Maybe dancing."

Know what else he told me that night? He said, right before we went to sleep, he wasn't looking at me, he said he'd been thinking what would happen if I died, and he said he thought how he'd be at my funeral, all my family and my friends from high school and my little brother would all be around at the front and he'd be at the edge in the cemetery, nobody'd even know who he was.

I was in that crack, breathing the air between the bed and the wall. Cold and dusty. Yeah, we're having sex. I don't know. It's good. Sweet. He says he loves me. I have to remind myself. I talk to myself in my head while we're doing it. I have to say, it's OK, this is just Glenn, this is who I want it to be and it's just like rubbing next to someone. It's just like pushing two hands together, so there's no air in between.

I cry sometimes with Glenn, I'm so grateful.

My mother called and woke me up this morning. Ms. I'm-going-to-be-perfect. Ms. Anything-wrong-is-your-own-fault. Ms. If-anything-bad-happens-you're-a-fool.

She says if she has time, she *might* come up and see my dorm room in the next few weeks. Help me organize my wardrobe, she says. She didn't bring me up here, my dad did. I wanted Danny to come along. I love Danny.

But my mother has *no* pity. She thinks she's got the answers. She's the one who's a lawyer, she's the one who went back to law school and stayed up late nights studying while she still made our lunch boxes. With gourmet cheese. She's proud of it, she tells you. She loves my dad, I guess. She thinks we're like this great family and she sits there at the dinner table bragging about us, to us. She Xeroxed my grade card first quarter with my Chemistry A+ so she's got it in her office and she's got the copy up on the refrigerator at home. She's sitting there telling all her friends that and I'm thinking, you don't know it, but I'm not one of you.

These people across the street from us. Little girl, Sarah, eight years old. Maybe seven. Her dad, he worked for the army, some kind of researcher, he decides he wants to get a sex-change operation. And he goes and does it, over at Stanford. My mom goes out, takes the dog for a walk, right. The mother *confides* in her. Says the thing she regrets most is she wants to have more children. The little girl, Sarah, eight years old, looks up at my mom and says, "Daddy's going to be an aunt."

Now that's sad, I think that's really sad. My mom thinks it's a good dinner table story, proving how much better we are than them. Yeah, I remember exactly what she said that night. "That's all Sarah's mother's got to worry about now is that she wants another child. Meanwhile, Daddy's becoming an aunt."

She should know about me.

So my dad comes to visit for the weekend. Glenn's dad came to speak at UC one night, he took Glenn out to dinner to a nice place, Glenn was glad to see him. Yeah, well. My dad. Comes to the dorm. Skulks around. This guy's a *businessman*, in a three-piece suit, and he acts inferior to the eighteen-year-old freshmen coming in the lobby. My dad. Makes me sick right now thinking of him standing there in the lobby and everybody seeing him. He was probably looking at the kids and looking jealous. Just standing there. Why? Don't ask me why, he's the one that's forty-two years old.

So he's standing there, nervous, probably sucking his hand, that's what he does when he's nervous, I'm always telling him not to. Finally, somebody takes him to my room. I'm not there, Lauren's gone, and he waits for I don't know how long.

When I come in he's standing with his back to the door, looking out the window. I see him and right away I know it's him and I have this urge to tiptoe away and he'll never see me.

My pink sweater, a nice sweater, a sweater I wore a lot in high school, was over my chair, hanging on the back of it, and my father's got one hand on the sweater shoulder and he's like rubbing the other hand down an empty arm. He looks up at me, already scared and grateful when I walk into the room. I feel like smashing him with a baseball bat. Why can't he just stand up straight?

I drop my books on the bed and stand there while he hugs me.

"Hi, Daddy, what are you doing here?"

"I wanted to see you." He sits in my chair now, his legs crossed and big, too big for this room, and he's still fingering the arm of my pink sweater. "I missed you so I got away for the weekend," he says. "I have a room up here at the Claremont Hotel."

So he's here for the weekend. He's just sitting in my dorm room and I have to figure out what to do with him. He's not going to do anything. He'd just sit there. And Lauren's coming back soon so I've got to get him out. It's Friday afternoon and the weekend's shot. OK, so I'll go with him. I'll go with him and get it over with.

But I'm not going to miss my date with Glenn Saturday night. No way. I'd die before I'd cancel that. It's bad enough missing dinner in the cafeteria tonight. Friday's eggplant, my favorite, and Friday nights are usually easy, music on the stereos all down the hall. We usually work, but work slow and talk and then we all meet in Glenn's room around ten.

"Come, sit on my lap, honey." My dad like pulls me down and starts bouncing me. *Bouncing me.* I stand up. "OK, we can go somewhere tonight and tomorrow morning, but I have to be back for tomorrow night. I've got plans with people. And I've got to study, too."

"You can bring your books back to the hotel," he says. "I'm supposed to be at a convention in San Francisco, but I wanted to see you. I have work, too, we can call room service and both just work."

"I still have to be back by four tomorrow."

"All right."

"OK, just a minute." And he sat there in my chair while I called Glenn and told him I wouldn't be there for dinner. I pulled the phone out into the hall, it only stretches so far, and whispered. "Yeah, my father's here," I said, "he's got a conference in San Francisco. He just came by."

Glenn lowered his voice, sweet, and said, "Sounds fun."

My dad sat there, hunched over in my chair, while I changed my shirt and put on deodorant. I put a nightgown in my shoulder pack and my toothbrush and I took my chem book and we left. I knew I wouldn't be back for a whole day. I was trying to calm myself, thinking, well, it's only one day, that's nothing in my life. The halls were empty, it was five o'clock, five-ten, everyone was down at dinner.

We walk outside and the cafeteria lights are on and I see everyone moving around with their trays. Then my dad picks up my hand.

I yank it out. "Dad," I say, really mean.

"Honey, I'm your father." His voice trails off. "Other girls hold their fathers' hands." It was dark enough for the lights to be on in the cafeteria, but it wasn't really dark out yet. The sky was blue. On the tennis courts on top of the garage, two Chinese guys were playing. I heard that *thonk-pong* and it sounded so carefree and I just wanted to be them. I'd have even given up Glenn, Glenn-that-I-love-more-than-anything, at that second, I would have given everything up just to be someone else, someone new. I got into the car and slammed the door shut and turned up the heat.

"Should we just go to the hotel and do our work? We can get a nice dinner in the room."

"I'd rather go out," I said, looking down at my hands. He went where I told him. I said the name of the restaurant and gave directions. Chez Panisse and we ordered the most expensive stuff. Appetizers and two desserts just for me. A hundred and twenty bucks for the two of us.

OK, this hotel room.

So, my dad's got the Bridal Suite. He claimed that was all they had. Fat chance. Two-hundred-eighty room hotel and all they've got left is this deal with the canopy bed, no way. It's in the tower, you can almost see it from the dorm. Makes me sick. From the bathroom, there's this window, shaped like an arch, and it looks over all of Berkeley. You can see the bridge lights. As soon as we got there, I locked myself in the bathroom, I was so mad about that canopy bed. I took a long bath and washed my hair. They had little soaps wrapped up there, shampoo, may as well use them, he's paying for it. It's this deep old bathtub and wind was coming in from outside and I felt like that window was just open, no glass, just a hole cut out in the stone.

I was thinking of when I was little and what they taught us in catechism. I thought a soul was inside your chest, this long horizontal triangle with rounded edges, made out of some kind of white fog, some kind of gas or vapor. I could be pregnant. I soaped myself all up and rinsed off with cold water. I'm lucky I never got pregnant, really lucky.

Other kids my age, Lauren, everybody, I know things they don't know. I know more for my age. Too much. Like I'm not a virgin. Lots of people are, you'd be surprised. I know about a lot of things being wrong and unfair, all kinds of stuff. It's like seeing a UFO, if I ever saw something like that, I'd never tell, I'd wish I'd never seen it.

My dad knocks on the door.

"What do you want?"

"Let me just come in and talk to you while you're in there."

"I'm done, I'll be right out. Just a minute." I took a long time toweling. No hurry, believe me. So I got into bed with my nightgown on and wet already from my hair. I turned away. Breathed against the wall. "Night."

My father hooks my hair over my ear and touches my shoulder. "Tired?"

I shrug.

"You really have to go back tomorrow? We could go to Marin or to the beach. Anything."

I hugged my knees up under my nightgown. "You should go to your conference, Dad."

I wake up in the middle of the night, I feel something's going on, and sure enough, my dad's down there, he's got my nightgown worked up like a frill around my neck and my legs hooked over his shoulders.

"Dad, stop it."

"I just wanted to make you feel good," he says, and looks up at me. "What's wrong? Don't you love me anymore?"

I never really told anybody. It's not exactly the kind of thing you can bring up over lunch. "So, I'm sleeping with my father. Oh, and let's split a dessert." Right.

I don't know, other people think my dad's handsome. They say he is. My mother thinks so, you should see her traipsing around the balcony when she gets in her romantic moods, which, on her professional lawyer schedule, are about once a year, thank god. It's pathetic. He thinks she's repulsive, though. I don't know that, that's what I think. But he loves me, that's for sure.

So next day, Saturday—that rabbity guy, Paul's his name, he did my shift for me—we go downtown and I got him to buy me this suit. Three hundred dollars from Saks. Oh, and I got shoes. So I stayed later with him because of the clothes, and I was a little happy because I thought at least now I'd have something good to wear with Glenn. My dad and I got brownie sundaes at Sweet Dreams and I got home by five. He was crying when he dropped me off.

"Don't cry, Dad. Please," I said. Jesus, how can you not hate someone who's always begging from you.

Lauren had Poly Styrene on the stereo and a candle lit in our room. I was never so glad to be home.

"Hey," Lauren said. She was on her bed with her legs propped up on the wall. She'd just shaved. She was rubbing in cream.

I flopped down on my bed. "Ohhhh," I said, grabbing the sides of the mattress.

"Hey, can you keep a secret about what I did today?" Lauren said. "I went to that therapist, up at Cowell."

"You have the greatest legs," I said, quiet. "Why don't you ever wear skirts?"

She stopped what she was doing and stood up. "You think they're good? I don't like the way they look, except in jeans." She looked down at them. "They're crooked, see?" She shook her head. "I don't want to think about it."

Then she went to her dresser and started rolling a joint. "Want some?"

"A little."

She lit up, lay back on her bed and held her arm out for me to come take the joint.

"So, she was this really great woman. Warm, kind of chubby. She knew instantly what kind of man Brent was." Lauren snapped her fingers. "Like that." Brent was the pool man Lauren had an affair with, home in LA.

I'm back in the room maybe an hour, putting on mascara, my jeans are on the bed, pressed, and the phone rings and it's my dad and I say, "Listen, just leave me alone."

"You don't care about me anymore."

"I just saw you. I have nothing to say. We just saw each other."

"What are you doing tonight?"

"Going out."

"Who are you seeing?"

"Glenn."

He sighs. "So you really like him, huh?"

"Yeah, I do and you should be glad. You should be glad I have a boyfriend." I pull the cord out into the hall and sit down on the floor there. There's this long pause.

"We're not going to end up together, are we?"

I felt like all the air's knocked out of me. I looked out the window and everything looked dead and still. The parked cars. The trees with pink toilet paper strung between the branches. The church all closed up across the street.

"No, we won't, Daddy."

He was crying. "I know, I know."

I hung up the phone and went back and sat in the hall. I'm scared, too. I don't know what'll happen.

I don't know. It's been going on I guess as long as I can remember. I mean, not the sex, but my father. When I was a little kid, tiny little kid, my dad came in before bed and said his prayers with me. He kneeled down by my bed and I was on my back. *Prayers.* He'd lift up my pajama top and put his hands on my breast. Little fried eggs, he said. One time with his tongue. Then one night, he pulled down the elastic of my pajama pants. He did it for an hour and then I came. Don't believe anything they ever tell you about kids not coming. That first time was the biggest I ever had and I didn't even know what it was then. It just kept going and going as if he were breaking me through layers and layers of glass and I felt like I'd slipped and let go and I didn't have myself anymore, he had me, and once I'd slipped like that I'd never be the same again.

We had this sprinkler on our back lawn, Danny and me used to run through it in summer and my dad'd be outside, working on the grass or the hedge or something and he'd squirt us with the hose. I used to wear a bathing suit bottom, no top—we were this modern family, our parents walked around the house naked after showers and then Danny and I ended up both being these modest kids, can't stand anyone to see us even in our underwear, I always dress facing the closet, Lauren teases me. We'd run through the sprinkler and my dad would come up and pat my bottom and the way he'd put his hand on my thigh, I felt like Danny could tell it was different than the way he touched him, I was like something he owned.

First time when I was nine, I remember, Dad and me were in the shower together. My mom might have even been in the house, they did that kind of stuff, it was supposed to be OK. Anyway, we're in the shower and I remember this look my dad had. Like he was daring me, knowing he knew more than I did. We're both under the shower. The water pasted his hair down on his head and he looked younger and weird. "Touch it. Don't be afraid of it," he says. And he grabs my thighs on the outside and pulls me close to him, pulling on my fat.

He waited till I was twelve to really do it. I don't know if you can call it rape, I was a good sport. The creepy thing is I know how it felt for him, I could see it on his face when he did it. He thought he was getting away with something. We were supposed to go hiking but right away that morning when we got into the car, he knew he was going to do it. He couldn't wait to get going. I said I didn't feel good, I had a cold, I wanted to stay home, but he made me go anyway and we hiked two miles and he set up the tent. He told me to take my clothes off and I undressed just like that, standing there in the woods. He's the one who was nervous and got us into the tent. I looked old for twelve, small but old. And right there on the ground, he spread my legs open and pulled my feet up and fucked me. I bled. I couldn't even breathe the tent was so small. He could have done anything. He could have killed me, he had me alone on this mountain.

I think about that sometimes when I'm alone with Glenn in my bed.

It's so easy to hurt people. They just lie there and let you have them. I could reach out and choke Glenn to death, he'd be so shocked, he wouldn't stop me. You can just take what you want.

My dad thought he was getting away with something but he didn't. He was the one who fell in love, not me. And after that day, when we were back in the car, I was the one giving orders. From then on, I got what I wanted. He spent about twice as much money on me as on Danny and everyone knew it, Danny and my mom, too. How do you think I got good clothes and a good bike and a good stereo? My dad's not rich, you know. And I'm the one who got to go away to college even though it killed him. Says it's the saddest thing that ever happened in his life, me going away and leaving him. But when I was a little kid that day, he wasn't in love with me, not like he is now.

Only thing I'm sad about isn't either of my parents, it's Danny. Leaving Danny alone there with them. He used to send Danny out of the house. My mom'd be at work on a Saturday afternoon or something or even in the morning and my dad would kick my little brother out of his own house. Go out and play, Danny. Why doncha catch some rays. And Danny just went and got his glove and baseball from the closet and he'd go and throw it against the house, against the outside wall, in the driveway. I'd be in my room, I'd be like dead, I'd be wood, telling myself this doesn't count, no one has to know, I'll say I'm still a virgin, it's not really happening to me, I'm dead, I'm blank, I'm just letting time stop and pass, and then I'd hear the sock of the ball in the mitt and the slam of the screen door and I knew it was true, it was really happening.

Glenn's the one I want to tell. I can't ever tell Glenn.

I called my mom. Pay phone, collect, hour-long call. I don't know, I got real mad last night and I just told her. I thought when I came here, it'd just go away. But it's not going away. It makes me weird with Glenn. In the morning, with Glenn, when it's time to get up, I can't get up. I cry.

I knew it'd be bad. Poor Danny. Well, my mom says she might leave our dad. She cried for an hour, no jokes, on the phone.

How could he *do* this to me, she kept yelping. To her. Everything's always to her.

But then she called an hour later, she'd talked to a psychiatrist already, she's kicked Dad out, and she arrives, just arrives here at Berkeley. But she was good. She says she's on my side, she'll help me, I don't know, I felt OK. She stayed in a hotel and she wanted to know if I wanted to stay there with her but I said no, I'd see her more in a week or something, I just wanted to go back to my dorm. She found this group. She says, just in San Jose, there's hundreds of families like ours, yeah, great, that's what I said. But there's groups. She's going to a group of other thick-o mothers like her, these wives who didn't catch on. She wanted me to go to a group of girls, yeah, molested girls, that's what they call them, but I said no, I have friends here already, she can do what she wants.

I talked to my dad, too, that's the sad thing, he feels like he's lost me and he wants to die and I don't know, he doesn't know what he's doing. He called in the middle of the night.

"Just tell me one thing, honey. Please tell me the truth. When did you stop?"

"Dad."

"Because I remember once you said I was the only person who ever understood you."

"I was ten years old."

"OK, OK. I'm sorry."

He didn't want to get off the phone. "You know, I love you, honey. I always will."

"Yeah, well."

My mom's got him lined up for a psychiatrist, too, she says he's lucky she's not sending him to jail. I *am* a lawyer, she keeps saying, as if we could forget. She'd pay for me to go to a shrink now, too, but I said no, forget it.

It's over. Glenn and I are, over. I feel like my dad's lost me everything. I sort of want to die now. I'm telling you I feel terrible. I told Glenn and that's it, it's over. I can't believe it either. Lauren says she's going to hit him.

I told him and we're not seeing each other anymore. Nope. He said he wanted to just think about everything for a few days. He said it had nothing to do with my father but he'd been feeling a little too settled lately. He said we don't have fun anymore, it's always so serious. That was Monday. So every meal after that, I sat with Lauren in the cafeteria and he's there on the other side, messing around with the guys. He sure didn't look like he was in any kind of agony. Wednesday, I saw Glenn over by the window in this food fight, slipping off his chair and I couldn't stand it, I got up and left and went to our room.

But I went and said I wanted to talk to Glenn that night, I didn't even have any dinner, and he said he wanted to be friends. He looked at me funny and I haven't heard from him. It's, I don't know, seven days, eight.

I know there are other guys. I live in a dorm full of them, or half full of them. Half girls. But I keep thinking of Glenn 'cause of happiness, that's what makes me want to hang on to him.

There was this one morning when we woke up in his room, it was light out already, white light all over the room. We were sticky and warm, the sheet was all tangled. His roommate, this little blond boy, was still sleeping. I watched his eyes open and he smiled and then he went down the hall to take a shower. Glenn was hugging me and it was nothing unusual, nothing special. We didn't screw. We were just there. We kissed, but slow, the way it is when your mouth is still bad from sleep.

I was happy that morning. I didn't have to do anything. We got dressed, went to breakfast, I don't know. Took a walk. He had to go to work at a certain time and I had that sleepy feeling from waking up with the sun on my head and he said he didn't want to say goodbye to me. There was that pang. One of those looks like as if at that second, we both felt the same way.

I shrugged. I could afford to be casual then. We didn't say goodbye. I walked with him to the shed by the Eucalyptus Grove. That's where they keep all the gardening tools, the rakes, the hoes, the mowers, big bags of grass seed slumped against the wall. It smelled like hay in there. Glenn changed into his uniform and we went to the North Side, up in front of the chancellor's manor, that thick perfect grass. And Glenn gave me a ride on the lawn mower, on the handlebars. It was bouncing over these little bumps in the lawn and I was hanging on to the handlebars, laughing. I couldn't see Glenn but I knew he was there behind me. I looked around at the buildings and the lawns, there's a fountain there, and one dog was drinking from it.

See, I can't help but remember things like that. Even now, I'd rather find some way, even though he's not asking for it, to forgive Glenn. I'd rather have it work out with him, because I want more days like that. I wish I could have a whole life like that. But I guess nobody does, not just me.

I saw him in the mailroom yesterday, we're both just standing there, each opening our little boxes, getting our mail—neither of us had any— I was hurt but I wanted to reach out and touch his face. He has this hard chin, it's pointy and all bone. Lauren says she wants to hit him.

I mean, I think of him spinning around in his backyard and that's why I love him and he should understand. I go over it all and think I should have just looked at him and said I can't believe you're doing this to me. Right there in the mailroom. Now when I think that, I think maybe if I'd said that, in those words, maybe it would be different.

But then I think of my father—he feels like there was a time when we had fun, when we were happy together. I mean, I can remember being in my little bed with Dad and maybe cracking jokes, maybe laughing, but he probably never heard Danny's baseball in his mitt the way I did or I don't know. I remember late in the afternoon, wearing my dad's navy-blue sweatshirt with a hood and riding bikes with him and Danny down to the diamond.

But that's over. I don't know if I'm sorry it happened. I mean I am, but it happened, that's all. It's just one of the things that happened to me in my life. But I would never go back, never. And what hurts so much is that maybe that's what Glenn is thinking about me.

I told Lauren last night. I had to. She kept asking me what happened with Glenn. She was so good, you couldn't believe it, she was great. We were talking late and this morning we drove down to go to House of Pancakes for breakfast, get something good instead of watery eggs for a change. And on the way, Lauren's driving, she just skids to a stop on this street, in front of this elementary school. "Come on," she says. It's early, but there's already people inside the windows.

We hooked our fingers in the metal fence. You know, one of those aluminum fences around a playground. There were pigeons standing on the painted game circles. Then a bell rang and all these kids came out, yelling, spilling into groups. This was a poor school, mostly black kids, Mexican kids, all in bright colors. There's a Nabisco factory nearby and the whole air smelled like blueberry muffins.

The girls were jump-roping and the boys were shoving and running and hanging on to the monkey bars. Lauren pinched her fingers on the back of my neck and pushed my head against the fence.

"Eight years old. Look at them. They're eight years old. One of their fathers is sleeping with one of those girls. Look at her. Do you blame her? Can you blame her? Because if you can forgive her you can forgive yourself."

"I'll kill him," I said.

"And I'll kill Glenn," Lauren says.

So we went and got pancakes. And drank coffee until it was time for class.

I saw Glenn yesterday. It was so weird after all this time. I just had lunch with Lauren. We picked up tickets for Talking Heads and I wanted to get back to the lab before class and I'm walking along and Glenn was working, you know, on the lawn in front of the Mobi Building. He was still gorgeous. I was just going to walk, but he yelled over at me.

"Hey, Jenny."

"Hi, Glenn."

He congratulated me, he heard about the NSF thing. We stood there. He has another girlfriend now. I don't know, when I looked at him and stood there by the lawn mower, it's chugging away, I felt the same as I always used to, that I loved him and all that, but he might just be one of those things you can't have. Like I should have been for my father and look at him now. Oh, I think he's better, they're all better, but I'm gone, he'll never have me again.

I'm glad they're there and I'm here, but it's strange, I feel more alone now. Glenn looked down at the little pile of grass by the lawn mower and said, "Well, kid, take care of yourself," and I said, "You too, 'bye," and started walking.

So, you know what's bad, though, I started taking stuff again. Little stuff from the mailroom. No packages and not people I know anymore.

But I take one letter a Saturday, I make it just one and someone I don't know. And I keep 'em and burn 'em with a match in the bathroom sink and wash the ashes down the drain. I wait until the end of the shift. I always expect it to be something exciting. The two so far were just everyday letters, just mundane, so that's all that's new, I-had-a-pork-chop-for-dinner letters.

But something happened today, I was in the middle, three-quarters way down the bag, still looking, I hadn't picked my letter for the day, I'm being really stern, I really mean just one, no more, and there's this little white envelope addressed to me. I sit there, trembling with it in my hand. It's the first one I've gotten all year. It was my name and address, typed out, and I just stared at it. There's no address. I got so nervous, I thought maybe it was from Glenn, of course, I wanted it to be from Glenn so bad, but then I knew it couldn't be, he's got that new girlfriend now, so I threw it in the garbage can right there, one of those with the swinging metal door, and then I finished my shift. My hands were sweating, I smudged the writing on one of the envelopes.

So all the letters are in boxes, I clean off the table, fold the bags up neat and close the door, ready to go. And then I thought, I don't have to keep looking at the garbage can, I'm allowed to take it back, that's my letter. And I fished it out, the thing practically lopped my arm off. And I had it and I held it a few minutes, wondering who it was from. Then I put it in my mailbox so I can go like everybody else and get mail.

LOOKING AT HIM

GLORIA FRYM

Good Morning ―――――――――――――――――――――――

He could leap out of bed called by an alarm only he could hear. He could saunter into the shower. He could shut the shower door and rattle the tiny wired hexagons of glass. I could see him in silhouette, soaping down his private places. He could step out of the shower and rub his shoulders with the white towel. He could stand in front of the steamy mirror brushing his teeth, with the towel draped around his waist. He could comb his hair but leave it wet and slicked back, the moisture gravitating down to the ends, a few drops stuck to his cheeks below his sideburns. He could sashay into the kitchen and put the kettle on to boil. He could call out, "coffee," in a throaty voice. I could moan back, "uh-huh." He could return to the bedroom and stand in front of the open closet. The towel could slip from his hips. He could bend over to pick it up and throw it on the bed. I could feel the weight of the towel land on my ankles. His straight hair could curl slightly behind his right ear. I could follow the curl down the side of his neck around to the ten or fifteen strands of russet fuzz on his chest. He could have a faint vertical line of down running from his chest to his lower stomach, branching into his red pubic mound. The red telephone could ring and he could stand by the bed with his right hand on his white hip just below his tan line. He could slowly sit down on the bed and even more languorously lay his head on the pillow as he continued to speak into the phone. I could lean over and kiss his left shoulder which could smell like English lavender. I could bend my head down and kiss his tightening thigh. I could let my tongue move all the way down his thigh to his ankle. I could grab both his ankles and spread his firm legs apart. I could hear his voice quiver into the phone. I could crawl in between his legs, I could nest my head between his thighs, I could make him late for work.

○○ ○○ ○○

LESLIE SCALAPINO

How can I help myself,   as one woman said to me about wanting

to have intercourse with strange men,   from thinking of a man

How can I help myself,   as one woman said to me about wanting
to have intercourse with strange men,   from thinking of a man
(someone whom I don't know) as being like a seal. I mean I see a
   man
(in a crowd such as a theatre) as having the body of a seal in the way
a man would, say, be in bed with someone, kissing and barking,
which is the way a seal will bark and leap on his partly-fused hind
   limbs.
Yes. Am I not bound, I guess, (I say to myself) to regard him
   tenderly,
to concentrate on the man's trunk instead of his face, which in this
   case,
is so impassive.   Seriously,   I am fascinated by the way a seal moves.

LAURA CHESTER

Loving My Boys ───────────────

I have to be careful in loving my boys, to do so with distance, as from my desk, where I sit now, hearing him bellow, gleeful, as he drives the tractor and his full young voice bounces against the forest, the edge of which he cuts. My big boy, as tall as I am, with his twelve-and-a-half size shoe—I watch him in our Levi jacket, as he takes his lariat and ropes a chair on the patio, returning a call from "Wendy." He's got a date tonight, my baby, only thirteen. My friend Francine says he's going to be a killer, with that look in his eye, and he's got the meat already. I like to push on him to feel the playful resistance, the teen-force in him, ram-like. He walks into my bedroom first thing in the morning, looking for his brother to shoot. They kill each other, over and over, using red and blue ink that dries without a mark. They drag each other across the lawn, hoist one another from the downstairs up, by an ankle on a rope. My younger son is still innocent enough to come crawl into bed, and I gather his warmth, his blondness, into my arms, even hug him in with a leg, and often we fall back to sleep that way, arms around each other's necks. Soon, he too won't be able to come to me, tenderness met with a shrug, "Oh Mom!" They will be loved by many girls. I was simply the first. They both have heart as well as head. They both will undoubtedly devour sex. But leaving the nest is never graceful. My applause holds back, as they tumble and wave. I know I will have to let go, the hardest act—pretending to turn away, as if I had someone better to love. And it is already beginning. This summer my eldest flew off to the Tetons. When he returned, he had veins in his arms, the way a man has muscles and veins. My younger son *leaps*. I imagine a baby. They will go into manhood with their good bodies, confident, ready, whole. Take life on and plunge it. Make it thrive and yield.

oo oo oo

SHARON OLDS

The Connoisseuse of Slugs ───────────

When I was a connoisseuse of slugs
I would part the ivy leaves, and look for the
naked jelly of those gold bodies,
translucent strangers glistening along the
stones, slowly, their gelatinous bodies
at my mercy. Made mostly of water, they would shrivel
to nothing if they were sprinkled with salt,
but I was not interested in that. What I liked
was to draw aside the ivy, breathe the
odor of the wall, and stand there in silence
until the slug forgot I was there
and sent its antennae up out of its
head, the glimmering umber horns
rising like telescopes, until finally the
sensitive knobs would pop out the ends,
delicate and intimate. Years later,
when I first saw a naked man,
I gasped with pleasure to see that quiet
mystery reenacted, the slow
elegant being coming out of hiding and
gleaming in the dark air, eager and so
trusting you could weep.

LYDIA DAVIS

Break It Down _____

He's sitting there staring at a piece of paper in front of him. He's trying to break it down. He says:

I'm breaking it all down. The ticket was $600 and then after that there was more for the hotel and food and so on, for just ten days. Say $80 a day, no, more like $100 a day. And we made love, say, once a day on the average. That's $100 a shot. And each time it lasted maybe two or three hours so that would be anywhere from $33 to $50 an hour, which is expensive.

Though of course that wasn't all that went on, because we were together almost all day long. She would keep looking at me and every time she looked at me it was worth something, and she smiled at me and didn't stop talking and singing, something I said, she would sail into it, a snatch, for me, she would be gone from me a little ways but smiling too, and tell me jokes, and I loved it but didn't exactly know what to do about it and just smiled back at her and felt slow next to her, just not quick enough. So she talked and touched me on the shoulder and the arm, she kept touching and stayed close to me. You're with each other all day long and it keeps happening, the touches and smiles, and it adds up, it builds up, and you know where you'll be that night, you're talking and every now and then you think about it, no, you don't think, you just feel it as a kind of destination, what's coming up after you leave wherever you are all evening, and you're happy about it and you're planning it all, not in your head, really, somewhere inside your body, or all through your body, it's all mounting up and coming together so that when you get in bed you can't help it, it's a real performance, it all pours out, but slowly, you go easy until you can't anymore, or you hold back the whole time, you hold back and touch the edges of everything, you edge around until you have to plunge in and finish it off, and when you're finished, you're too weak to stand but after a while you have to go to the bathroom and you stand, your legs are trembling, you hold on to the door frames, there's a little light coming in through the window, you can see your way in and out, but you can't really see the bed.

So it's not really $100 a shot because it goes on all day, from the start when you wake up and feel her body next to you, and you don't miss a thing, not a thing of what's next to you, her arm, her leg, her shoulder, her face, that good skin, I have felt other good skin, but this skin is just the edge of something else, and you're going to start going, and no matter how much you crawl all over each other it won't be enough, and when your hunger dies down a little then you think how much you love her and that starts you off again, and her face, you look over at her face and can't believe how you got there and how lucky and it's still all a surprise and it never stops, even after it's over, it never stops being a surprise.

It's more like you have a good sixteen or eighteen hours a day of this going on, even when you're not with her it's going on, it's good to be away because it's going to be so good to go back to her, so it's still here, and you can't go off and look at some old street or some old painting without still feeling it in your body and a few things that happened the day before that don't mean much by themselves or wouldn't mean much if you weren't having this thing together, but you can't forget and it's all inside you all the time, so that's more like, say, sixteen into a hundred would be $6 an hour, which isn't too much.

And then it really keeps going on while you're asleep, though you're probably dreaming about something else, a building, maybe. I kept dreaming, every night, almost, about this building, because I would spend a lot of every morning in this old stone building and when I closed my eyes I would see these cool spaces and have this peace inside me, I would see the bricks of the floor and the stone arches and the space, the emptiness between, like a kind of dark frame around what I could see beyond, a garden, and this space was like stone too because of the coolness of it and the gray shadow, that kind of luminous shade, that was glowing with the light of the sun falling beyond the arches, and there was also the great height of the ceiling, all this was in my mind all the time though I didn't know it until I closed my eyes, I'm asleep and I'm not dreaming about her but she's lying next to me and I wake up enough times in the night to remember she's there, and notice, say, once she was lying on her back but now she's curled around me, I look at her closed eyes, I want to kiss her eyelids, I want to feel that soft skin under my lips, but I don't want to disturb her, I don't want to see her frown as though in her sleep she has forgotten who I am and feels just that something is bothering her and so I just look at her and hold on to it all, these times when I'm watching over her sleep and she's next to me and isn't away from me the way she will be later, I want to stay awake all night just to go on feeling that, but I can't, I fall asleep again, though I'm sleeping lightly, still trying to hold on to it.

But it isn't over when it ends, it goes on after it's all over, she's still inside you like a sweet liquor, you are filled with her, everything about her has kind of bled into you, her smell, her voice, the way her body moves, it's all inside you, at least for a while after, then you begin to lose it, and I'm beginning to lose it, you're afraid of how weak you are, that you can't get her all back into you again and now the whole thing is going out of your body and it's more in your mind than your body, the pictures come to you one by one and you look at them, some of them last longer than others, you were together in a very white clean place, a coffeehouse, having breakfast together, and the place is so white that against it you can see her clearly, her blue eyes, her smile, the colors of her clothes, even the print of the newspaper she's reading when she's not looking up at you, the light brown and red and gold of her hair when she's got her head down reading, the brown coffee, the brown rolls, all against that white table and those white plates and silver urns and silver knives and spoons, and against that quiet of the sleepy people in that room sitting alone at their tables with just some chinking and clattering of spoons and cups in saucers and some hushed voices her voice now and then rising and falling. The pictures come to you and you have to hope they won't lose their life too fast and dry up though you know they will and that you'll also forget some of what happened, because already you're turning up little things that you nearly forgot.

We were in bed and she asked me, Do I seem fat to you? and I was surprised because she didn't seem to worry about herself at all in that way and I guess I was reading into it that she did worry about herself so I answered what I was thinking and said stupidly that she had a very beautiful body, that her body was perfect, and I really meant it as an answer, but she said kind of sharply, That's not what I asked, and so I had to try to answer her again, exactly what she had asked.

And once she lay over against me late in the night and she started talking, her breath in my ear, and she just went on and on, and talked faster and faster, she couldn't stop, and I loved it, I just felt that all that life in her was running into me too, I had so little life in me, her life, her fire, was coming into me, in that hot breath in my ear, and I just wanted her to go on talking forever right there next to me, and I would go on living, like that, I would be able to go on living, but without her I don't know.

Then you forget some of it all, maybe most of it all, almost all of it, in the end, and you work hard at remembering everything now so you won't ever forget, but you can kill it too even by thinking about it too much, though you can't help thinking about it nearly all the time.

And then when the pictures start to go you start asking some questions, just little questions, that sit in your mind without any answers, like why did she have the light on when you came in to bed one night, but it was off the next, but she had it on the night after that and she had it off the last night, why, and other questions, little questions that nag at you like that.

And finally the pictures go and these dry little questions just sit there without any answers and you're left with this large heavy pain in you that you try to numb by reading, or you try to ease it by getting out into public places where there will be people around you, but no matter how good you are at pushing that pain away, just when you think you're going to be all right for a while, that you're safe, you're kind of holding it off with all your strength and you're staying in some little bare numb spot of ground, then suddenly it will all come back, you'll hear a noise, maybe it's a cat crying or a baby, or something else like her cry, you hear it and make that connection in a part of you you have no control over and the pain comes back so hard that you're afraid, afraid of how you're falling back into it again and you wonder, no, you're terrified to ask how you're ever going to climb out of it.

And so it's not only every hour of the day while it's happening, but it's really for hours and hours every day after that, for weeks, though less and less, so that you could work out the ratio if you wanted, maybe after six weeks you're only thinking about it an hour or so in the day altogether, a few minutes here and there spread over, or a few minutes here and there and half an hour before you go to sleep, or sometimes it all comes back and you stay awake with it half the night.

So when you add up all that, you've only spent maybe $3 an hour on it.

If you have to figure in the bad times too, I don't know. There weren't any bad times with her, though maybe there was one bad time, when I told her I loved her. I couldn't help it, this was the first time this had happened with her, now I was half falling in love with her or maybe completely if she had let me but she couldn't or I couldn't completely because it was all going to be so short and other things too, and so I told her, and didn't know of any way to tell her first that she didn't have to feel this was a burden, the fact that I loved her, or that she didn't have to feel the same about me, or say the same back, that it was just that I had to tell her, that's all, because it was bursting inside me, and saying it wouldn't even begin to take care of what I was feeling, really I couldn't say anything of what I was feeling because there was so much, words couldn't handle it, and making love only made it worse because then I wanted words badly but they were no good, no good at all, but I told her anyway, I was lying on top of her and her hands were up by her head and my hands were on hers and our fingers were locked and there was a little light on her face from the window but I couldn't really see her and I was afraid to say it but I had to say it because I wanted her to know, it was the last night, I had to tell her then or I'd never have another chance, I just said, Before you go to sleep, I have to tell you before you go to sleep that I love you, and immediately, right away after, she said, I love you too, and it sounded to me as if she didn't mean it, a little flat, but then it usually sounds a little flat when someone says, I love you too, because they're just saying it back even if they do mean it, and the problem is that I'll never know if she meant it, or maybe someday she'll tell me whether she meant it or not, but there's no way to know now, and I'm sorry I did that, it was a trap I didn't mean to put her in, I can see it was a trap, because if she hadn't said anything at all I know that would have hurt too, as though she were taking something from me and just accepting it and not giving anything back, so she really had to, even just to be kind to me, she had to say it, and I don't really know now if she meant it.

Another bad time, or it wasn't exactly bad, but it wasn't easy either, was when I had to leave, the time was coming, and I was beginning to tremble and feel empty, nothing in the middle of me, nothing inside, and nothing to hold me up on my legs, and then it came, everything was ready, and I had to go, and so it was just a kiss, a quick one, as though we were afraid of what might happen after a kiss, and she was almost wild then, she reached up to a hook by the door and took an old shirt, a green and blue shirt from the hook, and put it in my arms, for me to take away, the soft cloth was full of her smell, and then we stood there close together looking at a piece of paper she had in her hand and I didn't lose any of it, I was holding it tight, that last minute or two, because this was it, we'd come to the end of it, things always change, so this was really it, over.

Maybe it works out all right, maybe you haven't lost for doing it, I don't know, no, really, sometimes when you think of it you feel like a prince really, you feel just like a king, and then other times you're afraid, you're afraid, not all the time but now and then, of what it's going to do to you, and it's hard to know what to do with it now.

Walking away I looked back once and the door was still open, I could see her standing far back in the dark of the room, I could only really see her white face still looking out at me, and her white arms.

I guess you get to a point where you look at that pain as if it were there in front of you three feet away lying in a box, an open box, in a window somewhere. It's hard and cold, like a bar of metal. You just look at it there and say, All right, I'll take it, I'll buy it. That's what it is. Because you know all about it before you even go into this thing. You know the pain is part of the whole thing. And it isn't that you can say afterwards the pleasure was greater than the pain and that's why you would do it again. That has nothing to do with it. You can't measure it, because the pain comes after and it lasts longer. So the question really is, Why doesn't that pain make you say, I won't do it again? When the pain is so bad that you have to say that, but you don't.

So I'm just thinking about it, how you can go in with $600, more like $1,000, and how you can come out with an old shirt.

DORIANNE LAUX

China ——————————————————

From behind he looks like a man
I once loved, that hang dog slouch
to his jeans, a sweater vest, his neck
thick veined as a horse cock, a halo
of chopped curls.

He orders coffee and searches
his pockets, first in front, then
from behind, a long finger sliding
into the slitted denim like that man
slipped his thumb into me one summer
as we lay after love, our freckled
bodies two plump starfish on the sheets.

Semen leaked and pooled in his palm
as he moved his thumb slowly, not
to excite me, just to affirm
he'd been there.

I have loved other men since, taken
them into my mouth like a warm vowel,
lay beneath them and watched their irises
float like small worlds in their opened eyes.

But this man pressed his thumb
toward the tail of my spine
like he was entering
China, or a ripe papaya
so that now when I think of love,
I think of this.

oo oo oo

ERICA JONG

from: *Fanny: Being the True History of the
Adventures of Fanny Hackabout-Jones*

Fanny plays the man . . .

A Noble Beginning; but then the Twig snapp'd! 'Twas
no Matter, for just at that Moment, there came a Knock upon the Door,
and, like a Conjurer at a Fair, I flipp'd the Tablecloth o'er to its clean
Side, secreted the charcoal Twig in my Boot Top, and call'd:

"Enter!"

'Twas Polly with my roast Capon.

"If you please, Sir," said she.

"Thankee kindly, Polly," said I.

"Thank *you*, Sir," said she, flashing her Eyes at me. Whereupon she
tuckt a linen Napkin into my Shirt Front, taking care to expose her
fine, plump Bosom, just below my Nose, and I receiv'd a most Pow'rful
Odour of Attar of Roses, and honest female Sweat, o'er and above the
Odour of roast Capon: so much so that, 'twas fortunate I was not the
Man I seem'd to be, for certainly the mingl'd Lusciousness of their
entrancing Odours would have caus'd me to ravish Polly forthwith.

Instead, I made ready to ravish the Capon.

"Sit ye down, Lass," said I, "and talk to me whilst I have my Supper."

"Oh, Sir," said Polly, flutt'ring her Lashes. "I'm sure I daren't. The
Landlord would surely turn me out o'Doors for such."

Now, our Polly was not one of those Slender Wenches who put one
in mind of an Anatomist's Skeleton, and who would probably seem
more like Broomstaffs than Women if one embraced 'em in Bed. No.
She was, on the Contrary, so juicy and plump that she seem'd bursting
thro' her tight Stays, e'en as the Flesh of the delicious roast Capon was
bursting thro' its sewn Trussing. For a Moment, I almost fancied I *was*
a Man and susceptible to her Charms. 'Twas all I could do to stop
myself from thrusting an eager Hand into that luscious Cleavage.

"Are you quite well, Sir?" she askt, bending o'er me with Solicitude
(for, perhaps I lookt as queer as I felt). "Shall I cut your Capon for
you?"

"Yes, Lass, please do so, for I have had a most wearying Journey
and I can scarce find the Strength to do it myself."

She leant o'er me to pierce the juicy Flesh of the Capon; and, unable to contain myself any longer, I clapp'd my Mouth to the tender Valley betwixt the white Mountains of her Breasts and there insinuated my darting Tongue.

"Sir!" she cried with Alarm.

"A thousand Pardons!" I cried, sinking to my Knees, and kissing the Hem of her Garment. "A thousand Pardons. But I have this Day lost my own dear Mother and Grief hath left me distracted."

"Sir," she says, "I'll have you know I'm no Strumpet!" But i'faith, I could feel her softening a little at this Tale of Grief—which was, indeed, not so very far from being true.

I need hardly say, Belinda, that I was astonish'd by my own Behaviour, and yet, somehow I could not desist. Perhaps 'twas Grief that drove me to seduce a Maid when I was a mere Maid myself; perhaps 'twas something stranger still. Perhaps 'twas the wretched Influence of the God of the Witches (whom some call the Devil), or perhaps 'twas some long-lasting Result of the Flying Unguent, or yet perhaps some Madness brought on by the Horrors I had witness'd. Perhaps e'en 'twas my Muse's Way of showing me to feel both Man's and Woman's Passions. Or perhaps 'twas the mischievous Working of that Great Goddess in whom I only half believ'd.

At any Rate, I threw myself at Polly's Feet, and kiss'd her Hem, and then her Ankles, and then, since she made but little Resistance, her Knees, and then, since she seem'd to sigh and invite it, her Thighs, and then, since she sat down upon a Chair and spread those Thighs (all the while protesting *No! No! No!* in the self-same Tone as *Yes! Yes! Yes!*), the sweet tender Ruby-red Cleft of her Sex itself, which lay expos'd to my View, since the Wench wore nothing at all 'neath her Shift and Petticoats.

Ah, the poor Capon lay deserted and steaming upon the Table (and 'neath that lay hidden my poor, scarce-started Epick), whilst I bent my Lips to Polly's tender Cleft and play'd Arpeggios with my own astonish'd Tongue. 'Twas salt as the Sea and tasted not unlike sweet Baby Oysters pluckt from the Bosom of the Deep.

"O Sir! O! O! O!" cries Polly, as I dart my Tongue in and out, inflam'd by her Words as well as her lovely ruby Slit. But, since by now her Petticoats are o'er my Head, I cannot fondle the twin Hillocks of her Breasts, but instead make free to stroke her milky Thighs, whilst her Petticoats make a sort of Tent in which I hide from all the Horrors of Mankind.

How warm and sweet it is inside a Petticoat! What Refuge from the Terrors of the World! What great Good Fortune to be born a Man and have such Refuge e'er within Grasp, within the warm World of a Woman's Hoop!

oo oo oo

BERNADETTE MAYER

Carlton Fisk Is My Ideal ——————————

He wears a beautiful necklace
next to the beautiful skin of his neck
unlike the Worthington butcher
Bradford T. Fisk (butchers always
have a crush on me), who cannot even order veal
except in whole legs of it.
Oh the legs of a catcher!
Catchers squat in a posture
that is of course inward denying orgasm
but Carlton Fisk, I could
model a whole attitude to spring
on him. And he is a leaper!
Like Walt Frazier or, better,
like the only white leaper,
I forget his name, in the ABA's
All-Star game half-time slam-dunk contest
this year. I think about Carlton Fisk in his
modest home in New Hampshire
all the time, I love the sound of his name
denying orgasm. Carlton & I
look out the window at spring's first
northeaster. He carries a big hero
across the porch of his home to me.
(He has no year-round Xmas tree
like Clifford Ray who handles the ball
like a banana). We eat & watch the storm
batter the buds balking on the trees
& cover the green of the grass
that my sister thinks is new grass.
It's last year's grass still!
And still there is no spring training
as I write this, March 16, 1976,
the year of the blizzard that sealed our love
up in a great mound of orgasmic earth.
The pitcher's mound is the lightning mound.
Pudge will see fastballs in the wind,
his mescaline arm extends to the field.

70

He wears his necklace.
He catches the ball in his teeth!
Balls fall with a neat thunk
in the upholstery of the leather glove he puts on
to caress me, as told to, in the off-season.
All of a sudden he leaps from the couch,
a real ball has come thru the window
& is heading for the penguins on his sweater,
one of whom has lost his balloon
which is floating up into the sky!

ANNE WALDMAN
from: Iovis Omnia Plena _____

My older brother's wife rips up the photograph of his earlier daughter. I struggle in heart with the little godchild my lover commands with him into my world. The male makes us suffer for his heart of hearts. I sleep with my older brother's brother not my blood but who yet resembles him, after sitting on my brother's lap in what seems like a long taxi ride (it was raining) home. My mother is trying to keep us apart. We go to Hotel Earle with old man lobby, whore at the door and make illicit love something like incest, unskilled in a burning urge to forge a link. The beautiful god is in town a few days, heading out west. Can I really make love to this yet again another Greek? Too cerebral, unsatisfied. It's the dark connection in this one. I always wore a black turtleneck then. I speak confidently.

The blond on the telephone is a long story, like my younger another brother who confesses desire for drugs & men. He takes my virginity as we used to say and we are cheerful in a sullied bed. Because my mother died I can speak these things I state again this is for fathers, brothers, lovers, husbands, son for that is next of kin alive & changing in a fluid world. It is a palpable motion towards them from one who slumbered many years in the body of a man and in herself a turf of woman becoming Amazonian in proportions (I grow larger even as I write this) as she spans a continent takes on the wise mother as she dies. I gave birth to a son to better understand the men whose messages pour out of me.

• • •

All is full of Jove, he fucks everything
It is the rough way to prove it
The male gods descend & steal power
How does it happen
How does it happen Blanche Fleur & Heart Sorrow?

Here's how:

I lie back & take him in. He wounds me after a fashion. A new sensation of art & stimulus, for I watch us both & participate after a fashion until we are spent & the man is melted in arms, and no longer to do battle on this bed stage. The bed is the book is the bed is the book where sheets record every muscle tear sweat ooze of life & groan. It is the playground of the senses for this artist as sweet rehearsal for the non-existent pages that will honor this rumbling & panic and lost-ness. I want to say to dear male lovers living & dead not anger made this but with due respect in spite of the crimes of which your sex is prone. I honor the member who is a potential wand of miracles, who dances for his supper, who is the jester & fool and sometimes the saint of life. But she, me, who takes it, who responds clasping with cunt teeth, the receiver, the mountain, whatever it could be called, the emptying, the joining of this most radiant sphere where the chakras glow under the sheets or else they are fucking in water, she is witness in this brave act. It feels like the great sperm whale entered me.

oo oo oo

LOUISE SHIVERS

from: *Here to Get My Baby Out of Jail* ————————

Rainwater splashed out of the sides of the big basin, and although I'd sworn to myself that I wouldn't think about him, one of the water splotches on the porch floor was shaped like the soft brown birthmark on his face. I lifted a straight chair out into the flower garden and sat in the sun. Bending over with my head between my knees, I brushed hard with long, sweeping strokes and gave myself to the thoughts of him that reached into my brain like fingers.

The fingers pulled me back to another Saturday, one in May when the plants were still tender in the fields. He'd been standing on the back porch washing himself out of an enamel pan. Making up the bed in the back room where the window faced out onto the porch, I'd looked up and seen him. He jerked his undershirt off over his head like an impatient boy and slung it to the floor. The sheen of the hair growing down his torso in the shape of a tree trunk was brighter than the streaked red hair on his head.

I'd stopped fluffing the pillow in my hand. He soaped and washed his sloping chest and lean arms as unself-consciously as if he were at his own stream in some deep forest. He threw back his head as if to taste the spring air when he saw my watching face. For the first time we looked straight into each other's eyes. Slowly he began washing again, keeping my eyes. I could feel the smoothness of the washrag slide down his arm and then up the white underarm into the shocking nest of armpit. People moved around us in the house, but it was as if we were in a little box sealed with beeswax and couldn't stop the breath-holding communication until there was the loud sound of a pickup truck driving into the yard and Neb's voice calling out: *"Jack!"*

Now the hot summer sun that ripened the tobacco leaves to their gold dust dried the cocoon of my hair.

"Roxy . . ." I dropped my towel and the brush that was full of tangled black tufts of hair, and, of course, it was him standing there when I thought he was halfway to Raleigh. Him standing there feet apart, calves hard, eyes watching me.

Dear God, I must die from the sickness of wanting wanting.

"He gone into town?" Jack asked.

I must die, there is no way of holding back.

He took hold of my hand, and we moved to the shade of the shed. There was no thought of going inside the house or any other hiding place. The tobacco fields were fences. We lay down together in the fragrant dirt of the flower bed. Cotton clothes were no matter; an overflowing gourd dipper was tilted to the angle for him to drink. Our motions were like the unrollings of a Persian rug of many colors. Our tongues were the tenderest chameleons of spring. He put himself high up inside me as naturally as a silver shoehorn easing a silk slipper.

By the time Daddy's car pulled into the yard, Jack had gone down to the tobacco barns. I was bathed and lying across my bed, napping, with a whisper in my brain. The muslin robe that covered my body lay on me like broomstraw.

By the end of June the heat had settled over the county. The tobacco was ripe in the fields, and every week, every day, was centered around getting the leaves out of the fields at their peak before the sun burned away their brightness. "Burned up" were words that were always whispered in this part of the country because they could mean only two things: burned up in the fields because the harvesting wasn't done quickly enough, or the feared sight in the night of a wooden barn full of golden tobacco bursting into flames because someone sleeping there hadn't watched the stoked wood fires closely enough.

Helpers came out from town—maids, factory workers, children out of school for the summer, all glad to get the good pay and the change from town. Callie and Raider and sometimes Gyp came out to earn extra spending money. Daddy visited all over. He liked to see how each farm's crop was doing. He'd stay an hour at one place, then ride on to another, then back to the funeral home.

It seemed like Aaron's complete attention was on his crop. When the smell of curing tobacco from the first barn was in his nose, he walked around with a half smile on his face and whistled through his teeth. He worked every day until he was so tired all he could do was wash off and drop into bed. Jack worked hard, too, in the fields, with the mules, but he seemed to save a part of himself.

When the "putting-in" started, Aaron and Jack alternated nights at the barn. Whichever one slept there slept in the big net-covered cot and kept the fire going and the barn temperature even. Whichever one slept there slept in snatches.

At first we'd just be together the nights when Aaron was at the barn. Without saying any words, Jack would take me into the spare room and do quiet things to me with his mouth. Once we started doing it, we just couldn't stop.

Barning tobacco was good, close, clean, hard work, with everybody doing his part. The men and mules in the field cropping and bringing the arrowhead-shaped leaves to the little sheds near the tobacco barns, the women and children waiting to take the leaves from the burlap-sided truck, to hand them in little bunches to the loopers, one on each side of the truck. The loopers slapped the leaves onto tobacco sticks that sat on wooden sawhorses, slapped and tied the harvested leaves onto the stick with cotton twine. A pattern and a relay from the field to the rafters of the barn established itself quickly, and hot day after hot day followed one after the other. The sound of summer voices, laughing, telling stories about hants and lost loves, passing the time as quick hands moved, filled the air and drifted on whatever stir of breeze passed by over Tar County, into the town.

But all of it rolled out in front of me like some kind of dream. I couldn't get enough of Jack.

All summer the radio in the kitchen played

> *I will pawn you my watch,*
> *I will pawn you my chain,*
> *I will pawn you my gold wedding ring,*
> *Oh, warden, you know I want my baby out of jail.*

In the daytime I was like a sleepwalker—walking slow, my blood thick as honey. I could hear the tobacco truck's wooden wheels rattling in the ruts coming out of the fields toward us at the barn. The tow-sack sides were high and the cropped leaves piled up. Here we stood working on the truck under the shed: Slap-hand-sling-twine-tie.

I looped on one frame horse and Gyp on the other, her black face shiny with sweat. Old Mama handed out the leaves, ready to take my place when I went to the house to start dinner.

Quiet as velvet, I could hear my own blood. I'd remember pulling his head down, groping in his hair, while his sun-cracked lips searched around the blanched thin skin to the earth color to the center—moving, tasting, drawing from the nipple the way to the well inside that holds water never hauled up in its own bucket before, but now moved even by the daydream of him.

Jerking up, my mind would come back, and I'd realize that the chicken was lying floured and unfried on the kitchen table while I'd been across the quilt in a trance. The field hands, Aaron, the children, all would be coming in for dinner in no time. My feet would light across the lino-leum, moving with haste. By the time Raider, always the first, came bounding up the porch chanting *Roxanna, Georgeanna, ripe banana, Alabama,* the chicken would be fried, the cornbread sliding out of the oven, the tomatoes sliced and the butter beans dipped up.

I'd keep my eyes down as Jack washed, scrubbed the black tobacco gum from his hands. I'd keep busy pouring tea, glass after glass, for the thirsty workers, and I'd only nod when Jack would speak.

Pass me some more of those butter beans.

But I'd inhale his body from across the long table, know his dusty cured smell from all the others.

After everyone left to go back to the barns, I'd pick up the heavy workshirt he left behind—the one he wore for top cover at daybreak to go into the fields to crop the clammy leaves. I'd pick it up and burrow my face in it and inhale the wood-smoke smell of him until I'd realize I was moaning out loud. Baby'd start repeating my sounds. I'd look at her and listen to the strange imitations. Bird mocking a cat. My eyes would blur, and even when I'd reach to touch her, I'd realize that my own little baby seemed no more real to me than a picture in a catalogue.

By July I'd start slipping down to the barn. It seemed there was just no way we could get enough of each other. It was dangerous, terrible. Every chance we'd get we'd snatch at each other, slip, hide—and when we couldn't, it was hard not to be cross or surly. We'd stare across the kitchen at each other—our eyes dry and cagey. Watching. Waiting. I'd realized by then that the fond feeling I'd had for Aaron was just a weak hum compared to the raging thing in my chest now. I didn't think about the rest of my life. I didn't care. I had to have him. The way his eyes looked at me across the room told me he felt the same.

○○ ○○ ○○

JULIA VOSE

---

       mmmmMMMMmm . . . Let there be slips Let trees go
sideways Let him lie "maybe" Let him be surprised when he takes
Let eyes happen blue over a string of lies Let the lies be his true
Take his comfort when the cat's mauled Take a call in the middle of
the night Take him home Take your clothes off with him Let your
bed see if somebody wants to drive him off Let him walk away Let
him out of your sight Let him leave the country Let him live alone
Let him run out of money Let him borrow money Let him get fucked
over Let him cook Let him clean Let him build Let him want you
Let him dream of losing you Let him eat Let him shit Let him
masturbate Let him want a man Let him want a lesbian Let him
want a literary bride Let him want to Let him want you Let him
tear your clothes off Let him see how fat you really are Let him be
dirty Let him sleep in another room Let him eat alone with you
there Let him reject you Let him find you again Let him off the
hook Let him go Let go of him Let him be a century Let him be
the other side of the country Let him hate his mother Let him love
men Let him love women Let him dress like a rat Let him be bald
Let him grow hair Let him shave Let him have face fair Let him
call you any name he needs to Let him go crazy Let him be six weeks
old Let him have someone take your picture while he sneaks up on
you in a mask Let him suck you in bed like a baby Let him wear
panties Let him talk himself out Let him fool himself Let him sit
down Let him have time Let him have time for wisdom Let him
make a place for you in his house Let him give you a good room
Let him come to you Let him work Let him build for himself Let
him build himself partly for you Let him take a walk Let him walk alone

        you do, don't you?
        you do receive him

oo oo oo

KATHLEEN FRASER

Because You Aren't Here to Be What I Can't Think Of _____

Because you aren't here to be what I can't think of I need most.
Because you aren't pouring me a Scotch with your hands all over the
ice cubes.
Because the moon's another streetlight and your lights are off, and on
in someone else's.
　　　　　Because you warned me thinking you were good
　　　　　but you weren't.
Because I imagine your almost skinny legs and ideal ass from the
back
as you put more Debussy on the stereo with the 10 A.M. sun
deliciously
licking you.
　　　　　Because I'm in trouble, hot-headed, bored with the
　　　　　necessary
and can't put on my jogging shoes in spite of their blue Nike stride.
Because your mouth is wistful, off on the grand tour and I want to be
every stop, because you won't stop
long enough to get really scared when you see how deep you
　　go in me,
how deep I come inside you, inside you, let me go
　　　　　　　　　　　　inside you and
　　　　　　　　　　　　come up
for more because there are the soft syllabic fruits of Brazil
yet to taste and our twenty juicy fingers' amaroso

on a white cotton shore in what country, is it, meant for us.
Because we are changing
　　　　　　　each other's proportions and how much
　　　　　　　there is
to know, because you still believe you are always in control, oh
a syllogism is a safe place to be but not as mysterious as a rare
　　Chablis.

Because I keep trying to be ambidextrous and adapt to this double
　　vision,

but my eyes hurt and in the last dream you came right in
and went to sleep on my floor.
Because I want to tell you the truth and you think of yourself
as not truthful enough, but you listen, and are sometimes coming
    nearer.
Because the old stories, you know them backwards, you know them
    forwards
and they need more pictures in them with windows and doorways
    and
smoke drawn in pencil curling out the chimney.

Because it's getting
late

and you know you can fool almost anyone but me, but so what.
There you are now in your fabulous brown Italian shoes and
    Egyptian cigarettes,
the man whose soul I love and chest (under cotton shirt) which I bite
    into
with this thought, in spite of those not quite open eyes
so intent on their hiding you are careful of.
Because there's a saxophone playing between our telephones but you
    can't
pick it up

because of your other life, the life that came first,

that
comes

first tonight, even in our city, life I came after, and other lives
that I continue to come after, because logic always dictates an order,
reasonable, one before two, two before three, because I will not
    always
be she who is willing to be logical, not always be two, three.
Because I love the new, in you, and the years of us,

but listen closely

when you tell yourself to me, how you never want to hurt again,
someone. As though only one of us were some one.

Because I want to do it, let's do it to a brassy Salsa trumpet,
because I'm not on a dancefloor with you, but here,
hanging out with my shadow over a city of windows,
lit-up, imagining another kind of life almost like this one.

○○ ○○ ○○

ANNE RICE

from: *The Vampire Lestat* _____

Lestat's childhood friend Nicholas has discovered that he and his mother, Gabrielle, are vampires . . .

When I awoke I heard his cries. He was beating on the oaken door, cursing me for keeping him prisoner. The sound filled the tower, and the scent of him came through the stone walls: succulent, oh so succulent, smell of living flesh and blood, his flesh and blood.

She slept still.

Do not do this thing.

Symphony of malice, symphony of madness coming through the walls, philosophy straining to contain the ghastly images, the torture, to surround it with language . . .

When I stepped into the stairwell, it was like being caught in a whirlwind of his cries, his human smell.

And all the remembered scents mingled with it—the afternoon sunshine on a wooden table, the red wine, the smoke of the little fire.

"Lestat! Do you hear me! Lestat!" Thunder of fists against the door.

Memory of childhood fairy tale: the giant says he smells the blood of a human in his lair. Horror. I knew the giant was going to find the human. I could hear him coming after the human, step by step. I was the human.

Only no more.

Smoke and salt of flesh and pumping blood.

"This is the witches' place! Lestat, do you hear me! This is the witches' place!"

Dull tremor of the old secrets between us, the love, the things that only we had known, felt. Dancing in the witches' place. Can you deny it? Can you deny everything that passed between us?

Get him out of France. Send him to the New World. And then what? All his life he is one of those slightly interesting but generally tiresome mortals who have seen spirits, talk of them incessantly, and no one believes him. Deepening madness. Will he be a comical lunatic finally, the kind that even the ruffians and bullies look after, playing his fiddle in a dirty coat for the crowds on the streets of Port-au-Prince?

"Be the puppeteer again," she had said. Is that what I was? *No one will ever believe his mad tales.*

But he knows the place where we lie, Mother. He knows our names, the name of our kin—too many things about us. And he will never go quietly to another country. And *they* may go after him; *they* will never let him live now.

Where are *they?*

I went up the stairs in the whirlwind of his echoing cries, looked out the little barred window at the open land. They'll be coming again. They have to come. First I was alone, then I had her with me, and now I have them!

But what was the crux? That he wanted it? That he had screamed over and over that I had denied him the power?

Or was it that I now had the excuses I needed to bring him to me as I had wanted to do from the first moment? My Nicolas, my love. Eternity waits. All the great and splendid pleasures of being dead.

I went further up the stairs towards him and the thirst sang in me. To hell with his cries. The thirst sang and I was an instrument of its singing.

And his cries had become inarticulate—the pure essence of his curses, a dull punctuation to the misery that I could hear without need of any sound. Something divinely carnal in the broken syllables coming from his lips, like the low gush of the blood through his heart.

I lifted the key and put it in the lock and he went silent, his thoughts washing backwards and into him as if the ocean could be sucked back into the tiny mysterious coils of a single shell.

I tried to see *him* in the shadows of the room, and not *it*—the love for him, the aching, wrenching months of longing for him, the hideous and unshakable human need for him, the lust. I tried to see the mortal who didn't know what he was saying as he glared at me:

"You, and your talk of goodness"—low seething voice, eyes glittering—"your talk of good and evil, your talk of what was right and what was wrong and death, oh yes, death, the horror, the tragedy . . ."

Words. Borne on the ever swelling current of hatred, like flowers opening in the current, petals peeling back, then falling apart:

". . . and you shared it with her, the lord's son giveth to the lord's wife his great gift, the Dark Gift. Those who live in the castle share the Dark Gift—never were they dragged to the witches' place where the human grease pools on the ground at the foot of the burnt stake, no, kill the old crone who can no longer see to sew, and the idiot boy who cannot till the field. And what does he give us, the lord's son, the wolfkiller, the one who screamed in the witches' place? Coin of the realm! That's good enough for us!"

Shuddering. Shirt soaked with sweat. Gleam of taut flesh through the torn lace. Tantalizing, the mere sight of it, the narrow tightly muscled torso that sculptors so love to represent, nipples pink against the dark skin.

"This power"—sputtering as if all day long he had been saying the words over with the same intensity, and it does not really matter that now I am present—"this power that made all the lies meaningless, this dark power that soared over everything, this truth that obliterated..."

No. Language. Not truth.

The wine bottles were empty, the food devoured. His lean arms were hardened and tense for the struggle—but what struggle?—his brown hair fallen out of its ribbon, his eyes enormous and glazed.

But suddenly he pushed against the wall as if he'd go through it to get away from me—dim remembrance of their drinking from him, the paralysis, the ecstasy—yes he was drawn immediately forward again, staggering, putting his hands out to steady himself by taking hold of things that were not there.

But his voice had stopped.

Something breaking in his face.

"How could you keep it from me!" he whispered. Thoughts of old magic, luminous legend, some great eerie strata in which all the shadowy things thrived, an intoxication with forbidden knowledge in which the natural things become unimportant. No miracle anymore to the leaves falling from the autumn trees, the sun in the orchard.

No.

The scent was rising from him like incense, like the heat and the smoke of church candles rising. Heart thumping under the skin of his naked chest. Tight little belly glistening with sweat, sweat staining the thick leather belt. Blood full of salt. I could scarce breathe.

And we do breathe. We breathe and we taste and we smell and we feel and we thirst.

"You have misunderstood everything." Is this Lestat speaking? It sounded like some other demon, some loathsome thing for whom the voice was the imitation of a human voice. "You have misunderstood everything that you have seen and heard."

"I would have shared anything I possessed with you!" Rage building again. He reached out. "It was you who never understood," he whispered.

"Take your life and leave with it. Run."

"Don't you see it's the confirmation of everything? That it exists is the confirmation—pure evil, sublime evil!" Triumph in his eyes. He reached out suddenly and closed his hand on my face.

"Don't taunt me!" I said. I struck him so hard he fell backwards, chastened, silent. "When it was offered me I said no. I tell you I said no. With my last breath, I said no."

"You were always the fool," he said. "I told you that." But he was breaking down. He was shuddering and the rage was alchemizing into desperation. He lifted his arms again and then stopped. "You believed things that didn't matter," he said almost gently. "There was something you failed to see. Is it possible you don't know yourself what you possess now?" The glaze over his eyes broke instantly into tears.

His face knotted. Unspoken words coming from him of love.

And an awful self-consciousness came over me. Silent and lethal, I felt myself flooded with the power I had over him and his knowledge of it, and my love for him heated the sense of power, driving it towards a scorching embarrassment which suddenly changed into something else.

We were in the wings of the theater again; we were in the village in Auvergne in that little inn. I smelled not merely the blood in him, but the sudden terror. He had taken a step back. And the very movement stoked the blaze in me, as much as the vision of his stricken face.

He grew smaller, more fragile. Yet he'd never seemed stronger, more alluring than he was now.

All the expression drained from his face as I drew nearer. His eyes were wondrously clear. And his mind was opening as Gabrielle's mind had opened, and for one tiny second there flared a moment of us together in the garret, talking and talking as the moon glared on the snow-covered roofs, or walking through the Paris streets, passing the wine back and forth, heads bowed against the first gust of winter rain, and there had been the eternity of growing up and growing old before us, and so much joy even in misery, even in the misery—the real eternity, the real forever—the mortal mystery of that. But the moment faded in the shimmering expression of his face.

"Come to me, Nicki," I whispered. I lifted both hands to beckon. "If you want it, you must come..."

I saw a bird soaring out of a cave above the open sea. And there was something terrifying about the bird and the endless waves over which it flew. Higher and higher it went and the sky turned to silver and then gradually the silver faded and the sky went dark. The darkness of evening, nothing to fear, really, nothing. Blessed darkness. But it was falling gradually and inexorably over nothing save this one tiny creature cawing in the wind above a great wasteland that was the world. Empty caves, empty sands, empty sea.

All I had ever loved to look upon, or listen to, or felt with my hands was gone, or never existed, and the bird, circling and gliding, flew on and on, upwards past me, or more truly past no one, holding the entire landscape, without history or meaning, in the flat blackness of one tiny eye.

I screamed but without a sound. I felt my mouth full of blood and each swallow passing down my throat and into fathomless thirst. And I wanted to say, yes, I understand now, I understand how terrible, how unbearable, this darkness. I didn't know. Couldn't know. The bird sailing on through the darkness over the barren shore, the seamless sea. Dear God, stop it. Worse than the horror in the inn. Worse than the helpless trumpeting of the fallen horse in the snow. But the blood was the blood after all, and the heart—the luscious heart that was all hearts—was right there, on tiptoe against my lips.

Now, my love, now's the moment. I can swallow the life that beats from your heart and send you into the oblivion in which nothing may ever be understood or forgiven, or I can bring you to me.

I pushed him backwards. I held him to me like a crushed thing. But the vision wouldn't stop.

His arms slipped around my neck, his face wet, eyes rolling up into his head. Then his tongue shot out. It licked hard at the gash I had made for him in my own throat. Yes, eager.

But please stop this vision. Stop the upward flight and the great slant of the colorless landscape, the cawing that meant nothing over the howl of the wind. The pain is nothing compared to this darkness. I don't want to . . . I don't want to . . .

But it was dissolving. Slowly dissolving.

And finally it was finished. The veil of silence had come down, as it had with her. Silence. He was separate. And I was holding him away from me, and he was almost falling, his hands to his mouth, the blood running down his chin in rivulets. His mouth was open and a dry sound came out of it, in spite of the blood, a dry scream.

And beyond him, and beyond the remembered vision of the metallic sea and the lone bird who was its only witness—I saw her in the doorway and her hair was a Virgin Mary veil of gold around her shoulders, and she said with the saddest expression on her face:

"Disaster, my son."

oo oo oo

MARGARET ATWOOD

Variation on the Word *Sleep* ⎯⎯⎯⎯⎯⎯⎯

I would like to watch you sleeping,
which may not happen.
I would like to watch you,
sleeping. I would like to sleep
with you, to enter
your sleep as its smooth dark wave
slides over my head

and walk with you through that lucent
wavering forest of bluegreen leaves
with its watery sun & three moons
towards the cave where you must descend,
towards your worst fear

I would like to give you the silver
branch, the small white flower, the one
word that will protect you
from the grief at the center
of your dream, from the grief
at the center. I would like to follow
you up the long stairway
again & become
the boat that would row you back

carefully, a flame
in two cupped hands
to where your body lies
beside me, and you enter
it as easily as breathing in

I would like to be the air
that inhabits you for a moment
only. I would like to be that unnoticed
& that necessary.

TO GIVE AND
HAZARD ALL

ERICA JONG

from: *Serenissima* _____

Suddenly Will runs in to me, wearing his motley. He turns for me, showing it off. He drops his mask, then puts it back on, doing a little dance around the room, miming the perfect Harlequin. Then all at once he banishes the maids in a stern, masterly voice. They flee from the room bowing and tittering. My heart pounds as if it should fly out of my bosom. Then it happens—all in a rush—he takes me in his arms (I still dressed in my boy's doublet), holds me fast, and kisses me with molten sweetness.

"Jessica, Jessica," he says, enfolding me. The tight rosebud between my thighs, furled for so many celibate months, wants nothing more than to explode, but my mind races ahead as minds will. Perhaps when animals mate it is all a matter of blood and nerves, scents and synapses, vessels filling and vessels emptying (although sometimes I doubt even that); but humans love within the context of that great convention "Love," that well-worn metaphor "Love," that gaudy tapestry "Love" woven through the ages by the poets and artists, dyed in our nerves, imprinted on our brains, accompanied by sweet familiar music.

Oh, I had loved and lusted, loved and "Loved." And sometimes I was not sure whether I had loved "Love" or the man in question, myself and my role as Innamorata, or just the adrenaline rush of love, that most powerful of all drugs, that highest of all highs—kickier than cocaine, more euphoric than opium, dizzier than dope. For sometimes we create a lover out of a parti-colored fool just to feel that rush again—and when the rush is over, we look at him and laugh, asking ourselves why.

But at its truest, love is altogether another matter: a matter of gods and goddesses, or spirits merging, of a holy communion in the flesh. And one never knows, before making that leap of faith, whether one will find pure spirit or mere motley, holy communion or sexual aerobics, gods and goddesses, or goats and monkeys. "Who chooseth me must give and hazard all he hath"—the essence and the test of love.

JOYCE CAROL OATES

from: *You Must Remember This* _____

Enid's uncle Felix visits her in the hospital after her suicide attempt . . .

So you want to love me, Felix said.

So you thought you'd kill yourself to punish me, Felix said in a voice just loud enough for Enid to hear.

In the hospital room when they were alone together he stroked her hand in secret, slowly he drew his fingers along the curve of her waist, her thigh. She felt his touch through the bedclothes, staring at him weak with love. At these times he said nothing, a kind of trance was upon them both, a languorous blood-heavy extinction of their minds. She saw he was angry with her, he was sick with desire for her, the rest of the world was distant, obliterated. Enid felt a shuddering sensation of the kind she had felt sinking into sleep, into Death. Except she had not died. They had hauled her back as one might haul a fish out of the water with a net. So you thought you could escape us!

You're never going to do that again, are you, Felix said.

Enid's lips moved numbly. No.

Are you?

No.

Are you?

No, Felix.

And they stared at each other half perplexed, trembling with anticipation, a desire so keen it must surely have charged the air in the room and anyone blundering inside would have known. Felix's color was high, warm, his smile seemed involuntary, he was the one who had brought Enid Stevick the twelve creamy-white roses wrapped in tissue paper and smelling of cold; he was the one who had brought the Swiss chocolates in the plump red satin box there on the windowsill for Enid's visitors to sample. Of all Enid Stevick's relatives the nuns were most taken with her young Uncle Felix.

He promised her he wouldn't hurt her he wouldn't really do anything to her until he thought she was ready, no matter that Enid, crying her hot spasmodic tears, squirming eel-like and ravenous in his arms, demanded love, adult love; she *was* ready, she said, the taste of wine oddly dry in her mouth, sweat running in rivulets down her sides. Felix stroked and caressed her, he kissed and tongued and sucked her breasts, her nipples, he liked even to suck her underarms, he liked her sweat, the tastes of her body—there was nothing of her body he didn't adore! He might kiss and nuzzle the soft rather bruised flesh of the inside of her elbow, the flesh behind her knee, he kneaded her buttocks, the small of her back, her belly, always he stroked and kissed and tongued her between the legs, he loved making love to her in any way he might, rubbing his erect penis in its thin tight rubber sheath slowly between her legs, slowly slowly again again again kissing her with his tongue deep in her mouth until Enid couldn't bear the powerful waves of sensation, orgasm overcame her quick and terrible, her eyeballs rolling in their sockets and her lips drawn back in a death's-head grimace from her teeth. She heard herself cry out helplessly, crazily—the delirious words *I love you I love love love you* or no words at all, only frightened sounds like those of a small child being beaten. Their faces were hidden from each other, Felix's weight on her was profound as the very weight of the world, she wanted it never to be lifted.

Sometimes it was a glass of red wine he urged her to drink, sometimes straight vodka, he gave her only a shot glass of vodka it was such powerful stuff he warned but it should loosen her up. And it did.

He was risking jail for her, he must be crazy, he said, baring his teeth in a mirthless laugh, but what the hell: it was something they needed to do. When they weren't together he seemed to be thinking about her all the time, he'd wake in the middle of the night thinking of her, he knew what that meant, it meant this, and this, and this, *this*—he was going to teach her to like it as much as he did.

Elsewhere his life didn't interest him. The hotel at Shoal Lake was doing fairly well in its first season, better than they'd expected; he was bored with it however and had to be moving into other things, investments, he had a few ideas he was working on, he'd see. Sometimes he talked to Enid about his life, particularly about his boxing career or the prospects of Jo-Jo Pearl's boxing career, but he didn't like her to question him. There were afternoons, entire hours, when he didn't talk to her at all, he was all feeling, emotion, desire, rarely did he respond to anything she said at such times, very likely he didn't hear.

Repeatedly he cautioned her: she wasn't to expect anything from him, not anything, did she understand, yes honey but do you *understand*, he'd give her things, presents, sure, he was crazy about her wasn't he, he was paying for her piano lessons, hoping Lyle wouldn't get suspicious, that wasn't what he meant, he meant he just wasn't making any promises. It wasn't love it was just something they needed to do, he didn't intend to harm her but he wasn't making promises of any kind, did she understand, this isn't a relationship that can last. And Enid said, reckless, teasing, to show she wasn't hurt: Except I'll always be your niece, won't I.

In the beginning it worried him, their close relation, being blood kin as they were, not once did he say the word "incest" nor did Enid allow herself to think much about it. It was just a word out of the dictionary! The main thing about being blood kin, Felix said, was of course you didn't want to have children and she wasn't going to get pregnant, that was damned sure.

Though in a few months he stopped worrying about their blood tie, or talking about it. Maybe he even liked it, he hinted, that she was his niece—it showed how much of a shit he was. He'd always wondered.

Still he was superstitious about seriously making love to her. Breaking her hymen, penetrating her as deeply as he could. Wouldn't it then mean too much to them both! She'd be getting married someday, he said. Enid said, hurt, I don't want to get married—I love you. Felix took such remarks lightly, he didn't really hear. He said, Sure you're going to get married someday, sweetheart—what else are you going to do?

Another time he told her he didn't want to ruin her life. And Enid said her life was already ruined, wasn't it—she had only him to make it well again.

LAURIE DUESING

Send Pictures, You Said . . . _____

On the subject of nude bodies, my father asked,
"What's the big deal? Everybody has one!"
commentary I always agreed with until you told me
to send some nude photographs while you were away
on the job in Georgia. I rummaged through
those old black and whites I took of myself 8 years ago
for an assignment in my photography class.
Beautiful and discreet, they were almost glacial
in their "I am nude" perfect, predictable poses,
their attitude of I-have-no-clothes-on but it's O.K.
because I am being artistic. I knew you didn't want
art: you wanted the body
which accounts for the snapshots I took of myself in the mirror.
It was the end of the roll and I figured so what.
Now I am looking at these 4 × 6 inch prints, shocked
by the way every fleshy part of me lifts and leans
toward the mirror, toward an idea of love.
I didn't know my lower lip was that full, my nipples
that large, my body so at ease with itself, so sure
of its desire. I did not know what a woman looks like
when she is inviting a man inside her. Besides,
it was your passion which impressed me,
a feeling so large I thought you generated it yourself,
that it drove you to me and into me.
Now, as I look at these pictures,
I see the body of a woman that pulled you into it.
You had no choice. I remember that first night
when you took off your clothes and sat on the edge
of the bed, waiting. So stunned by your beauty,
I turned my back so I could concentrate
on taking my clothes off. When I turned around,
I walked to you and rested my hands on your shoulders,
thinking, "If this is all I ever have of him, it's enough."
You dropped to your knees, wrapped your arms around
my legs, rested your head on my belly. I felt
your warm tears on my skin. All I knew

was that I was beginning something that would never end.
If I had paid more attention to those tears,
these photographs would have told me nothing.
But then I had no idea, I had no idea.

oo oo oo

CAROLEE SCHNEEMANN

Up Is One Direction _____

(to J.T.) 1965

      sweet love, beautiful man, my joy freeing all desire, re-
newing light of day, shadow night trembling, planed for our loving
(line where snow has fallen, branch touching windows, sun spot or
beating rains, hearts. . . . . . red valentine wind swung . . . unending or
bent spruce fingers shaking . . . your lips.)
everywhere I am you are. all I can be I am to you. there is nothing
I desire beyond what we find together, bring to one another in clear
expression (there can be no waste, uselessness, terror or fear or longing
residues). come in come in everywhere anywhere. whatever you wish
of me I can give to you; whatever I need you bring to me. you flower
tree, ramrod, lightning rod face fingers mine yours, paw pads, rolling
buttocks, finger furrow balls, fissures, breathing tissue, sweet curving
cock head, tiny eye kiss you, eat bite melt flesh of you me, roar juice
and wetness where you are I am combined (and even so our cylinder
walls—wash board ridged one of the other marvelously) so when you
fill me you do so fill me UP is one direction we go. all paths of us
are open to us. (all intricacies of me—sex, emotion, thought—and
strangeness, all details drawn luminous by your fire, light.
LOVE is YOU. love is how
  we grew to all expectations and more than I could long for, hope
for, hope to be, to be allowed being as I am I am for you. . . . . . how I
need to be and becoming together we are each one two.

oo oo oo

SUE MILLER

from: *The Good Mother* _____

As for me, it was his wildness, his openness which in-
trigued me, which I wanted. But it was that very quality which scared
me at the start, and the security of his being *like me* in some way—
professional, educated—that had let me move over the edge into his
world. As for what kept me there, it was, of course, still his wildness,
but it was also things like the whiteness of his skin, the way it filmed
over during sex and seemed to grow paler from within; the way his
hair curled over his neck when he bent once to tie my shoes after
helping me get dressed. It was the fact that during sex I lost track of
the boundaries between us, thought of his cock as a feeling inside me,
thought of my cunt as a part of his body, his mouth. And because I
became with him, finally, a passionate person.

We fought a lot about work, about what it meant to each of us. And
sometimes in the heat of those fights, I'd feel a claustrophobic sense of
the familiarity of the kind of standard he set for himself, for me. I'd
feel I'd come full circle, back to the expectations of my childhood. I can
remember raising my voice over a screaming train to yell at him that
those issues were completely extrinsic to a relationship, were things
individuals worked out for themselves. That people loved each other
for other reasons than that.

As the train's noise faded from under it, my voice suddenly sounded
harsh, strained. We sat staring at each other across the startling silence
in the dining room, and he shook his head slowly.

"It ain't like that in my experience, Anna," he said softly. "People
love each other *for* things, at least in part. Not after you leave your
mom's house do you get unconditional love, love without all those
things you think are so fucking extrinsic."

My sudden teariness took me back to the time before I'd left my
mother's house, to a yearning for a kind of love I felt I hadn't had even
then. But it was even with some sense of release that I felt the wash
of self-pity—or more precisely, pity for the little girl who also had
been so exacting of herself. In sorrow for her then, I started to cry; and
Leo, somehow able to sense that my sorrow reached beyond what was
happening between us, held me until I'd stopped.

No fight was worse than the first one, in part because I was still in
the euphoria of getting to know him, which denied even the possibility
of such a thing. It was one of our earliest weekends alone together—

Brian was with Molly—and we'd gone to a restaurant in Harvard Square to celebrate. Leo had given me a pink silk blouse, loose, low-cut and draped across the bosom (he thought I dressed too suburban and had given me a number of presents designed to transform me: rhinestone earrings, suede pants). I was wearing it, and feeling very beautiful. We parked the car on Acacia Street and walked through a fine spring rain to the restaurant.

We'd been making love all day and hadn't eaten anything. The wine with dinner affected us both almost immediately. We were loud and silly through the meal. Over coffee, I was talking about my piano students. I was amused with myself, very conscious of how pretty I looked in the blouse, and was, I thought, amusing him too; but slowly I noticed that he'd fallen silent. I stopped talking and there was a blank moment between us.

"I'm sorry," I said. "Was I talking too much?"

He pretended to be startled. "No," he said. "Not at all. I was enjoying it."

"I thought I'd noticed that you stopped, though. Enjoying it."

He shrugged. "I guess." I looked across at him. In the dim light I couldn't see where his pupils ended and the near-black of his iris began. He looked away. "I guess I just get tired of kind of the *way* you talk about your work."

"What do you mean?"

He shrugged again, and turned slightly in his chair, as though trying to end the conversation. "It just seems so . . . limited. Like it's just background noise in your life."

I sensed a great danger, an oddly familiar pit I could fall into. I tried to push it away with an attempt at objectivity. "Well, I suppose there's some sense in which that's true. But I *like* my work."

"But it's all pretty interchangeable isn't it? I mean, the rats, the piano students, you know."

I shrugged now. "Well, maybe almost. Not quite. I think I feel more utilized in the piano lessons."

Slowly, as though suppressing more violent motion, he leaned back in his chair, tossed his napkin onto the table. "Jesus," he said softly. "Utilized."

The contempt in his voice stung me into a silence that lasted for perhaps a minute. Then I started to feel angry. "Are you objecting to my choice of words?" I asked.

He looked across the restaurant for a moment, as though he hadn't heard me. Then abruptly, he turned to face me. Quietly he said, "It's just that I can't stand the way you think about your work, your life.

You don't care about it. I mean, you don't even *have* work in the sense that I'm talking about."

"What sense is that?" I could hear the polite contempt in my voice too.

He leaned forward and spoke intensely. "And don't talk to me in that fucking ladylike tone," he said. "I'm talking about passion. About some kind of commitment to something else besides a way to put food on the table. I mean, when I first met you, I thought you were a musician, that you cared about music."

"I do."

"But you *don't*. I mean, I look for some kind of parallel to the way I feel about my work and there just isn't one."

"Why should there be?"

"Because that's what I *want*, dammit. I want a woman who has that powerful a commitment to something outside herself."

"I have a commitment like that."

"To music?"

"To Molly. And to doing carefully and well what I do."

He looked at me for a moment. I thought of how he'd looked when we made love that afternoon in his light-flooded studio. "We can't even talk about it," he said. He picked up the bill and began rifling through his wallet.

I leaned forward and put my hands on his. He looked up. "Listen to me," I said. I moved my hands but stayed hunched across the table. "It used to be that men would say, 'I want a woman who' and the list would be a little different. 'Who cooks, who sews, who can entertain my friends.' But it's the same impulse. The same impulse. It's still *your* judgment, *your* list, your game. Just all the rules have changed." I was suddenly aware of my breasts, pushed together and nearly fully revealed in the low-cut blouse. I leaned back. "You're still saying I'm just an extension of you, that I'd better look good to the world so I make you look good. That's all it is."

He shook his head. "You're missing it, Anna. That's not it."

"What is it then?"

"It's really that having those parallel interests, those parallel passions, makes life more *interesting*."

"So I bore you."

"I just don't get the way you talk about your work."

"Because it's different from the way you talk about yours."

"Right."

"And if I *were* a real musician, a ... what? A performer? A composer? What would do the trick?"

"Don't make fun of me, Anna."

"No, I'm wondering. Really. Because I might have been, you know. I've told you that. That was the plan for me. And I just *wasn't* that good. That's all." I had begun to cry, but strangely, it didn't, at least for the moment, seem connected to me. I could feel tears springing from my eyes and running down my cheeks, but it was as though they were glycerin, movie tears. "And so I've made another kind of life for myself. But I *hate*, I really *hate* to be told there's no honor in it. Especially by someone as lucky as you are, with the good *luck* to be as good as you are at what you do."

I pushed my chair back quickly, stood up and crossed the restaurant. A few people looked up at me and then quickly away as I passed their tables. I wiped at my face with my hands.

It was still raining outside, the streetlight's garish aureole making Mt. Auburn Street ugly. I turned off into Hilliard Street, and the sudden absence of that purple softened and darkened the world. Yellowish light seeped mistily from the houses. In one of them, a woman bent over a table to turn off a lamp. For a moment she appeared all grace in the orange glow. Then she was gone, the windows black, glistening with raindrops.

I heard footsteps behind me. Leo caught up with me, put a coat over my shoulders.

"You left your raincoat behind."

I turned to him, and let him hold me against his chest. I felt a wild grief, a pain in my throat like a deep cut, but no sound came out and my tears had stopped.

"Anna, I'm sorry," Leo said. His hand ran over my hair again and again.

"Please don't say that," I said. "It's what you meant. You're only sorry it hurt me, not that you feel it."

"I'm not sure what I feel," he said. After a moment, we began walking, half-stumbling, half-embracing on the rain-slicked, bumpy bricks.

When we got to the truck, he unlocked my side and let me in, then walked around. I slid across the seat to unlock his door, and when he got in, I clambered over him, sat across his lap, ground against him, kissing him. The rain drummed steadily on the truck, and the sound of our breathing, the wet, light clicking of our mouths sliding over each other's was intensified in our tiny world. The windows began to fog lightly, and Leo reached up to find my underpants, to pull them down.

"It's a body-stocking," I whispered. "It's all one piece."

I lifted my skirt to show him. He arched up, unsnapped his pants. I raised myself slightly, let him unzip himself and pull his stiff penis out. I bent over and reached between my legs, pulled the body stocking to one side. I moved towards him, onto him, and he came in me a little way, guiding himself with his hands. I rose off him, then down again, each time a little deeper, until he was all the way inside me. I let my weight go and felt him almost like pain, deep in me. I touched his face, moved freely on him. The windows silvered with our breathing, and when he came he cried out my name over and over. In the panting silence that followed, we could hear doubled footsteps, voices passing by closely on the street outside. "Richard," a man's voice said. We didn't move, didn't speak until they'd gone.

Molly liked him too, though it wasn't until I realized that this was the case that I also realized how much it meant to me that she did. Initially with her he was much less impetuous, much less active. Around her he was even, instinctively it seemed, less active with me. He let her occupy the center of my life, as she always did, and modeled his behavior on mine.

But as he grew to know her, he got more comfortable and seemed more himself. The third time he came over when she was awake, he brought me flowers, and a box of Band-Aids, three hundred of them, for her, because he'd noticed her affection for one on her knee. For days she was covered in them. At the slimmest excuse she'd slap on one, and I didn't interfere. They were hers, I told her. She could make her own rules for when she needed them. She put Band-Aids on her toys, on me, and finally, one night, on Leo. It was a turning point, her first spontaneous gesture towards him. He had a cold, was honking and sneezing into a Kleenex and complaining about his nose being about to fall off his face. She taped it on, soberly, with four or five big ones.

"God, I can't tell you how grateful I am, Moll," he said. "If *your* nose is ever about to drop off, I hope you'll tell me, so I can return the favor."

Slowly she let him touch her, started to be affectionate to him. They began to have routines they'd go through, just as she'd had with Brian. He'd stop her on her way through the kitchen. "Just a second, Molly," he'd say, frowning. "You've got something in your *ear*, here." And then he'd pull a nickel or a dime out. "My God, Molly," he'd say. "Look at this, that I found in your ear. Can you believe it? It must be . . . magic!" And she would grin at him, charmed, but dubious.

"Now, Moll," he'd say. "Who would you say a nickel like that *belonged* to? Does it belong to the person who found it? Like me? or does it belong to the person whose *ear* it was in? For example, like you?"

And she'd have to claim the nickel, claim the magical ear, which she always did, but with a little edge of honest worry.

Three weeks after I'd slept with Leo for the first time, I bought a queen-size mattress and box spring and folded up the rollaway bed, and he began to sleep with me at our apartment. At first he would leave late at night. Then more and more, he'd set the alarm and leave at dawn. We almost always made love in that clean half-light, and it was then, in the mornings in my room, that I began to come predictably with Leo. Often I'd wake with his caressing me, entering me, and begin to get there before I was even conscious of desire. Perhaps it was the absence of all those layers of conscious judgment; perhaps it was the utter hopelessness of worrying about all the things I'd always worried about with sex—how things looked, smelled, tasted. In those early mornings it all tasted of sex after a few moments. The sheets would get tangled and sweaty. The whole room seemed full of our commingled, complicated smells. And over and over again I'd come, sometimes still nearly asleep.

Then once or twice when we were very rushed, he asked me to bring him off with my hands or mouth. I did, quickly at first, and a little fastidiously. But then I discovered that I wanted him that way too. All my initial passivity, all his energy, I realized, had made our lovemaking seem in a sense like masturbation. He was so like a fantasy, like someone I might have conjured in my solitary mornings of coming alone. I could simply lie back, as though dreaming a sexual dream, and be made happy.

But now I discovered a different kind of appetite, a kind of active hunger for his body. I loved watching him come in my hands, or feeling him, tasting him, in my mouth, the even more intense connection with him sexually that came from understanding exactly how he came the moment that he did, from helping him get there. All of that made my love for his body more intense, more absolute. I felt there was nothing I didn't want to do for him, wouldn't want him to do to me. We got wilder and wilder, even when we were simply doing it straight. It felt like some shift in dimension, not just the addition of new techniques. Once he kissed the back of my neck softly in the kitchen, and with a little gasping upheaval, I came. Sometimes just looking at his hands circling a coffee cup could stir me nearly to moan aloud.

Still we were trying to keep it from Molly. We didn't discuss it much, and by now Leo was spending three or four nights a week in my bed, but he got up faithfully each morning he slept over and was out of the house before she emerged from her room. Once or twice it was the noise of her beginning to putter in her room which woke us, but then Leo would kiss me, rise swiftly from the bed and pull on his clothes, and be gone barefoot down the long hall nearly as quickly as the half-formed memory of my dreams faded from me.

I'm not sure why we didn't tell her. She seemed irrevocably to like Leo, so it wasn't the fear that it would threaten their friendship. Perhaps part of it was simply that I didn't understand what significance it might have to her to know that he and I were sleeping together, and so wasn't sure how to explain it. As for Leo, he was again following my lead. It was a fatal part of his sweetness to follow me, even in my confusion, to assume always that I knew what I was doing with her, around her. I fostered it. I never articulated to him my anxiety, the sudden rush of feeling I sometimes had with her that I was doing everything wrong. He saw my mothering her, her relationship with me, as implacably monolithic, a given, what was meant to be, and took all his cues from that. Even the grace of his uncomplaining rising in the morning—the quick tilt back of his hips to zip his fly, the wings of his half-buttoned shirt flying out as he turned to enter the hallway—seemed emblematic to me of his assumption of rightness in whatever I was doing with Molly.

But the truth also was that I felt less confusion with her then, that I asked myself fewer questions. When I think about the whole period of time I spent with Leo, I try to rewrite it in a sense, to bring Molly more into the foreground. Surely she nibbled at my conscience, my unconscious, as she had before, as she certainly has since. Surely I always thought of her, I never took her growth, her happiness, for granted.

I don't know, really, but I think there is some sense in which during my passion for Leo, I *forgot* Molly. Maybe in no worse a way than mothers of three or four children sometimes forget one of them for a while, or women living in a time which didn't make them concentrate such energy on the issue of their children's emotional life could and perhaps did sometimes forget them. But the sense of blankness about Molly that thinking of Leo conjures for me now is as horrifying, as accusatory as the memory of her scratched and screaming in the back seat of the car at Sammy Brower's house.

At any rate, one cool night in May, long after Leo and I were asleep, something woke Molly and she came and got into bed with us. I was too soundly asleep to realize the implications of this, or perhaps some part of me was glad for the resolution it would offer and pushed consciousness away. I made room for her and fell deeply asleep again, my arm around her, Leo's body warm and smooth against my back.

When she woke in the morning, she seemed to think it was perfectly natural to find him there too. Her excitement was almost entirely transferred to the idea of having him join us for breakfast. He played along with her by insisting that that's what he was there for: to make breakfast for all of us.

And he did. Shirtless, barefoot, in jeans, his hair wild around his head, he made Molly's favorite, French toast. After that it became, as

DEEP DOWN · · ·

things did under Molly's stern aegis, a ritual. When Leo spent the night, he got up first, leaving me sleepy, love-satisfied, in our bed. Then he woke Molly, and it was only after I heard their voices, smelled coffee and the sweet vanilla odor of French toast cooking, that I'd rise and pull on clothes to join them.

I felt I'd never been so happy, and perhaps I never was. Our lives seemed magically interpenetrated, commingled, even as we each separated into all the day's complicated activities. I had never expected it to seem so graceful and easy, but Molly's seemingly complete comfort with Leo was like a benediction on all aspects of the relationship, even the sexual.

I remember one night her getting up (and that seemed to be the only symptom of possible trouble—that her sleep became sometimes disturbed, she appeared slightly more frequently at my bedside than before Leo came). Leo and I had been making love, and it's possible that the noise disturbed her. He had come into me from behind, and I was up on my hands and knees pushing back against him, when I heard her shuffle in the hallway. I stilled myself, and that stopped his motion. Together we lowered ourselves, and as the bedroom door swung open, I turned towards the little halting figure. She came and stood by the bed, her face inches from mine, recarved, narrowed to maturity in the dark. She was having a bad dream, she said. Her voice was thin with terror. I held the covers up to welcome her, and she clambered in and lay down next to me. Though Leo wasn't very deep in me, I was wet, and he could easily move gently, slowly, in and out of me. I asked Molly about her dream. I held her in the curve of my upper body and smelled the damp sweetness of her hair and skin. She explained to me how she'd been playing a game when Jerome, another crazy man at day care, came and took all her toys away. She'd started a different game, and he did it again. "*Every time*, he did that, Mumma," she said, a vibrato shaking her tiny voice.

I started to talk to her about what would happen in her waking life if Jerome did that. We speculated about which teachers would help her; I got her to imitate what they might say to bad Jerome. Her voice got dreamier, the intervals between confidences longer. Leo moved sometimes, and then lay still. I can remember feeling a sense of completion, as though I had everything I wanted held close, held inside me; as though I had finally found a way to have everything. We seemed fused, the three of us, all the boundaries between us dissolved; and I felt the medium for that. In my sleepiness I thought of myself as simply a *way* for Leo and Molly and me to be together, as *clear*, translucent. I drifted off.

JANET HAMILL

Open Window ———————————————————

The air is cool. coming
with the tourmaline sea
into my symphonic interior
caresses. both yours
and the breeze's lingering
longer days of dazzling
light. flood the room
above the Avenue of Palms

a bed with the imprint
of your body on it. sugar
almonds on a silver tray
posing as if for a painting
before a moorish screen
four goldfish swim in a bowl
on fire. my skin is blushing
pink. like a battle of roses

after a bath. the charged
idleness accompanying your
absence wraps around me. in
the silk of a white kimono
in the frame of the open
window. I can see my buoyant
heart. sailing the Mediter-
ranean with a wind caught
under its wings

oo oo oo

MARILYN HACKER

from: *Love, Death and the Changing of the Seasons*

NOCES

First, I want to make you come in my hand
while I watch you and kiss you, and if you cry,
I'll drink your tears while, with my whole hand, I
hold your drenched loveliness contracting. And
after a breath, I want to make you full
again, and wet. I want to make you come
in my mouth like a storm. No tears now. The sum
of your parts is my whole most beautiful
chart of the constellations—your left breast
in my mouth again. You know you'll have to be
your age. As I lie beside you, cover me
like a gold cloud, hands everywhere, at last
inside me where I trust you, then your tongue
where I need you. I want you to make me come.

SOURCES

Didn't Sappho say her guts clutched up like this?
Before a face suddenly numinous,
her eyes watered, knees melted. Did she lactate
again, milk brought down by a girl's kiss?
It's documented torrents are unloosed
by such events as recently produced
not the wish, but the need, to consume, in us,
one pint of Maalox, one of Kaopectate.
My eyes and groin are permanently swollen,
I'm alternatingly brilliant and witless
—and sleepless: bed is just a swamp to roll in.
Although I'd cream my jeans touching your breast,
sweetheart, it isn't lust; it's all the rest
of what I want with you that scares me shitless.

105

FUTURE CONDITIONAL

After the supper dishes, let us start
where we left off, my knees between your knees,
half in the window seat. O let me, please,
hands in your hair, drink in your mouth. Sweetheart,
your body is a text I need the art
to be constructed by. I halfway kneel
to your lap, propped by your thighs, and feel
burning my hand, your privacy, your part
armor underwear. This time I'll loose
each button from its hole; I'll find the hook,
release promised abundance to this want,
while your hands, please, here and here, exigent
and certain, open this; it is, this book,
made for your hands to read, your mouth to use.

BLOOMINGDALE'S

"If I weren't working, I'd sleep next to you
an hour or two more. Then we'd get the car
and drive a while, out of Manhattan, to
a quiet Bloomingdale's in Westchester.
If we saw anything we liked, we'd buy it!
We'd try things on, first, in one cubicle.
You'd need to make an effort to be quiet
when I knelt down and got my fingers full
of you, my mouth on you, against the wall.
You'd pull my hair. You'd have to bite your tongue.
I'd hold your ass so that you wouldn't fall.
Later, we'd take a peaceful walk along
the aisles, letting our hands touch every chance
they got, among the bras and underpants."

GRAMERCY PARK

Denim and silk pooled at our feet upstairs
in the hotel room. Everybody wore a
hot outfit for the weekend's diaspora.
... I called it that, and you assented. There's
cold heat in love that exiles make. Despair's
under the glistening surfaces. Who cried
after she came; who came after she cried?
Streetlights went off, then on again outside.
The landless lovers hit the tiles in pairs.
The icons of our ceremony are
glasses smashed underfoot in a gay bar
whose shards are swept out with the morning's trash.
"Where do the black girls dance?" Why do the Jews
go in for telegrams and wads of cash
close to the thigh? Our home is in the car
today. Baby, our home is in our shoes.

ANOTHER SUNDAY

Sometimes, when you're asleep, I want to do
it to myself while I'm watching you. It
would be easy, two fingers along my clit,
back, in, back out. Your skin's heat comes into
me, adjacent. Through the mussed chrysanthemum
petals, your big child's sleep-face, closed around
its openness, gives me your mouth to ground
on, but only with my eyes. I could come
like that, but I don't—take you against your will,
it seems like, and I wouldn't; rather wait
adrowse in sunlight with this morning heat
condensing, a soft cloud above my groin
gently diffusing brightness there, until
you wake up, and you bring it down like rain.

○○ ○○ ○○

CHRISTINE SCHUTT

About Her Love —————————————————

Only the calves are shapely and the girl-slim ankles; the rest of the boy is slumbering: his voice full of summer heat and the rasped sound of grass. Odd notes leap when he speaks. His stories tilt upward. Everything in question, turned up at the end—mouth, nose, brows—why not? He wants. He wants a bite of what I've got; but he eats it whole and doesn't seem to taste. He just wants more. Mothers in the park offer fruit. They lust after him. Should have been a girl, they say. Thick hair like that. They want him up close and wag bags of carrots. They want to touch him, this blond boy, so big for his age.

"Mom!" He yells out, "Come in here."

My son not yet ten, likes to loll in his own skin after a shower. When he sees me, he throws out his arm. "Scratch," he says. Sly pickerel smile: makes *me* smile. I start singing the Beatles, "Love, love me do," finger his innie, play with his breasts. I love every part of this boy, and he sees it. My feelings shame me. I roll him like a carpet onto his belly, tickle the noontime dimples on his ass. A big boy fished from a pool of big people. His Daddy says he's growing up; his Grandma says he's fine, just money in the bank. Sure, I say, he's hungry.

He was six when his father and I separated, and he began to act up at school. He was punching kids, so the school sent us to a doctor who told us what he saw: a boy afraid of everything, disconnected, hollow, *hungry*. (The doctor used that word. I'm sure of it.) Treat him like a baby, he said. Make him feel secure. Fat chance, I thought, giving my ex the finger. (Oh I was angry when my little boy was six, his father flitting around town with one of those lady-banker types—butch haircut, fuck-me shoes.) But the doctor said, Try, and I did. It was easy.

Very soon the leached and rutted fingernails grew smooth; the rucked brow flattened. He let me hold him for long stretches, and his body eased into mine. We fit together. Every night, running my hands over parts of him, his strong shapely legs, smooth feet. I wriggled my fingers through spatulate toes, then spidered up the legs to pinch the squint-eyed nipples. The urge to touch him everywhere was powerful in me, and I saw how a thing could happen.

He begins to wiggle when I count the moles on his back, "Hold still."

"What are they?"

"They're beauty marks."

"Oh Mom," he says, "I'm not beautiful."

He raises his head to look at the picture of Rambo taped to his wall. His shoulders bunch as he considers this man.

"I want to be an actor. Then when I'd go back to school they'd be surprised."

"You mean if you were in a movie, people in your school would want to know you?"

"They'd be surprised to *see* me. I want to be in the movies now."

He's better looking than his father, and although he does things like the man, sneaks up to a song on the radio as if he were fly catching, no expression until he's almost there and all of a sudden dancing. He dances by himself. He turns up the tunes and leers and sings along and rides his bike and strums his cock. His Dad just wiggled his ass.

I sometimes think of a genetic code as looking like paper swissed by a hole punch and my son's paper almost matching his father's. This thought makes me anxious for my own future and some girl's. Men go on, I think; it's the women who get stalled.

After dinner his father calls. They talk—about school, movies, things my son wants to buy. Today it's some new game.

"Don't badger the man."

"You talk then," he hands me the phone, and we talk mechanically because his girl is in the background, whistling. I hear pots bang. The kitchen tiles, my son told me, are black and white. Sometimes on the phone I try to walk through his new life but all I see are the backs of people. Once he showed me his new camera. It made me crazy. "What the hell is there to photograph?" I screamed. Now all I hear is this whistling, so I agree to all-day Sunday but nothing on Saturday. Then I get off the phone and go looking for my son.

He is hunched over his desk, drawing pictures and talking to himself. His figures have small heads, squared bodies. They are all armed. Many of them smoke. Trails of ash and fire are the loose horizontals on a page of upright men standing in thin air. He never sketches ground, trees, homes, birds; his figures are headquartered in corners.

"Reload!" one man cries to another. "Son of a bitch."

"These people are always in trouble," I say.

He doesn't look up but keeps on talking. "Fuck!"

"Don't say that."

"He just lost his leg, Mom!"

"I don't care."

"You tell Dad about Art Club?"

"No." He's been suspended again. "I thought you should."

"Bring more ammo," he says, speaking for the man with no leg. "They're moving in."

I stand behind him, watching the bad guys advance past land mines and fires and hooded snakes. A sky full of menace he draws, both hands fisted, his right gripped almost to the pencil lead. My heart tightens to see him, and I want to uncurl his fingers and lick the nails grown smoother now. When the doctor told us this boy was disconnected, hollow, hungry—those *were* his words—I felt as threatened as my boy's one-legged man. Love him, the doctor said, and I thought, what does this man *mean*, love him!

My boy presses so hard the lead breaks and the pencil flips out of his hand. His concentration snaps just as quickly and he says, "Let's read in bed."

When I finish the chapter, his face is slack and dreamy. He's almost lost his voice. He says, "Scratch me, Mom," and I do. He says, "Stay," and I will. In this instant the world is easy, and I feel dizzy and sentimental, almost near tears, when I see his sweet face darken. He looks at me; his eyes glint with some idea. "Scratch here?" he says, pointing to his cock, smiling his sly, pickerel smile.

"No!" I shout, and then I'm straddling him as he kicks and laughs and squeals in protest. "No. No. No," I say, and his whys bounce off my voice. "Because I love you. I love you in other ways," I say, when what I'm thinking is I wish I knew how.

oo oo oo

ERIN MOURÉ

La Gueule _____

This morning, a small
halo of hope worn around the ankle, as the word *worn* is worn,
soft, chewed leather against the skin,
worn as the marble stairs of the courthouse become art gallery,
worn minds of its prisoners & judges, the artists & board of
    directors,
worn as my shirt is worn, frayed at the sleeve & shoulder
& not discarded or sent away,

as I have been wearing a small crown of sunlight
& sent away,

wearing a piccolo of feathers & sent away,

wearing the word "of" as if all embellishment
is carried on the back of this small word,
its round mouth & tall skeleton, bent over
under the weight of what we make it say.

The woman with yellow airplanes small from her ears,
the restaurant *La Gueule*, with its beautiful vowels
& white fan on the ceiling.
The shirt worn around the neck with its arms joined.
Hope is the word we use when we have given up on the objects,
given up on the after-life, Consumer's Reports

Hope is a thin note sung hard in the chest between
the seven bones of the body's harp, the ribs,
a halo of light
around the ankle, it is the woman's smile
as she crosses the street, that burns into the ribs until the breasts
    ache,
& lights the body up, at its restaurant table, like a rice-paper kite,
or lantern

LAURA CHESTER

Crazy ───────────────────────────

My darling always thought he'd like to be a sex object until I made him into one. Now he thinks of strategies of escape before he dares stir in the morning, how he will pretend to go brush his teeth, and then quickly pull on his Levis. Seeing the disappearance of those muscular calves is like watching good wine being wasted, wanting more kiss than compensation, wanting his rough morning face in my hands. I lunge when he calls me, *"Messhuga,"* though I know he could throw me right over this bed. He has come to expect my fawning, my can't-keep-my-little-hands-off you, and I'm used to his pushing these gestures away, because I find him too irresistible. He answers that all the women he ever dated did, so I cuff his hat and feel miserable, which leads him to anger and unkind things—"I can't take this aggravation in my life anymore!" I suffer a spell of insomnia that lasts until 4 A.M. Thank God he understands the subtlety of my longing, "If you don't fuck me I will kill myself!" I also recently gave up cigarettes and agreed to on one condition, that my kisses would taste sweeter than apples and he'd take a big bite more often, but I have noticed a gradual falling off, and when I confront him about this, he pops miniature marshmallows into his mouth. I'm too young to be replaced by junk food. I'm too old for unrequited love. The snow has been falling for ages, and he's like someone who was built to hibernate, and I'm blamed for keeping him awake. The thimble is a humble symbol, but I'd rather pick the cannon or the horse. He says something about my being a banana, and my mind slips, and I think I'll rip his shirt off, just to get a whack of his skin, but instead he holds me down with one hand, whips out the scissors to his army knife and snips off a lock of my hair. If he were Italian he might at least have kept it, the way I'm tempted to save the wads of kleenex he inevitably leaves in bed. Even such remnants affect me. His pheromone's my one cologne. I think we were made for each other, an exchange of crazy casseroles, if only it were the dinner hour, and the spoons were back under the covers, especially now that it's supposed to snow forever and I'm editing this collection of erotica. Sometimes I wonder who hung the terra cotta angel from the ceiling of his bathroom, and where went all the women of his bachelor's past, and how will I become one any different. He tells me how there's no one he would rather see, but how he truly dreaded coming over. He seems to say everything in two directions and the intersection is my head. I know he will have to leave me, intending to return, but maybe I'll be buried in snow by then, lost in this winter like his underwear in the big white mounds of his mind, snowed-in by him, this man who has driven me crazy, sex mad, snow blind, approaching irrelevant, because he wants to break me God dammit he does, because he thinks I always want things *my way*. Pot call the kettle black much? Suddenly, I just stop caring, and then he's all over me. Nothing's wrong as far as he's concerned. All male, oh man, he makes his move, to grapple and to pin me. His physical love's a vise wherein I struggle to return to sanity with him, until I just lie there, smitten.

oo oo oo

MARY MACKEY

Golden Cords: Erotic Attachment and the Pain of Separation _____

One night about ten years ago, while lying next to a lover and dear friend, I felt a shimmering in the air over my head, and as I looked at it, the shimmering condensed into a tangle of golden cords, as thick as fingers, arched above the two of us like a rainbow only moving and pulsating, as if a coil of strange, exotic snakes had found its way into our bedroom. At first I was taken aback, almost frightened, but the cords were so radiant, so obviously benevolent that my fear dissolved. Listening I heard that they were making sounds, high and clear, producing a sweet strange music that filled me with energy.

When I looked down at my own body, I saw that half the cords were coming out of me, part from my chest more or less in the region of my heart and part from my abdomen around the area of my navel. Crossing the space between me and my lover, they had rooted in his heart and abdomen, attaching us together in a long, pulsating tangle. The other half of the cords was coming from my lover, rooting in me, grafting to my flesh, growing through my skin to my womb and stomach, until I could feel myself filled inside by hundreds of thin tendrils.

I saw all of this for a minute, maybe more, and then the cords disappeared, and our bed became merely a bed again in an ordinary room, in a perfectly ordinary town. The next morning I was sure I had only been dreaming—certainly the most reasonable explanation—but something had changed in me, something odd and slightly disturbing. Now, whenever we made love or were especially close, I felt new cords growing into my flesh; other times, when we were angry or separated, I felt an uncomfortable sensation as if someone were tugging at me. From time to time, I had a quick glimpse of the cords again, full of light when things were going well, dull and listless when there was tension and misunderstanding.

When my lover and I finally broke up for reasons beyond our control, I was in pain for a long time, unable to eat or sleep, full of nostalgia and regrets so intense that they verged on nausea. Everything reminded me of him: a red blouse I had worn on one particularly happy day we spent hiking, music we had listened to together, stir-fried vegetables with seaweed (one of his favorite dishes), even the stars because we had once picked out the constellations together. The whole situation was both tragic and profoundly ridiculous. My friends shook their heads and offered calcium tablets and herb tea. I was advised to get on with my life, but from my point of view I had no life worth getting on with.

Then one evening crying over a plate of stir-fried vegetables in a Niagara of self-pity, I saw the cords again—or rather a set of cords and a set of scars. The scars were where my lover's cords had entered my body; they were wounds, the size of pennies, half-healed but very painful. The remaining cords were mine. Suddenly I realized what was wrong: I was still attached to him, even though he was no longer attached to me. All my energy was running out of my body, and nothing was coming in. I was being dragged around as he moved into his new life, no longer considering me, the hundreds of miles between us stretching and pulling until they had very nearly pulled me apart.

I decided that whether these cords were imaginary or real, I had to cut them somehow simply to survive. After thinking the situation over, I decided that I would try fighting a vision with a vision; that is to say, I would try imagining a great pair of scissors slicing through every attachment I still had to my lover; I would pretend to see the cords snap, and then I would imagine pulling them back into me, rerooting myself in my own flesh and healing the scars.

Now that I knew that I had suffered not just a separation but a physical injury, I was more gentle with myself, more willing to give myself time to heal and recover, but day by day it seemed to work and I began to feel the relief of growing whole and self-contained.

The day finally came, of course, when all the cords were cut, but the experience taught me several things that I still do my best to remember. First, I became aware that sex is the major cause of cording—especially when sex comes in the form of a full-blown erotic attachment combined with love. Not all sex, of course, casts cords from one lover to another, but the potential is there and that knowledge makes me reluctant to be involved in casual relationships. I'm more humble now in a way, more aware that things may be happening on another level in some other dimension that I am only occasionally aware of. If the cords are real, who knows what other unknown factors are produced by intimacy. Perhaps we dream each other's dream at night; perhaps we have non-physical bodies; perhaps the electrical energies of our brains mingle; perhaps we are capable of tearing open each other's auras.

And perhaps, of course, all of the foregoing is nonsense. Perhaps my so-called vision is merely imagination heightened by sentimentality. I only know that cording is a useful way of explaining to myself both the pleasure of intimacy and the pain of separation. To tell the truth, I still see the cords occasionally, and the knowledge that I could become so physically entangled with another human being has made me very, very selective.

oo oo oo

DANIELA GIOSEFFI

Toward the Greater Romance, Please Place Roses in my Skull (A Tantric Love Song) _____

Oh my love, I will carry
your lantern ahead,
whispering light for your steps.
Please touch me to come to you.

Toward the light, Father/Mother,
shining harbor ahead,
all grievance closed on our breasts,
sound coloring words to breath.

Glide with me through my river.
I've come this way, too,
slithering out as new flesh.
Our bodies burst into bloom.

Hands know silk, skin, and petals,
wet mouth, apple's breath.
Place roses into my skull.
Our bones are white, pupils black.

Oh my love, shine with my life,
be as my brother,
yin and yang flowing bright milk
from autumn leaves in the grass.

Oceans swirl, marble blue earth,
hear, taste, feel, see, heal,
toward the explosion of light,
eyes opening souls from death.

oo oo oo

KATHLEEN FRASER

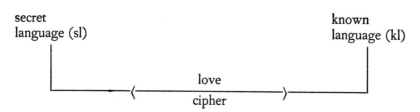

secret
language (sl)

known
language (kl)

love

cipher

your sky against my starfish I know how big
your body covering me down
foot to foot and knees inside of
knees your cock be smooth French cork
oh tight I'm *La Cour*
Pavillon, La heart
and everywhere ooze
where your little bites
                         set loose hunger
such as never
              How wide this soul
you grow in dark windowlight,
hiss of steam and deep blanket of siren
(I could walk around in it so hot)
                              In you
I want the long stride   wet and tongue
as far as your sky goes
how big you can let me

CAROL BERGÉ

from: *Secrets, Gossip and Slander* _____

A RESOLUTION—OF SORTS

They were walking on level ground now but to Rachel it was clearly uphill. How odd that he seemed so Jewish to her at this moment, so like her uncles, with their commitments to the traditions of Judaism, their reverence for the scholarly, the considered, the philosophical, the historical. Although John rarely gave her the answers she wanted, she had already become accustomed to going to him for an opinion—a *responsah*—as if he were a *rabbi* who knew the Talmud and the Mishnah—as in fact John did. It was John, wasn't it, who'd pointed out to her the similarity between Mishnah and the *koans* she worked with, in her own life, wasn't it?

In the dark silence Rachel blurted out: But if you love someone, aren't you *supposed* to want to live with them? And he said, No, not if it's going to kill that love. You know we don't want to do that. Why can't we, she said, and she and he both were hoping she wasn't going to whine. Well, he said, imagine that I am allergic to something and I would go into an extreme reaction if I were around it constantly. You don't mean *me*, do you? said Rachel, angrily. No, I don't mean you, John said, I'm being theoretical, to make my point. Bear with me. You remember Eleanor and Warren, my old friends whom you met last month—well, he was extremely allergic to something and for months the doctors couldn't figure out what, and it turned out he'd become allergic to her hair; quite a problem, eh?

Rachel had visions of the wives in the *shtetls*, with their shaven pates and *sheitlech* ... I'd recommend a good shrink, she said, I don't believe in allergies. They're real, John said. As a metaphor—No, said Rachel, as a metaphor, for *us*, it stinks. Do we have to love each other's lifestyle in order to live together? No, it's the other way around, said John, we don't need to compromise, you have your lifestyle and I have mine, neither of us has to accommodate to the other, and we don't live together, and we don't get married.

Well, said Rachel, our signs aren't compatible anyway. You don't believe in that garbage, do you? asked John. No, Rachel said carefully. I *use* it, to work with understanding people. Nonsense, said John, it's just mumbo-jumbo. You need to say that, said Rachel, because you don't use it. How you do pick and choose! Your own mother used to plant her garden by the signs—and you're always talking about The

Devil, as if that were something real. Every religion has its devils, John said. Not mine, said Rachel, we don't have somebody ugly and threatening sitting on our shoulders telling us it's wrong to enjoy life. Yes, you do, said John, or where would you get your concept of *trafe*? That's based, Rachel said, on old dietary laws. But today we extend it. For example, my mother would say you're *trafe*, because you're a *Goy*. God, I'm glad to get that said.

They were at a place where the dirt road ended and became pavement. Nor are we out of it, mumbled Rachel. What's that? said John. Nothing, it's—The Devil made me say it. What? said John, again. That's a Flip Wilson line, she said. Who's he, asked John. Nobody you'd know, my purist, somebody on TV. You do waste your time, said John. Go to hell, she replied, it beats me, how you can live in a modern culture and intentionally cut yourself off from what's happening in it —No, he said, if you know the cycles of history, the details fall into place. You grew up with TV and you take it for granted. I don't. I'd rather read. But you read trash, she said, along with the other stuff. I own my TV, it doesn't own me, I own all my artifacts, I can turn it off. I can have it on even when I'm studying or working, if I choose not to hear it. Then why have it on? said John. If I don't have one, I don't have to turn it off, or even on. More mortification, said Rachel reminds me of the kind of scarification the—

Never mind, he said, closing the subject. Why couldn't she understand? Classic case of youth being wasted on the young. So stubborn. He felt an anger at her insistence. The familiar tension. She would not look up at him, he began to want her, his cock began to swell in his trousers. Perfect, he thought. He would have her, and for as long as he wished, on his terms. He reached out for her. She twisted away, then caught the smell of him, the good animal he was, no aftershave, just his own smell (he counted on her being downwind). He was sweating and so was she, by now. Damn you to hell, she said, if that's not where you are already. There, there, he said, his hands on her, knowing she was beginning to get wet. Let's just not argue any more, it's late. Knowing the argument would go on, all the way to his place. She was a conditioned animal by now and so was he. It would take something, someone quite powerful to change this.

This was a concept she was only beginning to learn about, this tension: that nobody could couple without this opposition. His theory. Hatred and love in dynamic chemistry, and the resultant tension, and then sex and new life on earth. Rachel was nattering on now about Pat, how they'd discovered their menstrual patterns were in total coincidence. Of course, said John, close women friends—How much better, she said, I really *like* women as friends, they're reasonable, they're imaginative, they're vulnerable—they're really much more trustworthy as friends. That's the way it's supposed to be, said John, you're supposed to feel *safe* with other women, nonthreatened. But, said Rachel, doesn't that depend on what kind of mother one had?

He was constantly amazed at the information she was "discovering," and which he had known for ages, from studies or from experience. If you knew all that, she said, why didn't you tell me? It never came up, he said. Thinking, I would never spoil it for you, it would spoil the tension, and we wouldn't survive a day without it, my pretty little student-of-life. How can I tell you what I've learned in my time? You wouldn't agree, you wouldn't believe it, you'd disagree just on principle. And that's just fine, just this amount.

She's a Breughel, isn't she, and I'm a Leonardo line drawing. He smiled in the dark, pleased with the image. Breughel evidenced the excesses of peasants. Whereas DaVinci achieved excellence through purity. John was exceeding his own background by being a scholar. He had not yet overtly added to the field, but he was sure the book he was working on now would do it. On his desk right now, his own theory, developing it slowly, methodically, 2,343 pages of longhand already, only some of it footnotes; it sat in boxes under his desk and he added to it almost every night; he'd awaken and work on it, in the wee hours, long after Rachel and the rest of the town were asleep elsewhere, long before he himself would have to waken to do classes. Sometimes two, often three hours a night. It would be a great work, it would make his reputation finally, it put together all of his theories, his wisdom, his readings, conversations with other scholars in the field, it would be his success. It would prove—

She feared it, this work he was doing, it took him away from her, put him in even more competition with her, existed as a barrier between them. She hated the drinks he took when he awoke to work on his tome, the stacks of yellow paper, the boxes, and the ideas therein. She thought the whole theory, as he expounded it, dreadful and erroneous. A theory that natural relationships were of necessity based in friction rather than in affection, that attraction to the opposite sex was based in polarization, and that dominance depended on intuited signals which were implicit rather than explicit but which could be defined and categorized. That the survival of humanity, in fact, depended on like "marrying" unlike and then procreating. Clearly all of the great lovers had been unlike. Friendship and sexual attraction were mutually exclusive.

But do you have to go two damn thousand pages to say it? Rachel howled. That's the way theories have to be explicated, he said, smiling. You have to state your sources, the research that's laid the groundwork for the new concept, even more so than you're doing in your thesis, he said to her. It has to be comprehensive. Disgusting, she said, why not just say out what you think, and a few things about what other people said on the subject to back it up, and publish it as an article? That's not the scholarly process, he said. What it is is *boring*, she said. I don't think so, he said, I love it.

It was the first time she could recall his using that word, no, it was the second, the first had been about Margery and that had been long after the fact, the act ... They reached John's apartment; the front porch-light had gone out but by now they both knew the count of the steps upward; the front door, open, would give them illumination, the hall-light enough to get the key turned. He'd left no lights on. She always left a light on. He was always glad not to waste money having a bulb lit when no one was there; she was always glad to have a light already waiting when she came home ... he slept in the dark, she slept with that same light lit.

He reached for her without putting the light on. It would be one of those nights: she was pleased for the darkness so that he could not see her expression. She was smiling sardonically. He was so predictable. If he put the light on, it meant they would have to sit and make some preamble social conversation before getting it on. If not, it meant he was ready pronto and they'd cut out the preambles. She was never consulted about whether or not she was ready. Meantime, John was sure she was ready; he'd had enough signs from her on the way. No use wasting time. They both had to get up for early classes.

He stripped in the darkness. Enough light came in through the door's glass panel so that she could see his beautiful, long back and thigh and his risen hard-on as he turned toward her. She left her clothing on and lay down. Let him do the work, why make it easy? He put his hands into her jeans and her shirt. Baby, why don't you take those off, it's time. I don't think so, she said. But then she did, what was the use of it, she wanted him for sure, without knowing why. She fell back on the bed and he put his flat palm across her mound, moving it slightly, subtly. She thought she would go crazy. Why was it that half the time she wanted him into her at once and the rest of the time she thought he didn't do enough foreplay? Come *on*, she said. And then it happened—as he turned from her side and began to climb on top of her to enter her, he groaned slightly, the groan of an old man who is making an effort.

That could stop her. If she let it. If she became annoyed and turned off, if she considered the abnormally soft, smooth texture of the skin under her hand, the skin of a person who has passed sixty, is moving toward death, who chews the cud of what used to be, so sure of everything—Who was he, and who was she, what was she doing in this bed with this old man who unconsciously groaned as he lifted his still remarkably beautiful lanky skeleton to climb onto her young and round body and put his body inside of hers to make this gesture for pleasure—

She moved to open under him. He had no fantasies, he was pleased with the moment, he owned it and her; he would not admit, even now, even to himself, how rich this process was and how important to him. Her firm cunt closed around his cock and he moved, thus, murmuring, Wonderful, come on, pretty bitch, and dug his fingernails slightly into her back, put his mouth on her breast, felt her contracting on his shaft. She studied the process as if from another room, as if they were both in one of those porn magazines of his, and felt herself pleased to come. But did he? What kind of man is it that makes no sign when he comes? Repressed, yes, she thought, against his arm, but that much isn't— normal. Don't worry about me, he said once, it doesn't matter, it's being with you that counts. I don't believe you, she said. That's your problem, he said, and not mine, I know how I feel. But I don't, she said. Why do you have to? he asked. Because—don't you *know* why? I—she started, and then fell asleep. Just before she slept, she had a strong, clear image of David's face. A man she had not yet made love with, slept next to. As if it were he. Next to her.

When she dreamed, it was David's face, surrounded by John's silvery, swept-back hair. David's face had a netting of tiny, broken veins at the cheekbones and along the cheek, as John's did. David's face had a tiny patch of silvery stubble at the edge of the right mandibula, as John did when he often missed that spot in shaving. It was David, not as he would look thirty years from now, but as he would look if he were both David and John in one man. As if there were a split and clone, a composite formed of each and both. How can this be, she said to herself in the dream, I didn't even tell John ... that David and— The words formed with no more sound than would a bubble in water. She woke, into total darkness. John was gently snoring, his back to her.

He was swimming in his own dream: talking to Arthur about Rachel, or *was* it Rachel, and he was saying "us," to Arthur, and Arthur was arguing with him, saying, There's no such thing as "us," "us" is not a real condition, it's a temporary one, it's a word we make up to fill our need for such a word, and John was arguing back, No, but you have to understand, I mean me and Rachel, I don't mean Margery, not any more. Don't be a silly old ass, Arthur said, it's certainly Margery, just look. No, it's not, said John, Margery never wanted to fuck and Rachel likes to fuck, so it has to be Rachel when I say "us." And don't call me a silly old ass, or that makes you one too, you're my age and more and you're easily as silly, my friend. Arthur said, age isn't what makes someone an ass. Well, said John, why didn't you call me that when I came to your house and you were crying? You wouldn't have heard me, said Arthur. That's right, and I don't want to hear you now, either. Shut up and move your Queen, Arthur said. It's *your* Queen has need of moving, said John, or I'll—No way, said Arthur, I have no Queen, some friend you are, won't even teach me how to be alone.

And when he said "alone," the word spun out into a silvery fuzz, a threaded zone that covered both their heads. John couldn't breathe. It woke him. He needed to piss. Rachel was gone. She'd left one small light on with a note next to it. It said, Why can't we get married? Why can't we live together? John read it and then said softly, into the alone night, Because I don't want to lose you. He returned from the bathroom, had a stiff bourbon on the rocks, put on one more light and took out his most recent box of papers. Poured another bourbon and set it next to his typewriter. It was 2:40 A.M. He began to write.

oo oo oo
MARGE PIERCY

Raisin pumpernickel ⸻

You shine, my love, like a sugar maple in October,
a golden-orange overarching blaze of leaves,
each painted its own tint of flames
tossed on the ground bright as silk scarves.
So are you happy.

My curly one, my stubborn fierce butter,
down with the head and charge all horns
and the blattering thunk of bone head on bone,
the smoke and hot rubber stench of overheated temper.
So are you angry.

The tomcat is a ready lover. He can do it at dawn
when the birds are still yawning, he can do it
while the houseguest walks up the drive, do it after
four parties and an all-night dance, on a convenient floor.
So are you able.

Your love comes down rich as the warm spring rain.
Now it charges like a tawny dark maned lion.
Now it envelopes me in wraiths of silken mist.
Now it is a thick hot soup that sustains me.
So are you loving.

You're an endless sink of love, a gaping maw
into which I shovel attention like soft coal
into an old furnace; you're a limitless love source,
a great underground spring surging out of rock
to feed a river.

You cry your needs, bold as a six-week kitten.
You're devious as a corporate takeover and direct
as an avalanche. What ten years into this conversation
commands my interest? You're still the best novel
I've ever read.

Secretly we both think we were bred for each other
as part of an experiment in getting dreams made
flesh and then having to feed on the daily bread
of passion. So we die and die with loving
and go on living.

124

○○ ○○ ○○

EDNA O'BRIEN

Baby Blue _____

Three short quick death knocks resounded in her bed-
room the night before they met. He said not to give it a thought, not
to fret. He asked if she would like a kiss later on and she nodded. They
were alike in everything and they talked with their heads lolled against
the back of the armchairs so that to any spectators it was their throats
that would be readily visible. The others had gone. He had been brought
in unexpectedly by a friend, and as she said, somewhat frankly, it wasn't
every day that one met an eligible man. He for his part said that if he
had seen her in a restaurant he would have knocked over tables to get
to her. Her hand was on the serge of his knee, his hand on the velvet
of hers, and they were telling each other that there was no hurry at all,
that their bodies were as perfectly placed as neighboring plants.

She escorted him to the corner to get a taxi, and on the way they
found a pack of cards on the wet road, cut them there and then, and
cut identically. Next day he would be making the short flight across the
Channel to his home, which sounded stately, with its beech trees, its
peach houses, its asparagus bed, and Corinthian pillars supporting the
front porch. In time she would be acquainted with the rooms, she would
ask him to describe them one by one—library, kitchen, drawing room,
and last, but very last of all, bedroom. It was his wife's house. His wife
was her coloring and also five foot seven and somewhat assertive. His
children were adorable. He had thought of suicide the previous summer, but that was over, meeting her had changed all that. It was like
Aladdin, magical; his hair would begin to grow again and he would
trim his black beard, so that by the next weekend his lips would feel
and imprint hers. He worked as a designer and had to come back each
week to continue plans for a little theater that was being built as part
of a modern complex. It was the first thing he had done in years.

The card he sent her was a historic building going up in flames and
she thought, Ominous, but because of the greetings on it she was in
an ecstasy.

He would arrive on Fridays, telephone from the airport, and in the
hallway, with his black mohair bag still in his hand, he would kiss her
while she bit at his beard and got to the secrecy of his lips. Then he
would hold her at a distance from him and tilt her head until she became flawless. There she would be, white-skinned, agog, and all of a
blush, and there he would be, trying not to palpitate so hard. His smell

was dearer to her than any she could remember and yet it was redolent of some deep, buried memory. Her mother, she feared. Something of the same creaminess and the same mildness united them as if poised for life's knife. He plaited her hair around his finger, they constantly swapped plates, glasses, knives, forks, and were unable to eat, what with all the jumping up and down and swapping of these things. He took her hands to his face, and she said all the little pouches of tension would get pressed away, and not long after this, and during one of those infinite infinities, he cried and she drank in two huge drops of very salty tears. He confessed to her that when he was little and got his first bicycle he had to ride around and around the same bit of safe suburban street so that his mother would not worry about his getting run over on a main road. She said that fused them together, that made him known to her throughout, and again she thought of slaughter and of some lamb waiting for life's knife.

"Will it last, Eleanor?" he said.

"It will last," she said.

She never was so sure of anything in her life. In the bedroom she drew the pink curtains, and he peeled the layers of her clothing off, and talked to her skin, then bones beneath it, then to her blood, then their bloods raced together.

"I can't stop my wife coming to London to shop," he said, getting out of bed, dressing, and then undressing again. He scarcely knew what he wanted to do. He had a migraine and asked if she ever suffered from that. She said go, please go. They had known each other for six weekends and he intended to get her a ring. Her mascara was badly crusted on her lashes and had smeared onto her lids.

This was no way to be. She had left her earrings on and knew that the crystal would have made a semblance of a gash on each side of her neck. They had gone to bed drunk, and were drunk oftener than they need be. He used to intend to go early to the family he was supposed to be staying with, but always his resolution broke and he stayed with her until breakfast time, or later.

"Go, please go," she said it again.

His smile was like a cowl placed over a very wretched face.

The next weekend it didn't work out too badly. It was a question of him running back and forth to her, and from her, helping his wife with shopping, getting his daughter a diary, getting his son some toy motors, once having to fail her by not showing up at all, and then in a panic ringing her from the flat in the middle of the night—presumably his wife was asleep—saying, "I have to talk to you, I will see you tomorrow at ten; if you are not there I will wait, I will see you tomorrow at ten, I have to talk to you, if you are not there I will wait . . ."

At ten he arrived and his complexion was that of an old gray sock.

"What is it?" she said sympathetically, and still relatively in control of herself. If only she had crystal-gazed.

"I dread looking into my wife's eyes and telling her that I am in love with another woman."

"Then don't," she said.

"Do you love me anymore?" he asked.

"Yes," she said, and they sat in the dining room, on a carved chair, looking out at the winter trees in the winter sky, feeling sad for each other, and for themselves, and remembering to the future when the trees would be in leaf, and they would walk in the gardens together and there and then, a bit teary, unslept, and grave beyond belief, they started to build.

Christmas comes but once a year, and when it does it brings families together. He went home and, as the friend who had introduced them said, was probably busy, dressing the tree, going to parties, pulling crackers, and, as she silently added, looking into his wife's eyes, or his old cat's eyes, putting drops into his cat's eyes, doing his duty. He used to tell her how he sat on the stairs, talking to his cat as if it were her, and then biting one of his whiskers. No letter. She didn't know it but the huge gilt mirror in their hall fell, broke, and just missed his wife by inches; she did not know it then, but that miss was relevant. New Year's Eve saw her drunk again and maudlinly recalling dead friends, those in the grave and those who were still walking around. She would not leave the restaurant but sat all night at the corner table until the waiter brought her coffee and a little jug of warm milk in the morning. He found her curled up in her fox cape.

"Gigo, am I old . . . ?" she said.

"No . . . not old, well-looking," he said.

He knew her well and had often helped her out with her parties. He knew her as a woman who worked for a public relations firm, and brought them nice customers and did lots of entertaining. They sat and talked of towns in Italy—Siena, Pisa, Padua, Fuerti di Marmi, Spoleto. At the mention of each town he kissed the air. On the twelfth day—little Christmas—he wrote to say, "Only that I love you more and miss you desperately, I am in a spruce wood and it is growing dark." It was. She saw that but she refused to comprehend.

When she saw his wife she thought that yes she would have known her and felt that the scalded expression and marmalade hair would make an incision inside her brain. "I will dream of this person," she said warningly to herself as they shook hands. Then she handed him the bottle of white wine but kept the little parcel of quails' eggs, because they looked too intimate and would be a revelation in their little nest of chaff, speckled, freshly boiled an hour before, blue-green with spots of brown, eggs as fresh as their sex. It was at his hospital bedside, and there beside him were these two women and above him a little screen denoting the waver of his heart. It was all a bit unreal to Eleanor. No two people looked more unsuited, what with his shyness and his wife's blatancy, his dark coloring and hers, which had the ire of desert sand. For a moment she felt there was some mistake, it was perhaps his wife's sister, but no, she was busying herself doing a wife's things, touching the lapel of his pajamas, putting a saucer over the jug of water, acknowledging the flowers. The lilies of the valley that Eleanor had sent him were in a tumbler, the twenty sprays dispatched from Ascot. Asked by his wife where they had come from, he said an "admirer" and smiled. He smiled quite a lot as he nestled back against the pillows, seeming like a man with nothing on his mind except the happy guarantee that there would be hot milk at ten, two sleeping pills, and oblivion. She kept eying his wife, and the feeling she got was of a body, tanklike, filled with some kind of explosive. His wife suddenly told them that she was something of a seer and he asked politely if he would recover. The wine she brought they drank from cups. Exquisite, chilled white wine, such as she and he had often drunk, and such as he had drunk with his wife in the very first stages of their courtship. He was a man to whom the same thing was happening twice. The nurses were beginning to busy themselves and bade good night overloudly to one lame visitor who was getting up to leave. The man in the next bed begged if he could have his clothes in order to go home to his own house, whereupon the night sister gave him a little peck on the cheek.

"I must go," Eleanor said, and looked at him as if there were some means of becoming invisible and staying.

"So must I," his wife said, and it was apparent that she wanted them to go together, to have a chinwag perhaps. Eleanor touched the counterpane beneath where his feet were and left hurriedly, as if she were walking on springs instead of high-heeled patent shoes. No chinwag, no nothing with this self-claimed seer. Yet something in her wanted to tell it, to have it known there and then, to have each person speak their mind. She ran down the stairs, crossed the road, and stood trembling in the porchway of the pub, dividing her glance between the darkness of the hospital doorway and the welcoming soft pink light inside the pub itself. When she saw the woman, the wife, emerge in a black coat with a little travel bag, she felt momentarily sorry for her, felt her defeat or perhaps her intuition in the way she walked down the street. She watched her and thought that if they had been at school together or were not torn between the same unfortunate man, they might have some crumb of friendship to toss at one another.

Back at his bedside making the most of the two minutes the sister had allowed her, she looked at him and said, "Well."

"What did you think?" he said.

"She talks a lot," she said.

"Now you see," he said, and then he held her and she knew that there was something that she did not see, something that existed but was hidden from her. Some betrayal that would one day come out.

"I am not jealous," she said.

"How could you be?" he said, and they sobbed and kissed and rocked back and forth, as if they were in their own room.

"I would like you to have a baby," he said.

"I'll have twins," she said.

"My wife says if it was anyone but you."

"But me," she said, and she could feel herself boiling.

His wife had gone on a short holiday in order to recoup her strength so that they could finalize the marriage. Eleanor had flown over to see him and was staying in a hotel a few miles from where he lived.

"She won't let me see the children," he said.

"That's what everyone says, that's standard."

"I had to lie about your key."

"How did she find it?"

"In my pocket," he said, then asked if he should demonstrate it.

"No," she said, "don't."

The question escaped out of her: "Do you sleep together?"

"Once . . ." he said. "I thought it was honorable."

"Don't," she said.

"It's a big bed, it's almost as big as this room."

Although she meant to hold her tears at all costs, they accrued, dropped onto the toasted sandwich and into the champagne that he had bought her and onto the orange-colored napkin. They were like rain softening the paper napkin. He squeezed her hand and led her back to the hotel room; there he undressed her, washed her, powdered her, and put her to dry in a big towel, then told her he loved her, that he would always love her, and she lay inside the towel listening to the crows cawing, then the rain pelting off the roof, and the old trees with their old branches groaning, then the spatters against the windowpane, and she thought of the daffodils getting soaked as he clasped her through the warm towel and begged of her to let him in, always to let him in. Later that evening when she caught the plane back he simply said, "Soon, soon." All through the journey, talking to a juggernaut who sat next to her, she kept thinking, Soon, and yet there was one little niggle that bothered her, his saying that he would have to tax the car next day, because his wife liked everything to be kept in order.

The night his wife returned he phoned her from a booth and said he was never in all his life so incensed. He said he had no idea what he might do next. She did not know it then but he had a black eye caused by a punch from a ringed finger, and wounds around the thighs where he was ridiculed for being a cunt. She said he ought to leave at once, but he was too drunk to understand. The next day when he phoned he said everything was going to be more protracted but that he would phone when he could, and that she was to be well, be well. He was with her within twenty-four hours, sitting on the swivel chair, pale, bruised, and so disheveled that she realized he had known more ordeal in a day than in the sum of his life. He kissed her, asked her to please, please, never pull his hair by the roots, because he minded that more than anything. They made love, and on and off throughout the day and in his short sleeps he kept threshing about and muttering things. He dreamed of a dog, a dog at their gate lodge, and when he told her she felt inadequate. She would have to replace wife, children, animals, a sixteen-room house, the garden, cloches, the river, and the countryside with its ranges of blue-black mountains. As if he guessed her thoughts, he said sadly that he owned nothing, and the little stone he once gave her would be the only gift he could afford for a while. The theater design was complete, but no other offers of work loomed. That was the other thing that galled. He had busied himself in craven domesticity and let his work slide. He had beggared himself.

He would telephone her when he was out and say he was on his way "home, so to speak." He was seeing various friends and, though she did not know it, getting communiqués from his wife to come back, to come back. The evening he broke it to her, he first asked if she had seen a rainbow in the sky and described how he saw it when standing in a bus shelter. Then he coughed and said, "I rang my wife," and she gulped.

"My wife isn't like you, she never cries, but she cried, she sounded ill, very ill," he said.

"She's a maneuvering liar," she said.

"I have to be there," he said.

"Go now," she said, not wanting the ritual of a wake, and in fact he had forestalled her in that, because his wife was flying at the very moment and they had arranged to meet in a friend's house, empty, as it happened.

Then followed their first dirty quarrel, because he had told her so many hideous things that his wife had said about her, so many outrageous untruths.

"She's mad," she said. "It's a madhouse."

"I'll tell you what a madhouse it is," he said, and proceeded to describe how as a farewell barter his wife had induced him to make love to her and was now in the process of looking for an abortionist.

"You mean you did," she said.

"In the morning I'm always, a man is always . . ."

"You went in."

"I didn't ejaculate."

"She stinks."

"It stinks," he said, and as he left she clung to his sleeve, which must have been clung to a few mornings earlier, and she saw his hair so soft, so jet, his eyes bright hazel and overalive, and then she let go without as much as a murmur.

"I'll always love you," he said.

She walked with him in imagination up the road, to the house where his wife waited, to their embrace, or their quarrel, or their whatever, and all night she kept vigil, expecting one or the other of them to come back to her, to consult her, to include her, to console her, but no one came.

The Sunday he was due to arrive back, she went into the country, both to escape the dread of waiting and to pick flowers. She picked the loveliest wildflowers, put them all around the house, then put the side of salmon in a copper pan, peeled cucumber, sliced it thin as wafers, proceeded to make a sauce, and was whipping, stopping every other minute for the sound of the telephone, when in fact the doorbell rang. He was in a sweat, carrying a bag of hers that he had once borrowed. Yes, his wife had insisted on coming with him and was in the friend's house a mile away, making the same threats about writs, about custody, about children, about his whoring. They drank and kissed and ate dinner, and it was the very same as in the first wayward weeks when he kept kneeling by her, asking for special favors, telling her how much more he loved her. Around midnight he said he had no intention of going back to the house where his wife was, and falling half asleep and still engaged in the tangle of love, he thanked her from the bottom of his heart and said this was only the beginning. Next day when he telephoned, his wife demanded to see him within the hour, but he decided not to go, said, "Let it stew."

They were invited by friends of Eleanor's to the country, and he chose what she should wear, he himself having only the clothes that were on his back, his suitcase being in his wife's possession. It was a beautiful house and he had some trepidation about going.

"Look, black swans," she said, pointing to the artificial lake as they drove up to the avenue and stepped out onto the very white gravel, her shoes making a grating sound. The butler took their bags, and straightaway, with their hostess, they set out for a walk. The lawn was scattered with duck droppings and swan droppings and fallen acacia petals. It was a soft misty day, and the black swans were as coordinated and elegant as if they were performing a pageant. It was perfect. A few last acacia flowers still clung to the bushes and made a little show of pink. In the grotto one of the guests was identifying the hundreds of varieties of rock there. Had they stayed outside they could have watched a plane go by. He loved planes, and for some reason to do with portent, she kept count of them for him. When she entered the dark and caught him by surprise, their two faces rubbed together and their breaths met. That night in a different bed, a four-poster, they made love differently, and he told her as he tore at the beautiful lingerie that she had bought for the occasion that never had he loved her so much as earlier in the dark grotto, with her big eyes and her winged nose looming over him. The torn silk garments fell away from her and she felt at last that they had truly met, they had truly come into their own.

He went back, but in his own time. Each night when he phoned he said there was no question now of their losing each other, because he was recovering his self-esteem. Then he returned sooner than she expected, in fact unannounced. She was hemming curtains, lovely cream lace curtains that she had bought with him in mind. They went to the kitchen and he said yes, that his wife had come again and was making the same contradictory threats, one minute telling him to get out, the next minute begging him to stay, showing him her scarred stomach, scars incurred from all her operations. He was wearing a striped seersucker jacket, and it was the first time that she saw him as his wife's property, dressed expensively but brashly. He was restless, and without knowing it, she kept waiting for the crisis.

"I can't phone you in the future," he said.

"You can," she said, coaxing him.

"They listen at the exchange," he said.

"I insist," she said, and began in jest to hit him. All of a sudden he told her how he had thrown his wife out of a room the night before and how he realized he wanted to kill her.

"And?" she said.

"She came back to say she was bleeding from the inner ear."

"And?" she said.

"Good, I said."

There was a dreadful silence. They sat down to eat a bit of bread and cheese, but the jesting was over. Next day he went to inquire about work, and when he came home in the evening, everything was friendly but something needed to be said. He was going to be incommunicado, he said, thus making it impossible for his wife to find him. Next night they went to a party and she made certain not to cling to him, not to make him feel hemmed in. Yet they had to rush to the little cloakroom to kiss. He lifted her dress and touched her lingeringly, and she said wasn't he the philanderer, then. On the way home she expressed the wish to be in Paris, so they could have breakfast and dawdle all day. What she really wished was not Paris but a place where they could be free. It was a midsummer night, and they decided to go into the square and sit under a tree where the pigeons were mildly cogitating. He gave her a borough council rose and said would she keep it forever, even when it crumpled. He said there was no doubt about it but that she was psychic, that his wife, who always wore girdles, was now buying the same panties as her. He had seen them in a case—white, brown, and cream, with the maker's name on them and little borders of lace. She asked a question. He said no, there had not been a reunion, but that he went into the bedroom to get his book from the bedside table and there they were on the top of the opened suitcase.

"I would like to be there, just once, invisible," she said.

He shook his head and said all she would see would be himself at a table trying to draw something, his wife in her cashmere dressing gown, coming in, snatching it out of his hand, saying, "You cunt, don't forget that, you louse," then going on about *her* worth, *her* intelligence, the sacrifice she had made for him, leaving the room to down another glass of wine, coming back to start all over again with fresh reinforcements, to get into her stride.

"Are you hiding something, Jay?" she said.

"Only that I love you passionately," he said, and together they held the rose, which was dark red and vibrant as blood.

A few days later he was remote, refused to eat or drink, and was always just short of frowning when she entered the room. He sat and watched cricket on television, and sometimes would get up and mime the movement of the batsman, or would point to one of the fielders who were running and say how miraculous it was. A few times he went upstairs to kiss her, kisses of reassurance, but each time when she commenced to talk, he was gone again. Young love, outings to the country, a holiday, all those things seemed improbable, a figment. They were too racked by everything. She was glad that there was a guest for dinner, because he became his old self again, warm and friendly; then he sang and in the course of singing put one lock of her hair behind his ear, which made him look like a girl. They met each other's glance and smiled and it was all like before. The friend said no two people were so well matched and they drank to it. In bed he tossed and turned, said it would have been better if he stayed in a hotel, so as not to disturb her sleep, said all in all he was a very spoiled person and that he would have to get a steady job. He said he had to admit that his wife was now nothing, no one, although he had dreamed of her the previous night, and that he was hoping that she would go far away and, like a Santa Claus, send back some of her money. Yes, it was like that. All his past life was over, finished; then he doubled over with pain and she massaged him gently, but it gave no relief; he said the pain went right through to the fillings of his teeth.

"You have something to tell me?" she asked.

"Yes." He said it so quietly that the whole room was taut with expectation. The room where eight months previously she had heard the unfathomable death knocks, the room to which they climbed at all hours, drinking one another in, the room where the sun coming through the gauze curtains played on the brass rungs of the bed and seemed to reveal and scatter imaginary petals, the room where he gave her one drop of his precious blood instead of a gold wedding ring. What he had to tell her was that he was giving it all up, her, his wife, his family, his beautiful house, the huge spider's web that he had got himself into. For a moment she panicked. He once told her that he would like to go to a hotel room and write to the people concerned—herself, his children, his wife—and, as he implied, put an end to himself. She thought not that, not that, no matter what, and for a second rehearsed a conciliatory conversation with his wife where they would both do everything to help him. He could not be allowed to.

"I'll leave here tomorrow," he said.

"Where will you go?" she asked.

"I'll go home to say goodbye." And in those few words she knew that he would go home not to say goodbye but to say "Hello, I'm back." She prayed that by the morrow he would change his mind and feel less conclusive about things.

I am not dead, she thought, and clutched at objects as if they could assure her of the fact. Then she did rash things, went outdoors, but had to be indoors at once, and barely inside was she than suffocation strangled her again, and yet out in the street the concrete slabs were marshy and the spiked railings threatening to brain her. It was the very same finality as if someone had died and she could see, without looking, his returned latchkey, its yellow-green metal reflected in the co-green of her ring stone. The ring she had taken off the previous night in order for her fingers to be completely at one with his fingers. It was not long after that he said it, and it seemed to her that she must have precipitated it in some mysterious way, and that maybe she had made him feel lacking in something and that it need never have happened, but that it had happened and he had suddenly announced that there was no room for her in his life, that she was not someone he wished to spend his life with, that it was over. Instantly she was off the cliff again. The night and the morning were getting crushed together: the night, when he told her, and the morning, when he had packed every stitch while she was having a shower and had his bag down in the hall and was whistling like a merry traveler.

"I can't," she kept saying, "can't, can't," and then she would refer to his hair, his brown tweed jacket, and the beautiful somberness of him, and then again she would remember the words, the fatal words, his Adam's apple moving, juggling, and the way she bit at it out of love, out of need, and in the morning—yes, it was morning—when she folded his two legs together and kissed as much of him as protruded, and he asked would she do that when he was very old and very infirm and in an institution, and for a moment they both cried. He left. She knew in her bones that it was final, that he had deceived her, that all those promises, the reams of love letters, the daily pledge, "You, I hold fast," were no longer true, and she thought with wizard hatred that perhaps they never had been true, and she thought uselessly but continuously of his house with the fawn blinds drawn down, his getting home after dark, putting his bag on a chair, throwing down the gauntlet at last, saying he was back for good and all, had sown his wild oats. That would not be for a few hours yet, because he was still traveling, but that is what would happen. To get through until dark, she asked of God, as if dark itself had some sort of solution to the problem. Two women held her pressed to a chair, and said commiseratingly to each other that it was impossible to help someone. Judging by their startled faces and by the words that flowed out of her mouth, she knew that she was experiencing the real madness that follows upon loss.

"We're here, we're here," her friend would say.

"Where is he, where is he?" she said, rising, stampeding.

The swivel chair was like a corpse in the room and she threw the paperweight at it. What had once been a dandelion clock inside pale-green glass was now pale-green splinters and smithereens. If he had had a garden, or rather, if he had tended their own garden, he would only cultivate green-and-white flowers, such things as snowdrops and Christmas roses. Between her tears she tried to tell them that, so they would have some inkling of what he was like, and what had gone on between them, and for a moment she saw those Christmas roses, a sea of them, pale and unassuming in a damp incline from the opposite side, and he eerily still.

She went to a friend's house to write it, being too afraid to do it in her own house, in case he might telephone. She used a friend's foolscap paper and over that hour filled three full pages. It was the most furious letter she had ever written, and she wished that she had a black-edged envelope in which to post it. There was no tab on the postbox telling the time of the next collection, so she went into a nearby shop to ask if it was reliable. It was a lighting shop. Long glass shades hung down like crystals, like domes, like translucent mushrooms, reminding her of some nonexistent time in the future when she would entertain him. After posting the letter she went back to the friend's house to finish her tea, and as she was being conveyed up the street, they saw an elderly woman with a big sheepdog in her arms, holding it upright, like a baby, and she wanted to run across and embrace both of them.

"That woman saw her father being run over when she was fourteen and hasn't been the same since," her friend said.

"And we think we're badly off," she said.

She felt curiously elated and began to count, first in hours, then in minutes, then in seconds, the length of time before he received the epistle.

He was sleeping in his wife's bedroom again. That was part of the pact, that, and a vow that he would never travel abroad without her, that he would pay attention to her at parties, appreciate her more than he had been doing. He said yes to all her demands and thought that somehow they would not be exacted once she was over her fit. He slept badly. He talked, shouted in his sleep, and in the morning while being rebuked about it, he never inquired in case he might have said the other woman's name. Her photo, the small snapshot of her that he had kissed and licked so many times, was in the woodshed along with the one letter that he had brought away out of the pile that he had left in her study for safety. It was the night of his thirty-fifth birthday, and they had been parted but a week. He stood over his son's bed telling himself that what he had done was the right thing. The little boy had one finger in his mouth and the other hand was splayed out like a doll's. "It's the hands that kill you, isn't it?" said his wife, who had crept in to enjoy the moment of domesticity.

He kept going to the front door long before the visitors were due to arrive, and he was even in two minds about nipping the lead off to the master telephone, because he was in dread of its ringing. At the party he sang the same songs as he had sung to her, in fact, his repertoire. His wife drank his health, and the old nanny, who had been in the habit of hearing and seeing the most frightful things and had seen bottles flying, thought how changeable a thing human nature can be. Even staggering to bed he thought he heard footsteps. His wife dared him to fuck her, but it was a drunken dare and drunkenly dismissed; in fact, it made them laugh. She didn't sleep well, what with her thirst, his tossing and turning, and those son-of-a-bitch snores. She was downstairs sipping black coffee, putting a touch of varnish on her nails, when the footsteps came over the gravel.

Early Monday, she thought, and went out to open the door for the postman, who always said the same dumb thing—"Fine day, ma'am," regardless of the weather. Now more than ever his letters concerned her, and her own letter from her sister in Florida took mere second place as she looked at the two business envelopes and then the large envelope with its deceiving blue-ribboned type. She decided to read it outdoors.

"Drivel," she said, starting in on the first stupid nostalgic bits, and then in her element as she saw words she knew, words that could have been her own, the accusation of his being a crooked cunt, the reference to his wife's dandruffy womb, to his own idle, truthless, working-class stinking heart, and she knew that she had won.

"What's that?" she said, and snatched the letter from him. She read it with a speed that made him think for a minute she had written it herself. He saw her eyes get narrower and narrower, and she was as compressed now as a peach stone. She pursed her lips the way she did when entering a party. She got to the bits referring to herself, read them aloud, cursed, and then jubilantly tore it up and tossed the pieces in the air as if they were old raffle tickets. She danced, and said what whoopee, and said "kiss-kiss," and said he'd be a good boy now. He got out of bed and said he had to go to the hotel, have a drink, and not to forget that they were going to a party that night and not to get "drunkies" early in the day, as there were plenty of parties for the summer vacation. As he left she was phoning to ask the girl in the boutique to send up some dresses, a few, and then she started discussing colors.

"Wait a minute ... hey ..." He turned around in order to be asked if pale blue and baby blue were one and the same thing.

"Just asking my beau," she said to the girl on the telephone, but he was unable to give any reply.

In the driveway he tried to remember the letter from start to finish, tried to remember how the sentences led from one to another, but all that he could remember were single vicious words that flew up into the air; it was the very same as if the black crows had turned into great black razors and were inside his head, cutting, cutting away. He would stay in the hotel for as long as possible, all day, all night maybe, and he would go back tomorrow and the next day, and maybe one day he would take a room and do the thing he wanted to do, maybe one day.

They were simply little slabs of stone laid into and just beneath the level of the grass, about a hundred of them almost begging for feet to dance, or play hopscotch. Here and there was a vase or mug filled with flowers, mostly roses. She asked one of the gardeners what the slabs signified and he said each one covered someone's ashes. "There's two boxes in some, where was a husband and wife, but most of 'em there's one," he said. The words went straight to her heart. Not long after, she found a tomb with Jay's name on it and nearby was his daughter's name. These names swam before her eyes. She wished that her name were there, too, and began to search. She went around and around the main graveyard, then to that part where the meadowsweet was so high, the tomb and the stone effigies were all covered over, and she could not read a thing. Some French children, on a conducted tour, were running back and forth, amused at what they saw and even more amused when they went in under the redstone ruin that had a big sign saying DANGEROUS STRUCTURE. A few hundred yards away they were setting up wagons for the weekend's amusement fair, and men in vests with big muscles were laying aluminum tracks for the Dodg'em cars. Graveyard and pleasure green were side by side, with a tennis court and a miniature golf course at the northern end. The caravans had arrived, the women were getting out their artificial flowers, their china plates, and their bits of net curtain, to set up yet again their temporary dwellings. She tried to hold on to life, to see what she was seeing, these people setting up house for a day or two or three, muscles, burial places, schoolchildren with no thought of death. It was a windy day, and the roses in the containers kept falling over and girls kept bullying each other to come on or not come on. In the Church of St. Nicholas she looked at the altar, at the one little slit of light from the aperture above, under half of which was stained and half was clear. Then she looked at oddments in a glass case, bits of tiling, and one tiny bit of bone as perfect as a pillar that had been found by a schoolchild whose statement it bore. Outside, the lawn mowers were full on, and those plus the shrieks of the visiting children tried to claim her head; she hoped that they would, thereby banishing forever the thought of all that had gone before. The sun came in fits and starts, the tiers of yellow bulbs were all bunched up, waiting to be lit, the haunted caravan with its black skull and its blooded talons looked a little ridiculous, since no wicked ogre lurked within. She had come on a train journey to consult a faith healer but was much too early. All was still, and only the bright garish daubs of paint suggested that by Saturday all would be in motion, and for better or worse people would go and get on the Dodg'ems and the mad merry-go-round.

What would she have not given to see him for a moment, to clasp him utterly silent, no longer trusting to speech.

It will pass, she thought, going from grave to grave, and unconsciously and almost mundanely she prayed for the living, prayed for the dead, then prayed for the living again, went back to find the tomb where his name was, and prayed for all those who were in boxes alone or together above or below ground, all those unable to escape their afflicted selves.

SHE FLUVIAL

LAURIE DUESING

Blossoming ————————————————

She told me she opened up
like a flower. I said that
to you while I was sitting
in the swing in your loft.
I wore no clothes and bent my knees
trying to swing higher.
You thought I meant sex
but that was too obvious.
I was talking about childbirth,
the way she felt when her baby
came. When you put your hands
on my thighs, the swing stopped.
Perhaps I was beautiful
because you knelt, put your mouth
over me, your tongue inside.
Though you misunderstood,
you wanted me
to open up like that.

○○ ○○ ○○
ALICIA OSTRIKER

Greedy Baby ————————————————

Greedy baby
sucking the sweet tit
your tongue tugging the nipple tickles your mama
your round eyes open appear to possess understanding
when you suckle I am slowly moved
in my sensitive groove
you in your mouth are alive, I in my womb
a book lies in my lap I pretend to read
I turn some pages, when satiated
a moment you stop sucking
to smile up with your toothless milky mouth
I smile down, and my breast leaks
it hurts, return
your lashes close, your mouth again clamps on
you are attentive as a business man
your fisted fingers open relaxing and
all rooms are rooms for suckling in
all woods are woods for suckling in
all boulevards for suckling
sit down anywhere, all rivers
are rivers for suckling by—
I have read that in all wars, when a city is taken,
women are raped, and babies stabbed in their little bellies
and hoisted up to the sky on bayonets—

LOUISE ERDRICH

from: *The Beet Queen* _____

*Twelve-year-old Sita brings her younger cousin Mary, who has
unexpectedly come to stay, to meet her best friend Celestine.*

"Mary," I said, "aren't you going to tell Celestine what
was in the little blue box you stole out of your mother's closet?"

Mary looked right at me. "Not a thing," she said.

Celestine stared at me like I was crazy.

"The jewels," I said to Mary, "the rubies and the diamonds."

We looked each other in the eye, and then Mary seemed to decide
something. She blinked at me and reached into the front of the dress.
She pulled out the cow's diamond on a string.

"What's that?" Celestine showed her interest at once.

Mary displayed the wonder of how the light glanced through her
treasure and fell, fractured and glowing, on the skin of her palm. The
two of them stood by the window taking turns with the cow's lens,
ignoring me. I sat at the table eating cookies. I ate the feet. I nibbled
up the legs. I took the arms off in two snaps and then bit off the head.
What was left was a shapeless body. I ate that up too. All the while I
was watching Celestine. She wasn't pretty, but her hair was thick and
full of red lights. Her dress hung too long behind her knees, but her
legs were strong. I liked her tough hands. I liked the way she could
stand up to boys. But more than anything else, I liked Celestine because
she was mine. She belonged to me, not Mary, who had taken so much
already.

"We're going out now," I told Celestine. She always did what I said.
She came, although reluctantly, leaving Mary at the window.

"Let's go to our graveyard," I whispered, "I have to show you something."

I was afraid she wouldn't go with me, that she would choose right
there to be with Mary. But the habit of following me was too strong
to break. She came out the door, leaving Mary to take the last batch of
cookies from the oven.

We left the back way and walked out to the graveyard.

"What do you want?" said Celestine when we stepped into the long
secret grass. Wild plum shaded us from the house. We were alone.

We stood in the hot silence, breathing air thick with dust and the
odor of white violets. She pulled a strand of grass and put the tender
end between her lips, then stared at me from under her eyebrows.

Maybe if Celestine had quit staring, I wouldn't have done what I did. But she stood there in her too-long dress, chewing a stem of grass, and let the sun beat down on us until I thought of what to show her. My breasts were tender. They always hurt. But they were something that Mary didn't have.

One by one, I undid the buttons of my blouse. I took it off. My shoulders felt pale and fragile, stiff as wings. I took off my undervest and cupped my breasts in my hands.

My lips were dry. Everything went still.

Celestine broke the stillness by chewing grass, loud, like a rabbit. She hesitated just a moment and then turned on her heel. She left me there, breasts out, never even looking back. I watched her vanish through the bushes, and then a breeze flowed down on me, passing like a light hand. What the breeze made me do next was almost frightening. Something happened, I turned in a slow circle. I tossed my hands out and waved them. I swayed as if I heard music from below. Quicker, and then wilder, I lifted my feet. I began to tap them down, and then I was dancing on their graves.

RACHEL BLAU DUPLESSIS

from: Eurydice _____

1.

Since the narcissus bud,
eye of a bird,
of a girl,
almond shaped eye,

when not yet open,
smells more of its
rich flower
than
when it has opened,

she desires never to be open.

a hidden bird   mistaken
for a leaf on a young tree.

2.

She will lie naked
where sea touches sand;
her own body
the border; the edge
dividing ocean and land
against itself; but of one body.

And tides come over her.
Then she will be turned
into a smooth stone
salt white as an egg,
shiny as an eye.

She will turn
over and over on herself,
body balancing ocean and land,
throwing the stone

down

a deeper and deeper well.

3.

Back arched like a bow
lips like arrows stinging.

And then you wet me with your tongue.

This is my fragrance.
You say
honey tastes sour
after.

You sing to me
that I am a fresh pool.

4.

Where is the bird?
fallen from flying

Where is the arrow?
hard in the wound

Where is the stone?

Songs are his,
melody like a great linked chain.
Touch is his,
outlining the edge of my dance.

I cannot find my center
I cannot find my path.
Now he can make me open, shut and open

Now I have lost myself.

NOTE: As a whole, in its eleven sections, this quest poem makes a critique both of
patriarchal uses of sensuality and of the relation of Orpheus to Eurydice in
the classic myth.

oo oo oo

RACHEL BLAU DUPLESSIS

Mirror Poem _____

Your thick metallic menstrual aroma
Your changes

My desire to enter the knowledge of your changes.
The symbol of fountains.

Stains on the bed are siena pink.
I embrace the shell-round space you arise from.

I have swum through fish lakes and fish oceans
being nibbled by mouths bubbling O's of air

I have climbed calendars like mountains

Walked down many a white road.

I dream of women.

I touch them, take their hands as they come toward me.
One is paler than in life; one has hennaed her hair.
I take their hands and ask
how is it in your life, how is your life.
One slides away from me as she has always done;
We cannot make contact, yet we have created each other.

We touch our finger tips as equals across a lengthening space.

Accept women; accept the love of women; accept loving women.
There I saw her at her window
early morning, white nightgown
when I looked out of my window
early morning, white nightgown.

Another morning looks out of the morning.
We could kiss each other. It would be no surprise.

oo oo oo
LILY POND

Ovulation _____

I have a convocation of crows
in my cunt
I have a convocation of crows
in my cunt   cawing
I have a convocation of crows

I have a basket of snakes
in my cunt
I have a basket of snakes
in my cunt   sliding
I have a basket of snakes

Screaming the infants
the mouths of the infants   birds
screaming for worms
wide as the stretch of a cunt
I have a convocation of crows
I have a basket of snakes

I have a black bat
I have a bat in my cunt
I have lizards
I have peonies
I have grasshoppers
I have a convocation of crows
I have a basket of snakes

I have no regard
I have no regard in my cunt
for time or poetry
for I have no petals
I have flame
I have the dragon
I have the fire
I have the conflagration

and the heat will not settle
(I have the snakes)
I would see you
but the flames are too high

I have the flames
in my cunt
and would burn everything
to get to you

SUSAN GRIFFIN

Viyella _____

An erotic story. For one thing I am in a rage at my lover. And for another my neck muscles are in a spasm so painful that moving in any direction frightens me. And making love requires movement. But this of course is a metaphor. I am going through profound changes in my soul. I know this. I can describe them to you on a minute level. But I won't. Not here or now. Suffice it to say that my muscles are in spasm because I am terrified of the changes taking place inside me. And in this state of mind I sit down to write a story about Eros.

I am writing this in a conversational style. In the language of the female realm of experience. Kitchen-table talk. This is the only way I can enter the erotic honestly. I have spent years trying to be what I thought I should be. This seems to be the only sentence I can begin with, as I try to speak of erotic feeling. Now, finally, at the age of forty, I know that I am a lesbian. This does not mean that I have no sexual feeling for men. But rather that my most profound longings and desires, for intimacy, to know, to touch and be inside the body and soul of another, becoming and separating from, devouring and being devoured, that wild, large, amazing, frightening territory of lovemaking, belongs for me not with men, but with women.

What is the story? The erotic story. The story will have to be a story about two women making love. It will have to take place sometime in a woman's life after she has been married and had a child and ended that marriage, and realized that for whatever other reasons her marriage failed, it also failed because her real passion and her deepest feelings of love did not belong to men. Which is to say it will have to take place after a certain change has transformed a woman's soul. After she has decided that she will stop trying to be what others have said she should be. After she has decided to stop lying about who she really is.

Which is, by the way, part of the problem with my neck. But I am not going to tell you about my present difficulty. It is part of my private life, which is to say it is delicate and vulnerable and does not yet belong on a page nor to the eyes of strangers. And at any rate, I have made my mind so tired by going over and over again the terrain of the present, I am aching with it, aching with rage and love. I want to reach back into the past. And I want to change that past. Not lie about it. But re-create it in a slightly different medium of fact and circumstance than that in which it actually occurred.

And why? The first reason is complex, the second simple. The first reason arises out of my knowledge of the imagination and our relationship to the past. I know that depending on who we are at the moment, we reshape the past into new meanings. And the second reason, the simple one? I do not want to reveal the private life of another woman, one who once trusted me, and whom I once loved, and still do, in another part of my soul, always will, love.

I will call her Viyella. The name appeals to me. It is not of course her real name. But I like it so that I have carried it around with me for weeks. This name has made me fall in love with this character. I am at this moment entering a real love affair with her, Viyella. This name is not anything like the name of my real lover, from the past. But she could have been named Viyella. And now the name is part of the character I create who resembles someone I actually did love, make love with, hold in my arms. This woman whom I create took the name for herself, and this is part of her character. She has a sense of drama, she and the real woman she takes after. She likes to invent a persona. She has airs.

When I knew her (the real woman or Viyella? Does it matter any longer?) she had a Southern accent. This was not put on. This was the realest part of her. She was from a small rural town in Georgia where the soil is red, and I loved to hear her talk about it and her family in those soft Southern tones that seemed warm and red like the earth itself. But she had been to the Sorbonne. The way she put it, she had upped and left all that Sorbonne shit—this is the way Viyella talked—because, honey, it was the phoniest thing in the world she'd ever met up with, it just wasn't her, she was ready to go back with the real folk, the kind she grew up with. Well, not exactly, because she was now living in Berkeley, California. She wore flannel shirts. And soft blue jeans. And her hair flowed around her head like wildlands. Her face had a kindness and a plainness, not the plainness of lack of beauty, but that American plainness which made you think of old farmhouses, the wood cut simply and then left to be shaped by the weather. Everything about her was very soft, and I feel a softness inside me even now as I remember the way she looked. Something essential about her, in the way she sat and gestured, was womanly, though she had a cocky boy's walk, and hunched her shoulders, as if her frail body were ready for a fight, and she wore boys' tennis shoes. She was a photographer, who worked as a volunteer on a women's newspaper. She collected food stamps and welfare. Did things basic (she would say), had no need for fancy stuff. But she wanted you to know she had seen better and rejected it.

Stories about Paris and the Sorbonne glittered in her normal conversation the way gold or silver mixed in eye shadow shines from a woman's eyelids. She mixed French phrases in her talk. A lovely French really. Not mispronounced so much as touched ever so lovingly by Georgia. *Ça va?* meaning *Okay?* got drawn out a little longer so that one heard Saaah vaah? It was nice. She had been there, she said, to study French literature. She had memorized quotations from Baudelaire and would toss off a line or two at certain moments. She had been working on her doctorate, the story went. Only Paris became more interesting to her than school. She wanted to build a life like the one she had in Paris again, only in Berkeley, and therefore she spent an inordinate amount of time at cafés, drinking coffee, which was not good for her, since she had problems with her heart. She decided to leave the Sorbonne, she said, because she did not want to be a dry academic. She wanted adventure. She wanted more of life. And anyway, she needed to go back to her roots, to see again the real people of this earth. And this is why she returned to her own country. This and the fact that she had to face the truth that the woman she had fallen in love with in Paris would never be anyone's lover, really.

But there was another side to Viyella. Another part of the picture she painted of herself. She talked about how she loved her MaMa and her MaMa never quite loved her back. That took my breath away when she talked like that. A woman sitting there, saying right out in that Southern accent, flecked so glamorously with a bit of French, how she wanted mother love, and how she felt rejected, how she never got enough of that love, and still wanted it. Wanted it still. I didn't say to myself, here is an honest person. Here is a person of great strength, someone who can look into her soul and see her own forbidden desires. Someone who can admit to her vulnerability, her tenderness, her childlikeness. I did not say this to myself. Nor did I say that I was so pleased that she had been a scholar before she gave the scholarship up. That she had proved to herself and the world that she could be someone. Someone recognized by European professors as being brilliant. Someone certified in the world as accomplished. Someone who spoke French, after all, who knew things. Who could dazzle and impress and then say with a shrug, "None of that shit really matters, does it?"

I did not say any of that to myself, nor other things, things I knew, really all along, about who Viyella really was. I had doubts and worries. The first time I saw Viyella she seemed at the end of her rope. I felt she was desperate and lost and looking for someone to fix her. But I forgot this first impression, or rather hid my memory of it from myself. I silenced my own doubts, and in that silence, I fell in love.

I was lavish. I brought her flowers. Sent her beautiful letters. Dressed in my best clothes and introduced her to special places to eat. I would kiss her and hold her hand in public and she admired my outrageousness. I had held back my love for women for so long that once I broke free from this taboo, there was no stopping me. I did not care what strangers on the street thought. I even imagined they liked the sight of one woman in love with another woman and kissing her on the mouth, pressing her body into the other woman's body, so that the softness of their breasts made one fine softness you might sink all the way into like heaven. I even imagined this soft feeling leaked out into the atmosphere and made people around us as happy as we were.

We became lovers. She pretended, as women are trained to do, to be not entirely available. When I called to ask her out she paused to look at her calendar, and said no first, and then, reconsidering and juggling, said yes. This increased my sense of panic. When she did not leap to say yes, I felt as if I had become the condemned, as if I were doomed to be forever turned away by those to whom I express love. This was an agony, very old. Someone I loved did not love me. I was the mirror image then of Viyella in her description of herself, a child who loved her mother and was not loved back, rejected.

But finally, finally. We went out. Kissed. And then one night we were in my bedroom together. And together we took off our own and each other's clothes, playfully, with some embarrassment, and swiftness. We seemed like boys trying to unfasten their first brassieres and laughed at ourselves. But we were not boys, we were women who knew far more than boys and hiding what we knew. Yet whatever we allowed ourselves to know then, what happened first was that a kind of miracle took place just between the surfaces of our two naked skins before they even touched. A kind of radiance happened in the tiny almost invisible place between our bodies. And when we touched, my arms around her, our unclothed breasts against each other (we were the same height), her belly against mine (the same weight) and pressing lightly, that agony in me that I felt when I was not sure she loved me became an open valley in me, a hollow weeping, a cry of such longing that had you heard it as a song you would never be able to erase it from your memory. And the valley filled with all the pain of loneliness I ever felt going back to what age? So young. So young. But now the pain was good. It was the feeling of a body expecting to be touched, to be moved into even deeper feeling. It was desire, and known in that moment also by her body, and so growing in intensity, as the desire echoed from my body to her body. Her body. Its skin, that soft flesh meeting mine took right up into it all that I was, all that I knew and tried to hide from myself, or kept secret, and all that her body knew in me was blessed. While at the same time, my body felt all she had ever felt, and wept for what she had suffered. I was led in my soul to an infinite tenderness for her. I wanted her. Wanted to reach inside her, even as I ached to have her put her hands, her mouth, in me. I reached with my hand. I touched her. I can't really tell you because I can't quite remember, can't quite imagine anything of that moment now, except that I had finally reached into her lips, into the red canal between her soft thighs which surrounded and met my hand as it went there. And I was astonished. Because she was so open. It was so easy to enter. And I was frightened to discover no resistance but only will-ingness. I was not used to this. It was as if every wish I had ever wished had come true. As if the world had turned upside down and I no longer understood gravity. And then she said to me sweetly and calmly in that same Georgian voice how she was not always so open. But that was how she felt now. And since we were standing there, she said, perhaps we had better get into the sheets, into the bed, perhaps this would be better. So we did, and we made love. She put her mouth to me, her hands to me, her self to me. I reached into and around her and sank into someplace with her, and there was such a degree of wanting that we both cried out and then that ecstasy which happens inside a woman's body happened to the two of us, not at the same time, but one time after another, and then again, as waves, up the length of the body, and then the heat, and the heaviness, and the scent, and then the looseness as if still another layer of clothing had been removed, as if we had come finally into a world which had for a mo-ment frightened us, and now caressed us, we were so glad, as if now we were unafraid of all we had ever feared, and laughing.

Because of that night, and many others that followed, and days, and time spent just sitting together, near each other, in an ease of bliss, or glancing into the face that held that bliss, the memory and the promise, there was something in this love that was right. Despite the pain that came after. Despite it all. For it, like the joy, was considerable.

In the beginning, as is so when one is in love, life was like paradise. With Viyella, everything seemed more beautiful. All that was fraught with complexity or tension seemed simple now. I loved everyone more. One evening we stood out in the cold night to watch an exquisite sunset. I could not bear to go inside for even a moment to fetch a jacket. Viyella shielded me with her arms. I imagined we were angels.

But here is the irony! We were on earth. I caught cold. And now Viyella was elaborate with her plans for caring. She was going to stay with me. Order my house. Answer the telephone. Make me breakfast, lunch and dinner. But like her plans to put on a show of her photo-graphs, very little of this came true. She would say, "I'll come to make you dinner." And at first I was surprised when she came by, looking sheepish, or worse, pretending not to remember her promise, at eleven at night. I began to expect failure from her. And at the moment of this failure I felt, like a tidal pull, her wish that I comfort her for having failed. This was a pattern. A scenario which would have to be played out many times and with no ultimate end in sight. But though I knew this, I pretended to myself that I did not know. I lied to myself, so that I could go on being with Viyella and her failed promises.

But finally there was another promise more essential to our union which I could not ignore when it was broken. Viyella failed to be the person I had convinced myself that she was. I told myself that I found this out by accident. But really I had for a long while had suspicions, and thus I made a plan to catch her in a lie. Instead of asking her openly, "Viyella, are you really a scholar of French literature?" I plotted. Pretending only the wish to share with her a phrase from French literature, I said one day, *"Mais où sont les neiges d'antan?"* She responded as I feared she would. She knew neither how to translate this line nor where it came from. I saw a look of panic pass over her face which told me everything and she in turn saw a look of dismay and betrayal pass over my face. "Where are the snows of yesteryear?" I translated the line for her, explaining to her that it was one of the most famous lines in French poetry. She left me sadly, pretending that she had known this all along. And though I could see her sorrow, all I could feel was anger, that she was lying to me even now.

Who was she really then? I didn't ask. There were a few days of separation. She came back to me more honest. All her life, she said, she had exaggerated the truth. She wanted to be a scholar, this part was true. And she was, for a week, *at* the Sorbonne, and if she was not really a student, still she had sat in lecture halls, straining to translate. I only knew that I had lost the woman I had fallen in love with—the one who so gallantly gave up academic success for a world of real people.

I tried to love her still, but I did not succeed. Though my body went on loving her. At the thought of leaving her a grief came into my heart which was as palpable as physical pain. Despite the fact that I withdrew from her, a radiance still existed between us, a joy and even a healing, inside skin and bones, this feeling we call tenderness.

Finally weeping, even sobbing, I left her. I told her that what was between us was now finished for me. At first she pretended not to care, just as, in the beginning, she had pretended to be too busy to see me. But in a few hours, she was at my door pleading to talk it over again. I would not see her. I was afraid to see her. Afraid my body might go back to her and make my mind try to live with the deception that had been making me wake with dread every morning.

After nine months I discovered that Viyella had lied to me. But it was years before I knew that I had lied to myself. I knew from the beginning that what she told me could not be true. In the first moment I met her I knew I encountered a different Viyella. I lied to myself about what I knew and even asked her, I believe, in that unspoken way that we make demands on each other, to tell me the lies she told about herself. I wanted her to weave a fantasy for me of someone I could admire. I never told myself that just as she needed to impress me with her fantasies, I needed to impress the world with a fantasy lover. And in the same way, I did not own what in myself was lost, like Viyella, buried and broken.

This tale is a story both true and not true. It did happen in the past, not just once but many times over, not only with Viyella but with others too. And it happened before I ever met Viyella or imagined her. Many, many years ago someone I loved was not who I wished her to be. She had wanted to be for me what she could not be. She made promises to me she could not keep. To comfort myself, I wove a fantasy of her, out of her illusions and mine. She was my mother but could not mother me. All her promises failed. In my child's mind I knew this, but I could not bear the despair of this knowledge. For me, the habit of lying to myself was an old one.

"Viyella," I wrote her, a few weeks after we separated, "we can never get back together again. I don't even know who you are." And I was right. But now, after the passage of time, I would add another line: "The truth has many faces." I did know Viyella and love her in my body and I can never forget this love. I do not wish to forget it. Her openness when I reached into her and how that openness changed the shape of the world for me. There is no way to love without being changed. There is no way to write about love without changing the shape of your mind and your heart. You, sitting across the table from me, can see this in my face now. If I was feeling a rage at my lover, this has become grief. Yet even grief has a different dimension now. Can you feel it?

oo oo oo

ALICE WALKER

She Said: ———————————

She said: "When I was with him,
I used to dream of them together.
Making love to me, he was
making love to her.
That image made me come
every time."

A woman lies alone
outside our door.
I know she dreams us
making love;
you inside me,
her lips on my breasts.

AMY GERSTLER

Ups and Downs _____

Carola couldn't stop watching.
The model looked stunning and vulnerable,
as she withdrew three potato chips,
wrapped in a paper napkin, from her purse,
and eyed them lovingly, her blue irises
alive with the chaste lust of a Catholic
about to receive communion. "I haven't
eaten in a week, 'cause of today's shoot,"
the model apologized, her body curved like
a sapling, or the letter C. With an
almost inaudible crackle, she consumed her
meal. The elevator reached the *Vogue* office,
twenty-fifth floor. She shook her frizzed
hair. She looked like a lit match. Carola felt
momentarily hollow, as though she'd been x-rayed,
or had just given blood (type O).
Don't leave me now, she implored the model,
via blonde to blonde ESP. *My heart has
stopped at your floor. What do I need?
A fur bracelet, a mango facial, brawn to
ballast my brains, a year long sauna?*
The model stepped past our heroine, cupped
her wan palm to Carola's right cheek, kissed
the left, and though it was noon, softly
wished her goodnight.

oo oo oo

AMY GERSTLER

A Lecture on Jealousy

Jealousy can be smelled, if you've a nose for it, like mildew, garlic, or the fear-scented sweat rabid dogs find humans to bite by. Jealousy makes pastry taste bad, hobbles your gait, causes your right hand to write checks for sums your left hand never had. Jealousy can make sufferers hate harmless objects. Matchbooks, letters, eyebrow pencils—innocuous props we all need to fidget with, become EVIDENCE. The only known cure for this wasting disease is to cultivate a love for your rival. Earnest, passionate admiration, with all the tremblings and trimmings. Sleepless nights spent wondering "What does she have that I don't have/What does she leak that I've run dry of?" must be given over to serious research. Her white neck, her slender wrists, her great taste in A-line skirts, her confusion at stoplights, her old hands and young feet, her perfume—or is it coconut soap, the deft motion with which she flicks cigarette ashes hither and yon, her loud red blouse, her love of cherry tomatoes, her sneeze, her eggs benedict, her secrecy, the drone of her hair dryer, the amazing way she always looks like she's had her hair cut yesterday . . . see how easy it is? Her drug problem, her insomnia, her dress size, her polka-dot bikini, her pony skin wallet, her saliva which tastes so great . . . for god's sake, somebody stop me.

oo oo oo

ROCHELLE OWENS

Devils Clowns and Women _____

for Willem de Kooning

I was the one   who found you   who brought
you to America   I was wearing   red silk   when you
brought me to America   I was wearing a white cotton
dirndl   that you had made   you always
gave special care   to me
in the evening   you would   read to me   I remember
the small hotel   on top of a mountain
where we spent a night   we watched
the sunrise with the sun shining   on the mountain top
while the country down   below   was still
in darkness

I remember
that white dirndl that I made
for you   it had lace   lace is so inviting to the touch
the texture of rounded edges   so pleasing
fifty years ago society ladies   displayed their
collections   on gold-edged boards   a
popular tea-time diversion   Tanya wore black lace
her skin   luminous   even the jasmine
flowers become dull compared to her skin   wouldn't
you like to be alone with her and take all
her   clothes off
nourished by the purity of childlike
beauty
you'd like to photograph Tanya   wouldn't you
you'd have as much control over yourself
as a moth flying   around   a   candle
As long as you kept a camera
in your hands   you'd be safe   Tanya is every
red-blooded man's dream
where is she?   did you see her?   you said vicious
things to her   you have an ugly heart
it was night time   she
couldn't see the look on   my face   tucked away
in a far corner   of my brain lie the

soft tender feelings   I stand in horror of them
wind-swept deserts
and gypsy caravans   that's what Tanya brings to mind
delicious in white
I want to take Tanya   for a day of
swimming
in the countryside
hello   hello   my darling girl
she'll come to me   we'll watch the trees   breathe
I'll hand her an orange
she'll eat it   pulp & rind   we'll let desire run into
our bodies   she will not be a cold girl
she will not want to miss out   on any   of my stories

You know   when I first met her
I knew she was a rare woman   she moved
like an athlete   strong firm legs   I
was resigned   detached   Well   you've got your girl
I'll teach you how to cook
a traditional Sunday dinner   succulent roast
beef   you will wallow in envy   In Thailand   when you
kissed me   you told me that the soft space
above the corner of my lips was
shockingly erotic   I'm just a carcass of evil
next to you   let me comb your hair
the miracle of you
is unequaled after a thousand years   I am part
of a long migration of fearless lesbians hardly
ever recognized   except as the witch
in fairytales   concocting
potions of flowing menstrual
blood   eating young virgins
You excite me   your hunger
your yearnings   happy now?   You're
a sleeping beauty
But I am all tangled impulses
I am not detached   You and I in every
pose   sexual tender   our hands and teeth
our noses   close together   And I will hold
your curving body   taut with desire
We should sing praises
to the loveliness of young girls   Queens
and their daughters   we don't know where

we are going to die   sacred responsibilities
to give care & protect
                    In Thailand   you accused me
of trying to blind you   you had gotten an eyelash in your
        eye   under the lower lid   you were trying
to remove it   I went over to help you   while
    I was moving your eyelid up and down   gently
                to dislodge the eyelash
you said   don't stand behind me   I don't like to
                feel only a presence
                        I have bad nerves   there's a
head-on fiery battle   In a poor land   I longed
        for you   for want of your fair   hand   as a little
    girl I gathered springflowers for the monks   for
spite I hid a chicken head in a bouquet
                        the monk's reaction made me numb
        cold   distorted   he simply said   I see it all
    I see everything   you're a little
                            butterfly
        I take you with a grain
                    of salt
                I take each step   as if   it was
the last   to avoid the falsity   as best I can
    no matter what its form   woman like
                fire & water makes   the truth live
                        within herself
                    What did he do?
                    He made a pass at me
                    O he did did he?
                    What did he do?
                    Did he whistle at ya?
                    He ogled me
                    Ogled you? I thought
                    maybe he diddled you
                    You know when he first
                    saw you he asked me
                    if you were the wife
                    He didn't say is she your wife?
                    He said is she the wife?
                    He said that you looked like
                    a hot piece
                        Roses whose haunting beauty

164   DEEP DOWN · · ·

echoes thy lips   you have the dirtiest mouth
      of any woman that I've ever seen

                    She is my sole source   to feel her is
to feel a snarl   of honeysuckle   sometimes to annoy me
    she would tap her foot incessantly   I would
        grab her knee under the table   holding her leg
          down   we played a game   she'd hoist
me up with her feet   she'd lie on her back   brace
        her feet against my thighs and fly
                        me through the air   and the light
    scattering around her hair   sweet rituals

                    What did she wear?   What was her face like?
  Her hair?   Her body?   Proud   strong   she wore a black
  lace dress   a twisted coal-black bead choker   bright
        blue beads   the night I was with her
after dessert   when coffee was served   He reached inside
    his jacket and withdrew a cigar   the whore reached
          across the table and took   it from him
He smiled   she bit off the end of the cigar with slightly
      parted lips   exposing white teeth   moistened it
          with the tip   of her tongue   and slowly
lit it   She threw back her head   and blew smoke
                    toward the ceiling
                            a binge with a whore
    with childlike beauty
                    I'll tuck a patchwork quilt around you
we'll drink steaming mugs of   hot buttered rum
                        what could be more cozy
        than that?
                    you should pile   your hair
atop your head   so that it falls   in beguiling tendrils
      around the nape   of your sweet neck   you look
so wan   so tragic   let me help you slip   into
      the silk kimono that   I bought for you   from Thailand

                    Just when you think
                    that she is your pal
                    you look for her
                    and find her hangin'
                    'round some other gal

what were you when
I found you
a gal whose arteries
and veins are made
of rusty wire and sticky
eggshells
convicted of drug smuggling
burglary and murder

I eat the same food   that the inmates eat   I sleep
where they sleep   I hold them   they walk by the
guards   at the iron gate   a prisoner with tattoos from
                her neck to her waist   she pulls up
        her skirt   and shows me a scar   on her abdomen
            she asks me   if I can get her some   medicine
another prisoner pulls down her lower lip and requests
        special bridgework   another asks me for warm milk
                I calm them   and listen
                            to them cry
            they tell me their names   aliases   and crimes
            there was   a little girl   who had a
                            little curl right in the

middle of her face
                        According to Benjamin Franklin
                        there are only three faithful
                        things   an old wife   an old dog
                        and ready money
                        leave things the way they are
                        quoth the Lord of battle
                        chieftain   mercenary   sorcerer
                        street commando   gangster-daddy
                        Doc Holliday

                        She takes me for granted
            I'm too too generous   with her   I don't know why
        she rips up my needlepoint   years ago   she cut my belt
        in half   it was navy-blue leather   she said she
    needed a belt   she took it without   asking   I found
                        it later   she had cut a piece off
        & punctured a hole into it   so it would fit around
                            her small waist
                Tanya singing   her moist oval lips
                        like a Christmas caroler in the snow

166   DEEP DOWN · · ·

Why couldn't I fall into   her arms   without
                    falling into her hands
                              What happened?
          you got burned
                    She would sit   with me   for
hours   her hands resting   on her knees   attentive   sensitive
                              I loved her then
          who loves the most   dear
                              No matter what her age
          she'll have that skin   life is too short &
                         winter too long to go
          without my darling girl

                    I was thinking of the photo
                    my mind drifts in and out
                    she was nude except for
                    a white mink coat draped
                    around her shoulders   fur
                    against her skin   she was
                    standing with her back
                    towards the camera   her
                    rump gleamed in the moonlight
          her what?   her rump
                              body & soul   I love to dance
abandoned to dreams   legends   mysterious divinities
          remembrances of silken touches   sunlight warm on
                              my breasts   the lacy
          butterfly at her bodice   quite a bit of gorgeous
     ass   temptation abounds   the color   subtle   twilight
     lavender   come close   touch it   touch it
                         the trees   the gardens   the pool
               lovely soft warm colors   a cloud of dried
                         baby's breath

                    I hate autumn   the first chill
          my skin hurts   let's make a fire
                              you love the rust and gold
of trees   don't you?   I'm cold   my legs are cold
               I can't sleep   scrub the bathtub
I want to do it   because I can't sleep   it's three A.M.
                    he stands on her grave
                    his legs wide apart
                    witch face witch face

                    boar tusks protrude from
                    her cheeks   mud & plant
                    fibers leak from her
                    nipples faces & forms
                    of demons devils clowns
                    women spooks spooks
       Tanya is splendid   Tanya's skin is taut   smoothed
to perfection   healthy   woman   matron   model
            of proper behavior   tawdry slut   buffoons that
make me laugh   ugly   I shit in her cunt   I will buy
    my stunning piece jewels for her   gleaming satin skin
                then cherish it   then cherish it
                                she harasses me   she is like a sack
of hate that stretches shifts & changes shape
                        mask   fetish   cult figure   volcano
                                    rock cunt
she was smiling at me when I gave her the earrings
            of gold & diamonds   I carried her over
                the threshold of our new home
                                    she's home   it takes
just a fraction of a breath   to say
                                home

oo oo oo

TONI MORRISON

from: *Song of Solomon* _____

Jealous Hagar, who has been trying to kill her lover Milkman, meets his mother . . .

A woman sat on a bench, her hands clasped between her knees. It was not Pilate. Ruth stood still and looked at the woman's back. It didn't look like death's back at all. It looked vulnerable, soft, like an easily wounded shin, full of bone but susceptible to the slightest pain.

"Reba?" she said.

The woman turned around and fastened on her the most sorrowful eyes Ruth had ever seen.

"Reba's gone," she said, the second word sounding as if the going were permanent. "Can I do something for you?"

"I'm Ruth Foster."

Hagar stiffened. A lightning shot of excitement ran through her. Milkman's mother: the silhouette she had seen through the curtains in an upstairs window on evenings when she stood across the street hoping at first to catch him, then hoping just to see him, finally just to be near the things he was familiar with. Private vigils held at night, made more private because they were expressions of public lunacy. The outline she'd seen once or twice when the side door opened and a woman shook crumbs from a tablecloth or dust from a small rug onto the ground. Whatever Milkman had told her about his mother, whatever she had heard from Pilate and Reba, she could not remember, so overwhelmed was she in the presence of *his* mother. Hagar let her morbid pleasure spread across her face in a smile.

Ruth was not impressed. Death always smiled. And breathed. And looked helpless like a shinbone, or a tiny speck of black on the Queen Elizabeth roses, or film on the eye of a dead goldfish.

"You are trying to kill him." Ruth's voice was matter-of-fact. "If you so much as bend a hair on his head, so help me Jesus, I will tear your throat out."

Hagar looked surprised. She loved nothing in the world except this woman's son, wanted him alive more than anybody, but hadn't the least bit of control over the predator that lived inside her. Totally taken over by her anaconda love, she had no self left, no fears, no wants, no intelligence that was her own. So it was with a great deal of earnestness that she replied to Ruth. "I'll try not to. But I can't make you a for-certain promise."

Ruth heard the supplication in her words and it seemed to her that she was not looking at a person but at an impulse, a cell, a red corpuscle that neither knows nor understands why it is driven to spend its whole life in one pursuit: swimming up a dark tunnel toward the muscle of a heart or an eye's nerve end that it both nourished and fed from.

Hagar lowered her eyelids and gazed hungrily down the figure of the woman who had been only a silhouette to her. The woman who slept in the same house with him, and who could call him home and he would come, who knew the mystery of his flesh, had memory of him as long as his life. The woman who knew him, had watched his teeth appear, stuck her finger in his mouth to soothe his gums. Cleaned his behind, Vaselined his penis, and caught his vomit in a fresh white diaper. Had fed him from her own nipples, carried him close and warm and safe under her heart, and who had opened her legs far far wider than she herself ever had for him. Who even now could walk freely into his room if she wanted to and smell his clothes, stroke his shoes, and lay her head on the very spot where he had lain his. But what was more, so much more, this thin lemon-yellow woman knew with absolute certainty what Hagar would willingly have her throat torn out to know: that she would see him this very day. Jealousy loomed so large in her it made her tremble. Maybe you, she thought. Maybe it's you I should be killing. Maybe then he will come to me and let me come to him. He is my home in this world. And then, aloud, "He is my home in this world."

"And I am his," said Ruth.

"And he wouldn't give a pile of swan shit for either one of you."

They turned then and saw Pilate leaning on the window sill. Neither knew how long she'd been there.

"Can't say as I blame him neither. Two growed-up women talkin 'bout a man like he was a house or needed one. He ain't a house, he's a man, and whatever he need, don't none of you got it."

"Leave me alone, Mama. Just leave me alone."

"You already alone. If you want more alone, I can knock you into the middle of next week, and leave you there."

oo oo oo

DAPHNE MARLATT

from: *Touch to My Tongue* _____

KORE

no one wears yellow like you excessive and radiant store-
house of sun, skin smooth as fruit but thin, leaking light. (i am climbing
toward you out of the hidden.) no one shines like you, so that even
your lashes flicker light, amber over blue (*amba*, amorous Demeter, you
with the fire in your hand, i am coming to you). no one my tongue
burrows in, whose wild flesh opens wet, tongue seeks its nest, amative
and nurturing (here i am you) lips work towards undoing (*dhei*, female,
sucking and suckling, fecund) spurt/spirit opening in the dark of earth,
yu! cry jubilant excess, your fruiting body bloom we issue into the light
of, sweet, successive flesh . . .

EATING

a kiwi at four a.m. among the sheets green slice of cool
going down easy on the tongue extended with desire for you and you
in me it isn't us we suck those other lips tongue flesh wet wall that gives
and gives whole fountains inner mountains moving out resistances you
said ladders at the canyon leap desire is its way through walls swerve
fingers instinct in you insist further persist in me too wave on wave to
that deep pool we find ourselves/it dawning on us we have reached the
same place "timeless" you recognize as "yes" giving yourself not up
not in we come suddenly round the bend to it descending with the
yellow canyon flow the mouth everything drops away from time its
sheets two spoons two caved-in shells of kiwi fruit

IN THE DARK OF THE COAST

there is fern and frost, a gathering of small birds melting
song in the underbrush. close, you talk to one. there is the cedar slant
of your hair as it falls gold over your shoulder, over your naked, dearly
known skin—its smell, its answering touch to my tongue. fondant,
font, found, all that melts, pours. the dark rain of our being together at
last. and the cold wind, curled-up fronds of tree fern wanting touch,
our fingers separate and stiff. we haven't mourned enough, you say,
for our parting, lost to each other the last time through. in the dark of
this place, its fire touch, not fern but frost, just one of the houses we

pass through in the endless constellation of our being, close, and away from each other, torn and apart. i didn't know your hair, i didn't know your skin when you beckoned to me in that last place. but i knew your eyes, blue, as soon as you came around the small hill, knew your tongue. come, you said, we slid together in the spring, blue, of a place we'd been. terra incognita known, *geysa*, gush, upwelling in the hidden Norse we found, we feel it thrust as waters part for us, hot, through fern, frost, volcanic thrust. it's all there, love, we part each other coming to, geyser, spouting pool, hidden in and under separate skin we make for each other through.

○○ ○○ ○○

ERIN MOURÉ

Aspen _____

Woman whose arms are the bones of the poem,
full of indispensible marrow

Her mouth is a lone cry behind
an aspen, the weeds grown tangled, cow parsnip, brown canes of
raspberry, sunlight,
I touch her with my mouth

& our two cries flutter,
impossible havoc, heat, haven, have-not of the body,
our tensions in its arms & folded openings in its centre,
where we touch the cry
without knowing its sense
finally
deep inside the marrow
Hushed in each other for a moment, the leaves still

before we separate
& it begins again, each cry
behind its aspen, each aspen
clattering its leaves in sunlight, dropping silver onto the floor

ERIN MOURÉ

She Touched Me ───────────────

I saw it
I heard it
It had a voice
Two people jumped up & congratulated me
Their seats were empty
It had a beautiful voice
It touched me

I touched her
Her mouth tasted like salt
I held my tongue in her
Her voice was a thread in my mouth
Her hand touched my ear
I heard it

They jumped up
The bleachers were yellow & red
The roof of the stadium
vanished
I held her with my mouth
A voice heard me

The tide was down
Wood was high on the shore
They stood out of their seats
They saw me
I heard it
It had a beautiful voice

The ramps of the new bridge were empty
I heard the voice
It woke me
Her hand touched my breast where I was
moving
They stood up

The train pulled into the station
A false creek stopped it
The wood on the shore began singing
I heard it
It had a voice
The water was far away
The train let go

Their seats were empty

She touched me

oo oo oo

LESLIE SCALAPINO

from: Floating Series ————————————

FLOATING SERIES 1

the
women—not in
the immediate
setting
—putting the
lily pads or
bud of it
in
themselves

a man entering
after
having
come on her—that
and
the memory of putting
in
the lily pad or the
bud of it first,
made her come

having put
the
lily pad in
herself—
encouraging the man
to
come inside
her

a man to
come on the woman
gently—her
having
put the lily pad in
herself

with him not
having entered
her yet

or
having
put in the bud of
it
and
the man not
having
entered her
coming first

that in
the city as in
the middle—to
someone who's
death comes from
age

FLOATING SERIES 2

to foresee
the man's
response—when
the woman had
come—him not
having
done so—and
had
the bud of it in her still

THIRD PART

having
swallowed the
water
lily bud—so having
it in
him—when he'd
come on some
time with her

a man'd
swallowed
the bud
of the water lily—and
had
it in
him that way

oo oo oo

MAUREEN OWEN

from: Amelia Earhart Series _____

"Assholes!"   her eyes seem grey in this soup   the hangars
chalk   & grey   sound of the engines grey   & far off   I
craved those fogged-in afternoons   just the two of us   getting
high   &   hanging out   We'd work on the Electra   some
have a beer or two   then share our last joint   under the fuselage
& shoot the breeze   the reward for marriage is getting a
man's name   we decided   Mrs Donald Roscoe Jr.   Mrs
Kenneth Norton the III   Vowing the next time we ran   into
Ginger   & Tootie   on the street   we'd hail them   as   Don!
& Ken!   the old levitation trick   first anger crushes
then leaves you   light as air   arm   squashed into doorjamb
step out   & up it goes   Finally we'd laugh till we were sick
guffawing out of control   going spaz in the spilled beer   &
oil   hugging   pawing each other wildly   we'd laugh till
we sloshed   tumbling in spilt motor oil   spazzing out we'd
laugh till we were sick   pouring the rest of the beer in
each other's hair   hugging & sloshing in spilled motor oil—
We always   wore khakis   & boots.   & if I smoked   I'd
tuck my deck   in my rolled   t shirt sleeve   the way poets
do   or stash a homemade behind my ear   like in the films
While   AE'd stand out there   in   visibility   zero
Hooting   the long letters of her name   A M E L I A . . . .
E A R H A R T . . . .

                  aviator   aviator   aviator

○○ ○○ ○○
LYN LIFSHIN

Penthouse Playboy

no women wear under
wear   show their
beautiful bush thru
a hole in the kitchen
floor to workmen in
the cellar who've
come to fix a crack
and of course do
No body ever has a
period or hair
where it shouldn't
be. Cocks are always
9 inches and throb
bing and women's
tits point to the
sky they never
have to worry a
bout lawbriefs or
poems or food but
hang out at rallies
drug stores and
on planes in their
blond hair like
vampires under
a full moon that
starved for hot
blood they rip
zippers bulging
jeans and the mounds
under wool open with
their white teeth
it doesn't matter
if there's a druggist
or people buying
dramamine or voting
democratic even
in a crowded elevator

between floors these
women dive thru
leather with their
own crotch hairs
always dripping
like a porpoise

oo oo oo

NICOLE BROSSARD

Sous La Langue
Under Tongue _____

Translated by Susanne de Lotbinière-Harwood

The body salivates, yet nothing is foreseen, not the wealth of touching, nor the furtive slowness, the exact frenzy of mouths. Nothing is foreseen yet at eye level is where the body first touches everything without foreseeing the naked skin, and it needs saying, without foreseeing the softness of skin that will be naked even before the mouth signals the state of the world.

Nothing here to suggest that at the slightest touch the gaze already falters wanting already to foresee such a *rapprochement*. Nothing is foreseen other than the breathing, the sounds resounding flesh to flesh. Does she frictional she fluvial she essential does she, in the all-embracing touch that rounds the breasts, love the mouths' soft roundness or the effect undressing her? Nothing is foreseen yet at body's uttermost the skin will image the body for without image there is nothing at body's uttermost images shatter the state of the world.

You cannot foresee so suddenly leaning towards a face and wanting to lick the soul's whole body till the gaze sparks with furies and yieldings. You cannot foresee the body's being swept into the infinity of curves, of pulsings, every time the body surges you cannot see the image, the hand touching the nape of the neck, the tongue parting the hairs, the knees trembling, the arms from such desire encircling the body like a universe. Desire is all you see. You cannot foresee the image, the bursts of laughter, the screams and the tears. The image is trembling, mute, polyphonic. Does she frictional she fluvial she essential does she all along her body love the bite, the sound waves, does she love the state of the world in the blaze of flesh to flesh as seconds flow by silken salty cyprin*.

You cannot foresee if the words arousing her are vulgar, ancient or foreign or if it is the whole sentence that attracts her and

_____

*Female sexual secretion. From the French *cyprine* [fr. Gk. Cyprus, birthplace of Aphrodite]. We are proposing *cyprin* for English usage. T.N.

182

quickens in her a desire like a scent of the embrace, a way of feeling her body as truly ready for everything. Nothing is foreseen yet the mouth of bodies commoving aroused by the words by instinct finds the image that arouses.

You cannot foresee if the state of the world will topple over with you in the flavour and surging motion of tongues. Nothing is foreseen yet the shirt is half-open, the panties barely away from the cleft and yet the closed lids and yet the inner eyes are all astir from feeling the tender in the fingers. You cannot foresee if the fingers there will stay, motionless, perfect, for a long while yet, if the middle finger will move o ever so slightly on the little pearl, if the hand will open into a star shape at the very moment when the softness of her cheek, when her breath at the very moment when the other woman's whole body will weigh so heavily that the book where it rests gives way under the hand, the hand, at the very moment when balance will become precarious and thighs will multiply like orchids, you cannot foresee if the fingers will penetrate, if they'll forever absorb our fragrance in the image's continuous movement.

Nothing is foreseen for we do not know what becomes of the image of the state of the world when the patience of mouths lays being bare. You cannot foresee from among the waves the one the unfurling one the split second that will image in the narrative of bodies whirling at the speed of the image.

You cannot foresee how the tongue wraps round the clitoris to lift the body and move it cell by cell into a realm unreal.

TOI DERRICOTTE

Touching/Not Touching: My Mother ⸻

I.

That first night in the hotel bedroom,
when the lights go out,
she is already sleeping (that woman who has always
claimed sleeplessness), inside her quiet breathing
like a long red gown. How can she
sleep? My heart beats as if I am alone,
for the first time, with a lover or a beast.
Will I hate her drooping mouth,
her old woman rattle? Once I nearly
suffocated on her breast. Now I can almost
touch the other side of my life.

II.

Undressing
in the dark,
looking,
not looking,
we parade before each other,
old proud peacocks, in our stretch marks,
with hanging butts. We are equals. No
more do I need to wear her high heels to step
inside the body of a woman.
Her beauty and strangeness no longer seduce
me out of myself. I show my good side, my
long back, strong mean legs, my thinness that
came from learning to hold back
from taking what's not mine. No more
a thief for love. She takes off her
bra, facing me, and I see those gorgeous
globes, soft, creamy,
high; my mouth waters.
How will I resist
crawling in beside her, putting
my hand for warmth
under her thin night dress?

DEAR ENEMIES

○○ ○○ ○○
DEENA METZGER

from: *What Dinah Thought* _____

As soon as he opens the door from his inner office and
enters the room where I am working, I smell sweat which is saturating
his clothes. Then I feel his breath on my neck, a little moist and heavy
with tea and sandwiches. Mayonnaise, soggy lettuce, kosher breast of
chicken. Swee-touch-nee tea, two cubes of sugar, one rectangular, one
square, two carrot sticks, a piece of honey cake. His breath is just a
little fetid, just a little unwashed as are his clothes; it's summer, noon
and hot, the windows are closed against the noise, and there is no air
circulating in the room. He twirls the buttons of his robe. It's a nervous
habit so some are popped and the threads stand up alarmed, a bit of
white undershirt peeking through the empty hole of his vest, the white
of an eye. He bends closer; he says he can't see. "Shall I take it out of
the typewriter for you, Rabbi?"

"No, don't bother. I don't want you to lose your place, then it won't
line up correctly and you'll have to start again."

He is quite certain there is a spelling error or something he'd like to
alter, or he is not sure that my phrasing is correct in the section he
asked that I add. That sentence is awkward. Am I certain I didn't alter
the text he gave me? He leans over my shoulder, pointing at the error.
I can't see it. My vision blurs. I think it is his sweat dripping into my
eyes. He drops the pencil just as I lean forward to examine the letter
better, but his hand is already in my lap, looking for the pencil. He
can't find it. It has dropped to the floor but he pulls me back not wanting
to disturb me, to soothe me. It doesn't matter. It's only a spelling error,
it won't ruin the letter, he isn't worried because he knows I'll find it
later and correct it, it doesn't matter about the carbons, they don't need
the spelling corrected, and it doesn't matter that he's lost the pencil,
but maybe it is still in my lap not on the floor, he didn't hear it drop,
his hand is on my shoulder pressing me back into the typing chair so
he can look in my lap, among the folds of cloth, my skirt is very pretty,
he is glad I am earning a lot of money, he thinks the minimum wage
is very generous to young people and I can buy myself nice work
clothes but did I think over his proposal that I donate some of my
salary to the Yeshiva because those boys are doing God's work for all
of us, he always liked pleats, but they hide so many things. Did the
pencil fall down my blouse, it was his favorite pencil, the blouse is very
loose, did I know, sometimes he thinks women do not dress carefully

187

enough, it's one of the banes of the orthodox tradition to try to instruct girls so that they will not violate God's laws. So often the mothers are lax or have forgotten all the injunctions, and what is a man to do, it is his duty, but still it is awkward, the pencil was a mechanical pencil that is why he's making such a fuss though he's sure it isn't lost and maybe he left it on my skirt, didn't I, it has one of those retractable points that is protected within the metal casing when it is not in use, and it slides in and out very easily, but he thinks he ought to show me how to tie my blouse better, he'll look for the pen later when I get up, the blouse needs to be tighter or higher, though he agrees the style is very pretty, his mother always wore peasant blouses and now it is the fashion, imagine that. He is glad it has draw strings, not elastic, so that they can be opened and tied tighter, no not up to the neck, but still a little tighter, there, let's see, he pats the blouse to see how it looks and lets the strings go so that it falls open and sees that I'm upset, silly, he wants to calm me, please, it's only a spelling mistake and your blouse was not that open, not as open as it is now, but he'll fix it, no, don't touch it, he'll do it, he has to measure it, to see that it is exactly perfect, and he doesn't have a mirror for me to look in, better for girls to be without mirrors, but he can see exactly everything that he is doing, please don't cry, it's only a spelling mistake and a blouse, here, he'll soothe me, he'll pet me a little like he does his daughters to soothe me, calm me, he pushes my head back against his fat belly, relax, close your eyes, get calm or you won't be able to type and I'll just rub these little breasts, first one and then the other, you'll be surprised how very soothing this will be, just lean back in the chair, let it hold you as it is designed to do, it will catch me in the small of the back and if I raise my legs, I'll see, it will bend back-wards, and he'll support me, it will be as if I'm taking a little nap and forgetting everything, I can just lie down and let him rub my little breasts, for as long as I want, until I'm calm and not crying, just breath-ing deeply with my eyes closed, or until the nipples stand up very hard and tall and then get very soft again, it will take a little while but not too long, he's breathing hard, and rocking the chair back and forth against his thighs, and then, then, just another moment, oh what sweet breasts, we must keep them hidden but he won't tell anyone how sweet they are, as his hands rub my breasts and nipples inside my blouse and brassiere, it's too tight, it must be uncomfortable in this heat, here he'll take my brassiere off, pull my arms out of the sleeves of my blouse, no the blouse doesn't have to come off altogether, just a minute, he knows I'm so hot, I'll faint, he doesn't want me to faint, and he's unable to open the window or unlock the door into the corridor to let in air, there the brassiere is off and the blouse is down to my waist but he pulls it up and puts my hands back into the sleeves so he can put his hands back into the blouse, the brassiere is in the wastepaper basket, he'll throw it away somewhere else later, no, he doesn't think I ought to wear it, an undershirt perhaps or a little white camisole, it's not good for the lungs, the body needs to be free, and he thinks it is OK because my little nipples don't show through the cloth, because I'm just a little girl so it doesn't matter, and it is also proper for a little girl like I am always to wear white, no, don't cry, just rest and lean back against me and I'll rock you, while I put my hands in your lap, I'm sure the pencil is here, there, spread your feet just a little and we'll see, there, that's the girl, and rest against me and soon everything will be soft and then you'll be easy.

○○ ○○ ○○

TOI DERRICOTTE

Saturday Night ────────────────────

We come home from the movie, and you head for the TV.
I peek out of the bathroom to hear you move around in there.
I'm screaming: "You're sick. I can't take it anymore. You've been
   with machines all day—computers, TV. You don't want anything
   to do with me."
You deny this. You had only gone into that room to put down your
   wallet.
I want to kill. Am crazed with the smell of my own blood.
"I don't need this. You think I need you like before?"
I hear you in the bathroom cutting your toenails, it takes a long time.
   I wonder if you are on the toilet.
"You're so used to me being the one to need you, it's a game. But
   games can be stopped," I scream.
I grab a magazine and get into bed, flipping through. I want to attack
   until I feel you in my hands, cut through to the other side, like
   diving toward a light.
Will you save me? Will you reach out your hand and save me? Just
   one finger on my arm . . .
You pull back the covers and come into bed, gazing up at the ceiling.
I want to touch you, but can't move. How can I stay in a room too
   small to stand or sit or lie in, cramped in a fetal posture?
I want to threaten until God takes back his lies of paradise, till the
   sun cracks open and lets us die.
We are packed in a frame bed like a child's wagon in the middle of a
   tornado.
"Games can be stopped," I repeat softly. "But it hurts."

"I am so lonely," I say. "So lonely."

NTOZAKE SHANGE

comin to terms _____

        they hadnt slept together for months/ the nite she pulled the two thinnest blankets from on top of him & gathered one pillow under her arm to march to the extra room/ now 'her' room/ had been jammed with minor but telling incidents/ at dinner she had asked him to make sure the asparagus didnt burn so he kept adding water & they, of course/ water-logged/ a friend of hers stopped over & he got jealous of her having so many friends/ so he sulked cuz no one came to visit him/ then she gotta call that she made the second round of interviews for the venceremos brigade/ he said he didnt see why that waz so important/ & with that she went to bed/ moments later this very masculine leg threw itself over her thighs/ she moved over/ then a long muscled arm wrapped round her chest/ she sat up/ he waz smiling/ the smile that said 'i wanna do it now.'

mandy's shoulders dropped/ her mouth wanted to pout or frown/ her fist waz lodged between her legs as a barrier or an alternative/ a cooing brown hand settled on her backside/ 'listen, mandy, i just wanna little'/ mandy looked down on the other side of the bed/ maybe the floor cd talk to him/ the hand roamed her back & bosom/ she started to make faces & blink a lot/ ezra waznt talkin anymore/ a wet mouth waz sittin on mandy's neck/ & teeth beginnin to nibble the curly hairs near her ears/ she started to shake her head/ & covered her mouth with her hand sayin/ 'i waz dreamin bout cuba & you wanna fuck'/ 'no, mandy i dont wanna fuck/ i wanna make love to . . . love to you'/ & the hand became quite aggressive with mandy's titties/ 'i'm dreamin abt goin to cuba/ which isnt important/ i'm hungry cuz you ruined dinner/ i'm lonely cuz you embarrassed my friend: & you wanna fuck'/ 'i dont wanna fuck/ i told you that i wanna make love'/ 'well you got it/ you hear/ you got it to yr self/ cuz i'm goin to dream abt goin to cuba'/ & with that she climbed offa the hand pummelin her ass/ & pulled the two thinnest blankets & one pillow to the extra room.

the extra room waz really mandy's anyway/ that's where she read & crocheted & thot/ she cd watch the neighbors' children & hear miz nancy singin gospel/ & hear miz nancy give her sometimey lover who owned the steepin tavern/ a piece of her mind/ so the extra room/ felt full/ not as she had feared/ empty & knowin absence. in a corner under the window/ mandy settled every nite after the cuba dreams/ & watched the streetlights play thru the lace curtains to the wall/ she slept soundly the first few nites/ ezra didnt mention that she didnt sleep with him/ & they ate the breakfast she fixed & he went off to the studio/ while she went off to school he came home to find his dinner on the table & mandy in her room/ doing something that pleased her. mandy was very polite and gracious/ asked how his day waz/ did anything exciting happen/ but she never asked him to do anything for her/ like lift things or watch the stove/ or listen to her dreams/ she also never went in the room where they usedta sleep together/ tho she cleaned everywhere else as thoroughly as one of her mother's great-aunts cleaned the old house on rose tree lane in charleston/ but she never did any of this while ezra waz in the house/ if ezra waz home/ you cd be sure mandy waz out/ or in her room.

one nite just fore it's time to get up & the sky is lightening up for sunrise/ mandy felt a chill & these wet things on her neck/ she started slappin the air/ & without openin her eyes/ cuz she cd/ feel now what waz goin on/ ezra pushed his hard dick up on her thigh/ his breath covered her face/ he waz movin her covers off/ mandy kept slappin him & he kept bumpin up & down on her legs & her ass/ 'what are you doin ezra'/ he just kept movin. mandy screamed/ 'ezra what in hell are you doin.' & pushed him off her. he fell on the floor/ cuz mandy's little bed waz right on the floor/ & she slept usually near the edge of her mattress/ ezra stood & his dick waz aimed at mandy's face/ at her right eye/ she looked away/ & ezra/ jumped up & down/ in the air this time/ 'what are you talkin abt what am i doin/ i'm doin what we always do/ i'm gettin ready to fuck/ awright so you were mad/ but this cant go on forever/ i'm goin crazy/ i cant live in a house with you & not fu .../ not make love. i mean.' mandy still lookin at the pulsing penis/ jumpin around as ezra jumped around/ mandy sighed 'ezra let's not let this get ugly/ please, just go to sleep/ in yr bed & we'll talk abt this tomorrow.' 'what do you mean tomorrow i'm goin crazy' ... mandy looked into ezra's scrotum/ & spoke softly 'you'll haveta be crazy then' & turned over to go back to sleep. ezra waz still for a moment/ then he pulled the covers off mandy & jerked her around some/ talkin bout 'we live together & we're gonna fuck now'/ mandy treated him as cruelly as she wd any stranger/ kicked & bit & slugged & finally ran to the kitchen/ leavin ezra holdin her torn nitegown in his hands.

'how cd you want me/ if i dont want you/ i dont want you niggah/ i dont want you' & she worked herself into a sobbin frigidaire-beatin frenzy ... ezra looked thru the doorway mumblin. 'i didnt wanna upset you, mandy. but you gotta understand. i'm a man & i just cant stay here like this with you ... not bein able to touch you or feel you'/ mandy screamed back 'or fuck me/ go on, say it niggah/ fuck.' ezra threw her gown on the floor & stamped off to his bed. we dont know what he did in there.

mandy put her gown in the sink & scrubbed & scrubbed til she cd get his hands off her. she changed the sheets & took a long bath & a douche. she went back to bed & didnt go to school all day she lay in her bed. thinkin of what ezra had done. i cd tell him to leave/ she thot/ but that's half the rent/ i cd leave/ but i like it here/ i cd getta dog to guard me at nite/ but ezra wd make friends with it/ i cd let him fuck me & not move/ that wd make him mad & i like to fuck ezra/ he's good/ but that's not the point/ that's not the point/ & she came up with the idea that if they were really friends like they always said/ they shd be able to enjoy each other without fucking without having to sleep in the same room/ mandy had grown to cherish waking up a solitary figure in her world/ she liked the quiet of her own noises in the night & the sound of her own voice soothin herself/ she liked to wake up in the middle of the nite & turn the lights on & read or write letters/ she even liked the grain advisory show on tv at 5:30 in the mornin/ she hadda lotta secret nurturin she had created for herself/ that ezra & his heavy gait/ ezra & his snorin/ ezra & his goin-crazy hard-on wd/ do violence to ... so she suggested to ezra that they continue to live together as friends/ & see other people if they wanted to have a more sexual relationship than the one she waz offering ... ezra laughed. he thot she waz a little off/ til she shouted 'you cant imagine me without a wet pussy/ you cant imagine me without yr goddamed dick stickin up in yr pants/ well yr gonna learn/ i dont start comin to life cuz you feel like fuckin/ yr gonna learn i'm alive/ ya hear' ... ezra waz usually a gentle sorta man/ but he slapped mandy this time & walked off ... he came home two days later covered with hickeys & quite satisfied with himself. mandy fixed his dinner/ nothin special/ & left the door of her room open so he cd see her givin herself pleasure/ from then on/ ezra always asked if he cd come visit her/ waz she in need of some company/ did she want a lil lovin/ or wd she like to come visit him in his room/ there are no more assumptions in the house.

oo oo oo

KATHLEEN FRASER

Bestiality. . . . (from The Leda Notebooks) _____

A man said, a man who was a friend said, "It's too bad that women can't participate in animal sexuality. If you have a penis you just stick it into this warm animal. Animals are not so far from humans, really. A very fine line." The line is made by a graphite pencil which draws in the dark. A small notebook at the opera, or "you could have it next to the bed." Michelangelo cuts and polishes the stone of Leda's instep to catch a certain light which another finger wants to touch. He lifts her body slightly from the couch, her back leaning against its marble cushion and supported by her left arm pulled backwards over a draped cloth which, in a picture, could be white satin with little cunt folds and openings. The swan is busy inside her thighs, pulling at the lower lip of her mouth with his beak. Her weight seems to be tilted against nature, towards the right buttock, in order to accommodate his thrust. Her thigh muscles as well as the pectoral support of her breasts could be a man's. The toes opening and closing, as well as the soft breast (from here, a white pear) and the elaborately plaited hair, give her sex away, in his eyes. "You don't know anything about animal sex. You just like to fuck but you don't know what goes on in the world. Women like horses because they have big cocks." Each time she steps out of the bath she covers herself with either the red towel with black borders or the thicker blue terrycloth with this year's moving dashes. Even though he's seen her naked only minutes before, she covers herself with the towel, wrapping it around her body and carefully tucking it in just next to the right arm above the breast. "You don't know what happens when doctors graduate. They get a woman and twenty of them fuck her. Or they bring in a dog or a horse." They lower the horse on pulleys. They wind up its legs on internal hinges, pointing them towards the ceiling, to bring the cock into relief. Then they roll the woman in. "She always smiles as if looking into the future. She always stands up straight, because she's getting paid. It is our animal nature which we can only confer and then take away."

FAYE KICKNOSWAY

Mr. Muscle-On, _____

talking his cock, talking
his legs straight across the planet. every
step gives flowers, onion, and garlic.
he piss big

as an elephant. make shit in balloon race. good
for you. carries his eyes like tiny baskets
of thistles and snakes. walks pre-occupied
through your body. takes

large bites of your hair and your hands. needs
you. got so much cold in him, kills stars. mr.
walking straight up. mr.
meat factory. mr.
kill them cows with a single beat of mah heart,
baby. momma, o

momma, rain coming from her mouth all over his face, spit
like you make a dog your dog, mouth
to mouth, holy joining, momma—the tit factory—holy, holy,
the centerfold alive like a picture show in every drop of cock
juice. momma, miss doughnut of 1942. miss show her knees
for the war effort, open-toe wedgies wet
as his dreams, spit them rivets
in them airplane blues: momma. a real

pair. boobies up his ass where it feels
so good, she's
his motorcycle, his cold metal tit, where it counts, right
between the legs. fascinating. balling

through traffic, wide-screen, panavision, technicolor cum
backing up his kundalini,
snotting from his nose, day-glo
women with fluorescent tongues sucking it off
his face. should

charge them cash for what they get. better
than whiskey. mr. holy virgin, vulture man. mr.
balls big as dishpans man. got

hands like helicopter blades, comes
quiet to your body, his mica blood 20 degrees
below zero. normal range. unchanging. says
hydrochloric words. webs you with them. look out.
pulls his cock out of his ass and rams it
down your throat. gets mad at you his cum don't crack
you open, kill you dead on the spot. mr.

white powder man, bad
dreams like armpit steam—your
burden—snort him up, he'll keep you

down, o!
what a ride; the heliograph of your heart
goes dead, cranberry juice—chilled—at 4:30 a.m.,
in texas, a menu saying, "thanks, call
again," is what's left of you, put
back by the salt, pepper, napkins, and ketchup. momma
did good

by her boy, got little jars of his insides
on the kitchen stove where she can eat
on them and know he's safe. momma don't allow no
birthday from her gut, she's all swole up
just thinking him back where he belongs.
mr. dildo. mr. silver bullet. mr. keep clean
for her. easy

does it when you're a transplant, when your face
is wallpaper with no wall behind it.
anything that comes to hand might fit. and he
don't know no better. momma got him dead
asleep. he's the metal claw she operates,

and she figures you as food. look out: her
old cunt chews
like it still had teeth.

ELIZABETH MCNEILL

from: *Nine and a Half Weeks* _____

I've never worn a garter belt, I tell him, though I've thought about buying one, off and on for years. Except, I tell him, I can't remember ever imagining myself in black, that would have been . . . pink, maybe, or white; we're both laughing again. He describes the dignified saleswoman who waited on him, a woman our mothers' age: large-bosomed, impeccable, glistening-mouthed, coolly uninterested. She had spread a bewildering array before him and had pointed out salient features: adjustable straps; an elastic inset at the back of this one—better fit; special darts, here; small rosettes of contrasting fabric and color enhancing the snaps on yet another one; all, naturally, cold-water-washable. "You've chosen one of the two best-selling models, sir," she had told him. He had wanted to ask her what the other one was but had decided against it when she had said, "Will there be anything else?" in what had seemed to him a near-venomous voice.

"Now look in the other box," he says, gleefully, and pushes the low table away from the couch. He is sitting with his legs apart, bare feet planted on the carpet, toes pointing outward; an elbow on each knee, his chin in the palm of his hands, his two ring fingers rubbing the skin at the outer corners of his eyes. His hair, dry now from the shower he took before dinner, lies soft above his forehead. A fine white cotton shirt, heavily frayed at the collar, unbuttoned, sleeves rolled up, chest hair curly and lower down less curly, disappearing into old and baggy tennis shorts. "You don't know what you look like, right now," I say. "A Crusoe, happy on his island, who'll never wear a suit again, I'm so in love with you."

He narrows his eyes and catches his lower lip with an upper canine, trying to mask a grin—shy and pleased and so utterly dear to me that my vision blurs. He leans into the couch, head bent far back onto the cushions; his arched throat gleams across the room. He pushes both hands through his hair and says to the ceiling—evenly, deliberately— "This has got to go on like this. All we have to do is just make it go on like this." And sitting up and hunching forward and waving an outstretched arm and pointed finger at me, in a booming voice: "Open the other bag, damn it, you wheedled and whined all evening, now look at you drag your feet!"

"All *right*," I say, "yes, *sir*!" The bag contains a shoe box from Charles Jourdan, a store I've only looked at from outside, acknowledging wisely that even my Bloomingdale's card is at times too much of a temptation. I lift the shiny beige lid. Swaddled in yet more tissue paper lies a pair of elegant, light gray suede pumps with heels so high I'm appalled. "*You* walk in these," I say, vehemently. "My *God*, I didn't even know they made heels like that." He ambles across the room and crouches beside me on the floor, grinning sheepishly. "Yeah, well, I see what you mean." "See what I *mean*," I repeat. "How can you *not*, you're sure these are supposed to be shoes?" "They're shoes all right," he says. "I guess you don't like them. Not at all? I mean, aside from the heels?" "Sure," I say, holding one shoe in each hand, the suede soft as velvet. "What's not to like, they're sensational. Course, it's hard to overlook such outlandish appendages, probably cost a fortune, too. . . ." He shrugs, suddenly awkward.

"Look," he says, "they're not really to wear, outside that is." He gestures at the Bendel's wrappings. "They're just for us. Me, really. Both of us. I wish you . . . what I mean is . . . but if you really hate them . . ." All at once he is a decade my junior, a very young man asking me to have a drink with him, expecting to be refused. I have not seen him like this before. "Darling," I say, overcome, in a rush, "they're lovely, feel this leather, of course I'll wear them. . . ." "I'm glad," he says, with a remaining trace of sheepishness. "I was hoping you would; there's always a chance you might get to like them." And buoyant again: "Put the stuff on."

So I do. As always until this evening—and tonight for the last time —I am wearing only a shirt, so it doesn't take long, though getting the seams straight is much trickier than I would have guessed. The shoes fit perfectly. "I took your black ones with me," he says. "And I insisted and they found a girl that size and she tried on nine pairs before I settled on these. Thank God you're an average size."

The heels make me so much taller we're nearly eye to eye. He hugs me lightly, runs his hands up my sides to my breasts, moves the palm of each hand, fingers extended, in small circles, a nipple at the center of each. His face is blank. The gray pupils on which mine are focused reflect two miniature faces. His hands move down my midriff to the garter belt. He traces its outlines around my body, then, one by one, follows each of the four straps down to where the stockings begin. It is almost dark. He switches on the floor lamp behind us, says, "Stay there," walks back to the couch, and sits down. "Now," he says, in a husky voice, "come over here. Take your time."

I walk slowly across the carpet. I take small steps, cautious, my body tilted into a foreign alignment. My arms hang awkwardly from their sockets. Something roars in my ears, amplifying each breath I take.

"Turn around now," he says when I'm a few steps away from the couch. I can barely hear him. "And lift up the shirt." I turn and stand very straight, holding the shirttails tucked up at my sides with my elbows. "Are you disappointed?" I say, in what turns out to be a high-pitched, flat voice. "Are you kidding, you're a sight," he murmurs behind me, "you're a sight, sweetheart." My eyes close. I listen to the roar in my ears, every square inch of my skin aching to be touched. Trying to clear my ears, I shake my head, hair catches in my mouth; please, I think, please.

"Get down on all fours," he says. "And pull your shirt up. Pull it up, I want to see your ass." I look at the tightly woven carpet, a rich gray, now only a few inches from my face. "Crawl around," he says, his voice very low. "Crawl over to the door. Crawl around." I move my right arm forward, my right knee, my left arm. I think: is it elephants that do this differently? My left knee. I am suspended in a silence that is broken by someone's muffled conversation in the corridor outside the apartment. A door slams. The cellist on the floor below begins to practice and I concentrate on his characteristic initial outburst with interest. I have always assumed that musicians warm up slowly, like joggers. This one starts out with great verve and volume and gradually winds down over the course of his three-hour run. He is bald and surly, I've seen him in the elevator. "I can't," I say.

It seems as if the sound of my voice has made my body crumple. For a second my face is flat against the carpet, which appears flawlessly smooth when seen from a standing height but is less soft to the skin than one might expect. I sit up. The height of these heels prevents me from sitting in the position I suddenly long for: my knees drawn up to my chin, my arms around me.

"Tell me," he says, neutrally. "I feel stupid," I say. "It makes me feel foolish." The one lamp at the other end of the room is not bright enough for me to be able to see the expression on his face. He folds his arms behind his head and leans back against the couch cushions. I get up, teeter, say, "This rug itches"—under my breath, but as if imparting valuable information—and sit down in the nearest chair. I cross my arms over the shirtfronts I have wrapped around me. One of the sleeves has come down and I tug the cuff over my fingers and curl my hand, inside the fabric, into a fist.

"It's not as if we haven't been through all this," he says, not looking at me. "I hate packing. I hate unpacking even worse. It took me a week to unpack that suitcase of yours, the last time around." The cello below erupts as if flayed by a madman.

"What I don't get is why you can't keep the idea of being hit in your mind, why it always actually has to be done to you. Before you say to me, no, I don't want to do that—why you don't picture me taking off my belt, in your head. Why you don't remember from one night to the next what it feels like when it comes down on you. We have to fucking negotiate each and every time and in the end you do what I tell you, anyway."

"No," I say, inaudibly first. "No," I say, "please ..." He leans toward me now, pushing hair off his forehead. "It makes me feel like a dog," I say, "crawling.... I'm scared you'll make fun of me."

"You *should* feel stupid," he says. "What a crock of shit. If I ever make fun of you I'll let you know." I shake my head, mute. Scowling and scrutinizing me closely, he walks toward and past me. I am sitting rigidly at the edge of the chair, my knees pressed together, my forearms tight against my stomach muscles. His hands are on my shoulders. I am pulled back until my shoulder blades touch the upholstery. Then his hand in my hair, massaging my scalp, closing into a fist, drawing slowly back until my face lies horizontal, the top of my head against his cock. He rubs the lower half of my face with the heel of his hand. My mouth soon opens. When I am moaning steadily he leaves the room and comes back with the riding crop. He lays it on the coffee table.

"Look at it," he says. "Look at me. In three minutes I can get you so you'll be in bed for a week." But I barely hear him. The inadequate, the miniscule, the fiber optics passage I have in my throat instead of a trachea allows me only quicksilver sips of air. My open mouth feels bruised.

"Crawl," he says. I'm on hands and knees again. I press my face hard into my right shoulder and feel how the trembling in my chin, instead of being steadied, transmits through bone after bone until my arms shake and my legs, down to my toes. I hear the tip of the leather-covered handle scrape against the tabletop. A white-hot pain leaps across the back of my thighs. Tears spring to my eyes, sudden as magic. Released as if from a dangerous stupor, I crawl from the chair to the bedroom door, limber and easily to the lamp in the far corner; a loudly purring cat weaves figure eights around my arms. Both stockings tear at the knees and I can feel a run creep jerkily up each thigh. When I've almost reached the couch again he overtakes me, pushes me down, turns me on my back.

It's the one time with him and the first time at all that I come at the same time as my lover. He licks my face then. Each spot is first warm and—when his tongue moves on—abruptly cold, sweat and saliva evaporating in the conditioned air.

When he stops I open my eyes. "But you beat me anyway," I whisper, "even when I do what you ..." "Yes," he says. "Because you like hitting me," I whisper. "Yes," he says, "and watching you flinch, and holding you down and hearing you beg. I love the sounds when you can't keep quiet, when you're past holding back. I love seeing a bruise on you and knowing where it came from, welts on your ass." I shiver. He reaches back and up and yanks down the old blanket he keeps folded under a cushion in the corner of the couch. He shakes it open and covers me with it and says, tucking the frayed satin binding under my chin, "And because you want it, too." "I do," I whisper. "Never *then* . . . never while . . ." "I know," he says, close to my ear, his hands deep in my hair, tight and soothing on my scalp.

JAYNE ANNE PHILLIPS

Slave _____

She wanted to have orgasms more and more often. She watched her men have orgasms with their eyes closed, sailing on their breath, and gone. She had the pleasure of helping them leave, and was left in possession of them until they returned. She had memorized faces in that moment of unconsciousness. Many times she was actually seeing that face rather than the face she was talking to, aware that this person whose face it was had never seen that face of himself. So the face became her secret. She herself had a tiny orgasm of fear when she saw someone she loved after a long separation, who usually no longer loved her. Something turned over once in her. She had the same turning ache when reading something suggestive or having a memory of arousal. She had it when she realized she wanted someone. When she masturbated she always had a brief intense orgasm, turning over ten times, and fell asleep released. But she seldom had orgasms with her men. She loved to make love with someone she wanted. They soared away from her arched and paralyzed and for an instant she had what she wanted. There was one man she liked to talk to, whom she didn't particularly want because he was so much like her. She already had what he had. She could get along without him, because when he came, there was no triumph of conquering their separation and winning him. So she told him that although she liked men she seldom had orgasms with them but only with herself. They talked about it patiently. After that she wanted to make love with him less because her power was exposed and solidified. He wanted to make love with her more but was self-conscious because he was unsure of his power. She felt he was no longer like her but was less than her, and she didn't want him. The relationship cooled. One day he called her on the phone and a fight ensued in which they each cataloged what was weak about the other. She was getting the best of him so he said Go fuck yourself, since you can do more for yourself than I can anyway. She sat there listening to the dial tone. She knew that he thought her power was uppermost because she could make him come but he couldn't make her come. He had the secret of what her power was about, but she had the secret of his powerlessness over her. That made him ashamed. He felt lonely but free because he thought there had to be two people to have the question of power. She knew her power over him happened because of her power over herself. The phone began bleeping frantically. Alone, she could feel her power holding her up. But what did that make her?

oo oo oo

KATHY ACKER

The Underworlds Of The World ──────────

Anwar Sadat climbs up a broken staircase, opens the door in front of him, looks into a dark stifling room, and says, "Are you alone now?"

"I'm always alone. Worse luck for me, deary, and better for you," a croak replies. "Come in, come in, whoever you are: I can't see you 'til I light this match, I recognize your voice I think. I know you, don't I?"

"Light that match and see."

"Oh oh deary I will oh oh, my hand is shaking so I can't put it on a match all of a sudden. And I cough so (cough cough) everytime I put these matches down they jump around, I never know where they are. Oh oh oh. They're jumping around, this damn cough, like living things. Are you planning to go somewhere, deary?"

"No."

"Not planning to go on a long trip?"

"No way."

"Well, there are people who travel by land and people who travel by sea. I'm the mother of both. I provide men with everything. Not like that Jack Chinaman Ludlow Street. He don't know what it is to father farther and mother. He don't know how to cut this, he charges what I charge and more, much much more, whatever he'll get. Here's a match, sweetie, uh-oh. Where's that candle? I never could stand electric lights. Everytime I start to cough, I cough out twenty of those damn matches before I get one lit. (She manages to light a match before she starts heaving again.) My lungs are gone! (Yellow phlegm) Oh oh oh!" While she's grabbing for her breath she can't see, all of her senses are dead, except the senses of coughing; now it's over—eyes open—life returning, "Oh, you."

"You're surprised to see me?"

"Aren't you dead?"

"Why do you think I'm dead?"

"You've been away from me for so long. How can you stay alive for three hours without me? Something bad must have happened to you?"

"Not at all. A relative died."

"Died of what, deary?"

"Probably, death."

Beginning her process and starting to bubble and blow at the faint spark enclosed in the hollow of her hands, she speaks from time to time, in a tone of snuffling satisfaction, without leaving off.

WHERE DO EMOTIONS COME FROM, ARE EMOTIONS NECESSARY, WHAT DO EMOTIONS TELL US ABOUT CONSCIOUSNESS?

She gives the man her brown leather bag.

She is sitting next to a man and her ass is bare on the taxicab fake leather.

He is reaching down into her blouse and making her pull off her clothes.

He's leaving her alone and she doesn't know how to handle an alien world.

He takes her somewhere she's never been before.

His hands are touching her sweater.

His hands are lifting her sweater up her back.

His hands are running down the outward slope of her ass.

His right hand's third finger is sitting in her asshole and his right hand thumb is an inch in her cunt.

He makes her cry out sharply.

His right hand is pushing her down.

His hard cock sticks into her hole.

He thrusts into her asshole without using any lubrication.

His knees stick into her face.

He explains to her she's not going to know.

His strong arm pulling on her arms is lifting her to her feet.

He shows her his whip.

One of his hands lies on her left shoulder.

He tells her she can expect he will hurt her mentally and physically.

He hurts her physically to give her an example.

He tells her there are no commitments and she has to let him make all the decisions, she won't make any more decisions.

IS THERE ANY NEED FOR EMOTION?

He says to her, "Nothing you have, even your mind, is yours anymore. I'm a generous man. I'm going to give you nothing."

She's turning around and catching his eyes staring at her as if he loves her.

She is sitting next to him and listening to him talk.

He is saying that it no longer matters what she thinks and what her choices are.

He is saying that he is the perfect mirror of her real desire and she is making him that way.

His eyes are not daring to meet her eyes.

He is walking back and down and in front of her.

He is dialing her phone number on the phone.

He's telling her to wait without any clothes on for him to come over.

He's telling her to throw out certain identities and clothes he doesn't like.

He's telling her he doesn't have any likes or dislikes so there's no way she can touch him.

He's telling her he's a dead man.

She's laying out her clothes and wondering which one's the softest.

She's wondering if she's going to die.

She is waiting for this man who says he's not her lover by trying to guess what he wants.

He is telling her iron becomes her.

He is seizing her by the throat and hair.

She is thinking that it is not a question of giving her consent and it is never a question of choice.

So what use is emotion? What use is anything? Oh, oh, she isn't understanding.

NOT ONLY IS THERE NO ESCAPE FROM PERCEIVING BUT THE ONLY WAY TO DEAL WITH PAIN IS TO KILL ONESELF TOTALLY BY ONESELF. SUICIDE HAS ALWAYS BEEN THE MOST DIFFICULT OF HUMANITY'S PROBLEMS.

Caress the tips of your nipples.

I'm giving you away so you have no choice who your teacher is.

Take off your skirt.

Suck me.

You don't care who you fuck.

Sex is only physical.

Play with your clit.

You'll obey me without loving me.

When you arrive, your eyes show happiness.

My hands are rubbing your breasts.

My lips are touching your breasts.

My lips are your lips.

When will you bring your whip?

I'm doing everything I can to understand.

I'm doing everything I can to control.

I'm doing everything I can to love (name).

My consciousness is letting loose every kind of emotion.

You will masturbate in front of me.

You are a whore.

All women are whores.

BLOOD SEEPS OUT OF ONE OF THE GIRLS' CUNTS WHILE HER LEGS ARE SPREAD OPEN

Hatless, wearing practically no makeup, her hair totally free, she looks like a well-brought-up little girl, dressed as she is in a very full wool tweed little boys' trousers and a box-cut matching jacket, or little hand-knit pale blue or red sweaters, tiny collars around the neck, flopping over full-cut velvet trousers, pale blue silk slippers tied around her ankles, or her evening narrow black knee-length dress. Everywhere Sir S takes her people think she's his daughter and her addressing him in the most formal terms while he acts familiarly with her underlines this mistake. Sitting in an all-night restaurant during the early morning hours before gray light starts to appear walking past the few trees that exist at the lower end of Fifth Avenue while the evening sky is unable to turn completely black, an old woman in the restaurant begins to talk to them the people on the street smile at them.

Once in a while he stops next to a concrete building and puts his arms around her and kisses her and tells her he loves her. THE FUTURE: once he invites her to lunch with two of his Italian compatriots. This is the first time he's invited her to meet any of his friends. Then he shows up an hour before he said he was going to.

He has the keys to her place. She's naked. She's just finished meditating. She realizes he's carrying what looks like a golf club bag. He tells her to open his bag.

The whips are pink silk and pale black fur and one plaster and leather with tiny double and triple knots so there're no expectations and dolls and a long light brown whip that looks like the tail of a thin animal.

The minute he touches her she begins to come.

For the first time he asks her what her taste is.

She can't answer.

He tells her she's going to help him destroy her. Whips don't exist and are ridiculous. Who could confuse orgasm with pain?

The three girls, in the school bathroom cold tiled floor, are giggling.

It's the first time he's taken her out and not treated her like a piece of shit.

The Swords Point Upwards

The man and the woman are sitting in the first restaurant he's ever taken her to. One of the man's friends is sitting in an armchair to her right, another to her left. The one on the left is tall, red-haired, gray-eyed, 25 years old. The man is telling his two friends he invited them to have dinner with the woman so they could do whatever they want with her in no uncertain terms because she's the most unnameable unthinkable spit spit. She realizes that she is at the same time a little girl absolutely pure nothing wrong just what she wants, and this unnameable dirt this thing. This is not a possible situation. This identity doesn't exist.

Her grandmother lifts up her pink organdy skirt to show the hotel headwaiter, "Look what my granddaughter's wearing! Her first new girdle! And only six years old!"

The first man doesn't recognize her humanity. All the men she has don't recognize her humanity. Kneel down suck off our cocks. While you're sucking them off, use the fingers of both hands with those quick feather ways you do. Then they all go away as quickly as possible while she's swallowing their cum.

The young boys being completely overwhelmed by her strength—her calm existing in such contradiction—tell her they want her to tell them everything. They give themselves over to her as if they're clay, not human. They fuck again and again. They can't get enough fucking. Then they turn on her. They hate her guts because she allowed them to be weak. They want to beat her up.

The following day, scared she'll leave him, he tells her the red-haired boy says he wants to marry her and so take her away from this unbearable contradiction in which she's living.

It's always her decision. She tells him she wants to become another, as if at this point it's even a question of a decision, though it always is.

Animality

Sparrow-hawk, falcon, owl, fox, lion, bull: nothing but animal masks, but scaled to the size of the human head, made of real fur and feathers, the eye crowned with lashes when the actual animal has lashes, as the lion has, and with pelts and feathers falling to the person-wearing-them's shoulders. A molded, hardened cardboard frame placed between the outer facing and the skins' inner lining keep the mask shape rigid. The most striking and the one she thinks transforms her the most is the owl mask because tan and tawny feathers whose colors are her cunt hairs make it; the feathery cape almost totally hides her shoulders, descending halfway down the back, and the front to the beginning of the breasts' swell.

"But O, and I hope you'll forgive me, you'll be taken on a leash."

Natalie returns holding the chain and pliers which Sir S uses to force open the last link. He fastens it to the second link of the chain stuck in her cunt. After she remasks herself, Sir S tells Natalie to take hold of the end of the chain and walk around the room, ahead of her. (being chained to the text)

"Well I must say," he remarks, "the Commander's right, all the hair'll have to be removed. Meanwhile keep wearing your chain."

What shocks and upsets the girl at the depilatory parlor the following day, more than the irons and the black-and-blue marks on her lower back, are the brand new whip marks. No matter how many times she repeats attempts to explain, if not what her fate (decision) is, at least that she's happy; there's no way of reassuring this girl or allaying her feelings of disgust and terror. No matter how much she thanks these people how polite just like a little girl she acts when she's leaving this parlor where for hours she's lain her legs spread as wide as possible not to get fucked but to get love, it doesn't matter how much money she gives all of them; she feels they're rejecting her rather than her walking out of a business appointment. She realizes that there's something shocking in the contrast between the fur on her belly and the feathers on her mask just as she realizes that this air of an Egyptian statue which the mask lends her, and which her broad shoulder narrow waist and muscled legs serve only to emphasize, demands her flesh be absolutely hairless.

Stared at them with eyes opened wide, deaf to human language and dumb. People seeing her, with expressions of horror and contempt turn and flee. Sir S is using O model to demonstrate. Stone wax unhuman. Daybreak is awakening the asleep. Unfasten chains, remove masks.

The Beginning

As you and Sir S are walking out of the subway station, up to the street, a young cop or a young man who looks like a cop, as soon as he sees Sir S, steps forward from a large black Mercedes whose doors are locked. He bows, opens the rear car door, and steps aside. After you've settled in the back seat, your luggage in the front seat, Sir S' lips lightly brush your right cheek and he closes the door.

The car starts suddenly, so fast you don't know enough to grab him to call out. Although you throw yourself against the moving back window, he's gone forever you feel frenzy.

The car is rapidly moving westward into the countryside. You are oblivious to the outside world because you are crying.

The terrorist driver is tilting his seat so it's almost horizontal to pull your legs on to the front seat. Your legs are pressing the ceiling as he's plunging his huge cock into you. He doesn't stop for an hour. He moans loudly when he comes.

The driver is 25 years old. He has a thin narrow face, large black eyes. He looks very sensitive and at the edge of being weak. His mouth never approaches your mouth. There is a basic agreement that the act of kissing is far more explosive than that of fucking.

When he finishes fucking you, you pull down your skirt and then button your thin hand-crocheted linen sweater through whose lace delicate puckers of nipples can be seen. You carefully place red lipstick over your lips.

If you want to, you can reach out and grab armfuls of red foxgloves.

"The driver raped you. You're two hours late. You let him rape you."

"Everything happens as Sir S says. Is he going to come?"

"I think so. I don't know when."

The tenseness felt in all your muscles when you're asking this question slowly dissolves and you look at this woman gratefully: how lovely she is, how sparkling with her hair streaked with gray. She's wearing over black pants and a matching blouse, an antique Chinese jacket.

Obviously the rules which govern the dress and conduct of the terrorists don't apply to her.

"Today I want to have lunch with you. Go wash yourself. At 3 o'clock sharp I'll be back."

You silently follow her; you're floating on cloud nine: Sir S says he'll see you again.

In this female terrorist house which is disguised as a girls' school, you're free to move around. You're standing on the Delancey Street

DEEP DOWN · · ·

corner. It's raining lightly. You know you're older than the other girls. A man might not want you cause the skin on your face's slightly wrinkled. Men want young tight fresh girl skin. They want new. They want to own. They want to be amazed. You're gonna have to work three times as hard as the other girls to get your men. This work is creating an image which men will strongly crave. This image has to be composed (partly) of your strong points and has to picture something some men beyond rationality want. You have to keep up this image to survive.

You put all thoughts away. Thoughts can be present in those hiatuses when you're not a machine moving to survive. You are a perfect whore so you're not human.

Get off this. "Hi honey, I can do anything." Your hips wiggle far wider than any other whore's hips. You're stealing outright from the restaurants you're sitting in you're laughing in those faces of big businessmen who look like pigs when a bum's pulling a knife on you you say, "Honey, it's too short." Nothing can touch (hurt) you when you're moving this fast: a perfect image: closed.

This' why you're the best whore in the world. You have to make this image harder. While you're a whore, you can love someone. While you're a whore, it's impossible for anyone to love you.

Sir S wants you to prostitute to bring him money.

"Listen, O, I've heard quite enough. If Sir S wants you to go to bed for money, he's certainly free to do so. It's not your concern. Go to sleep now, baby, shut up. As for your other duties and obligations, we use the sister system here. Noelle will be your sister, and she'll explain all the procedures to you."

The whores spend most of their time with other whores and live in a steamy, hot atmosphere, a dressing room (perhaps one pimp who is a cardboard figure over whom they obsess just like the pupils in an all-girls' school and the one male religion teacher), here at the edge of being touchable. Their knowledge of how vulnerable each of them is defines their ways of talking to each other and creates a bond, the strongest interfemale bond women know, between them.

Women's sexuality isn't goal-oriented, is all-over. Women will do anything, not for sex, but for love, because sex isn't a thing to them, it's all over undefined, every movement motion to them is a sexual oh. This is why women can be sexually honest and faithful. This is why women look up to things, are amazed by things. Women hate things the most.

Running the tip of his riding crop over the skin of your breasts.

"Why didn't you bring your whips tonight? At least you can slap my face."

Takes hold of your large nipples and pulls.

Calls you "a whore."

You're tightening around the flesh pole that fills and burns you. The pole doesn't move out.

"Caress me with your mouth."

You enjoy prostituting with this stranger.

She kisses the tip of one of your breasts through the black lacework covering it.

"They won't tell me their names," she says. "But they look nice, don't they?"

The men are embarrassed and vulgar. Their third drink has made them drunk.

They take a table for four. Just as they're finishing dinner, the man who took you last night walks into the restaurant. He discreetly signals and sits by himself.

"Shall we go upstairs?"

One of the hotel waiters shows you to a room. Without being asked, you walk over to your customer to offer him your breasts. You're slightly astonished to see how easy it is to offer your tits to this unknown man.

He tells you to undress, then stops you. Your irons impress him. As he's pulling his cock out of your asshole he says, "If you're really good, I'll give you a fat tip."

There's no possibility that anyone'll love you anymore or that love matters. Because there's no hope of realizing what you want, you're a dead person and you're having sex.

He leaves before you're out of bed, leaves a handful of bills on a small white table. You walk back to the house after having neatly folded the bills and stuffed them in your cleavage.

Your chains are disappearing.

You can decide now whether to get dressed or not.

You can decide now whether to work for money or not.

You can decide now who to talk to.

He still whips you every day. When you complain another girl says, "You want to be whipped so why are you being querulous? You're not Justine."

Who you are is obvious. There's no one else but you. If you want to get whipped, like being whipped, girl.

You own me.

You control me.

I have nothing to do with you.

You're a murderer.

There's no such thing as a terrorist: there're only murderers.

I'm a masochist.

This is a real revolution.

Sometimes men bring straight women into the brothel. These straight women act like they're not looking down on the whores they see and yet, underneath this fake understanding or liberality, pure fascination lies. Fascination can involve no such intellectual judgment. These women tremble in front of the whores. Their eyes secretly follow around the corners of the doorways. Their eyes pin themselves on the long upper thighs, the cunt hair that might show, is it wet? How does she act when she's . . . with a MAN? Does she spread her legs very wide? What tricks does she use to make the man love her? Is she real? Is her underwear filthy? Does she drink piss in her mouth? Is she just an orgasming machine? Is she just a sink-into-flesh machine? What's it like to be without brains? Not to have any worries about how to get along in life how to keep up respect (among men) how to manage my career and children how to maintain my image and underneath the image . . . ? What's it like to live in that one (animal) place?

I'm not like HER? I'm a person. The beautiful woman adjusts her face. Her left hand lightly brushes over the top of her man's hand to show she and he are real: she's his woman because they're a twosome: real people in a real working world unlike these HOLES who DON'T EXIST.

You're watching the girls in the brothel:

A slender but well-proportioned girl, all white against the cunt-blood hangings, shaking, bearing on her hips for the first time the purple crop furrows. Her lover is a thin young man who's holding her, by her shoulders, back on the bed, the way Rene had held you, and watching with obvious pleasure and agony as you open your sweet burning belly to a man you've never seen beneath whose weight the girl's moaning.

They belong exclusively to members of the Club; they give themselves up to unknown men; as soon as they're ready, their lovers prostitute them in the outer world for no reason at all.

Other girls prostitute only for money, don't have pimps, and will never leave prison.

One girl is left in the brothel six months, then taken out forever.

Jeanne lived in the brothel a year, left, then returned.

Noelle stayed for two months, left for three months, returned totally broke.

Yvonne and Julienne who like you get whipped several times a day will not leave.

A man's making love to you.

He's giving you a ring, a collar, and two diamond bracelets instead of your irons.

He's saying he's going to take you to Africa and America.

"No! No!" you scream. You can't bear to have anyone love you. You can't bear another person's consciousness. You don't want anyone in your distorted desolated life.

"You're now free," the streaked-with-gray-haired terrorist says to you. "We can remove your irons, your collar, and bracelets, and even erase the brand. You have the diamonds, you can go home."

You don't cry; you don't show any sign of bitterness. Nor do you answer her.

"But if you prefer," she goes on, "you can stay here."

The jellyfish is the rapist. When O was 17 years old her father tried to rape her when she told him he couldn't rape her he weeps, "Your mother won't fuck me, those boys don't respect you enough, I'm the only man who's respecting you." This night O has a nightmare. A huge jellyfish glop who's shaped into an-at-least-six-story worm is chasing her down the main sand-filled cowboy street. All of her WANTS to get away, but her body isn't obeying her mind. Like she feels she's caught in quicksand so her body is her quicksand.

Nightmare: her body mirrors/becomes her father's desire. This is the nightmare.

Then O had a number of S&M relationships with guys who dug their fingernails into her flesh slapped her face then jellyfish wanted to become her whinedaboutttheirproblems wanted to become her. Then O almost killed herself by developing an ovarian infection.

Men are rapists because rape rope is something O doesn't want. Why do people kill? A person kills, not from impotence but because he or she doesn't see what he or she is doing. O had to either deny her father's sex and have no father or fuck her father and have a father. This event led O to believe that a man would love her only if she did something she didn't want to do. How can I talk about ignorance, what ignorance unknowing is?

A young prince enjoying the company of an enchanting woman; he receives a cup of wine, elixir of life, out of her hands.

Probably Timurid period, 15th century.

The period corresponding roughly to the 15th century takes its name from the great conqueror Timur or Tamerlane, whose armies overran the Near East between 1365 and his death in 1405, and whose descendants held court in Persia for the next hundred years. The classic style introduced by Ahmad Musa had reached its apex under the Jalayrid Sultan Ahmad, who ruled at Baghdad till its conquest by Timur. After that his artists seemed to have taken service with the Timurid princes, especially Iskandar Sultan under whose patronage the Timurid style may be said to have been formed:

oo oo oo

LYN LIFSHIN

With So Many Voices _____

the play switches so fast
I couldn't remember
what part I was cast
in, your words, like a lid
over my eye so I had
to feel where I was
going, learning which
tone curled like a lip,
like a polaroid in a
hot damp room rain
leaks in. I moved by
touch could have been
blind folded on a velvet
couch with no panties
on, legs on silk pillows
gilt chains spiralled
from, being entered
by strangers, my dark
parts throbbing like
a throat exploding
in a rash of roses

DEENA METZGER

from: *Skin: Shadows/Silence* _____

*Surely one has to create
against this
—The Diary of Anais
Nin, Volume III*

It is afternoon. You've heard this story before. This is the story I will tell twice and then again. It does not empty easily. This story has left a scar and the scar needs to be cut out. This story will be told again.

It is afternoon. I am alone. In an office. It is afternoon. I am alone. In an office. It is afternoon. I am alone.

There is a knock at the door. Or the sound of the door opening in the outer office. Or a knock and the sound of a door opening in the outer office this afternoon. I am alone. Thinking of things one thinks when one is alone in the afternoon. Almost a daydream. Allowed to think. Why should I be startled by a knock at my door or the sound of another door opening. Why should I hear the door or even interrupt my thoughts which are so pleasant this quiet afternoon. All the work is done.

Why bother to turn my head when I hear the floor creak? My thoughts are so pleasant, nothing can interrupt them. This is my time to muse. A rare afternoon alone. All the work is done.

Probably it is not a knock at the door that I hear and do not respond to. Probably it is the sound of a door opening quietly and of soft footprints across the floor. Or maybe it is the sound of a knock, a tentative tap to see if I am in. But it is a quiet afternoon and all the work is done and I am in to no one but myself, so I do not answer the door. Probably there is no sound. It is not that I refuse to be interrupted but that my dreams are so intense that I hear nothing, not the initial knock on the outer door (if indeed there was a knock—probably there was no knock) nor the sound of the lock turning, nor the cautious feet across the floor, nor the cautious turning of the lock to my inner office and the stealthy opening of the door, nor the hand raised against me. Nothing. It is afternoon and I hear nothing, suspect nothing, till the gun is pressed against my head and the hand muzzles my mouth.

"Say nothing," he whispers.

It is a gun which is against my head. There is a man holding it. I cannot see him. But I do not think I know him. He ties an unclean and wrinkled handkerchief across my mouth. I close my eyes because I am afraid to know him. Simultaneously I keep them open in order to see this man. But I think I can see nothing.

"Take your clothes off," he says. Everything he says is in a strained and I assume disguised voice. Perhaps he is someone I know. Which is more awful—an anonymous assault by a stranger or by a friend?

My hands are shaking and he is laughing. I am struggling to obey. My feet are shaking also.

I can only see his feet. I have told you before about his scuffed black shoes which look as if they have steel linings in the toes. They are laced with frayed black laces. His socks are white. Dirty white. His feet are wide. I suspect his legs are hairy and that the hairs are damp.

It is afternoon. A quiet afternoon. No one is about.

No one is knocking at the door. "Take off your clothes," he says. My body is shaking. The dress peels from me like skin, a heap of feathers disordered, plucked live from the skin, a mound of fresh leather in a corner. The animal is still alive. And the animal is still alive! And the deer stretches denuded flanks, twitching. I can see the blood run across the hooves.

I am naked. He is wearing clothes. I do not wish to see his legs hairy at the ankle bone. I cannot bear to see his clothes against my skin. I am naked. He is fully clothed.

I remember nothing. I will remember nothing. I tell you this without hearing my own voice. I tell you this again and again so I will never remember it. I remember how naked I am next to his clothed legs in order to forget everything.

Handprints on my back. Indelible markings. In later mirrors it seems my back grows away from his hands. An announcement in reversal. In recoil.

An invasion. A tree opening to fire. And a black hollow from which no twig can emerge again. Perhaps it is a gun penetrating me and orgasm will be a round of bullets. Pain is a relief. I cherish it as a distraction from knowing. I am an enemy country. Destroy me with fire. But there is no distraction. The cloth rubs against my legs. There is a gun resting on my shoulder. I do not forget that death is the voyeur at this encounter.

Turning. Turning. The flesh of the spitted deer crackles against the fire. I want to reach for a knife to carve myself into morsels, to divide into portions, to carve a slit downwards from my navel to my spine.

There is a circle of steel against my ear.

I have told this before. It is afternoon, a quiet afternoon, and the taste of my own meat smeared on unknown flesh is in my mouth. I choke upon it. It is afternoon. I do not know what is thrust in my mouth. What banquet is this? What severed leg? What joint? What goat, deer, bone? I wish blood were dripping down my throat now. How long can I hold his sperm in my mouth without swallowing it?

It is afternoon. I have told you this before. It is a quiet afternoon. I do not hear the sound of someone knocking at my door.

I try to say, "Come in." I would like someone to help me from the floor. I need a pillow under my head. Wrap me in a blanket. Turn the lights out.

It is early evening. It is night. It is tomorrow. I would like someone to help me up from the floor. I cannot say, "Come in," to the knock on the door. I cannot yell for help. I need to be wrapped in a blanket. I need a pillow under my head. And a night dress. And a cover of white cloth.

ANN BEATTIE

from: Four Stories About Lovers ⎯⎯⎯⎯⎯⎯⎯

II

The lover thinks that he is compared unfavorably to other lovers. In fact he is no longer her lover, but he remembers when he was, and that depresses him because he never intended to become her lover and he never intended to stop being her lover. She left because he got nasty. One time they argued—well, a lot of times they argued—but one particular time they argued walking into the house and he bent to make a snowball, then another, and another. He threw them all at her, and instead of running into the house she ran around the house and, of course, finally fell. He didn't realize that she had really been frightened until he put out his hand to help her up and she tried to scramble backward with that strange expression on her face. Then, of course, the martyrdom: he could save his energy by just kicking snow over her instead of pulling her up. Go on, go on . . . He wasn't opposed to kicking a little snow? She was afraid of him sometimes, but she still fought with him.

Pulling up in front of the house where she lives now, he tries to remember pleasant things. How they had watched the snow falling in the morning. The morning of the day he threw snowballs at her. The morning of the day she turned her ankle. He didn't turn the ignition off. One of the girls she lived with looked at his car from where she stood on the front lawn. She must have been surprised when he took off again. She must have wanted to get a good look at him because no doubt she had heard stories about the girl's lover.

"Heard any stories about me?" he asks pleasantly when he returns to the house.

The girl has. She looks at him without speaking. She must be a little afraid of him, though, because she gives a half nod. The girl has brown braids and wears a backless summer dress. He toys with the idea of asking if she wants a lover.

"It's your lover," he calls through the screen door.

She comes to the door smiling. One of the things she likes about him is his sense of humor. What does she think is funny about his having been her lover?

She shows him around. She says she is happy in the house. She points out a table she likes. This house is furnished. They had very little furniture in the other house, although that too was "furnished."

He tries to remember the inside of the other house and ends up remembering being her lover. He says nothing about the table she shows him. She asks if he has eaten dinner. Does he want to go out, then, or just listen to some music? Go out. Where will they go? It was always her fault—she was always so quick to be cynical. He thinks about telling her they can go out and throw snowballs so he can watch her face change—so he can notice something familiar about her face. This doesn't even look like her face. He remembers that she shares the house with three other girls. What do they look like? Maybe one of *them* was his lover.

When he drove away from this house the first time he came, he went to a liquor store and bought some bourbon and drank it. She must have guessed that. She once thought he had been drinking when she smelled Lysol in the house. Lysol! If she's as uncomfortable as he thinks she is, maybe she'll drink some. She drank, too, but she always had something to say about his drinking.

The girl with the brown braids calls to them: "Have a good time."

She doesn't approve. He goes across the lawn to where the girl is digging in the garden. He picks up a handful of moist dirt, shapes it into a ball and throws it at the front of her dress.

"Whose lover am I?" he hollers.

The girl scrambles, regains her balance and tears off, calling, "You're her Goddamn lover!"

Exactly right. He raises his eyebrows questioningly to his lover.

"You won't scare me this time," she says.

She turns and walks to the car, pulls open the door, and sits down. She leaves the door open for him to close. He does: click. The proper little date.

"Did you do that to scare me?" she asks. "You won't scare me any more."

"You feel you understand me well enough now to be my lover?" he asks.

"What is there to understand?" she asks.

She's trying very hard to act self-assured. The speeding and changing-lanes trick always gets her. She wants to give in. Why else would she have agreed to see him? He looks at her questioningly again. That unnerves her a little; she repeats her question.

○○ ○○ ○○
ALICIA OSTRIKER

Warning ─────────────────────

I will no longer lightly walk behind
a one of you who fear me:
                    Be afraid.
                    —June Jordan

Let them grow afraid
Not only in the dream
They do not consciously remember.

The dream is: Beautiful mother
Slices you up like cooked liver.
Although your shirt is on
She raises you
Writhing upon her fork prongs.
You try to hide
But you are skimming through the air
To look into the lit
Theater of her palate
Ringed like a cave and a cathedral,
Hanging while she casually laughs,
Saliva spraying you.
The dream is: Beautiful mother
Takes away her hot breasts
Her sweet stench and large eyes,
Their speaking lashes.
She takes away her fountain,
The dream is your own thirst.

Let them grow afraid
Not only in the dream
They do not consciously remember.

The fact is: Beautiful girl
Wearing a short skirt
And laced boots
Who strides across Washington Square
Taunting you,

Or dumb mud-eyed girl
Behind the Woolworth's counter,
Or fat mama on the fire escape
Sipping her beer,
Bosoms like five pound sugar sacks,
May be a warrior.
You do not know which ones are warriors.
They shall conceal themselves among us.
When you go to rape her
When you fling her open
And think to own her
And punish her,
When the bars of that prison cell sweat,
She may stab you,
Filthy fool,
Your own salt blood may fountain from your throat.

> Let them grow afraid
> Let them grow afraid
> In real life let them grow afraid.

ANNE RAMPLING

from: *Exit to Eden* _____

And when a door opened somewhere with a soft, almost inaudible click I felt the hairs rise on the back of my neck.

She had come out of the bath; I could smell the perfumed steam of the bath, one of those piercingly sweet floral scents, very nice, and some other aroma, something clean and smoky and mingled with the perfume: her smell.

She moved across the room into my field of vision without making a sound. She was wearing spike-heel slippers of white satin, like the black one discarded by the chair. And above that she wore nothing but a little lace-trimmed slip that came halfway down her thighs. The slip was cotton, bad luck.

I don't really care one way or the other about the feel of a body through nylon. But a body under sheer cotton drives me out of my head.

Her breasts were naked under the slip, and her hair hung down in a dark shadow about her shoulders, something like a Virgin Mary veil, and through the slip I could see the dark triangle between her legs.

Again I had that sense of a force emanating from her. Beauty alone couldn't account for the effect of her presence, even in this insane room, though beauty she certainly had.

I never should have sat back without her permission. And to look at her directly, that was a violation of the rules of the game, yet I did.

I looked up at her, though my head was slightly bowed, and when I saw her small, sharply angled face, her large brown eyes almost brooding as we stared at each other, the sense of her force intensified.

Her mouth was indescribably luscious. It was rouged without gloss so that the deep red appeared natural and the bones of her delicately sloping shoulders were for some mysterious reason as enticing to me as the full slope of her breasts.

But the current coming from her was not the sum of all the splendid physical details. No. It was as if she gave off invisible heat. She was smoldering in the skimpy little slip and the fragile satin slippers. And you couldn't see the smoke but you knew it was there. There was something almost inhuman about her. She made me think of an old-fashioned word. The word lust.

I looked down deliberately. And going on my hands and knees towards her, I stopped when I had reached her feet. I could feel the force coming from her, the heat. I pressed my lips to her naked toes, to her instep above the band of satin, and I felt that strange, baffling shock again that left a tingling in my lips.

"Stand up," she said softly. "And keep your hands clasped behind your back."

I rose as slowly as I could without breaking the movement, and when I obeyed, I was certain my face was really red. But it wasn't the old ritualized emotion. I stood over her, and though I didn't look at her again, I could see her perfectly, see the well between her breasts, and the dark rose-colored circles of the nipples under the white slip.

She reached up, and I almost backed away from her, feeling her fingers move into my hair. She clasped my head tightly, massaged it with her fingers, sending the chills down my back, and then brought her fingers slowly over my face the way a blind woman might, to see it, feeling of my lips and my teeth.

It was the touch of someone burning with fever, the hot dancing tips of her fingers, and it was further heated by some low sound she made, like a cat's purr without opening her lips.

"You belong to me," she said in something lower than a whisper.

"Yes, Madam," I answered. I watched helplessly as her fingers dropped to my nipples, and pinched them, pumping them as my body tensed. The sensation shot down through my cock.

"Mine," she said.

I felt this compulsion to answer her, but I didn't say anything, my mouth opening and then closing as I stared at her breasts. That sweet, clean smoky scent came to me again, flooded me. I thought, I can't bear this. I have to have her. She is using some altogether new weapon on me. I can't be tormented like this, in this silent bedroom, this is too much.

"Back up, there to the center of the room," she said in a low monotone, advancing as she spoke, her fingers still pressing and pulling at my nipples, pinching them hard suddenly so that I gritted my teeth.

"Oh, we are sensitive, aren't we?" she said. And our eyes met again, the heat blazing in hers, her red lips just parted to show the barest flash of white teeth.

I almost begged her, said "please." My heart was skipping as if I'd been running. I was on the very edge of bolting, just backing off from her—I didn't know what exactly—trying to shatter her power. Yet there wasn't the remotest possibility that I would or could.

She rose on tiptoe in front of me. I could see she had hold of something above me, and I glanced up to see the pair of white leather handcuffs with buckles dangling at the end of the white leather chain.

That I had forgotten about that stuff seemed a fatal error. But what did it matter, after all?

"Lift your hands," she said. "No, not too high, my tall beauty. Just over your head a little where I can still reach them. Fine."

I heard myself shudder. Little symphony of stressful admissions. I think I was shaking my head.

The leather went round my left wrist first, buckled very tight, and then around the right. My wrists were crossed, bound together. And as I stood as helplessly as if six men were holding me there, she went to the far wall, and pressed a button that silently made the leather chain above me retract into the ceiling, causing the cuffs to pull my wrists up well above my head before it stopped.

"It's very strong," she said, coming towards me again, her grace perfect in the spike heels. "Would you like to try to break loose?" The little petticoat slid up on her thighs, the little nest of hair prickling under the white cloth.

I shook my head. I knew she was going to touch me again. I couldn't stand the tension.

"You're impertinent, Elliott," she said, her breasts almost grazing me. Her fingers were spread out flat on my chest. "It is 'No, Madam' and 'Yes, Madam,' when you speak to me."

"Yes, Madam," I said. The sweat had broken out all over me. Her fingers moved down over my belly, her right forefinger pressing into my navel. I couldn't keep quiet. Quickly, she dropped her hand to touch my cock.

I moved my hips back away from her. And her left hand went up behind my neck. She moved to my side, her right hand pinching the loose skin of my scrotum very hard, the fingernails biting into it. I tried not to grimace. "Kiss me, Elliott," she said.

I turned my head towards her, and her lips nudged at my mouth, opening it, and that electric shock came again. My mouth locked tight on her. I kissed her like I wanted to swallow her. I kissed her like I had her on a hook. I could hold her that way, no matter how helpless she had me, that's how strong the current was. I could lift her by the sheer power of it, draw her out of herself, and when through this delirium I felt her breasts against my side, I knew I'd done it, that I had her. And the kissing was wet and luscious and sweet. Her nails pinched the flesh around my scrotum harder, but the pain mingled with the force passing out of me into her. She was up on tiptoe with her whole weight against my side, her left fingers clasping my neck, and I was feasting on her, my tongue inside of her, and my wrists ground into the leather cuffs trying to break loose beyond my control.

She pulled away, and I closed my eyes. "God," I whispered.

And I felt her wet sucking mouth on my underarm, pulling at the hair so hard that I winced. I was moaning out load. She'd gathered my balls up in her right hand, was massaging them, gently, ever so gently, her lips sucking on the skin of the underarm and I thought I'd go mad. My skin, all over, had come alive. She bit into the flesh, licked at it.

My body went rigid, my teeth gritted. I could feel her fingers letting go of my balls, and closing around the shaft of my penis, and stroking it upwards. "I can't ... I can't ..." I said between my gritted teeth. I danced backwards, straining not to come, and she let go, tugging my face around and kissing me again, her tongue going into my mouth.

"It's worse than being whipped, isn't it," she purred under the kisses, "being tortured with pleasure?"

I broke away this time, pulling free of her, and then I kissed her all over her face, sucking at her cheeks and her eyelids. I turned and thrust my cock at her, against the thin cotton of her slip. The feel of her through the cotton was too exquisite.

"No, you don't!" she drew back with a low, sinister laugh, and smacked my cock with the flat of her right hand. "And you never do that, until I tell you that you can do it." She slapped my cock again, and again.

"God, stop it," I whispered. My cock was pumping, hardening with each slap.

"You want me to gag you?"

"Yes, gag me. Do it with your tits or your tongue!" I said. I was shaking all over, and without meaning to, I yanked on the leather handcuffs as if I meant to try to break loose.

She laughed a low, vibrant laugh.

"You bad boy," she said. And there came those taunting, punishing slaps again. She brought her nail across the glans, and then pinched it shut. Yeah, just a rotten kid, I wanted to say but I swallowed it. I ground my forehead into my forearm, deliberately turning away from her. But she took my face in her hand and pulled it around.

"You want me, don't you?"

"Like to fuck the shit out of you," I whispered. In a quick darting motion, I caught her mouth again and drew on it before she could get away. I pumped at her again. Backing away, she walloped my cock again with the broad sweep of her hand.

She drew back, silently, across the carpet.

About six feet away she stood just looking at me, one hand out on the dresser, her hair fallen down around her face, partially covering her breasts. She looked moist and fragile, her cheeks beating with a deep flush, and the same flush on her breasts and her throat. I couldn't catch my breath. If I'd ever been this hard before I couldn't remember it. If I had ever been teased to this point before, I'd blotted it out.

I think I hated her. And yet out of the corner of my eye I was eating her up, her pink thighs, the arches of her feet in the white satin, spike-heeled slippers, the way her breasts swelled under the cotton lace, even the way she wiped at her mouth with the back of her hand.

She'd picked up something from the dresser. It looked at first glance like a pair of flesh-colored, leather-clad horns. I opened my eyes to see it clearly. It was a dildo in the form of two penises joined at the base with a single scrotum, so damned lifelike the cocks seemed to be moving of their own volition as she squeezed the soft massive scrotum the way a child would squeeze a rubber toy.

She brought it closer, holding it up in both hands like it was a sort of offering. It was marvelously well defined, both cocks oiled and gleaming, each with carefully delineated tips. For all I knew there was some fluid in the big scrotal sac that would come through the tiny openings in both of the cocks when she gave them the right twist.

"Ever been fucked by a woman, Elliott?" she whispered, tossing her hair back over her shoulder. Her face was moist, eyes large and glazed.

I made some faint protesting sound, unable to control it. "Don't do that to me ..." I said.

She gave another one of those low, smoldering laughs. She went back for a small padded stool that stood beside the dresser and she brought it with her and set it down behind my back.

I pivoted to face her, staring at that thing like it was a knife.

"Don't push me," she said cruelly, her eyes narrowing. And her hand flew up and smacked my face.

I turned a little, weathering the stinging shock of the slap.

"Yes, you'd better cower," she whispering.

"I'm not cowering, cutie," I answered. There came the slap again, amazingly hard, my face throbbing.

"Shall I whip you first, *really* whip you?"

I didn't answer her but I couldn't make my breathing quiet, couldn't stop my body from shuddering.

Then I felt her lips on my cheek, right where she had slapped it, her fingers stroking my neck, and a low, thumping feeling rolled through me, intensifying the sensation in my cock. Soft, silky kiss, and the knot in my penis doubled, and in my head something snapped.

"You love me, Elliott?"

Some protective membrane had been ruptured. My mind couldn't catch up with it. My eyes were wet.

"Open your eyes, and look at me," she said.

She had stepped up on the little stool, and she was only inches from me, and she held the double phallus in her left hand, while with her right she lifted the lace hem of her slip.

I saw her dark curly hair there, tiny curling wisps against the pink skin, and shy, delicate pubic lips, the kind that are almost demurely hidden by the hair. She lowered the phallus and pushed one end of it up and into herself, her whole body moving in a graceful undulation to receive it, the other end curving outwards, and toward me just exactly as if she were a woman with an erect cock.

The image was stunning: her delicate form and the gleaming cock rising so perfectly from the tangled curly hair, her face so seemingly fragile, her mouth so deeply rose red. I hardly saw her hands move, or reach up, until I felt her thumbs pressed into my underarms, her face very close to mine as she said, "Turn around."

I was making some soft angry and helpless noise. I couldn't move. Yet I was doing exactly what she said.

I felt the cock push against me, and I stiffened, pulling away.

"Stand still, Elliott," she whispered. "Don't make it a rape."

Then came that exquisite feeling of penetration, of being opened, that gorgeous violation as the oiled cock went in.

Too gentle, too delicious, up to the hilt, and then rocking back and forth, and a low buzzing pleasure coursing through all my limbs from that one heated little mouth. God, if she had only rammed it, made it a damned rape. No, she was fucking me. Which was even worse. She worked it like it was part of her, the soft rubber scrotum warm against me, just like her hot naked belly and her hot little thighs.

My legs had spread out. There was that overpowering sensation of being filled, being skewered, and yet that rich, exquisite friction. I hated her. And I was loving it. I couldn't stop it.

Her arms went round me, her breasts against my back, her fingers finding my nipples again and pressing them hard.

"I loathe you," I whispered, "you little bitch."

"Sure you do, Elliott," she whispered back.

She knew where she was driving it, rocking it. I was going to come, jerk right into the air. I was saying all kinds of little curses under my breath. Harder, she pushed, moving me forward, slapping me a little with her hips, then faster, ramming me, her fingers stretching my nipples, her lips open and sucking on the back of my neck.

It was building, and building, and I was making low, stuttering sounds, thinking she can't come like this, against me, with me not coming, and the thrusts started slamming me, almost knocking me off balance. And then she went rigid with a pure woman-in-ecstasy cry. The heat of her breasts beat like a heart against me, her hair falling over my shoulder, her hands holding tight to me as if she'd fall if she let go.

I stood paralyzed with desire and rage. I was locked out of her, and she was inside me. But abruptly, I felt the phallus slip out with a kind of searing sensation, and the soft, hot weight of her body move away.

But she was still very close to me. And unexpectedly, I felt her hands on the leather cuffs above. She unbuckled the cuffs, and released my wrists and laid my hands down at my sides.

I glanced over my shoulder. She had backed away from me. And when I turned I saw her standing at the foot of the bed. She didn't have the phallus in her anymore. Just that little slip barely covering her sex. Her face was rosy and her eyes glittering against all the whiteness. And her hair was a beautiful mess.

I could feel myself ripping off the little slip, pulling the hair of her head back with my left hand . . .

She turned her back to me, one strap of the little slip falling down over her shoulder, and parting the light cotton bed curtains, she climbed on the bed so that I saw her naked bottom and her tiny pink vaginal lips. Then she turned towards me, drawing her knees to one side almost demurely, her hair hanging down over her face, and she said, "Come here."

I was on her before I knew what I was doing.

I scooped her up in my right arm and lifted her up on the nest of pillows, and I drove into her instantly, impaling her, and slamming her as she had me.

The blood flush came over her face and neck instantly, the deceptive look on her face of tragedy, pain. Her arms flung out and she bounced against the mess of lace ruffles like a rag doll.

She was so tight, so wet and hot it astonished me, the sheath of convulsing flesh feeling almost virginal, driving me right up to the edge. I ripped at the slip, tore it over her head and threw it off the bed. And in some mad moment it seemed she had me again, this time with her glove-tight little vagina, and her naked belly and breasts sealed against me, and I was her prisoner, her slave. But I wasn't going to come until she came. I wasn't going to spend until I saw her shuddering and helpless, and I drew up, lifting her bottom with my left arm, lifting her and forcing her down on me, then slamming her under the full weight of my body, grabbing at her mouth with my mouth, kissing her, and making her face be still under mine. When I caught her like that, slamming her and kissing her, she exploded inside, the blood flush going dark, her heart stopping, full throttle into "the little death," her moans animalian, raw. And holding back nothing, I went on fucking her, spending into her, fucking her harder than I ever fucked anything or anyone—male or female, whore or hustler, or powerless phantom of the imagination—in my life.

PURE SEX

○○ ○○ ○○

SHARON OLDS

Sex Without Love _____

How do they do it, the ones who make love
without love? Beautiful as dancers,
gliding over each other like ice-skaters
over the ice, fingers hooked
inside each other's bodies, faces
red as steak, wine, wet as the
children at birth whose mothers are going to
give them away. How do they come to the
come to the   come to the   God   come to the
still waters, and not love
the one who came there with them, light
rising slowly as steam off their joined
skin? These are the true religious,
the purists, the pros, the ones who will not
accept a false Messiah, love the
priest instead of the God. They do not
mistake the lover for their own pleasure,
they are like great runners: they know they are alone
with the road surface, the cold, the wind,
the fit of their shoes, their over-all cardio-
vascular health—just factors, like the partner
in the bed, and not the truth, which is the
single body alone in the universe
against its own best time.

JULIA VOSE

Medusa _____

"You know how it rained in January, and the trees were just full of water, and then it froze, and some of them just burst open, and mostly all of their bark fell off, and of course the leaves are all over the ground. The eucalyptus trees are dead. I actually didn't know then, when I, in a particular thought, want it to be nice to go back there for another little go, but then I myself met nature, then, as now, and lay on the ground last year when there hadn't been a frost like that since before anyone planted the trees, and my smile was just a crooked stick too, and I actually thought when I went there, and took off my clothes, and lay on the ground this year when the water was seeping, actually rising up through the leaves when he pressed. I thought for a while we could just try it standing up, and I took off all my own clothes, and laid them aside, and lay in the seeping leaves, and pulled him down on me, I didn't know that all the roots weren't drinking, and the water was actually coming up, and this was on top of a mountain, and I lay down for him on the ground, and it was feeling all cool, and I spread my legs, and made my knees a cradle so that only the tips of his boots and the sides of his hands touched any of the ground. I tipped my hips up so that not even his balls should dredge the ground, and I was not afraid of one small bug, though I saw several before, falling on the ground, and we rocked and I moaned much, and this tricked him though I lay in the world and was just on it also, and he, and the sky, and his face looked like he hated about to crash!

"And then he sort of slid down to the end of the cradle, so that his knees did touch the ground and his face, a part of his true head, lay just below my breasts, and I brought my arms up around his head, so that my breasts and arms pressed this particular man's head in a circle, and I felt, over my heart, that I could let him know I feel my body, as it is, surround his head, to surround is alright, and even good to receive, but I guess the breeze just went up over the top of his pants that were bunched, and actually hobbling him. Wind went right up his leg hairs and smooth back and suddenly he was not covered. Suddenly he got up, and for a while I just displayed and displayed my cradle, for what it was with its surprisingly suddenly present on a pink surface with all its hunger, though it just be one of the doors. He made as he reared up to get up a tube with his two hands curled, and pretended to take my picture thus, and I got up and felt sick because Fuck the World!

and my instinct to complain. Clearly we walked away in shame after brushing as best we could all the wet dead leaves, and the sticky bits of last year's decayed leaves from my back and buttox and everything in my hair too for my head had writhed."

AUDRE LORDE

from: *Zami: A New Spelling of My Name* _____

Until the very moment that our naked bodies touched in that old brass bed that creaked in the insulated sunporch on Walker Road, I had no idea what I was doing there, nor what I wanted to do there. I had no idea what making love to another woman meant. I only knew, dimly, it was something I wanted to happen, and something that was different from anything I had ever done before.

I reached out and put an arm around Ginger, and through the scents of powder and soap and hand cream I could smell the rising flush of her own spicy heat. I took her into my arms, and she became precious beyond compare. I kissed her on her mouth, this time with no thought at all. My mouth moved to the little hollow beneath her ear.

Ginger's breath warmed my neck and started to quicken. My hands moved down over her round body, silky and fragrant, waiting. Uncertainty and doubt rolled away from the mouth of my wanting like a great stone, and my unsureness dissolved in the directing heat of my own frank and finally open desire.

Our bodies found the movements we needed to fit each other. Ginger's flesh was sweet and moist and firm as a winter pear. I felt her and tasted her deeply, my hands and my mouth and my whole body moved against her. Her flesh opened to me like a peony and the unfolding depths of her pleasure brought me back to her body over and over again throughout the night. The tender nook between her legs, moist and veiled with thick crispy dark hair.

I dove beneath her wetness, her fragrance, the silky insistence of her body's rhythms illuminating my own hungers. We rode each other's need. Her body answered the quest of my fingers my tongue my desire to know a woman, again and again, until she arced like a rainbow, and shaken, I slid back through our heat, coming to rest upon her thighs. I surfaced dizzy and blessed with her rich myrrh-taste in my mouth, in my throat, smeared over my face, and the loosening grip of her hands in my hair and the wordless sounds of her satisfaction lulling me like a song.

Once, as she cradled my head between her breasts, Ginger whispered, "I could tell you knew how," and the pleasure and satisfaction in her voice started my tides flowing again and I moved down against her once more, my body upon hers, ringing like a bell.

I never questioned where my knowledge of her body and her need came from. Loving Ginger that night was like coming home to a joy I was meant for, and I only wondered, silently, how I had not always known that it would be so.

Ginger moved in love like she laughed, openly and easily, and I moved with her, against her, within her, an ocean of brown warmth. Her sounds of delight and the deep shudders of relief that rolled through her body in the wake of my stroking fingers filled me with delight and a hunger for more of her. The sweetness of her body meeting and filling my mouth, my hands, wherever I touched, felt right and completing, as if I had been born to make love to this woman, and was remembering her body rather than learning it deeply for the first time.

In wonder, but without surprise, I lay finally quiet with my arms around Ginger. So this was what I had been so afraid of not doing properly. How ridiculous and far away those fears seemed now, as if loving were some task outside of myself, rather than simply reaching out and letting my own desire guide me. It was all so simple. I felt so good I smiled into the darkness. Ginger cuddled closer.

oo oo oo

OLGA BROUMAS

Tryst ──────────────────────────────

The human cunt, like the eye, dilates
with pleasure. And all that joy never named

now are priceless in the magnitude of the stars.
From are to are, have to have, beat subeternal.

By day, I found these on the beach, for you each
day and give. By night, remind me, I have

forgotten. Action replied by action, peace by peace.
Take you in all light and lull you on a sea

of flowers whose petals have mouths, mesmerized
centerfold, upsweep toward sleep.

oo oo oo

SUMMER BRENNER

from: *The Soft Room* _____

VINI

I'd love to tell you how it feels.

When it's riding you out to the sky, and your whole body is huddled in a point, and then it rockets away from you on waves. I guess something about the ocean says it best. The smell. The origin there. Conceived and then burst into a billion cells. I mean we have all been intimate with the deepest creative experience. We've all been born.

I think people who are lost. That's what they're most lost from. And sex. Well that is one of the simplest and most thrilling ways to get it back again.

Sometimes I think if I could make love once a week very awesomely, well that would really take care of it. But then when someone is around, I mean someone I love, then I want to do it a lot more. And then I think it's mostly for affection. Then the coming part is different. It's a level that can be thoroughly satisfying, but I don't have to have those stars. It's almost bureaucratic. If I don't *need* to come, I don't. Then there are some days when I wake up, and I know that at a certain second someone's going to touch me on the shoulder, and I'm going to quake. It definitely gets easier. It never happened at all with my first lover. There are those degrees. Where it's a certain kind of thing that doesn't shake the sides. And then the one that grabs you so hard and takes you all the way there. I believe it's really the easiest way to understand the state of grace. And then when the lover begins to hoot and holler because he knows you've got it, then that's the best. I've only met a few men who could really gauge a wave.

I decided I didn't care about making love with a lot of men because it takes so long to learn someone in that way. It always feels like such a big struggle, and then the best are always the ones you are going to love in manifold.

I used to be so afraid of being sexy. Now it really tickles me. I like to get to the part where I can wear a slip. It still takes me a while to get down. And I really only can with someone I like a lot. But then it's like the dance. And there's the step you do for yourself. And the step you do for your lover. And the step for the audience too. That's a push-up on white porcelain.

I guess certain people like certain things. I knew one who would

239

grab my hair just above the wedge and make like he was going to touch that in the triangle there. I loved the feeling of the tease. It wasn't technique. He was learning to play an instrument well.

Men say the biggest thrill is to make it good for a woman. I can see how they'd come to that. I'd really love to know what other people feel.

Kissing is my favorite part.

I like to stop before it all explodes. Just lying together and breathing together. Connected by a stick and a hole. If I concentrate on what the space in my sex is holding, I can feel like I have a penis. We used to laugh that it was like being both sexes at the same time. And it is.

Society definitely makes us shy. Women I mean. I bet those reports about women's sexual peaks at 30 have to do with it actually taking a decade to overcome a certain kind of timidity.

Last year I saw this man at a party. We weren't introduced but I found out his name. I thought about him passionately for three days. Then I called information and got his number. Called him up and casually invited him to meet me, explaining about the party we had been at together the weekend before. I was practically throwing up. But it was so instructive to realize what the social dating procedure feels like. He was busy and disinterested. After the phone call, it lost its significance for me. Except for the fat understanding of what men have to go through all the time. Meet a girl, make a date, get laid. It's terrifying. And obviously drives them to wanting to *get a little* as some compensation for the uneasiness of the situation. Consequently, a woman is expected to submissively ride alongside being sexually ignored and abused.

Until hopefully one day. She sees a clean sheet on the line with dry air blowing through it, and she decides that's the way she wants to feel.

oo oo oo
ROO BORSON

Lust _____

Certain dreams presage true events.
If a woman, for instance, in mid-life
dreams that from her own body,
attached and tingling, a penis buoys up
with such lust as has followed her all her days,
like a naughty, dangerous puppy,
always at the heels,
and should she dream then from the other side,
not of Lethe between life and death
but of another, unnamed river, then upon waking
her allegiances may be realigned
as utterly as the magnetic poles of the earth.

And should it, the next night, occur
that her lover, overtaken by lust as seldom before, require,
because the small-walled house is bright with invited strangers,
that they step out for a moment where the blackened woods
are tethered all around in the eye of the storm
which has not yet finished with them,
and that her garments be taken down under this new government
too about to fall, of stars unevenly revealed in the shaky coup,
then the Seven Sisters, the Pleiades, of whom there are truly eight
but the eighth is clairvoyant and sickly,
then the Seven Sisters look down upon this scene and are jealous.

And the third thing,
this light in the brain which is like the eighth Sister,
a shimmer, an urge, not to be lost but found, so strong
that the lazily unwilling fingers comply to write this down,
this third thing is like the eighth Sister or the persistently dimming
flashlight which ceased—and would always cease—
to shed sufficient light on what they were doing on their way to the
    woods.

LAURA CHESTER

Correspondence _____

I want you to be reading this, as I make love to your cock. I want you to be standing there, reading this, looking down at the top of my head, engaged in the act of loving you, maybe looking up myself, to smile through half-closed eyes, only to sink again, into the pleasure of mouthing you, and I can feel you getting harder, wanting to push it in a little bit deeper, and I am getting myself aroused, reaching up to touch from your chest, expanded, down with curving nails, to where I can hold the stalk, and lick the tip and kiss your tightening balls. I want you to be engaged inside my orifice. I want you to feel me feel the meat of your buttocks, as you plunge, withdraw and plunge, as you collect my hair and groan—I want it to be so good you want to free yourself in my mouth. I want you to fold this poem, as if you can't stand to stand uncertain anymore, but have to let it go, allow— And let the paper fall, just as I make (imaginary) love to you — Real in the mail.

CAMILLE ROY

Oct. 8 ──────────────────────────

Oct. 8, 1983

"I followed you. I think you're interesting." At her doorway I suddenly acquired my mother's clear bony pronunciation, an embarrassment. She took my shoulder, gently steered me into the house, and shut the door.

"I noticed you."

I followed her through a dark hall, though the rooms on either side seemed full of light. It led to a library, or living room. She seemed clear and unworried, picking up a few things, laying her coat over a chair. Her disdainful expression had shifted to amusement. I thought, I'm going to have to do most of the talking, felt fatigued. I leaned back cautiously on a brown velvet sofa.

"You caught us by surprise." This in a wry, but friendly, tone.

Writing this, a sharp sense of visibility decreasing. The literalness of my desire becomes disjoint, slides off from the target. All this breath between myself and the pleasure. You invited me in. The shock of that image disconnects me.

She became suddenly tense, but I knew I had only to let her know it was too late to get out from under it. Her caustic frown, the weary sliding away of her eyes made me pushy. When she asked, "Why are you here?" I was lighting a cigarette.

"I don't know, you asked me."

She shook her head irritably.

"Sorry. I get annoyed when I don't know what I'm doing."

I leaned back on the couch and put my feet on her coffee table. "Oh you know what you're doing."

She smiled sideways, a sharp smile of recognition not directed at me. "OK, sure." She swung around to the chair next to the couch. Sat down, leaned forward, and nudged my leg with her finger.

"So what's your name?"

"Tanya."

"Hah, like Patty Hearst."

Just as quickly she got up to pour drinks. For some reason this struck me as really funny and I smiled foolishly for a long time.

One thing I like about her is she makes me feel inexperienced. A relief. The room was warm, the books against the far wall seemed vague but secure in their built-in bookcases. Suddenly I wanted to talk for a long time, or else be very quiet on that soft brown couch, leaning back and studying the layer of whiskey in my glass.

When she came back she lifted my hair off my neck as if it were very heavy, gently grazed my neck with her lips, then her teeth.

The glass was in my hand.

She leaned against the back of the couch, looking serious, swirling the ice in her glass with her finger.

"How you doing? You ever done anything like this before?"

Have I ever—that's funny, I thought. "Yes," I said. The word felt weak, I sounded like a liar.

She shrugged and traced the outline of my lips with her finger, ran her hand down my throat.

"Whatever."

Leaning back, she draped her hand across her lap. That shift on her face I thought must be a smile, perhaps an ironic imitation. A sexual flare had followed her hand across my face, I wanted to cover myself. I thought of striking her, the interesting sparks off that hard, long life.

"Anything special I should know about?"

"No of course not."

It was a good time to get up and walk around the couch, get myself between her legs. But I seemed to move slowly, couldn't get used to the speed.

"No of course not," she said gently, mocking me. Hand on my shoulder, the slow approach was beginning to make me suffer. "We'll see."

October 9, 1983

Her mountainous perversity is like buckets of hair. Buckets of finally hair, at a time of night when I get my pronouns confused. It's the kind of image or scene you want to describe to your friends but it's so weird that no openings come up in regular conversation.

Overheard on the street:

Y: She's a sadomasochist. And that's a new one, I'm telling you. But what's appealing to me is that she's been doing it for so long that her style and attitude about it are completely immune to fashion.

X: . . .

Y: Very hot. But I mean she has a pure attitude. And a kind of macabre seriousness, that reminds me of that writer's party we went to.

October 10

Her hand on my shoulder, that first gesture of invitation, was so characteristic of her. Circular as a huge conscience, something to follow indefinitely. Her fingered goodbyes marked my body, a sexual technique. Even this story, its thin crust, marks her evasions.

So the room was either dark or light, or was two rooms. There were implements beyond my consciousness. Sharp cravings make narratives, also subjects. So it was easy to let her carve it, warble wobble. Only by turning on her with all my teeth bared could I regain ground already lost. Of course I did it. Of course yearning made it impossible. Pleasures of the rupture, rack and screw.

All over her, squall. Green rose wet, puff of smoke.

She had a collection of crops framed and under glass. Each one had a name under it: Lady Fastbuck, Mary Mountbatten. She said these were mementos of the days when she rode in steeplechases. "It is hard to do this," she said, kneading my breast in the rhythm of her breath.

My moment in the hallway: I wanted to sit on the French inlaid bureau under the crops and get fisted. Marks rise to the surface of my neck. She looks like her leather jacket is causing long prickly emotions down the back. The bedroom is a place to die I think, shiny and submissive death. Pulling her shirt off is attacking the decency of white cotton, is attaching myself via red lines I draw in her flesh.

She's pushing me towards the next room. I'm reluctant, want to say "SHUT UP," though she is silent. Instead I twist out of her grasp & lean against the window. Cool glass against my cheek and hardening nipples, then a grassy sloping garden. Her hands are on my hip bones, they slide down slow & firm as if following a groove. "Slow down," I say. "No." Her voice is calm and flat, then her teeth graze my neck. I laugh, breath fogs the glass. What slides up my cunt is a smooth genital pain, it unfolds. "Please baby," I say. "What?" I twist around to look at her face. A slight smile but her eyes are wide and full with desire. Slipping my arm beneath her shirt I run my lips along her jaw line. I whisper, "Fist me." Her hands tighten on my breasts, so hard they hurt. "Alright," she says, and leans back into the doorway, hips cocked.

Dropping item by item on the rug, I'm oddly comfortable with my body. "Display item." Content to sink into this wordless stomach she runs her fingers across. There's a curious sense of touching the thick carpet only with my heels, perfect rounds of skin. She is rubbing her crotch, she says "Let me see your tits."

If I'm going to abandon the real world, the one made up solely of dressed people, I want her to, also.

I drop the shirt for her, push my breasts together hard enough to feel their resistance.

Her hand disappears in my fur and I tighten my thighs around her leg to grasp it. Sliding down, riding her knuckles, the juices of my cunt crease her expensive pants. Hand on my shoulder, she looks down at the wet streak and laughs. I suddenly like her; this new affection streaks thru my body like aggression. I undo her hands and push them down; her clit is warm and wet under my tongue. She slides down the wall into a heap, leans her head to one side. "What do you think you're doing?" she says quizzically.

"Making advances," I say. She makes a little leap forward and we're rolling on the floor like dogs. Democratic cacophony. What orders the flow is a modulation of aggression, hers. Unlike bathing. She's not a sadist really, rather possessive. That's the deepest thickest point. Working this, I could draw out desire even when she's unwilling. I twist over guilty as a yawn (timid gesture). But she's grasping buttocks with both hands, hardly lingering. Bent over the edge of the body, lattice handiwork, the roseate palm smacking my tin flesh.

I'm getting rosier and rosier. There's no telling where we are. These large sensations come and go. I want to be a star, I want to be adorable. Instead the larger sensations, so open there is a sense of leveling. What is inside slips out and vanishes. So when I am finally on my back again and she fists me with her total possessiveness, I am wholly (not) there having left (come), fucked to heaven.

BERNADETTE MAYER

Work in Progress _____

First turn to me after a shower,
you come inside me sideways as always

in the morning you ask me to be on top of you,
then we take a nap, we're late for school

you arrive at night inspired and drunk,
there is no reason for our clothes

we take a bath and lie down facing each other,
then later we turn over, finally you come

we face each other and talk about childhood
as soon as I touch your penis I wind up coming

you stop by in the morning to say hello
we sit on the bed indian fashion not touching

in the middle of the night you come home
from a nightclub, we don't get past the bureau

next day it's the table, and after that the chair
because I want so much to sit you down & suck your cock

you ask me to hold your wrists, but then when I
touch your neck with both my hands you come

it's early morning and you decide to very quietly
come on my knee because of the children

you've been away at school for centuries, your girlfriend
has left you, you come four times before morning

you tell me you masturbated in the hotel before you came by
I don't believe it, I serve the lentil soup naked

I massage your feet to seduce you, you are reluctant,
my feet wind up at your neck and ankles

you try not to come too quickly
also, you dont want to have a baby

I stand up from the bath, you say turn around
and kiss the backs of my legs and my ass

you suck my cunt for a thousand years, you are weary
at last I remember my father's anger and I come

you have no patience and come right away
I get revenge and won't let you sleep all night

we make out for so long we can't remember how
we wound up hitting our heads against the wall

I lie on my stomach, you put one hand under me
and one hand over me and that way can love me

you appear without notice and with flowers
I fall for it and we become missionaries

you say you can only fuck me up the ass when you are drunk
so we try it sober in a room at the farm

we lie together one night, exhausted couplets
and don't make love. does this mean we've had enough?

watching t.v. we wonder if each other wants to
interrupt the plot; later I beg you to read to me

like the Chinese we count 81 thrusts
then 9 more out loud till we both come

I come three times before you do
and then it seems you're mad and never will

it's only fair for a woman to come more
think of all the times they didn't care

oo oo oo

ANNE RAMPLING

from: *Exit to Eden* _____

ON THE LOOSE

By the time we landed, I was ready to murder somebody. I was also a little drunk. She wouldn't move out of that window seat next to the two creeps from Argentina, and I nearly tore the felt on the pool table playing eight ball with myself while the flight attendant, who looked good enough to rape, kept filling my glass.

La Poupée, a terrific surreal French movie that I used to love, starring a dead Czech actor whom I also used to love, kept blazing silently away, ignored by everybody, on the giant picture screen.

But as soon as we set foot outside the New Orleans airport (naturally it was raining, it is *always* raining in New Orleans), the two Argentinians vanished, and we were sliding *alone* into the back of a ludicrously enormous silver stretch limousine.

She sat smack in the middle of the gray velvet seat staring at the blank little television set in front of her, with her knees very close together, hugging my book like it was a teddy bear, and I put my arms around her and knocked off her hat.

"We're going to be at the hotel in twenty minutes, stop it," she said. She looked terrible and beautiful, I mean like somebody at a funeral looks terrible and beautiful.

"I don't want to stop it," I said, and I started kissing her, opening her mouth, my hands all over, feeling her through the velvet, through the thick seams of the pants and the heavy sleeves of the jacket, and then reaching inside and pulling open her vest.

She turned towards me, pressed her breasts against me and there came that fatal voltage, that annihilating heat. I was rising up, pulling her up and against me and then we went down together full length on the seat. I was tearing at her clothes, or just sort of pushing them and shoving them, trying not to really hurt them but to get them open and I got a real taste of how hard it is to get a man's shirt off a woman or to really feel a woman through a man's shirt.

"Stop," she said. She had pulled her mouth away and she turned to the side, her eyes shut, panting as if she had fallen down from running. I tried to lift up a little so as not to hurt her with my weight, and I kissed her cheekbone and her hair and her eyes.

"Kiss me, turn around, kiss me," I said, and then I forced her head towards me, and that current started again. I was going to come in my pants.

I sat up and kind of turned her around and she scrambled into the corner, her hair spilling out of the twist.

"Look what you did," she said under her breath, but it didn't mean anything.

"This is like fucking high school, goddamn it," I said.

I looked out at the sagging, delapidated Louisiana landscape, the vines covering the telephone wires, the broken-down motels melting into the grass, the rusted fast food stands. Every emblem of modern America looked like a missionary outpost here, a piece of junk left over from a colonization attempt that had failed over and over again.

But we were almost into the city proper, and I love the city proper. She had her brush out of the overnight bag. And she whipped at her hair, her face flushed, the pins flying out as she brushed her hair free. I loved seeing it come down like a shadow enfolding her.

I grabbed her and started kissing her again, and this time she backed up, pulling me with her, and it seemed we were circumnavigating the whole car for a few minutes, me kissing her and kissing her, and just eating the inside of her mouth.

She kissed like no woman I'd ever kissed. I couldn't figure out exactly what it was. She kissed like she'd just discovered it or something, like she'd fallen from another planet where they never did it, and when she shut her eyes and let me kiss her neck, I had to stop again.

"I feel like I want to tear you to pieces," I said clenching my teeth, "I want to just break you into pieces, I want to just get inside."

"Yes," she said. But she was trying to button her shirt and her vest.

We were lumbering along Tulane Avenue in that silent unreal way limousines travel, like they are tunneling unseen through the outside world. And at Jeff Davis, we turned left, heading for the Quarter more than likely, and I grabbed her again, gauging, well, at least another delicious dozen kisses, and when she pulled away this time, we were in those narrow claustrophobic little streets of row houses, heading towards the heart of the old town.

○○　○○　○○

MAUREEN OWEN

Urban Cowboy Hat ————————————————

for Harvey

Side street   in the French Quarter   through
the Spanish grillwork   of a dancehall bar
I saw a girl on the bucking machine   Lick
her own tit!   I admire that   Myself
I never could quite reach   I always
figured probably my tongue is
abnormally short . . . .

oo oo oo

TONI MORRISON

from: *Song of Solomon* _____

"You ought to have a rest before you go trottin off any-where," Omar said, looking at him. "There's a nice lady up the road a ways. She'd be proud to take you in." The look in his eyes was unmistakable. "Pretty woman too. Real pretty." Vernell grunted and Milkman smiled. Hope she's got a gun, he thought.

She didn't, but she had indoor plumbing and her smile was just like her name, Sweet, as she nodded her head to Milkman's query about whether he could take a bath. The tub was the newest feature in the tiny shotgun house and Milkman sank gratefully into the steaming water. Sweet brought him soap and a boar's-bristle brush and knelt to bathe him. What she did for his sore feet, his cut face, his back, his neck, his thighs, and the palms of his hands was so delicious he couldn't imagine that the lovemaking to follow would be anything but anticlimactic. If this bath and this woman, he thought, are all that come out of this trip, I will rest easy and do my duty to God, country, and the Brotherhood of Elks for the rest of my life. I will walk hot coals with a quart of kerosene in my hand for this. I will walk every railroad tie from here to Cheyenne and back for this. But when the lovemaking came, he decided he would crawl.

Afterward he offered to bathe her. She said he couldn't because the tank was small and there wasn't enough water for another hot bath.

"Then let me give you a cool one," he said. He soaped and rubbed her until her skin squeaked and glistened like onyx. She put salve on his face. He washed her hair. She sprinkled talcum on his feet. He straddled her behind and massaged her back. She put witch hazel on his swollen neck. He made up the bed. She gave him gumbo to eat. He washed the dishes. She washed his clothes and hung them out to dry. He scoured her tub. She ironed his shirt and pants. He gave her fifty dollars. She kissed his mouth. He touched her face. She said please come back. He said I'll see you tonight.

MIRIAM SAGAN

Erotica _____

There is a story I've been haunted by for a long time, not a story, maybe, but an image that turns into a story. It's about sex, so I'll hesitate, hold back a little.

It's just something that my friend Michael once told me while we were eating red hot Szechuan green beans at that Chinese restaurant across from the Neon Chicken in San Francisco. Michael and I were never lovers, we never wanted to be lovers, we were never going to be lovers, and so we used each other as resources, as spies in the mysterious camps of love. We ran across enemy lines in the dark and when we returned, tired but intact, we told each other everything.

The thing that Michael told me was simple. He said that once when he was riding on a Greyhound bus he saw a woman stroke the fur collar of her coat in such a way that he wanted to make love to her then and there. He said he wanted to pass her a note saying that he loved the way she stroked that fur collar. And perhaps he thought of himself as a substitute fur collar, his curly head or his pubic hair being gently stroked by that unknown hand.

But if this were my story it wouldn't be a bus, it would be a train. Buses smell of piss and disinfectant and sandwiches wrapped in wax paper and cheap clothes and sleep. I know. I once took the bus from Albuquerque to San Francisco. But trains smell of plush and overripe fruit and coffee and the cold night of all the country between here and Chicago—and for this reason trains are sexy and buses are not. Plus, buses don't have enough privacy.

Of course one of the most shocking stories I ever heard was told to me by my now ex-lover Larry—Larry who was a friend of Michael's. Once Larry was on a Greyhound bus—apparently these men did nothing but ride across country—and it was night, the darkened bus rolled through acres of unseeable wheat and corn. And somehow—and as this was Larry's story he didn't have to fill in the details to satisfy me—he spotted this exotic looking woman across the aisle. And somehow, without words, or plot, or money, she came over to him, unzipped his fly, and climbed over him, hugging him with her thighs. The bus rolled on, babies whimpered, old women dreamed about Jesus, soldiers slept with their boots in the aisle, and this dark woman rocked over Larry, pressing his flesh in bone, until they both came together and she got off at the next stop, someplace unimaginable, Cheyenne, Wyoming.

I didn't want to believe Larry about that woman, her skirts, I could imagine her skirts—the denim one on top, then a red flannel one printed with small yellow stars, and then even further underneath, close to her long dark legs that were brushed with unshaven fur, a light white cotton voile petticoat with cut out lace, and then nothing at all, a fork, an opening, the womb like an upsidedown heart. What do I know. I wasn't there. I didn't slip between the two of them, that man who wore a white fedora, that woman. I only heard, long after flesh, after sperm, after the cold green reflection in the sealed windows. But I believed.

What I never believed was when people wouldn't make love to me. I mean even the cat, a red sweater, windchimes, purple sneakers. I think objects should make love to me. They might enjoy it. I think New Mexico should make love to me, and also Lodi, New Jersey, with its registry of Motor Vehicles. I think the war in Viet Nam should make love to me, also enchiladas. I want the past to make love to me because I've fallen out of the cities, like a stone falling out of the sky. I want the bar called the Saints to make love to me, where the most frightening women in the world play pool. And I want total strangers to make love to me on trains.

The woman unfolded the note that lay against the fur of her collar. She looked up—a tall man with dark eyes was watching her. In a leisurely manner she stood up, her black silk dress was from the forties—shoulder pads fit her narrow shoulders, the silk touched her large breasts, her wide hips, ended at her knees, where sheer black stockings appeared and slid down to her feet in a pair of red sling back pumps.

It's clothes that are erotic, more erotic than a plump woman sitting naked on a kitchen chair eating a muffin and spilling marmalade, although that is erotic too.

And now I am sitting in the train's observation car, a plastic dome above the silver swivel seats. I'm drinking pepsi cola and the bubbles catch in my nose. Outside it is snowing, steer are standing in the snow along the Mississippi, dark and patient. I'm glad I'm wearing my good wool cape, the ruby colored one with the torn satin lining. Gently I stroke the black velveteen collar, the buttons match, when the cape gets wet it smells like my mother did in the fifties.

A man comes down the aisle. Obviously it is you. You are wearing jeans with a heavy copper belt buckle and the two-headed snake bracelet I gave you. I wanted this to be about sex but it isn't anymore, it's about love. I look at you, I know everything about you, how you are missing a vertebrae, how you have a BB pellet under scar tissue on your back, how you got your ear pierced, why you have a tattoo, where your thigh bone is broken in two places. I look at you. We don't do anything. We don't touch each others' fingers or kidneys or nipples or nostrils or toenails or navels or earlobes or hairlines or diaphragms or lips or lungs.

We sit together.

Outside it goes on snowing.

oo oo oo

LYN LIFSHIN

The Midwest is Full of Vibrators ⎯⎯⎯⎯⎯⎯

you don't see them right off,
kind of the way grass ripples
in the prairie and you know
something's moving and then
it stops and starts again

love in the flat lands
matters more   the sky is
so huge it swallows,
claustrophobic as a
giant diaphragm

in the midwest they
think the east is smirking.
I could curl up for years
in a drawer where those
vibrators are kept

under flannel   waiting
for a tongue to spin
me smooth take me out of
my razzle dazzle New York
clothes   somebody who

wouldn't say much
or talk fast and nervously
as I do   someone slow
and hypnotic as an
Indiana tornado

oo oo oo

JAYNE ANNE PHILLIPS

Stripper ———————————————————————

When I was fifteen back in Charleston, my cousin Phoebe taught me to strip. She was older than my mother but she had some body. When I watched her she'd laugh, say That's all right Honey sex is sex. It don't matter if you do it with monkeys. Yeah she said, You're white an dewy an tickin like a time bomb an now's the time to learn. With that long blond hair you can't lose. And don't you paint your face till you have to, every daddy wants his daughter. That's what she said. The older dancers wear makeup an love the floor, touchin themselves. The men get scared an cluster round, smokin like paper on a slow fire. Once in Laramie I was in one of those spotted motels after a show an a man's shadow fell across the window. I could smell him past the shade, hopeless an cracklin like a whip. He scared me, like I had a brother who wasn't right found a bullwhip in the shed. He used to take it out some days and come back with such a look on his face. I don't wanna know what they know. I went into the bathroom an stood in the fluorescent light. Those toilets have a white strip across em that you have to rip off. I left it on an sat down. I brushed my hair an counted. Counted till he walked away kickin gravel in the parkin lot. Now I'm feelin his shadow fall across stages in Denver an Cheyenne. I close my eyes an dance faster, like I used to dance blind an happy in Pop's closet. His suits hangin faceless on the racks with their big woolly arms empty. I play five clubs a week, $150 first place. I dance three sets each against five other girls. We pick jukebox songs while the owner does his gig on the mike. Now Marlene's gonna slip ya into a little darkness Let's get her up there with a big hand. The big hands clap an I walk the bar all shaven an smooth, rhinestoned velvet on my crotch. Don't ever show em a curly hair Phoebe told me. Angels don't have no curly hair. That's what she said. Beggin, they're starin up my white legs. That jukebox is cookin an they feel their fingers in me. Honey you know it ain't fair what you do Oh tell me why love is a lie jus like a ball an chain. Yeah I'm a white leather dream in a cowboy hat, a ranger with fringed breasts. Baby stick em up Baby don't touch Baby I'm a star an you are dyin. Better find a soft blond god to take you down. I got you Baby I got you Let go.

oo oo oo

MARY MACKEY

The Kama Sutra of Kindness: Position No. 2 ————————

should I greet you
as if
we had merely eaten
together one night
when the white birches
dripped wet
and lightning etched
black trees on your walls?

it is not love
I am asking

love comes from years
of breathing
skin to skin
tangled in each other's dreams
until each night
weaves another thread
in the same web
of blood and sleep

       and I have only
       passed through you quickly
       like light

       and you have only
       surrounded me suddenly
       like flame

the lake is cold
the snows are sudden
the wild cherry bends
and winter's a burden

       in your hand I feel
       spring burn in the bud.

oo oo oo

ERICA JONG

from: *Parachutes & Kisses* _____

Talk about the Zipless Fuck! Talk about the impossible fantasy come true! Bean took to bed as a duck to water, a polar bear to snow, a starving man to a hunk of mutton. You'd have thought— from the way he went at Isadora's body—that he'd been starved for female bodies his whole life, though clearly that was not the case. He was so hungry, so horny (yet so oddly pure in his hunger and horniness that she wanted to say, "There, there—nobody's going to take it away from you," but she refrained, out of fear of being flippant about his prodigious sexuality). Nor did he have any kind of hang-ups about taste or smell. It was clear that he relished smells, juices, sweat, blood. He dove into her muff with great exuberance, parted it, found the white string that dangled chastely there and pulled her Tampax triumphantly out with his teeth.

"Aha! A string!" he said between clenched teeth. He chewed on the Tampax lightly, savoring its taste, then tossed it to the floor and dove in again, tongue-first. He played lusty tunes on her clitoris, plunged a practiced finger into her snatch, and reached all the way in until he found, on the anterior wall, the sweetest spot. By rubbing her expertly there, while his tongue trilled on her clit and the other hand pressed down on her belly, he brought her swiftly to the most palpitating climax she'd ever known.

She tried to close her legs to rest a while, but he forced them apart (ignoring her protestations) and rammed his cock inside her. He rocked her from side to side, touching parts of her insides she could have sworn were untouched before; then he pulled back suddenly, and rammed it in again. Now he began to pound her mercilessly. Raising himself on his arms, he went at her cunt with his ferociously hard cock as if he meant to annihilate all trace of any previous lovers. "For Josh," he said, ramming it in, "for Bennett, for Brian, for all of them." He pounded her so hard that she was about to come again, but just at that moment, he pulled back saying, "Not yet, baby, not yet," forcibly turned her over, smacked her hard on her bottom, and plunged into her from behind. He drew her up on her knees, and fucked the daylights out of her while his fingers found her clit and she came and came and came, screaming and covering his cock, the sheets, the quilt, the pillows, with blackly red menstrual blood.

He was triumphant. The sheets were mad with blood. His face, his

259

cock, his belly ringed with it. He wore a mustache of blood, a beard of blood, war stripes of blood on his cheekbones; and she wore blood all over her belly.

She tried to eat him, to lick off her own blood, but he pushed her back, threw both her legs over one of his shoulders, and began to fuck her again with outrageous determination and spirit. She had never known anyone—except herself, perhaps—to give himself so wholly. Usually in sex, there is a part of the other that tries to hold back, seeking detachment, cynicism, judgment—anything rather than a complete fusion with the lover. But Bean had no such need of detachment; he was wholly unafraid of sex, wholly confident of his own manhood in a way that Isadora supposed must have vanished with the Vikings. His face bore the most intent expression: he would have killed himself by skidding into a tree if he couldn't fuck her, and now he fucked her as if fucking her were a matter of life and death.

Holding her legs aloft, pinning her ankles behind his ear, he fucked her wildly. She could not choose the position, nor control it. She could not lead with this dancing partner—but curiously enough this excited her more than ever and she came repeatedly in positions which she had previously thought were not propitious for her.

He chortled and laughed whenever she came. He could feel her orgasm squeezing his cock—so perfect was their fit.

"You're my fit, my mate," he said, eyes wild with delight. "Have another one on me."

He kneeled above her, brandishing his cock like a lethal weapon. It was very red, covered with her blood, and it had a tantalizing curve to it, almost a bend at midpoint.

"I want to fuck the daylights out of you," Bean said, plunging in again. "I want to obliterate all the other lovers, all the other husbands," he said, "I want to be your *man*," he said on the next plunge, "your *man*, your *man*, your *man*."

Isadora gasped as he plunged into her. She gasped with pleasure and astonishment. Bean's eyes were wild.

"You madman," she said. "You maniac."

"I haven't even *begun* to fuck you," he said, pulling out, rolling her over, and starting to smack her bottom again.

"What a beautiful ass you have—but not red enough. I'm going to make it red."

He smacked her until the whole room resounded with smacks, until her buttocks smarted and tingled and the fiery feeling seemed to pass to her cunt. Then he rolled her over again and whipped her pussy with his hard cock. Again he thrust his cock into her and then pulled it out.

Again he whipped her clit. He kept this up until she was begging for him to plunge in again.

"Not yet, baby, not yet," he said.

He lowered himself between her legs and started to eat her again, revolving his tongue on her clit, filling both cunt and ass with fingers.

"I'm going to stick one finger deep inside until I can feel all the dark of you," he said; then he went back to eating her.

She was wild with desire, fatigue, desire. She wanted to fight it, not to favor him with another orgasm. She had lost count of how many she'd had—but she was somehow sure that it was the next one which would bond her to him forever, which would finish her, finish her freedom. She was determined to hold back. She tried to think of Josh, of Kevin; she even tried to conjure up a headache—but it was in vain. She felt herself going over the shuddering edge into another orgasm, an orgasm which seemed to raise the *kundalini*, and which made her legs go into convulsions and her hands grip the back of his neck until he cried out in pain.

Then he mounted her again and fucked her with an intensity even greater than before. He turned his head to one side and his face became contorted as if in pain. He raised himself on his arms again and slid, glided, flew in and out of her body as if he were blasting off into space.

"Fly, darling, fly!" she said.

"Baby, baby, baby, baby," he screamed, as he thrust into her, coming like mad, his pelvis and thighs convulsing as he came and one artery pulsed hotly in his thigh. He collapsed on top of her.

"My darling," he said, rubbing her head and neck again. "My darling, darling, darling, darling, darling."

They lay for a while in each other's arms, astounded by the intensity of their own coupling, astounded by the third creature they had made with their two bodies.

"I knew you were trouble," Isadora said, "but I didn't know you were so *much* trouble." She felt like Venus with Adonis in her arms, like Ishtar with her young consort, like Cleopatra with Mark Antony. This was the primal erotic experience, she knew—a woman in all her ripeness, and a young man who had not yet begun to lose the juice of life.

SHARON OLDS

Greed and Aggression _____

Someone in Quaker meeting talks about greed and aggression
and I think of the way I lay the massive
weight of my body down on you
like a tiger lying down in gluttony and pleasure on the
elegant heavy body of the eland it eats,
the spiral horn pointing to the sky like heaven.
Ecstasy has been given to the tiger,
forced into its nature the way the
forcemeat is cranked down the throat of the held goose,
it cannot help it, hunger and the glory of
eating packed at the center of each
tiger cell, for the life of the tiger and the
making of new tigers, so there will
always be tigers on the earth, their stripes like
stripes of night and stripes of fire-light—
so if they had a God it would be striped,
burnt-gold and black, the way if
I had a God it would renew itself the
way you live and live while I take you as if
consuming you while you take me as if
consuming me, it would be a God of
love as complete satiety,
greed and fullness, aggression and fullness, the
way we once drank at the body of an animal
until we were so happy we could only
faint, our mouths running, into sleep.

THE YIELD

○○ ○○ ○○

CHRIS TYSH

from: *Pornē* _____

> In the morning one often feels
> the ocean's milky babbling
> should one venture to stand
> in the middle of the room
> a momentary astonishing pleasure
> I imagine for you
> knowing what you know
> about the sameness of senses
> in the resilient unending autonomous flesh
> of the word

oo oo oo

SUMMER BRENNER

from: *The Soft Room* ———————————————

FATA MORGANA

The senses are much more fickle than the heart. It is their generosity that makes us twist and dive to get at it again.

Baby, you know what I like.

Every reality greeted with the divination of the senses. Smell the coffee. Smell the squealing tires. Smell the cloakroom. Where you fell on a pile of coats and came. Smell the tomato's leaf. Smell your smell before you get your monthly bleed. Smell sweat.

Now see. What do you see. The car tracking the edge of the highway around a concrete curve. The smile. At the gas station the way some of them smile. The stacked tiles. The pitched roofs. The window in the eave. The curtain in the window. The light in the curtain. And behind a thousand veils. Winesburg, Ohio. Gunga Din. The big Big Dipper. Dip dip dipping.

Sense is the stuff of our human being. Sensual. Risqué. Dirty. Sweet sensual love. Dirty slut. Loves her own smell too much.

It is that face. Those brows. That voice. Those hands. That back. Those thighs. That neck. Those breasts. That tongue. Those teeth. That chest. Those feet. That fur. Those paws. That tail. That beak.

Phantasmagoria. The body. Stand. Walk. Lay. Hunch. We touch. We don't stop.

In Paris on the Metro. Through the glass your eyes bolted mine. Drawn. Airtight. Shut out. Train east. Train west. My stop *Rue de Sèvres*. Yours the *Dix-huitième*. The single second of explosion from one lit orb, mine, to the other, yours. Love travels the speed of light. Train gone. No more. I almost jumped out to catch one back to find you. What did you look like. Heart of my hearts. Who took my face and ate it. Then threw it back through the subway window. A lesser reflection of myself without you, my double darkness.

The French inspire such things.

And us. All of us. Us the billions of Chinese. The Pygmies. The Kiwanis. We have our inspirations too. From the smell of old cheese. From the ocean. From cats in heat. From pigeons. From the stuff between the toes. From fresh-squeezed juice. From the choices. From taupe and midnight blue. Clean jade. Venetian red. Chinese silk.

Chemicals have done a lot to change our faces. Television is plastic surgery.

Get it. I can eat this rug. And you too. You're so sweet, I can eat you up.
Now come to your senses.
LO AND BEHOLD.

oo oo oo

Vegetable love ⎯⎯⎯⎯⎯⎯⎯⎯⎯⎯⎯⎯⎯⎯⎯⎯

Outside gnarled rough black,
the shaggy radishes talk louder
and longer of earth than the red globes
or the white pricks; inside hot,
properly hot. I grew up
eating thin slices like rose windows
I would hold up to the light
then smear with schmaltz.
These black lumps keep in the earth
all winter; we pull them from straw
and snow to warm us.
Sometimes happy in bed I think
of black radishes, round, hefty,
full of juice and hot within,
just like our love.

oo oo oo

CAROLEE SCHNEEMANN
Daily Paradise _____

(to C.E.) 1975

I do not "crouch" I run free I do not "crouch" I run free
and I come in my cunt in my cunt on the cock of my lover from the
wall of men where I fall free fall high to his cock that is paradise his
face mine in his hands before the wall of men we built light exploding
in my cunt coming free in my lover

Not death in my garden a beige doe in the garden shines light of my
cunt shines over corn beans tomatoes potatoes chard turnips parsley
lettuce and rutabagas onions red beets root there in the furrows I turn

My body *is* me I do not "show" it as you wrote I am my body I do
not "show" my garden it grows free in audacity in snow rain sun my
body runs free

I do not "slime" I cream milk glitter honey draw deep melt to fuse
I pour in my lover he pours in me glittering we shine in cunt in cock

A raccoon rolls apples across this porch the woodpecker drills the
Black Locust daily squirrels in the walls scratch as we sleep flowers
bloom in this house light cuts each stone where we shine in my cunt
in his cock deep in me typing a letter cutting a film cooking a goose

I cannot accept your words those words oppress heavy heavy weights
stones in a sling which could fly free heavy weights anus for cunts
spiders for eyes the static Beech where I see Ivy spiralling on Elm I do
not split apart to bury the archaic skull in maternal cycle tenderly I
cannot accept the absence of levity light rising free as cunt embrace of
cock where paradise can be

I do not "slime" I moisten I butter and cream we lick and we drink
in the house built by women the fortress built by men a love of cunt
and cock fly free by the hands of my father lifted high his blue eyes of
my lover father the tree where I spiral dreamed father blue eyes in my
lover butter cream burn blood and salt paradise streams my father spread
wide to his hands perfect trust his grip cock cunt holy father holy lover
paradise flies free dishes cups curtains chairs wild hair opened thighs
cunt bread butter milk meat

oo oo oo

SHERRIL JAFFE

They Go There Forever _____

He was outside her house. He knocked on the door. She invited him in. He stood with his hat in his hand. She asked for it. He examined the room. It was a small outer chamber, somewhat formal in its appointment, elaborately decorated, high cornices and wainscotting. He began to grow warmer as the room grew familiar. He examined each corner. It grew larger and larger. He came to a doorway. Beyond this room was another room. He passed through the opening, following her inward. Beyond this room was another room. He followed her forward. They went inward together, deeper and deeper. Beyond this room was another room, both smaller and larger, more than familiar, and beyond this is another room. They go there forever.

oo oo oo

JANE HIRSHFIELD

Of Gravity & Angels _____

And suddenly, again,
I want the long road of your thigh
under my hand, your well-travelled thigh,
your salt-slicked & come-slicked thigh,
and I want the taste of you, slaking,
under my tongue (that place of riding desire,
my tongue) and I want
all the unnameable, soft, and yielding places,
belly & neck & the place wings would rise from
if we were angels,
and we are, and I want the rising regions of you
shoulder & cock & tongue & breathing &
suddenness of you
opening
all fontanel, all desire, the whole thing beginning
for the first time again, the first,
until I wonder then how is it
we even know which part we are,
even know the ground that lifts us, raucous,
out of ourselves,
as the rising sound of a summer dawn
when all of it joins in.

LAURA CHESTER

from: *In the Zone* ———————————————

Barely gone seems too long when I think of you and remember how you loved me our last afternoon. You wanted me to drop the bathrobe, didn't you, and lie face down on the bed? It was warm, like spring, and soft together kissing you, though I started to shake before the quaking broke through, then quiet with your heartbeat on top of me. Hard to rise from your arms, though the clock said go — How could I cry at departure. It was more like the pain of the implement withdrawing— Only then do you feel the wound. I was almost in gear, in the car, when you said, "Let's kiss some more on the sidewalk." Then you did say the words that make her-his, before you held me goodbye— Now the words fill my head. It just doesn't get much better than this, and baby, you've got to believe me. I drove home to doo-wop and oldies but goldies, eating the knish as if it were your fine hind end, sweet meat of man, my William. Being with you is being "in the zone," where all is on, stroke after stroke. You stoke me, boy, with fuel to give, fresh fire to live, last bliss to hear your voice on the recorder, and know I've got a bit of you to get me through. I'll stay in the zone where you left me, Bill. It will be some place to return to.

oo oo oo

CAROL BERGÉ

from: *Secrets, Gossip and Slander* _____

A FAMILIAR REUNION

There was a knock at his door. Who, at this hour? It must surely be midnight. Everyone who knew him was forewarned that he did not like to be disturbed after ten at night. John stood up, realized his fly was unzipped, zipped it, ran a hand through his hair and went to the door. He was actually completely surprised to see Rachel standing there. He'd managed to get into another train of thought so completely that he'd forgotten his own suspense over whether she would receive his letter and whether she'd respond to what was in it, and if so, how. Oh, he said, smiling dumbly or thinking of himself that way, Rachel, how nice to see you. Won't you come in. And waved his hand in a wide gesture toward the room back of him.

How can he act like that, he must be drunk, thought Rachel. As if he's surprised to see me. Ridiculous. God, the room is a mess! How can he live like this? It's only been a couple of weeks, and already he's gone downhill this much, it's a *pit*. I guess he doesn't see it. That must be it. Okay. Here goes. Hi, John, I was just passing by and thought I'd drop in, she heard herself saying. Then she betrayed the whole thing by giggling one of her famous giggles. He did that wide grin of his. You've been smoking grass, he said. You found me out, she said. But that's okay, she said, you've been doing brandy, where'd you get that Courvoisier, you finally decide to spend some money on yourself? Naturally not, John said, with as much reserve as he could muster. Warren and Eleanor gave it to me.

Nothing wrong if you had, said Rachel provocatively. Speaking of Eleanor and Warren, actually I came by to find out an answer, a loose end, I just remembered something you said a long time ago that you never finished, and I need to know the answer. And what might that be, pray tell? asked John. It was about Eleanor and Warren, said Rachel.

May I offer you a glass? Don't mind if I do, said Rachel, very chivalrous of you indeed. He crossed in front of her to get the other glass from the drainboard of the little sink, and as he did, she got a whiff of him. My God, he hadn't bathed in a week! Then she noticed he hadn't shaved either, at least not today. Right, he said, pouring for her, I haven't bathed in a while. Haven't seen the need to. Is that all right with you, or do you have something to say on the subject, Mistress

273

Rachel? Oh, no, that's not my business any more, she said. Never was, he snapped.

We're off and running, she thought. This is more like it. The pattern. Leave it to him to get us on an edge. You *could* go in and shower now, she said, feeding the anger. I see no reason to, he said. I could think of a reason, she said. *Could* you now! he said. I doubt that very much. You barge in here, disturbing my peace and tranquility, with your— Never mind that, Rachel said, either you're going to take a shower or you're not. Which is it going to be? Not, said John. This is my palace, humble as it may be, and you're a guest here, and I say what happens and when. Fine with me, said Rachel. I didn't really want you to anyway. I was just testing. You're such a little girl, still, said John, shut up and drink your drink.

For once, she did as he ordered. But then, along with the whiff of him, she had the vision of how his cock looked when he was ready to do her. And it was irresistible. How awful. Must be the grass. She looked at him as he sat formally opposite her and she felt the same overwhelming lust for him that she'd felt for so many months past. Exactly the same texture. Pure and—well, you couldn't call it exactly simple, but it sure was pure. She forced herself to look from his crotch to his hand on the glass and then to his eyes. He was smirking. He knew. The rotten son-of-a-bitch *knew*. This was no good. She would have to get out of here while the getting was good. A damn trap, was all he was.

Forget it, he said, turning the smirk into a smile and smoothing the leg of his corduroys in that familiar gesture. She noticed that the nails on his left hand were dirty. You might at least take a shower, she said. As I am or not at all, he said, with that smile still going. Ah, but this was fun, he thought. They still needed at least ten minutes' worth of conversation.

She got up and moved toward his chair. Put her hand on the back of his hand. Did you miss me? she asked. Don't ask stupid questions, he said sharply, and sit down. Well, either you did or you didn't, she said, I think if you did you wouldn't tell me anyway. He said nothing. Why'd you write me that letter? she asked. I didn't write it *to* you, he said, I just *gave* it to you. There's a difference. Haven't you learned anything yet? Well, if you didn't miss me, you must've been getting off alone, like before you met me, she said, not looking at him. Ah so? he said. And pray tell what makes you think I got off alone, as you put it, before we met? The girlie magazines, she said. You're only partly right, he said. You must surely know there are other attractive people in the Department besides yourself. I'd never thought of that, said Rachel. That's disgusting, she said, you're on someone else's case already and the body's hardly cold in the ground. Not exactly, said John, watching her squirm.

You won't answer me directly, any more than you ever have, said Rachel. No need, said John, the subject is not uppermost on my mind. Bullshit, said Rachel, you've always had that subject uppermost. No, said John, in the lowest-voiced version of his patronizing tone. Not at all. You've forgotten the *koan* on that subject. Refresh me, said Rachel, not that I could stop you. Surely, said John. The two monks who've sworn chastity are walking on the road; they come to a stream and there's a maiden looking distraught and wanting to cross the stream. The older monk picks her up and carries her across and puts her down on the other side. The monks walk on further together, alone. Finally, the younger monk bursts out, How could you do that? You know we've sworn a vow to never involve in any way with females, and you touched her, you carried her. True, true enough, said the older monk. But look: I left her back at the stream. You're still carrying her with you.

Are you saying you left me back at the stream? asked Rachel. Exactly, said John. What a pompous lie, said Rachel. If you had, you wouldn't have written that letter. You'll figure it out in time, said John. He saw he'd gotten to her. She always looked for instant gratification, as if any explanation from him would immediately give her the solution to the problem at hand. Let it sit, he said to her, don't come running over here in the middle of the night demanding explanations. There are none forthcoming. You'll find one by yourself presently.

Okay, she said, not giving up, if you won't tell me about the letter, perhaps you'll deign to finish about Eleanor and Warren. Weeellll, he said, warming up to begin another of his long-winded stories. Don't make it lengthy, she said, I remember the beginning of the story and for that matter the middle as well—all I need is the answer to the question about what did they do because they discovered he was allergic to her hair. Did they have to shave it off and does she wear a wig now?

No, nothing like that, he said, slipping into that smile again. It wasn't the hair on her head. I'll bet you didn't think of that one, did you. You mean, she said, it was her body hair? Pubic hair, to be exact, said John, delighting. Her skull hair had absolutely no effect on him, and, oddly enough, neither did the hair beneath her arms. It was her pubic hair caused the skin eruptions he was suffering from. So? she said. I mean, what does a married couple do when one is allergic to the other's pubic hair?

What would you do, said John. They gave up sex. Simple as that. Warren realized he'd had it up to here with her complaints about how he didn't do her right in bed, and that was his way of saying he'd had enough of the whole mess. So then what did he do? after all, they were youngish, weren't they? He went *else*-where, said John drily. Meaning other women? asked Rachel. Only partly, said John. Oh, migod, you mean he went to men, too? Not just any men, said John. He wasn't the type who'd go finding some piece of ass in any men's room or toilet facility. What then, said Rachel, hoping not to hear the answer. He went to his friends, John said gently. Meaning you for one? said Rachel. Yes, said John. For one.

She was quiet. He knew she was mulling that over. And experiencing confusion and revulsion. Are you bisexual? she finally asked. What does that mean? he asked slowly. If it means I would have sex with any friend, without noticing if it's a male or a female so long as there's an attraction, then of course I am. You should have learned that, the night we were with Pat and Arnie. Unfair, she said, bringing that up now. It's apropos, he said. Isn't it? So you needn't act shocked.

I'm not shocked, she said, but she knew she was. Seeing Warren in her mind's eye. Picturing him with John in sex. Who was the leader? she asked. I mean—I know what you mean, said John, and there's no answer to that one, either. The question doesn't apply. Oh, I see, said Rachel, not seeing, but feeling as if she had to act more sophisticated. Don't worry about it, said John. Did Eleanor know, asked Rachel. I suppose she must've, said John, wouldn't you think? after all, she isn't exactly dumb. The evidence was there. You mean he brought people home? Rachel asked. No, no, no, said John, of course not. I meant, since he no longer had sex with her, and Warren was a young and highly sexual animal, he had to be with *someone*, right? So I suppose she just assumed.

And here I went along thinking of you as so limited, said Rachel finally. Goes to show you, said John. I'd have thought you'd know better. But you always—you seemed to—What? said John. Prefer the traditional, when I was with you? Yes, said Rachel. There were reasons for that, said John. And don't push me on that one. Not now. You don't have the right to muck about in my personal business any more. Oh yes, I do, said Rachel. What makes you think so, said John. Because I'm here, said Rachel. Because you wrote me that letter—oh, okay, you didn't write it to me, maybe, or so you say, but you gave it to me. So that means we still have something to say to each other. Nobody sends a communication unless it intends to communicate.

You have to bring that up again, said John. Certainly, said Rachel. I'm here to confront you. Oh, so that's what it's called now? said John.

Don't be smart, said Rachel. We have nothing to discuss, said John. You mean you're going to ignore me? Not that either, said John. What then? said Rachel. This, said John, getting up and pulling at her until she was sitting in his lap, in his chair.

She did not object. It felt so familiar. I thought you left me back at the bridge, she said, turning to face his eyes. No way, said John, putting his mouth on hers. It was good. It had been a long time, he thought. That rich mouth of hers, not just the fullness of it but the juices of her. He wanted her tit, that right one, the tiny nipple of it. He turned her shirt aside and went for it. She wound her hand into his hair. They struggled and the chair was too small for them. She felt his cock against her buttock as they moved in the chair. Should we go to the bed? he said. Are you asking me? she said, slipping off his lap. Because if you're asking—No, I'm not asking, he said, pulling her along.

I knew it, she said, I knew it would be like this. He said nothing; his mouth was busy, doing her nipple, the right one, and then the left one, which she'd always said was just a tad more sensitive than the other (though he preferred the right one, for the look of it, it looked to him like the nose of a puppy, he used to tell her, when they were together back then, all those times), and then her belly. And the sweetness of her cunt, with its amber curls around the dark red of her vulval folds. And the delicious smell of her. He noticed that she was smelling of come. She'd had sex with her new lover, then, before coming here, and had not washed. He found that idea tremendously exciting. Bitch, he said, audacious bitch, you fucked him and then you came here to me! Right, said Rachel, and you, you fucked Warren, didn't you, and you never told me till tonight. Well, tell me now. Show me now. What did you do? Show me. You're the teacher—well, show me, Teacher.

It was marvelous. He turned her over, not roughly, and pinned her arms with his hands. Spread, he said to her, I'll let you go just long enough to spread. You're not going to—Yes, I am, he said, and you'll love it. But we've never—I've never—High time, then, said John. Now, while you're good and hungry. Or did you get all you wanted with David, earlier? No, no, she said, I want you, I do want you. Good, he muttered, as he wet her asshole with his spit. Rubbed her with his hand, quickly, so she'd feel more pleasure. He would not be rough, even now. There, he said, beginning to enter her, feeling her tense around him. Be easy, he said, let me in, if you don't fight me it will feel good. There. Now you move. Take me in.

She felt him entering and it was very good—quite arousing and wonderful. That feel of him, that smell of him, and it was them, together again, familiar, even while it was unfamiliar. She felt needy of this from him. With him. She heard him talking to her at her shoulder.

Take me in, he was saying, I won't move until you're ready. She arched back to him and felt him moving further in. He had his hand under her from the side and was beginning to stroke her mound. Good, she said, so good, it's good, do that, do all of it. Don't say that again or I'll come, he said, gasping, and I don't want to come yet, not just yet. She stopped saying it. He said: Good, good, and stroked in and out of her slowly with each saying of the word. And touching her clit a bit with each stroke. I can't stand it, she said, I'm going to come. Come, then, John said, smiling. As she did. Oh, my God, she said, I've never—I know, John said, holding her, resting against her side. I know. It's quite another thing, isn't it. Is it ever, she said.

After a minute or two, she kissed him. He had not expected that. He wanted it to be cool, or rather cold and hot, but not warm, not that affection from her. With the heat of sex between them there could be a barrier. The limitation he needed. He could hold his grief to himself. But then she kissed him, and he began to weep. Aaaahh, aaaahhh, and turned his head aside. She took his head onto her shoulder and held him while he wept. You miss me, you do miss me, don't you, ah, John, dear John, why couldn't you have told me, you couldn't, you never did. Sweetie, why couldn't you have told me, something, anything—

He turned her to him then. I need you, he said, clearly. Maybe not to her eyes, since the room was in dim light from the one bulb lit in the lamp at the other end of the room. But it was clear and it was a statement. You mean you want me again? asked Rachel. That, too, said John. So she understood. He got up and went inside to wash and then returned to her quickly. And in the other way, their familiar way, began to make love with her. Slowly and with infinite delight. It was a wider space than they had known in their earlier time together. To him, it felt as if the two of them were moving down a river, swimming together in some vast river. Sometimes against the current; after all, that was part of their pleasure and pattern. Oh, he said to her at one point, you are such a great beauty. And she to him, I've missed you so, I didn't know that, I didn't want to remember. Ah, lady, he said, how could you forget this! It's what the rest is for.

They lay together afterward. Rachel was confounded. Usually, he would resist falling asleep, but tonight, he was asleep wholly, his head on her arm, minutes after he slipped out of her and onto his side. She didn't know what to do. Not disconnected totally from reality—David would be back by now—how could she explain—she would have to explain. Could she. How could this be explained. It was not to be written off as casual.

She didn't want to move. She had to go home, she was the one this time who felt compelled to leave. She was remembering how many times he had left her, when she'd wanted him to stay with her, sleep next to her. He was so peaceful. She turned and looked at him. He was not beautiful when asleep: all the tension and vivacity that held the flesh stretched over those elegant bones was softened. He was fully his age when he slept. But he was still John, and therefore totally beautiful somehow to her, as he had always been. The long, lean look of him. He didn't sprawl, even in sleep; he was his own original metonymy, container of the thing contained, the soul having shaped the form that held it, to this extent, this exactness. John, she thought, John, I can't leave you. Not this way and not that.

She slipped out of the side of the bed, out from under his massive head, with its weight of ideas and dreams, temper and arrogance. Stood naked next to the bed and looked at him again. This man she knew. Bad and good, she *knew* him. She remembered what he had said. Finally. He needed her and he had said so. The question was whether or not to trust him. He could renege, he could twist it so as to make it seem he'd never said it, if he decided it was a sign of weakness or in the event she would use his vulnerability, take advantage of his openness.

As she watched him and thought about it, he woke and looked up at her. Don't think it for a moment, he said. Don't even think it. If you walk out that door now, that's it. His eyes narrowed to slits as he said it. They understood each other perfectly, once again. The balance of power was on a fulcrum. She didn't hesitate. He had given that much. She pivoted and came back into the bed with him. They both slept.

Some time during the night, toward dawn, she woke, feeling totally at peace. He was asleep, and he was turned toward her. She was almost asleep again when she heard him say, again quite clearly: You can have both. Take your time.

oo oo oo

AI

Twenty-Year Marriage ——————————

You keep me waiting in a truck
with its one good wheel stuck in the ditch,
while you piss against the south side of a tree.
Hurry. I've got nothing on under my skirt tonight.
That still excites you, but this pickup has no windows
and the seat, one fake leather thigh,
pressed close to mine is cold.
I'm the same size, shape, make as twenty years ago,
but get inside me, start the engine;
you'll have the strength, the will to move.
I'll pull, you push, we'll tear each other in half.
Come on, baby, lay me down on my back.
Pretend you don't owe me a thing
and maybe we'll roll out of here,
leaving the past stacked up behind us;
old newspapers nobody's ever got to read again.

○○ ○○ ○○
AI

Reunions with a Ghost _____

for Jim Davis

The first night God created was too weak,
it fell down on its back,
a woman in a cobalt blue dress.
I was that woman and I didn't die.
I lived for you,
but you don't care. You're drunk again,
turned inward as always.
Nobody has trouble like I do, you tell me,
unzipping your pants
to show me the scar on your thigh,
where the train sliced into you
when you were ten.
You talk about it with wonder and self-contempt,
because you didn't die
and you think you deserved to.
When I kneel to touch it,
you just stand there
with your eyes closed,
your pants and underwear bunched at your ankles.
I slide my hand up your thigh
to the scar and you shiver
and grab me by the hair.
We kiss, we sink to the floor,
but we never touch it,
we just go on and on tumbling through space
like two bits of stardust that shed no light,
until it's finished
our descent, our falling in place.
We sit up. Nothing's different, nothing.
Is it love, is it friendship
that pins us down,
until we give in,
then rise defeated once more
to reenter the sanctuary of our separate lives?
Sober now, you dress,
then sit watching me

go through the motions of reconstruction—
reddening cheeks, eyeshadowing eyelids,
sticking bobby pins here and there.
We kiss outside
and you walk off, arm in arm with your demon.
So I've come through the ordeal of loving once again,
sane, whole, wise, I think as I watch you
and when you turn back, I see in your eyes
acceptance, resignation,
certainty that we must collide from time to time.
Yes. Yes, I meant goodbye when I said it.

○○ ○○ ○○

DEENA METZGER

from: *The Woman Who Slept with Men to Take the War Out of Them* _____

THE LOVER. You were telling me a story . . .
THE WOMAN. About the mermaid.

She smooths his skin running her hands down his hips onto his thighs, avoiding the center of his belly and his groin, smoothing down the skin turning opalescent under her fingers, the scales forming where she strokes him—thin, delicate armor, sharp, transparent petals, layered one on the other. The water follows her unimpeded, the scales directing the rivulets toward deepening pools. His feet join at the ankles, the toes thin and spread. The bones dissolve. Fins or seaweed emerge where his feet were. The bed is water. They absorb the common motion of the currents. Wherever she touches him, he alters. "I have always dreamed you this way," she says.

And at the waist, her flesh midriff against his chest, still flesh, her breasts against his nipples, their mouths make the fish, her hair carried damply across his face, the sweat is cool as sea water, they thrash about each other. Her skin glistens and his hands follow the light but that her tail slashes and the spray covers them. He enters where he can enter. Her mouth like the whale opens for what small fish will winnow through her teeth. When the jaw clenches behind, the probing finger can open it, and he jumps into the cavernous body across the pink ribs and into the salt-reeking dark among the smooth creatures, the odor of surf, shells pounded to sand by the thunderous ocean tail, the open bones, plankton, sea horses, jelly fish, all the transparent wonders are there. He holds her fingers up to the light to see the blood in her. Kelp winding itself about her body is the snake which holds her, the smooth rope which ties her, the live girdle encircling her, which turns her to the creatures which move in the dark. Ink to close her eyes and more hands than she can count.

Now he bridles her. The little pods of kelp break in her mouth. The cold tails beat in the water and the white foam passes the seeds through their water bodies. "I dream you this way," she whispers, her eyes opening from under the tide.

"I would be a moray eel," he answers. "I am so voracious."

"And your colors, what colors are you?"

He puts his fingers on her eyes and closes them. "Can you see," he strokes her, "the colors only the dark knows?" He slides into her, one fish opening its mouth and the other entering, this constant devouring; he is whole within her and yet he holds her. The beating tails keep them afloat; she extends to the shape he assumes, the tails flutter, and the spindrift catches them, tossing them whitely.

"You are more ravenous than I." Still he emerges unmarred. The tide pools are gentle. The anemones close or open to the sun.

MAY SWENSON

Poet to Tiger _____

The Hair
You went downstairs
saw a hair in the sink
and squeezed my toothpaste by the neck.
You roared. My ribs are sore.
This morning even my pencil's got your toothmarks.
Big Cat Eye cocked on me you see bird bones.
Snuggled in the rug of your belly
your breath so warm
I smell delicious fear.
Come breathe on me rough pard
put soft paws here.

The Salt
You don't put salt on anything
so I'm eating without.
Honey on the eggs is all right
mustard on the toast.
I'm not complaining I'm saying I'm
living with *you.*
You like your meat raw
don't care if it's cold.
Your stomach must have tastebuds
you swallow so fast.
Night falls early. It's foggy. Just now

I found another of your bite marks in the cheese.
I'm hungry. Please
come bounding home
I'll hand you the wine to open
with your teeth.
Scorch me a steak unsalted
boil my coffee twice

say the blessing to a jingle on the blue TV.
Under the lap robe on our chilly couch
look behind my ears "for welps"
and hug me.

The Sand
You're right I brought a grain
or two of sand
into bed I guess in my socks.
But it was you pushed them off
along with everything else.

Asleep you flip
over roll
everything under
you and off
me. I'm always grabbing
for my share of the sheets.

Or else you wake me every hour with sudden
growled I-love-yous
trapping my face between those plushy
shoulders. All my float-dreams turn spins
and never finish. I'm thinner
now. My watch keeps running fast.
But best is when we're riding pillion
my hips within your lap. You let me steer.
Your hand and arm go clear
around my ribs your moist
dream teeth fastened on my nape.

A grain of salt in the bed upsets you or
a hair on the floor.
But you'll get
in slick and wet from the shower if I let
you. Or with your wool cap
and skiing jacket on
if it's cold.
Tiger don't scold me
don't make me comb my hair outdoors.
Cuff me careful. Lick don't
crunch. Make last what's yours.

The Dream
You get into the tub holding *The Naked Ape*
in your teeth. You wet that blond
three-cornered pelt lie back wide
chest afloat. You're reading

in the rising steam and I'm
drinking coffee from your tiger cup.
You say you dreamed
I had your baby book
and it was pink and blue.
I pointed to a page and there
was your face with a cub grin.

You put your paws in your armpits
make a tiger-moo.
Then you say: "Come here
Poet and take
this hair
off me." I do.
It's one of mine. I carefully
kill it and carry
it outside. And stamp on it
and bury it.

In the begonia bed.
And then take off my shoes
not to bring a grain
of sand in to get
into our bed.
I'm going to
do the cooking
now instead
of you.
And sneak some salt in
when you're not looking.

MARILYN HACKER

Languedocienne _____

This morning the wind came, shaking the quince tree,
making trouble in the chicken-yard.

The attic door blew open, windows slammed their casements,
notebooks and envelopes slid off my work-table.

A poplar separating vineyards whispered over
olive and lavender cotton, two shades of summer brown.

Wind makes my head ache. I long for water
surfaces, light on four different river-banks,

silver trembling on the edge, a waterfall
come up inside me as I come down to you.

Early to the train station; slow bus back through Monday-shuttered
    towns;
apricots under the poplar, wind in the quince tree.

TONI CADE BAMBARA

My Man Bovanne ⸻⸻⸻⸻⸻⸻⸻

Blind people got a hummin jones if you notice. Which is understandable completely once you been around one and notice what no eyes will force you into to see people, and you get past the first time, which seems to come out of nowhere, and it's like you in church again with fat-chest ladies and old gents gruntin a hum low in the throat to whatever the preacher be saying. Shakey Bee bottom lip all swole up with Sweet Peach and me explainin how come the sweet-potato bread was a dollar-quarter this time stead of dollar regular and he say uh hunh he understand, then he break into this *thizzin* kind of hum which is quiet, but fiercesome just the same, if you ain't ready for it. Which I wasn't. But I got used to it and the onliest time I had to say somethin bout it was when he was playin checkers on the stoop one time and he commenst to hummin quite churchy seem to me. So I says, "Look here Shakey Bee, I can't beat you and Jesus too." He stop.

So that's how come I asked My Man Bovanne to dance. He ain't my man mind you, just a nice ole gent from the block that we all know cause he fixes things and the kids like him. Or used to fore Black Power got hold their minds and mess em around till they can't be civil to ole folks. So we at this benefit for my niece's cousin who's runnin for somethin with this Black party somethin or other behind her. And I press up close to dance with Bovanne who blind and I'm hummin and he hummin, chest to chest like talkin. Not jammin my breasts into the man. Wasn't bout tits. Was bout vibrations. And he dug it and asked me what color dress I had on and how my hair was fixed and how I was doin without a man, not nosy but nice-like, and who was at this affair and was the canapés dainty-stingy or healthy enough to get hold of proper. Comfy and cheery is what I'm tryin to get across. Touch talkin like the heel of the hand on the tambourine or on a drum.

But right away Joe Lee come up on us and frown for dancin so close to the man. My own son who knows what kind of warm I am about; and don't grown men call me long distance and in the middle of the night for a little Mama comfort? But he frown. Which ain't right since Bovanne can't see and defend himself. Just a nice old man who fixes toasters and busted irons and bicycles and things and changes the lock on my door when my men friends get messy. Nice man. Which is not why they invited him. Grass roots you see. Me and Sister Taylor and the woman who does heads at Mamies and the man from the barber shop, we all there on account of we grass roots. And I ain't never been souther than Brooklyn Battery and no more country than the window box on my fire escape. And just yesterday my kids tellin me to take them countrified rags off my head and be cool. And now can't get Black enough to suit em. So everybody passin sayin My Man Bovanne. Big deal, keep steppin and don't even stop a minute to get the man a drink or one of them cute sandwiches or tell him what's goin on. And him standin there with a smile ready case someone do speak he want to be ready. So that's how come I pull him on the dance floor and we dance squeezin past the tables and chairs and all them coats and people standin round up in each other face talkin bout this and that but got no use for this blind man who mostly fixed skates and scooters for all these folks when they was just kids. So I'm pressed up close and we touch talkin with the hum. And here come my daughter cuttin her eye at me like she do when she tell me about my "apolitical" self like I got hoof and mouf disease and there ain't no hope at all. And I don't pay her no mind and just look up in Bovanne shadow face and tell him his stomach like a drum and he laugh. Laugh real loud. And here come my youngest, Task, with a tap on my elbow like he the third grade monitor and I'm cuttin up on the line to assembly.

"I was just talkin on the drums," I explained when they hauled me into the kitchen. I figured drums was my best defense. They can get ready for drums what with all this heritage business. And Bovanne stomach just like that drum Task give me when he come back from Africa. You just touch it and it hum thizzm, thizzm. So I stuck to the drum story. "Just drummin that's all."

"Mama, what are you talkin about?"

"She had too much to drink," say Elo to Task cause she don't hardly say nuthin to me direct no more since that ugly argument about my wigs.

"Look here Mama," say Task, the gentle one. "We just tryin to pull your coat. You were makin a spectacle of yourself out there dancing like that."

"Dancin like what?"

Task run a hand over his left ear like his father for the world and his father before that.

"Like a bitch in heat," say Elo.

"Well uhh, I was going to say like one of them sex-starved ladies gettin on in years and not too discriminating. Know what I mean?"

I don't answer cause I'll cry. Terrible thing when your own children talk to you like that. Pullin me out the party and hustlin me into some stranger's kitchen in the back of a bar just like the damn police. And ain't like I'm old old. I can still wear me some sleeveless dresses with-

DEEP DOWN · · ·

out the meat hangin off my arm. And I keep up with some thangs through my kids. Who ain't kids no more. To hear them tell it. So I don't say nuthin.

"Dancin with that tom," say Elo to Joe Lee, who leanin on the folks' freezer. "His feet can smell a cracker a mile away and go into their shuffle post haste. And them eyes. He could be a little considerate and put on some shades. Who wants to look into them blown-out fuses that—"

"Is this what they call the generation gap?" I say.

"Generation gap," spits Elo, like I suggested castor oil and fricassee possum in the milk-shakes or somethin. "That's a white concept for a white phenomenon. There's no generation gap among Black people. We are a col—"

"Yeh, well never mind," says Joe Lee. "The point is Mama . . . well, it's pride. You embarrass yourself and us too dancin like that."

"I wasn't shame." Then nobody say nuthin. Them standin there in they pretty clothes with drinks in they hands and gangin up on me, and me in the third-degree chair and nary a olive to my name. Felt just like the police got hold to me.

"First of all," Task say, holdin up his hand and tickin off the offenses, "the dress. Now that dress is too short, Mama, and too low-cut for a woman your age. And Tamu's going to make a speech tonight to kick off the campaign and will be introducin you and expecting you to organize the council of elders—"

"Me? Didn nobody ask me nuthin. You mean Nisi? She change her name?"

"Well, Norton was supposed to tell you about it. Nisi wants to introduce you and then encourage the older folks to form a Council of the Elders to act as an advisory—"

"And you going to be standing there with your boobs out and that wig on your head and that hem up to your ass. And people'll say, 'Ain't that the horny bitch that was grindin with the blind dude?' "

"Elo, be cool a minute," say Task, gettin to the next finger. "And then there's the drinkin. Mama, you know you can't drink cause next thing you know you be laughin loud and carryin on," and he grab another finger for the loudness. "And then there's the dancin. You been tattooed on the man for four records straight and slow draggin even on the fast numbers. How do you think that look for a woman your age?"

"What's my age?"

"What?"

"I'm axin you all a simple question. You keep talkin bout what's proper for a woman my age. How old am I anyhow?" And Joe Lee slams his eyes shut and squinches up his face to figure. And Task run a hand over his ear and stare into his glass like the ice cubes goin calculate for him. And Elo just starin at the top of my head like she goin rip the wig off any minute now.

"Is your hair braided up under that thing? If so, why don't you take it off? You always did do a neat cornroll."

"Uh huh," cause I'm thinkin how she couldn't undo her hair fast enough talking bout cornroll so countrified. None of which was the subject. "How old, I say?"

"Sixtee-one or—"

"You a damn lie Joe Lee Peoples."

"And that's another thing," say Task on the fingers.

"You know what you all can kiss," I say, gettin up and brushin the wrinkles out my lap.

"Oh, Mama," Elo say, puttin a hand on my shoulder like she hasn't done since she left home and the hand landin light and not sure it supposed to be there. Which hurt me to my heart. Cause this was the child in our happiness fore Mr. Peoples die. And I carried that child strapped to my chest till she was nearly two. We was close is what I'm tryin to tell you. Cause it was more me in the child than the others. And even after Task it was the girlchild I covered in the night and wept over for no reason at all less it was she was a chub-chub like me and not very pretty, but a warm child. And how did things get to this, that she can't put a sure hand on me and say Mama we love you and care about you and you entitled to enjoy yourself cause you a good woman?

"And then there's Reverend Trent," say Task, glancin from left to right like they hatchin a plot and just now lettin me in on it. "You were suppose to be talking with him tonight, Mama, about giving us his basement for campaign headquarters and—"

"Didn nobody tell me nuthin. If grass roots mean you kept in the dark I can't use it. I really can't. And Reven Trent a fool anyway the way he tore into the widow man up there on Edgecomb cause he wouldn't take in three of them foster children and the woman not even comfy in the ground yet and the man's mind messed up and—"

"Look here," say Task. "What we need is a family conference so we can get all this stuff cleared up and laid out on the table. In the meantime I think we better get back into the other room and tend to business. And in the meantime, Mama, see if you can't get to Reverend Trent and—"

"You want me to belly rub with the Reven, that it?"

"Oh damn," Elo say and go through the swingin door.

"We'll talk about all this at dinner. How's tomorrow night, Joe Lee?" While Joe Lee being self-important I'm wonderin who's doin the cookin and how come no body ax me if I'm free and do I get a corsage and things like that. Then Joe nod that it's O.K. and he go through the swingin door and just a little hubbub come through from the other room. Then Task smile his smile, lookin just like his daddy and he leave. And it just me in this stranger's kitchen, which was a mess I wouldn't never let my kitchen look like. Poison you just to look at the pots. Then the door swing the other way and it's My Man Bovanne standin there sayin Miss Hazel but lookin at the deep fry and then at the steam table, and most surprised when I come up on him from the other direction and take him on out of there. Pass the folks pushin up towards the stage where Nisi and some other people settin and ready to talk, and folks gettin to the last of the sandwiches and the booze fore they settle down in one spot and listen serious. And I'm thinkin bout tellin Bovanne what a lovely long dress Nisi got on and the earrings and her hair piled up in a cone and the people bout to hear how we all gettin screwed and gotta form our own party and everybody there listenin and lookin. But instead I just haul the man on out of there, and Joe Lee and his wife look at me like I'm terrible, but they ain't said boo to the man yet. Cause he blind and old and don't nobody there need him since they grown up and don't need they skates fixed no more.

"Where we goin, Miss Hazel?" Him knowin all the time.

"First we gonna buy you some dark sunglasses. Then you comin with me to the supermarket so I can pick up tomorrow's dinner, which is goin to be a grand thing proper and you invited. Then we goin to my house."

"That be fine. I surely would like to rest my feet." Bein cute, but you got to let men play out they little show, blind or not. So he chat on bout how tired he is and how he appreciate me takin him in hand this way. And I'm thinkin I'll have him change the lock on my door first thing. Then I'll give the man a nice warm bath with jasmine leaves in the water and a little Epsom salt on the sponge to do his back. And then a good rubdown with rose water and olive oil. Then a cup of lemon tea with a taste in it. And a little talcum, some of that fancy stuff Nisi mother sent over last Christmas. And then a massage, a good face massage round the forehead which is the worryin part. Cause you gots to take care of the older folks. And let them know they still needed to run the mimeo machine and keep the spark plugs clean and fix the mailboxes for folks who might help us get the breakfast program goin, and the school for the little kids and the campaign and all. Cause old folks is the nation. That what Nisi was sayin and I mean to do my part.

"I imagine you are a very pretty woman, Miss Hazel."

"I surely am," I say just like the hussy my daughter always say I was.

oo oo oo

SHERRIL JAFFE

Ann Lay Naked _____

Ann lay naked in the sun. There was nowhere she had to be, no one she had to pick up, nothing she had to prepare for or endure. No one knew where she was or waited for her irritably. That morning she and Ben had put Bobby on a plane to his mother and now Ben himself was gone forever. The sun was warm, warmer than hands, and the wind in the trees sang a story deeper than a human story. Here sky was blue, bluer than she'd ever seen it, happy blue.

Behind her the French doors opened into the empty house, and the breeze came in, and the house breathed deep. Ann had opened every door and window, and the breeze blew through, and blew the greyness through, and the doors banged as the house breathed, and out the doors all the sadness fluttered, and out the doors and windows all the empty sadness blew.

oo oo oo

GLORIA FRYM

The Yield _____

the sun moves south like a transient lover
it's the last frontier of the year

oh children of final floral sex acts!

the pink light of autumn woos the
mountains, seasonal plunge is
what we stay for, it's what
I grab for
like a starving profligate
and gobble and spill and still
want more

lust for the pollen's suckling!
greed for the color, the honey!
and I want Fall to
drip slowly from the spoon to the touch
and I want huge bowlfuls
to stash away deep in my own
womb house

the pool of light in the
cupboard, the secret ingredient,
the golden unhomogenized thickness
drawing us, keeping us sweetly
alive and kicking

GLORIA FRYM

Manifesto _____

When the yearn redoubles itself out of nothing
better to do and at midnight telegrams stop seeming
the only way to get the continuous present
to you and the rhyme sits upon the line
like the skin upon the apple and the metaphor
is the thing and the idea disappears,
the long wait for the great poem
will be over. And I'll be over in a little while
to confirm the beginning of a new poetics,
plenty of broken lines among the prosaic,
smooth lengthy generous long-legged lines,
short compact circular lines,
lines on top of lines, lines moving sideways
into each other, lines rolling all over each other,
onto the floor, all disaffection, all indifference
moved to the next line and seduced back to innocence
by a strange music whose beat
is my pulse. And I will stop insisting I know
and simply do the expert thing
which at every moment in time
is to free these lines for you.

○○ ○○ ○○

WANDA COLEMAN

and when his good love is done
a man is a low-down, a troublesome thing
he'll leave you to sing

The Blues in the Night _____

She hates to see that western sun go down. Summer's heat mingles with desire/a sullen sweat that clings—a glistening second umber skin. It's too tight. It's too hot. She feels that primal yearn.

Whooowheee.

She aches for seduction/his lips pressing in on hers. She aches to yield to his manful grasp working her back, her shoulders, her breasts. She can almost inhale that pungent musk opening her nose, obliterating all thought. She can almost feel the touch of him—skin-to-skin/more than naked, the total loss of self as she submits/becomes a mass of sensation freed of the world and its psychotic quest for the new and orderly.

She suffers a euphoric vision: she and he embraced/one, a precise orchestration of hands and tongues amove in fevered rhythm/writhings in that sacred expanse/possessed. He and she arching, reaching through one another—he and she beyond exaltation—*there.* And the trumpet sounds and the walls yield. Decrescendo—a honeyed sopping slide down . . . down . . . down. Surrendered.

Oh—to once more smell that fish-stink after sex. That holy odor of gorged lust.

The children sleep unmindful of Mama's tortured restlessness. At times they've seen her bemoaning that past. At times they've seen her bemoaning their uncertain present. Now they awaken and surprise her, stumbling from the dark to suddenly quell those moans and sobs. And in their hapless/helpless concern comes the confused and loving whine of *Mama what's wrong.* She answers through tears and shudders. *Mama is sad is all. Don't be worried. Everything will be all right.* She hugs them and kisses them and sends them back to their dreams.

What could she tell them? She didn't know their marriage wouldn't last. She didn't know the kind of man he'd become. She didn't know she'd grow apart and part from him finally. And she didn't know the price she'd have to pay and keep paying. She didn't know, then, what would be demanded in sacrifice—or what it would extract in exquisite anguish. She had no idea of the limits of her fortitude or the strength of her weaknesses. But now she's growing aware—beginning to discover the fierce gluttony of flesh freed of matrimony:

That complexity of blood, bone, gristle, muscle and fat . . . that fiery vessel of steamy rut. That awareness that exudes sensuality and sex merely by being—effortlessly. And when she adds her mind to it, when love comes down on her, that's the worst time. That explicit urge overtakes/damns her.

She sits quietly on the floor by the stereo. She goes through her record collection, a stroll down memory lane. She needs some of that soothe for the beastly savage aprowl in her veins tonight. Something to lull/ temper/arrest it. A ritual dance through lost loves. Recollected moments—the cherished and the shameful. The first dance at a sock hop. The first house party. Prom night and the hymen breaking. The night he and she merged and conceived. Any memory to cling to, to keep her anchored and sane. Anything to relieve her of this raving heat. Anything to retrieve equanimity.

She searches for the proper sound, the one to counteract this particular mood—perhaps exorcise it. And she decides on the 45s. Some raw funk: Bobby Blue Bland goin' down slow, Syl Johnson only havin' love to give, the stomp down bump and grind of Mama's baby Daddy's maybe Swamp Dogg, James Brown grieving oh Mary don't you weep, Al Green in love and happiness, the Impressions inviting love to paradise, 'Spoon spewing bad bad whiskey losin' him a happy home, Otis Redding making admonitions about Cupid (he's not stupid), or the wicked Mr. Pickett's Mustang Sally refusing to slow her Mustang down.

She rises. She lets the music possess her and she cuts free, going for all she knows. Her head is soaked and her hair goes all the way back to Africa. She bends, turns, spins until she's one with that sound. One pulse. One throb hip-quaking—a frenzy working her way through steps she knows as intimately as the scars on her psyche: the shimmy, the hully-gully, the stroll, the skate, the four corners, the sophisticated sissy, the fat man, the charge, the bugaloo, the break down. She walks a dog and she shakes her tail feather. She mother popscorn in bare feet. The sound consumes her and she speaks in tongues.

Collapsed to the floor, she lies there for how long? Until summoned by the scratch of the needle's bounce at the end of a track, as the automatic return fails to re-activate. She can barely hear it above her heart still dancing inside her. And she groans. She wails. She chants *have mercy have mercy on me*. The hurt remains. And it is grown deeper than before. Down to her soul's bone.

She draws her bath. She's so hot the warm water begins to sizzle and bubble as she sinks into the tub. She bathes thoroughly but hastily. She can no longer wait. Her mind fixed on what she's driven to enact. She dries off quickly and liberally applies creams and potions to dispel ashiness, satisfied as her umber skin takes on satiny luster. She oils, braids and blow-dries her hair. It takes twenty minutes but the result is an ebony bush of silk. And now the smoky knit hose. And now the black strapless bra. And now the ebony mini-slip. And now an abbreviated top layer of gold lamé. She slips on black patent leather pumps. And her purse. What does she need? Her driver's license, her little money —enough for two drinks. It seldom takes long before some mother's son is paying her tab. The keys, her 'fro pick, a few tissues in the tiny shoulder bag. She won't have to ask anyone to watch her purse, it'll go right nicely with her on the dance floor.

In the mirror she feels beautiful—radiant—as she anoints herself in sterling silver and 14 carat gold.

She checks the windows. She checks the back door. She turns on the radio to ward off potential intruders. She'll leave the light on in the bathroom. She'll leave the television on as well. She'll leave a note taped to the telephone—in case . . .

She tiptoes to the children's room and looks in on them. She closes her eyes and envisions a white light around them. She opens her eyes and takes in their gentle breathing. She whispers, *Mama loves you*. She checks for and notes the pink glow of the night light protecting against an all consuming dark. She blows them a kiss and quietly closes the door.

It's so close—that midnight hour.

She secures the door behind her and high steps into the ultramarine cool of ghetto night as it licks her thighs. A jolt of expectation shoots through her as she hastens along that familiar avenue certain of her destination/that honky tonk haven, that urbane ubiety of flesh hunters and soulful survivors. She knows he's there waiting. She knows his voraciousness is mate to her own. She knows he is a lover of musics and madnesses—a man given birth by an upright piano, a guitar, a trombone, a set of skins and *beat me Daddy eight to the bar*.

She knows what his Mama done taught him. And she knows he no longer bothers with or cares what Mama said.

And her walk becomes a strut with a swing and a dip to her arrogant hip asway to the throb of traffic—to the staccato of her heels against that eternal pavement going clickitty-clack clickitty-clack echoing back. . . .

oo oo oo

LAURIE DUESING

Reprieve _____

> *What brought me to rest was your body.*
> *—Louise Gluck: "The Swimmer"*

I will deny everything
you think you gave me, except
the fact nothing ever got my attention
like your body
which I remember like a Russian novel:
when I read it, I felt it
but later could not imagine such things
happening to anyone.

It was not obsession
because it took too many years
and sex was only its form.
It was more like those irises
in my dream I blithely picked
to enter in the county fair.
I knew I would win.
And urgency: because we had so much of it,
there was none of it.

Those who say
you simply wore me out
forget how much fatigue and peace
resemble each other.
Think of the freedom weariness offers.
Oh, the things I have said
when I was tired.

After you left, someone told me
I looked confused.
For the first time, I had the confidence
to appear bewildered,
and those who consider stillness
a giving in cannot know
this ecstasy: the knowledge
I will never allow myself
to be hurried again.

oo oo oo

LAURIE DUESING

Wild and Blue _____

I want to be lifted, to meet the air
halfway—two reasons I can't forget
that gospel singer in her sassy
middle age. The way she mixed
everything up: black hair, bleached
red; tacky expensive dress; that muddle
of church and sex. But when the voice
of the Lord said, *Throw yourself into it,*
she did: jumped right into the air
and screamed. I didn't think a heavy woman
could get so far off the ground.

I want to rise under my own power
but the closest I've come
is the afternoon I threw myself
down on the ground and wept.
The scene was the woods and a person I loved.
That day, that place, that man
were not repeatable. *Why wait,* I thought
and gave in to grief.
The ground folded around me. I could not talk
but as I listened,
the earth began to stutter.

Perhaps direction does not matter
but before a woman can descend or rise,
before the universe can move her,
she must show she can pick up
the beat, the way people speaking
in tongues allow another voice to move
through their mouths while their lips
keep time. When I get the blues,
I am trying to show the earth I can reflect
her deepest colors, that I will take
whatever she sends through me.

I want to drive spirit into flesh,
a desire often confused with sex.
I once made love to a man
who had lost the woman he loved.
He sobbed and sobbed but I kept on
to show that when grieving stopped,
he would have something to look forward to.
If we are broken or forcefully
opened, it is only to get our attention.

Now I am rapt and looking for the still point
between earth and air. I am willing
to wait while the world turns red,
to watch while everything comes at me.

oo oo oo

LYNNE SHARON SCHWARTZ

from: *Disturbances in the Field* _____

Lydia and Victor have not been able to make love since two of their four children were killed in an accident...

"I'm so tired, Victor. Let's not tonight."

"Do you want to go to sleep? I'll turn out the light."

"No."

"What shall we do, then? Play cards? Battleships?" He turns to me quizzically and smiles anew. "I know. I have an activity to suggest." He puts a hand on my breast and circles the palm against the nipple. My eyes cloud over. He kisses me. "You're going to do it. You're going to like it, too," he says gently. Victor is starting to find his strength once more. I do not think I will be any match for him. Blighted, at least he is real.

"Do you really want to?" I ask. "I have the feeling you're just looking for something to do."

He finishes his bourbon, pours another quarter of an inch, and drinks that up. Then he glances over at me again. Very sexy, though he's not even trying. "I'll want to, after a while. I'll get there." The smile edges into that intimate, ironic, accepting grin. "Why don't you take off your nightgown? I'll look at you and be fired with passion."

I have to smile too, despite myself. I have no more resistance. I take off the nightgown while he gets up and locks the door.

He looks at me, and his eyes, the way they meander, are like hands. Yes, he is more himself, but I must try not to ... I must feel nothing. Fight it if I have to, for I know exactly what will happen otherwise.

He strokes my cheek with the backs of his fingers. "Do you remember," he says softly, "after you had Althea, those stitches, that first time? You pushed because you said there had to be a first time. You said it would only hurt once. You were right. I didn't like hurting you but you said go ahead, it's the best thing for it. Remember?"

"That was different. That was birth. I was all sore."

"Well, this ... You're sore again."

"I wish you wouldn't do me any favors, Victor. Do it for yourself, please. It's fine, I don't mind."

"You don't mind? A woman who doesn't mind? I don't need that. That's not you. You'll see in a minute who you are. I'll show you."

304

He moves down to get his face between my thighs, and he licks. Slowly. The sure-fire tactic. When in doubt, gentlemen ...

Well. I am only human. I have a long, reflexive history with this man. He pushes my legs further apart. After so long it feels very new, yet very familiar. It also feels like fire. The phases: craving and satiety. It throws apart and brings together again; advances and retires and advances till we reach the edge where, researchers have discovered, orgasm is inevitable. A subtle boundary, and really rather clever of them to have pinpointed it. It is inevitable, and sure I need it, I can't deny that. Except the more inevitable it grows, the more clearly the jumbled images come into focus, exactly what I expected and dreaded. I knew, I knew I shouldn't do this. Flames lick at the down jackets and the damp heavy corduroy pants. The burning books slide from their laps. Smashing noises, a shattering of glass, and we hurtle through the snowy air, hurtling torches past white-branched trees. We are stunned, falling, breathless, terrified, and I scream, "Stop! Stop! For God's sake, stop it!"

I have said stop before. A game: at that peak, pleasure slides easily across the border to pain and back again. The sensation can be played with to the point of mock danger, to the point where I nearly dissolve in a puddle like the Witch of the West. Victor has heard me say stop before. He likes it, why not? It makes him feel powerful, and when he stops—relents—he is a sultan showing mercy. But this ... he doesn't see ... this is no lovers' game with its moans for mercy, its teetering boundaries. I can't bear the fire any more! Her hair is aglow. Hair that easily ignites. Fine dark hair like mine. My baby, all alight.

He has to stop because there comes a pounding at the door. Althea, banging and yelling, "Mama! Mama! What is it? Open the door!" She hasn't called me Mama in fifteen years. Mother.

Victor looks up, gray with shock. And he thought he was doing so well. I raise myself to my elbows, still on fire.

"It's all right, it's all right," I call out to her.

"Open the door! Who's in there?"

Thank God he locked it. Did he know?

"No one, just me and Daddy."

She pounds. "Open the door!"

I get up and throw on a robe. Victor covers himself. I unlock the door and show myself intact.

Althea looks very small and suddenly still, standing at our doorway in a pink flowered granny nightgown that reaches to her ankles. Her taut neck rises, pale, from a white ruffled collar. Her face is pale and sharp, each feature as purely and delicately traced as in a Botticelli. Her pale hair is pulled back; her gray eyes are pale too. Caught short and frightened, the face looks about twelve years old. I gaze down at the rest of her: five feet two, narrow-waisted, full-breasted, slender wrists, small hands and feet. When I reach out to touch her shoulder she shrinks slightly from my touch.

"It's all right, dear. I'm sorry I woke you."

She is not twelve, she is seventeen, and as she stares at my flushed face and rumpled hair, my hand clutching the front of the robe together, my pupils probably large and ablaze, she is busy figuring, figuring, trying to work it all out in her head.

Down the hall, rubbing his eyes and stumbling around the door-frame, Phil appears. "Phil, it's okay, go back to bed. I had a dream." Phil shuffles to the bathroom, half asleep.

Althea stands as if frozen, her lips closed tight. I see she has not slept with Darryl or with anyone else.

"I'm sorry I woke you," I repeat softly, keeping my hand on her shoulder. She peers past me into the bedroom, but from that angle all she can see is the edge of the bed. As she steps back her eyes darken accusingly. A look of cunning comes into her face.

"It's not what you're thinking, Althea. It's not like that. Really, everything's all right." But what is she thinking? Love is not like that, I want to tell her. Do not catch by surprise and judge, like fire. But I cannot. Because love is—she has seen and heard for herself. At last she turns to go, tossing her ponytail, a pert aloofness in her walk. Still I'm throbbing. All the time I have faced her and talked to her I have never stopped feeling it, advancing and retiring, craving satiety.

I shut the door, lock it, and throw off the robe.

"Oh God," Victor says, clapping his hand to his head, as I switch the central light on so the room is bright. Blazing. "Does she think I —or we—"

I shrug and raise my eyebrows and fall onto the bed. Slowly, wickedly, we start to laugh, quiet hard laughs. For they are only our children; what do we care for children now? So easily lost, easy come, easy go. *This* is important. This is revenge.

"Well, finish up," I say in a hard low voice. "Do you mind finishing what you started? It wasn't quite finished."

He gets back to work. "Yeah, but listen, baby, not so loud this time." He has become Humphrey Bogart, lisping nasally out of the side of his mouth, to make us laugh. This time I keep my eyes as well as legs wide open and my heart closed—I keep a hand flat on my chest, holding it down—so there is no fire and no shattering glass and no hurtling through the snowy night, only wet furious pangs, nothing but biochemistry going about its business. I'm quiet, too. I'm experienced—four

DEEP DOWN · · ·

kids, always a sleeping baby in the house—I know how to keep quiet. I also know these bodies very well; if we stop at a certain instant and he gets inside me fast I can prolong it, make it seem endless. Oh, I know this system like a machine. So does Victor. At the right moment we bustle around efficiently. It works. But I'm not finished with him yet. The nights are long, I'll milk him dry. After a while there is a slight scuffle—he wants me on top now, but I decline the honor. We are a living contradiction to the sexual politics of our age: here nobody wants to be on top; here each one wants to be smothered. He wins, naturally, with a fifty-pound advantage—a gracious, grinning winner, gasping, "You'll have your way another time, kiddo." Finally he falls back exhausted, spreading his arms like a crucifixion. "Lydia, enough already. I'm a middle-aged man."

Yes, and you're screwing another woman besides. You have to husband your resources. We both have a drink of bourbon, straight, and he tells me he sees what I mean about doing it without the soul. My soul, in particular, was not in it. He says it uncritically, simply as an observation.

"So what? You got what you wanted, didn't you? You wanted to see me let go. You wanted to see me need you. Use you."

"Yes," he says. "Plus I saw the fire too. I know all about it. But I didn't stop."

"Oh. Is that the lesson? To walk right through the fire? No, thanks." To rescue them, yes, like Steffie. But now, what for?

Our bodies are coated with sweat and sticky patches. We lie in a close embrace on his side, sticking together, and tonight we will sleep well.

This land of ours, coarsened by blight, cannot endure. It's only a matter of time.

oo oo oo

JUDY GRAHN

a funeral
plainsong from a younger woman to an older
woman _____

a funeral: for my first lover and longtime friend
Yvonne Mary Robinson b. Oct. 20, 1939; d. Nov. 1974

i will be your mouth now, to do your singing
breath belongs to those who do the breathing.
warm life, as it passes through your fingers
flares up in the very hands you will be leaving

you have left, what is left
for the bond between women is a circle
we are together within it.

i am your best, i am your kind
kind of my kind, i am your wish
wish of my wish, i am your breast
breast of my breast, i am your mind
mind of my mind, i am your flesh
i am your kind, i am your wish
kind of my kind, i am your best

now you have left you can be
wherever the fire is when it blows itself out.
now you are a voice in any wind
        i am a single wind
now you are any source of a fire
        i am a single fire

wherever you go to, i will arrive
whatever i have been, you will come back to
wherever you leave off, i will inherit
whatever i resurrect, you shall have it

you have right, what is right
for the bond between women is returning
we are endlessly within it

and endlessly apart within it.
it is not finished
it will not be finished

i will be your heart now, to do your loving
love belongs to those who do the feeling.

life, as it stands so still along your fingers
beats in my hands, the hands i will, believing
that you have become she, who is not, any longer
somewhere in particular

we are together in your stillness
you have wished us a bonded life

love of my love, i am your breast
arm of my arm, i am your strength
breath of my breath, i am your foot
thigh of my thigh, back of my back
eye of my eye, beat of my beat
kind of my kind, i am your best

when you were dead i said you had gone to the mountain

the trees do not yet speak of you

a mountain when it is no longer
a mountain, goes to the sea
when the sea dies it goes to the rain
when the rain dies it goes to the grain
when the grain dies it goes to the flesh
when the flesh dies it goes to the mountain

now you have left, you can wander
will you tell whoever could listen
tell all the voices who speak to younger women
tell all the voices who speak to us when we need it
that the love between women is a circle
and is not finished

wherever i go to, you will arrive
whatever you have been, i will come back to
wherever i leave off, you will inherit

whatever we resurrect, we shall have it
we shall have it, we have right

and you have left, what is left

i will take your part now, to do your daring
lots belong to those who do the sharing.
i will be your fight now, to do your winning
as the bond between women is beginning
in the middle at the end
my first beloved, present friend
if i could die like the next rain
i'd call you by your mountain name
and rain on you

want of my want, i am your lust
wave of my wave, i am your crest
earth of my earth, i am your crust
may of my may, i am your must
kind of my kind, i am your best

tallest mountain least mouse
least mountain tallest mouse

you have put your very breath upon mine
i shall wrap my entire fist around you
i can touch any woman's lip to remember

we are together in my motion
you have wished us a bonded life

MARGARET ATWOOD

Late August _____

This is the plum season, the nights
blue and distended, the moon
hazed, this is the season of peaches

with their lush lobed bulbs
that glow in the dusk, apples
that drop and rot
sweetly, their brown skins veined as glands

No more the shrill voices
that cried *Need Need*
from the cold pond, bladed
and urgent as new grass

Now it is the crickets
that say *Ripe Ripe*
slurred in the darkness, while the plums

dripping on the lawn outside
our window, burst
with a sound like thick syrup
muffled and slow

The air is still
warm, flesh moves over
flesh, there is no

hurry

○○ ○○ ○○
LYDIA DAVIS
This Condition ————————————————————

In this condition: stirred not only by men but by women, fat and thin, naked and clothed; by teenagers and children in latency; by animals such as horses and dogs; by vegetables such as carrots, zucchinis, eggplants, and cucumbers; by fruits such as melons, grapefruits, and kiwis; by plant parts such as petals, sepals, stamens, and pistils; by the bare arm of a wooden chair, a round vase holding flowers, a little hot sunlight, a plate of pudding, a person entering a tunnel in the distance, a puddle of water, a hand alighting on a smooth stone, a hand alighting on a bare shoulder, a naked tree limb; by anything curved, bare, and shining, as the limb or bole of a tree; by any touch, as the touch of a stranger handling money; by anything round and freely hanging, as tassels on a curtain, as chestnut burrs on a twig in spring, as a wet teabag on its string; by anything glowing, as a hot coal; anything soft or slow, as a cat rising from a chair; anything smooth and dry, as a stone, or warm and glistening; anything sliding, anything sliding back and forth; anything sliding in and out with an oiled surface, as certain machine parts; anything of a certain shape, like the state of Florida; anything pounding, anything stroking; anything bolt upright, anything horizontal and gaping, as a certain sea anemone; anything warm, anything wet, anything wet and red, anything turning red, as the sun at evening; anything wet and pink; anything long and straight with a blunt end, as a pestle; anything coming out of anything else, as a snail from its shell, as a snail's horns from its head; anything opening; any stream of water running, any stream running, any stream spurting, any stream spouting; any cry, any soft cry, any grunt; anything going into anything else, as a hand searching in a purse; anything clutching, anything grasping; anything rising, anything tightening or filling, as a sail; anything dripping, anything hardening, anything softening.

oo oo oo

CONTRIBUTORS

KATHY ACKER has written several novels including *Blood and Guts in High School, Don Quixote, Great Expectations, The Childlike Life of the Black Tarantula,* and *Empire of the Senseless,* which will appear in '89. She has also done two plays with Richard Foreman and scripted the movie *Variety.* She currently lives in London.

AI is the writer-in-residence at College of the Holy Cross. She is the author of *Sin, Killing Floor,* and *Cruelty. Killing Floor* won the Lamont Prize in 1978, and she has also been the recipient of two NEA awards and a Guggenheim.

MARGARET ATWOOD was born in Ottawa, Ontario, and has taught English in many universities throughout Canada. She has received over twenty prizes and awards for her writing in both poetry and fiction. Her latest books include *Selected Poems II, Bluebeard's Egg, The Handmaid's Tale,* and a collection of her poetry will also be appearing in 1988.

TONI CADE BAMBARA was born in New York City, educated at Queens College, the University of Florence, and New York University. She has been a social worker, an instructor of English at City College, and writer-in-residence at Spelman College. The editor of the collection *The Black Woman,* her two volumes of short stories are *Gorilla My Love,* and *The Seabirds Are Still Alive.*

ANN BEATTIE was born in Washington D.C., and now lives in Charlottesville, Virginia. She has taught at the University of Virginia and at Harvard University. She is the author of the novels, *Chilly Scenes of Winter, Falling in Place,* and *Love Always.* Her collections of stories include *Distortions, Secrets and Surprises, The Burning House,* and, most recently, *Where You'll Find Me.*

CAROL BERGÉ's writing addresses relationships in intimate historical perspective: risk versus security in a fast-changes society. Most recent is the novel *Secrets, Gossip and Slander,* Reed & Cannon. She has received NEA and Caps Awards in Fiction. Reviews in the *New York Times, London Times, Village Voice,* and *Boston Globe* cite her twenty books from Bobbs-Merrill, Pocket Books, and other literary presses. A teacher and editor of *Center*, she is also a successful antiques dealer.

ROO BORSON was born in Berkeley, California, and currently lives in both New Mexico and Toronto. Her recent books include *The Whole Night, Coming Home,* and *The Transparence of November/Snow,* co-authored with Kim Maltman, Quarry Press, 1985.

SUMMER BRENNER is the author of *From the Heart to the Center* and *The Soft Room,* both published by The Figures. Her poems and stories have appeared in numerous periodicals. Currently she is working on a collection of short fiction and a novel.

NICOLE BROSSARD was born in Montreal, Quebec. Poet, novelist, and essayist, she has published more than twenty books since 1965. Her work has been regarded as some of the most significant in Quebec contemporary literature, and she has won the Governor General award for poetry twice. Her most recent titles, translated into English, include *Lovhers,* Guernica Press; *French Kiss,* and *These our mothers,* Coach House Press; her most recent novel is *Le Désert Mauve,* L'Hexagone.

OLGA BROUMAS is the author of *Soie Sauvage* and *Pastoral Jazz,* from Copper Canyon Press; *Black Holes, Black Stockings,* co-authored with Jane Miller, from Wesleyan; and her book, *Beginning With O,* was the 1977 Yale Younger Poets selection. She is the translator of *What I Love* and *The Little Mariner* by the Greek poet Odysseas Elytis, Copper Canyon. She lives in Provincetown, Massachusetts.

JOAN CHASE received a PEN-Ernest Hemingway Foundation Award for her first novel, *During the Reign of the Queen of Persia* in 1984. In October 1987 she won the Whiting Foundation Award. She is now finishing her second novel, *The Evening Wolves.* She lives in Massachusetts.

LAURA CHESTER is the co-editor of *Rising Tides: Twentieth Century American Women Poets* and editor of this anthology. Her most recent books include *My Pleasure,* The Figures, 1980; *Lupus Novice,* Station Hill Press, 1987; *Free Rein,* Burning Deck Press, 1988; and a large "collected" book of writing, *In the Zone,* will be available from Black Sparrow Press in the fall of 1988. She lives in the Berkshires with her two sons.

WANDA COLEMAN is the working mother of three children. She has published two books of poetry, *Mad Dog Black Lady* and *Imagoes,* both from Black Sparrow Press. Her work has appeared in many magazines including *Caliban, Enclitic, High Plains Review, Z Miscellaneous,* and *Callaloo.* Her most recent collected book of poems and stories, *Heavy Daughter Blues,* is also published by Black Sparrow.

SALLY CROFT's work has appeared in numerous small press publications, including *Seneca* and *The Bellingham Review,* and she has been anthologized in *Light Year '86.* Her work is also included in the recent *Introduction to Literature.* She is currently working on a novel.

ANN DARR was born in Iowa and now lives near Washington D.C. She has been a pilot in the Army Airforce, WWII, a radio writer/performer in New York, and teacher at the American University in D.C. Her books include *St. Ann's Gut* and *The Myth of a Woman's Fist,* both from Morrow; *Cleared for Landing,* Dryad; *Riding with the Fireworks,* Alice James; *Do You Take This Woman,* WWPH; and *High Dark,* a tape, from Watershed.

LYDIA DAVIS's collections of fiction include *The Thirteenth Woman,* Living Hand Editions; *Story and Other Stories,* The Figures; and, most recently, *Break It Down,* which was cited last year for the PEN Hemingway Award. She has received fellowships from the NEA and the Ingram Merrill Foundation, has taught at Bard College, Columbia University, UCSD, and currently lives in Brooklyn.

TOI DERRICOTTE's two collections of poems are *The Empress of the Death House,* Lotus Press, 1978; and *Natural Birth,* The Crossing Press, 1983. She is a recipient of a NEA, a fellowship from the New Jersey State Council on the Arts, and was a MacDowell Fellow. In 1985 she received the Lucille Medwick Memorial Award from the Poetry Society of America.

LAURIE DUESING was born in Milwaukee, Wisconsin, and now lives in Benicia, California, where she teaches creative writing and composition at Solano Community College. Her work has appeared in many small magazines, and a selection of her poems, *Three West Coast Women,* was published by Five Fingers Review in 1987.

RACHEL BLAU DUPLESSIS is the author of *Writing Beyond the Ending: Narrative Strategies of Twentieth-Century Women Writers,* 1985; and *H.D.: The Career of that Struggle,* 1986, both published by

Indiana University Press. Her poetry is collected in *Wells,* 1980; and *Tabula Rosa,* 1987, Potes & Poets Press. Her essays include, "For the Etruscans," and "Language Acquisition."

LOUISE ERDRICH, who grew up in North Dakota, is of German-American and Chippewa descent. Her first book was *Jacklight,* a volume of poetry. Her second, *Love Medicine,* was the winner of both the Book Critics Circle Award for Fiction and the Los Angeles Times award for best novel of 1985. Her new novel, *The Beet Queen,* was published in 1986. She lives in New Hampshire with her husband and their children.

KATHLEEN FRASER edits *HOW(ever),* a journal focused on innovative writing by women. Her books include *New Shoes,* Harper & Row, 1978; *Each Next,* narratives, The Figures, 1980; *Something (even human voices) in the foreground, a lake,* Kelsey Street, 1984; and *Notes Preceding Trust,* The Lapis Press, 1987. Fraser teachers at San Francisco State University, and lives in Rome part of each year.

GLORIA FRYM was born in Brooklyn, and now lives in Berkeley, California. She teaches in the Poetics Program at New College of California, San Francisco. Her book *Back to Forth,* The Figures, won the San Francisco State University Poetry Center Book Award. Her other books include *Impossible Affection,* Christopher's Books and *Second Stories,* Chronicle Books.

AMY GERSTLER is a poet and fiction writer living in Los Angeles. Her most recent books are *The True Bride,* Lapis Press, 1986; *Primitive Man,* Hanuman Books, 1987; and *Early Heaven,* Ouija Madness Press, 1985. She won second prize in *Mademoiselle* magazine's annual fiction contest in 1987 and is working on a children's book about the language of elephants.

DANIELA GIOSEFFI is a poet, novelist, and literary critic. Some of the poems in her collection, *Eggs in the Lake,* Boa Editions, 1979, won an award/grant from NYSCA of the NEA. Her novel, *The Great American Belly,* won critical acclaim here and abroad. Her poems, stories, and criticism have appeared in *The Paris Review, The Nation, Antaeus, The American Book Review,* and *Rising Tides.*

JUDY GRAHN's two latest books of poetry are *The Queen of Wands,* The Crossing Press, 1982, and *The Queen of Swords,* Beacon, 1987. Many of her early books have been collected in *The Work of a*

Common Woman, The Crossing Press, 1978. Grahn's major non-fiction work is *Another Mother Tongue*, Beacon, 1984. A prehistoric novel, *Mundane's World*, will be published by The Crossing Press in 1988.

SUSAN GRIFFIN is the author of *Woman and Nature: The Roaring Inside Her, Pornography and Silence: Culture's Revenge Against Nature,* and *Made F(f)rom T(t)his Earth,* a collection of her work. She has written a play, *Voices,* which won an Emmy.

MARILYN HACKER is the author of five books of poetry, most recently *Love, Death and the Changing of the Seasons* and *Assumptions.*

JANET HAMILL is the author of two books of poetry: *Troublante,* Oliphant Press, 1975; and *The Temple,* Telephone Books, 1980. She is also the author of a play, *Delouz Entango,* performed by St. Clements Church in 1978. Her poems have been anthologized in *Ordinary Women,* Ordinary Women Press; *Sweet Little Sixteen,* Rowoholt Taschenbuch; and *The Low-Tech Manual,* Low-Tech Press. She lives in New York City.

BOBBIE LOUISE HAWKINS was raised in West Texas, studied art in London, taught in missionary schools in British Honduras, and now lives in Bolinas, California. Her books include *Own Your Body,* Black Sparrow Press, 1973; *15 Poems,* Arif, 1973; and her two other books, *Frenchy and Cuban Pete* and *Back to Texas,* are included in her collected stories, *Almost Everything,* published by Coach House Press and Long River Books, 1982.

JANE HIRSHFIELD is the author of two collections of poetry, *Of Gravity & Angels,* Wesleyan University Press, 1988; and *Alaya,* QRL Poetry Series, 1982. She is the co-translator of *The Ink Dark Moon: Love Poems by Ono no Komachi and Izumi Shibiku,* Scribners, 1988. She has received a Guggenheim Fellowship and her work has appeared in such periodicals as *The New Yorker, The Atlantic Monthly,* and *The American Poetry Review.* She lives in Mill Valley, California.

SHERRIL JAFFE was born in Walla Walla, Washington, and now lives in Manhattan with her husband, Rabbi Alan Lew, and their two daughters. Her books include *Scars Make Your Body More Interesting, This Flower Only Blooms Every Hundred Years, The Unexamined Wife,* and *The Faces Reappear,* all from Black Sparrow Press.

ERICA JONG's books of poetry include *Fruits & Vege-tables*, 1971; *Half-Lives*, 1973; *Loveroot*, 1975; *At the Edge of the Body*, 1979; and *Ordinary Miracles*, 1983. Her novels are *Fear of Flying*, 1973; *How to Save Your Own Life*, 1977; *Fanny*, 1980; *Parachutes & Kisses*, 1984; and, most recently, *Serenissima*.

FAYE KICKNOSWAY grew up in Los Angeles and De-troit. She has taught creative writing at Wayne State and San Francisco University and currently teaches at the University of Hawaii. Her po-etry collections include *Asparagus, Asparagus, Ah Sweet Asparagus* and *She Wears Him Fancy In Her Nightbraid*, both from Toothpaste Press; *Who Shall Know Them*, Viking Penguin; and *All These Voices*, Coffee House Press.

DORIANNE LAUX lives in Berkeley, California, and has published widely in such magazines as *Beloit Poetry Journal, Tendril,* and *ZYZZYVA*. She is the winner of a 1987 Pushcart Prize, *Pushcart Prize XI: Best of the Small Presses*. Her most recent publication is *Three West Coast Women*, Five Fingers Poetry, San Francisco, 1987.

LYN LIFSHIN has had more than seventy books and chapbooks published including *Black Apples, Upstate Madonna, Kiss the Skin Off,* and, most recently, *Raw Opals* and *Rubbed Silk.* She has edited a series of books of women's writing, *Tangled Vines, Ariadne's Thread,* and forthcoming, *Unsealed Lips,* Capra. Her work has been the subject of a critical study by Hugh Fox, and she is the subject of a documentary film, *Not Made of Glass.*

AUDRE LORDE is a professor of English at Hunter Col-lege in New York. Her third book of poetry, *From a Land Where Other People Live,* Broadside Press, 1973, was nominated for the National Book Award. Her more recent books include *Coal,* 1976; *The Black Unicorn,* 1978; and *Chosen Poems—Old and New,* 1982. Her prose works include *Uses of the Erotic: The Erotic as Power,* Out and Out Books, 1978; *The Cancer Journals,* Spinsters Ink, 1980; and *Zami,* The Crossing Press, 1982.

MARY MACKEY is the author of *The Dear Dance of Eros,* a collection of erotic love poems, Fjord Press, and of *A Grand Passion,* a novel about love and ballet. She has written four novels, four books of poetry, and numerous reviews, essays, and critical articles. Her work has been translated into eleven languages. She lives in California.

DAPHNE MARLATT, currently living in Vancouver, has published numerous books of poetry and prose in Canada and the U.S. Her most recent work includes a novel, *Ana Historic,* Coach House Press, 1988; and a collection with poet Betsy Warland, *Double Negative,* Gynergy Books, 1988. She is founding member of the editorial collective, *tessera,* which publishes Québecoise and English-Canadian feminist theory and writing.

BERNADETTE MAYER is the author of ten books of poetry including *Midwinter Day,* Turtle Island Foundation; *Utopia,* United Artists; and *Mutual Aid,* Mademoiselle de la Mole Press. A director of the St. Mark's Poetry Project for several years, she now teaches poetry and science writing and works as a proofreader.

ELIZABETH MCNEILL is the pseudonym of the New York career woman who experienced and wrote about the *Nine and a Half Weeks* that began with a casual encounter at a Manhattan street fair, and ended in a disturbing climax.

DEENA METZGER is a poet, novelist, writer, and therapist. Her books include *The Woman Who Slept with Men to Take the War Out of Them & Tree,* Wingbow Press, Berkeley; and *Skin: Shadows/ Silence,* West Coast Poetry Review. Her article, "Revamping the World: On the Return of the Holy Prostitute," *Utne Review,* has been widely circulated. She has just finished a new novel, *What Dinah Thought.* The therapeutic approach to life-threatening diseases, which she developed, will be articulated in a new book, *Writing for Your Life.*

SUE MILLER is the author of the bestselling novel *The Good Mother*, 1986, and *Inventing the Abbotts*, 1987, a collection of short stories. She lives in Cambridge, Massachusetts.

SUSAN MINOT was born in Boston, Massachusetts. Her first novel, *Monkeys,* was published in 1986. Her story "Lust" received an O. Henry Award in 1985. Her stories have appeared in *The New Yorker, The Paris Review,* and *Grand Street*, and she has also been included in the *Pushcart Prize IX* collection and *The Best American Short Stories, 1984.*

TONI MORRISON was born in Lorain, Ohio, and now lives in Rockland County, New York. She is the author of five novels: *The Bluest Eye; Sula; Song of Solomon,* which won the 1978 National Book Critics Circle Award for fiction; *Tar Baby;* and, most recently,

Beloved. She is also the author of *Dreaming Emmett,* a play produced in 1986.

ERIN MOURÉ was born in Calgary, Alberta, Canada. She lived in Vancouver for eleven years before moving to Montreal in 1985. She has worked for the VIA Rail, and is interested in house repair and French feminist theory. Her books of poetry include *Wanted Alive,* Anansi, 1983; *Domestic Fuel,* Anansi, 1985; and *furious,* Anansi, 1987.

JOYCE CAROL OATES lives in Princeton, New Jersey, where she is on the faculty of Princeton University. She is the author of several books of stories published by Black Sparrow Press, as well as eighteen novels, including most recently *Them, Expensive People, A Garden of Earthly Delights, With Shuddering Fall,* and her latest book, *You Must Remember This.*

EDNA O'BRIEN lives in London, England. She is the author of fifteen books, including *Casualties of Peace, August is a Wicked Month, Girls in Their Married Bliss, The Lonely Girl,* and *The Country Girls.* A selection of her stories was gathered in *A Fanatic Heart* in 1984.

SHARON OLDS's books include *Satan Says,* 1980; *The Dead & The Living,* 1984; and *The Gold Cell,* 1987. She teaches at N.Y.U. and at Goldwater Hospital, Roosevelt Island, New York.

ALICIA OSTRIKER is the author of six volumes of poetry, most recently *A Woman Under the Surface,* Princeton; *The Mother/ Child Papers,* Beacon; and *The Imaginary Lover,* Pittsburgh Press. Her book on the women's poetry movement in American is *Stealing the Language,* published by Beacon. She teaches English and Creative Writing at Rutgers University.

MAUREEN OWEN's poems have appeared in many anthologies and magazines from *Anhoi* to *Z.* Her most recent books are *Hearts in Space,* Kulcher Press; *AE (Amelia Earhart),* winner of the Before Columbus Foundation's American Book Award, Vortex Editions; and *Zombie Notes,* Sun Press. She is the editor of Telephone Books Press. In 1979 she was awarded a poetry fellowship from the NEA.

ROCHELLE OWENS, recipient of Guggenheim, CAPS, Yale School of Drama, NEA and Rockefeller grants, has published twelve books of poetry and three collections of plays. A pioneer in the experimental off-Broadway movement, she has received numerous *Village*

Voice Obie awards and honors from the *New York Drama Critics Circle*. Her play *Futz* is considered a classic of the American avant-garde theatre. Her newest book is *How Much Paint Does the Painting Need*, Kulcher Press, 1988.

JAYNE ANNE PHILLIPS is the author of *Black Tickets, Machine Dreams,* and *Fast Lanes.* She is the recipient of the Sue Kaufman Prize for First Fiction from the American Academy and Institute of Arts and Letters, and two NEAs.

MARGE PIERCY's most recent novel, *Gone to Soldiers,* was published in 1987. Her poetry collection, *Available Light,* was published in 1988. Her other recent novels include *Fly Away Home, Braided Lives,* and *Vida,* and her recent poetry includes *My Mother's Body; Stone, Paper, Knife;* and *Circles on the Water.*

LILY POND has been publishing, editing, and designing *Yellow Silk: Journal of Erotic Arts* for the last six years, and now knows that it's more than another manifestation of prolonged adolescence. Her first twenty years were spent in Michigan, the second twenty, California, the next twenty? Anywhere she wants.

ANNE RICE, a.k.a. Anne Rampling, was born in New Orleans, and now lives in San Francisco with her husband, the poet Stan Rice. Her books include *Interview with the Vampire, The Feast of All Saints, Cry to Heaven,* and *The Vampire Lestat.* Under the pseudonym of Anne Rampling she wrote the novel *Exit to Eden,* as well as *Belinda.* Anne has also written a series of erotic novels under the name A.N. Roquelaure.

CAMILLE ROY has been living and writing in San Francisco for eight years. Her work has appeared in *HOW(ever),* and *Mirage,* among other publications.

MIRIAM SAGAN has published seven poetry chapbooks, including *Aegean Doorway,* Zephyr, 1984. Her work appears widely in magazines ranging from *Family Circle* to *Samisdat.* She is an artist in residence with the state of New Mexico, living in Santa Fe in an old adobe with her husband, Robert.

LESLIE SCALAPINO's books of poetry include *Considering how exaggerated music is,* 1982; and *that they were at the beach,* 1985; both published by North Point Press. A forthcoming book of poetry, entitled *way,* will also be published by North Point in the spring of 1988. Leslie Scalapino lives in Oakland, California.

CAROLEE SCHNEEMANN is a painter, performance artist, filmmaker, and writer. Her visual work appears in numerous private and museum collections, and her writings have been widely published. *More Than Meat Joy: Complete Performance Works & Selected Writings 1963–1979* was published by Documentext and *Carolee Schneemann: Early and Recent Work* was published by Hutchinson/Documentext.

CHRISTINE SCHUTT lives in New York City with her two sons. She is a Pushcart Prize winner, and her stories have appeared in numerous small magazines. Her poems have also appeared in *Folio, Intro #1,* and *Contempora.*

LYNNE SHARON SCHWARTZ is the author of several novels, including *Rough Strife* and *Balancing Acts,* as well as a collection of short stories, *Acquainted With the Night.* Her most recent work of fiction is *Disturbances in the Field,* 1983.

NTOZAKE SHANGE is a poet, playwright, and novelist. Her plays include *Spell No. 7, A Photograph: Lovers in Motion, Boogie Woogie Landscapes,* and the Broadway hit *for colored girls who have considered suicide/when the rainbow is enuf.* Her books of poetry include *nappy edges* and *Midnight Birds,* and she is the author of two novels: *Sassafras, Cypress and Indigo,* 1982, and *Betsey Brown,* 1985.

LOUISE SHIVERS was born one of ten children in eastern North Carolina. She now lives with her family in Augusta, Georgia, a mile from Tobacco Road. A member of the writers' group known as "The Six," who studied under Jean Witt Fitz, she has published poetry and short stories. *Here to Get My Baby Out of Jail* is her first novel.

MONA SIMPSON's short fiction has appeared in *The Paris Review, Ploughshares, The Iowa Review, The North American Review,* and other periodicals. Her stories have been selected for inclusion in *Best American Short Stories of 1986, The Pushcart Prize XI: Best of the Small Presses,* and *20 Under 30.* Her first novel, *Anywhere But Here,* was published in 1987.

MAY SWENSON was born in Utah and is now based in the New York City area. She has published nine books of poems since 1954. The newest, *In Other Words,* appeared in 1987. Among many awards to her work was a MacArthur Fellowship in 1987.

LYNNE TILLMAN is a writer and filmmaker who lives in New York City. Her writing includes *Haunted Houses,* Poseidon Press; *Weird Fucks,* Handshake Editions, Paris; *Living with Contradictions,* Top Stories; and *Madame Realism.* Her writing has appeared in many magazines and anthologies. She is co-director, co-producer, and writer of *COMMITTED,* an independent feature based on the life of Frances Farmer.

CHRIS TYSH resides in Detroit, Michigan, where she teaches Literature and Creative Writing. She is co-editor of In Camera, a small press concerned with experimental writing, sexuality, and politics. Her books include *Secrets of Elegance,* Detroit River Press, Detroit, 1981; and *Pornē,* In Camera, Detroit, 1984.

JULIA VOSE was born in Jacksonville, Florida, and raised in the San Joaquin Valley of California. In San Francisco she taught poetry writing at the University of California Extension, and was a Writer-in-Residence at Mount Zion Hospital. Her books include *Anne Sexton! What About It?,* Smoking Mirror Press; and *Moved Out On The Inside,* 1976, The Figures Press.

ANNE WALDMAN is the author of twelve books of poetry, including *Fast Speaking Woman, First Baby Poems,* and *Skin Meat Bones,* and a forthcoming *New and Selected* from Coffee House Press. She had performed her work internationally, collaborating with musicians and dancers. She currently directs the Master of Fine Arts program in Writing and Poetics at the Naropa Institute in Boulder, Colorado.

ALICE WALKER won an American Book Award and the Pulitzer Prize for her novel *The Color Purple.* Her other published works include two collections of stories: *In Love & Trouble* and *You Can't Keep a Good Woman Down.* She has written several other novels and volumes of poetry including *Horses Make a Landscape Look More Beautiful.* Born in Eatonton, Georgia, she now lives in San Francisco.

oo oo oo
ACKNOWLEDGMENTS

Kathy Acker: "The Underworlds Of The World" from *Great Expectations.* Copyright © 1982 by Kathy Acker. Reprinted by permission of Grove Press and Pan Books Ltd. Published in the U.K. in *Blood and Guts in High School Plus Two* (Picador).

Ai: "Reunions With a Ghost" originally appeared in *Quarterly West.* Reprinted by permission of the author. "Twenty Year Marriage" from *Cruelty* by Ai. Copyright © 1970, 1973 by Ai. Reprinted by permission of Houghton Mifflin Company.

Margaret Atwood: "Variation on the Word *Sleep*" from *Notes Toward a Poem That Can Never Be Written* from *Selected Poems II: Poems Selected and New 1976–1986* by Margaret Atwood (Houghton Mifflin), and from *True Stories,* copyright © Margaret Atwood 1981 (Toronto: Oxford University Press Canada, 1981). Reprinted by permission of Houghton Mifflin Company, Oxford University Press Canada, and Phoebe Larmore. "Late August" from *Circe/Mud Poems* in *Selected Poems 1965—1975* by Margaret Atwood. Copyright © 1976 by Margaret Atwood (Houghton Mifflin), and from *You Are Happy,* copyright © Margaret Atwood 1974 (Toronto: Oxford University Press Canada, 1974). Reprinted by permission of Houghton Mifflin Company, Oxford University Press Canada, and Phoebe Larmore.

Toni Cade Bambara: "My Man Bovanne." Copyright © 1971 by Toni Cade Bambara. Reprinted from *Gorilla, My Love* by Toni Cade Bambara, by permission of Random House, Inc. and The Women's Press Ltd.

Ann Beattie: from "Four Stories About Lovers" by Ann Beattie from the book *Distortions.* Copyright © 1974, 1975, 1976 by Ann Beattie. Reprinted by permission of Doubleday, a division of Bantam, Doubleday, Dell Publishing Group, Inc. and International Creative Management.

Carol Bergé: "A Resolution—Of Sorts" and "A Familiar Reunion" from *Secrets, Gossip and Slander.* Copyright © 1984 by Carol Bergé. Reprinted by permission of I. Reed Books.

Roo Borson: "Lust" originally appeared in *Poetry Australia.* Reprinted by permission of the author.

Summer Brenner: "Buttons and Knives," "Vini," and "Fata Morgana" from *The Soft Room* (The Figures, 1978). Copyright © 1978 by Summer Brenner. Reprinted by permission of the author.

Nicole Brossard: *Sous La Langue* (L'Essentielle, editrices and Gynergy Books, 1987). Copyright © 1987 by Nicole Brossard. Translation copyright © 1987 by Susanne de Lotbinière-Harwood. Reprinted by permission of the author and the translator.

Olga Broumas: "Tryst." Copyright © 1985 by Olga Broumas. Originally appeared in *LLCL.* Reprinted by permission of the author.

Joan Chase: two excerpts from *During the Reign of the Queen of Persia* by Joan Chase. Copyright © 1983 by Joan L.S. Chase. Reprinted by permission of Harper & Row, Publishers, Inc. and Virago Press Ltd.

Laura Chester: "Loving My Boys," "Crazy," "Correspondence," and excerpt from *In the Zone* printed by permission of the author.

Wanda Coleman: "The Blues in the Night" from *Heavy Daughter Blues*. Copyright © 1987 by Wanda Coleman. Reprinted by permission of Black Sparrow Press.

Sally Croft: "Blue" printed by permission of the author.

Ann Darr: "At Sixteen." Copyright © 1981 by Ann Darr. Originally appeared in *Poetry Now*. Reprinted by permission of the author.

Lydia Davis: "Break It Down" from *Break It Down* by Lydia Davis. Copyright © 1976, 1983, 1986 by Lydia Davis. Reprinted by permission of Farrar, Straus and Giroux, Inc. and the Harriet Wasserman Literary Agency. "This Condition" printed by permission of the author.

Toi Derricotte: "Touching/Not Touching: My Mother" and "Saturday Night" originally appeared in *Iowa Review*. Reprinted by permission of the author.

Laurie Duesing: "Send Pictures, You Said," "Blossoming," "Reprieve," and "Wild and Blue." Copyright © 1987 by Laurie Duesing. First published in *Three West Coast Women* (Five Fingers Poetry, 1987). Reprinted by permission of the author.

Rachel Blau DuPlessis: selections from "Eurydice" and "Mirror Poem" from *Wells* (Montemora, 1980). Copyright © 1980 by Rachel Blau DuPlessis. Reprinted by permission of the author.

Louise Erdrich: from *The Beet Queen* by Louise Erdrich. Copyright © 1986 by Louise Erdrich. Reprinted by permission of Henry Holt and Company, Inc.

Kathleen Fraser: "Because You Aren't Here To Be What I Can't Think Of" from *New Shoes* by Kathleen Fraser. Copyright © 1978 by Kathleen Fraser. Reprinted by permission of Harper & Row, Publishers, Inc. and Marian Reiner for the author. "Secret Language." Copyright © 1987 by Kathleen Fraser. Used by permission of Marian Reiner for the author. "Bestiality.... (from the Leda Notebooks)." Copyright © 1987 by Kathleen Fraser. Originally appeared in *Mirage*. Used by permission of Marian Reiner for the author.

Gloria Frym: "Good Morning" from *Back to Forth* (The Figures, 1982). Copyright © 1982 by Gloria Frym. Reprinted by permission of the author. "The Yield" from *Impossible Affection* (Christopher's Books, 1979). Copyright © 1979 by Gloria Frym. Reprinted by permission of the author. "Manifesto." Copyright © 1985 by Gloria Frym. Originally appeared in *Exquisite Corpse*. Reprinted by permission of the author.

Amy Gerstler: "The Unforeseen" and "Ups and Downs" printed by permission of the author. "A Lecture on Jealousy" from *The True Bride* (Lapis Press, 1986). Copyright © 1986 by Amy Gerstler. Reprinted by permission of the author.

Daniela Gioseffi: "Toward the Greater Romance, Please Place Roses in My Skull" printed by permission of the author.

Judy Grahn: "a funeral plainsong" from *The Work of a Common Woman*. Copyright © 1978 by Judy Grahn. Reprinted by permission of The Crossing Press, Freedom, CA.

Susan Griffin: "Viyella." Copyright © 1984 by Susan Griffin. First published in *Pleasures: Women Write Erotica*, edited by Lonnie Barbach (Doubleday, 1984). Reprinted by permission of the author.

Marilyn Hacker: six poems from *Love, Death and the Changing of the Seasons* (Arbor House, 1986). Copyright © 1986 by Marilyn Hacker. Reprinted by permission of the author. "Languedocienne." Copyright © 1987 by Marilyn Hacker. Originally appeared in *River Styx*. Reprinted by permission of the author.

Janet Hamill: "Open Window" printed by permission of the author.

Bobbie Louise Hawkins: "Running Set of Lies" from *Almost Everything* (Coach House Press and Longriver Books, 1982). Copyright © 1982 by Bobbie Louise Hawkins. Reprinted by permission of Coach House Press.

Jane Hirshfield: "Of Gravity & Angels" from *Of Gravity & Angels* (Wesleyan University Press, 1988). Copyright © 1988 by Jane Hirshfield. Originally appeared in *Yellow Silk*. Reprinted by permission of the author.

Sherril Jaffe: "They Go There Forever" printed by permission of the author. "Ann Lay Naked" from *The Unexamined Wife*. Copyright © 1983 by Sherril Jaffe. Reprinted by permission of Black Sparrow Press.

Erica Jong: from *Fanny: Being the True History of the Adventures of Fanny Hackabout-Jones* by Erica Jong. Copyright © 1980 by Erica Jong. Reprinted by arrangement with NAL Penguin Inc., New York, NY, and A.D. Peters and Co. Ltd. From *Serenissima* by Erica Jong. Copyright © 1987 by Erica Jong Productions, Ltd. Reprinted by permission of Houghton Mifflin Company and Bantam Press. From *Parachutes and Kisses* by Erica Mann Jong. Copyright © 1984 by Erica Mann Jong. Reprinted by arrangement with NAL Penguin Inc., New York, NY, and A.D. Peters and Co. Ltd.

Faye Kicknosway: "Mr. Muscle-On" from *All These Voices* (Coffee House Press, 1986). Copyright © 1973, 1974, 1978, 1982, 1983, 1986 by Faye Kicknosway. Reprinted by permission of the author.

Dorianne Laux: "China." Copyright © 1985 by Dorianne Laux. Originally appeared in *Yellow Silk*. Reprinted by permission of the author.

Lyn Lifshin: "Fitzi in the Yearbook" originally appeared in *Abraxus*. Reprinted by permission of the author. "Penthouse Playboy" originally appeared in *Naked Charm*. Reprinted by permission of the author. "With So Many Voices" printed by permission of the author. "The Midwest Is Full of Vibrators" originally appeared in *Madonna who shifts for herself*. Reprinted by permission of the author.

Audre Lorde: from *Zami: A New Spelling of My Name*. Copyright © 1983 by Audre Lorde. Reprinted by permission of The Crossing Press, Freedom, CA.

Mary Mackey: "Golden Cords: Erotic Attachment and the Pain of Separation." Copyright © 1984 by Mary Mackey. Originally appeared in *Yellow Silk*. Reprinted by permission of the author. "The Kama Sutra of Kindness: Position No. 2" from *The Dear Dance of Eros* (Fjord Press, 1987). Copyright © 1974, 1976, 1978, 1987 by Mary Mackey. Reprinted by permission of the author.

Maureen Owen: from "Amelia Earhart Series." Copyright © 1983 by Maureen Owen. Originally appeared in *HOW(ever)*. Reprinted by permission of the author. "Urban Cowboy Hat" from *Zombie Notes* (Sun Press, 1985). Copyright © 1985 by Maureen Owen. Reprinted by permission of the author.

Rochelle Owens: "Devils Clowns and Women" from *How Much Paint Does the Painting Need* (Kulcher Press, 1987). Copyright © 1987 by Rochelle Owens. Reprinted by permission of the author and Kulcher Press.

Jayne Anne Phillips: "Sweethearts," "Slave," and "Stripper" excerpted from the book *Black Tickets* by Jayne Anne Phillips. Copyright © 1975, 1976, 1978, 1979 by Jayne Anne Phillips. Reprinted by permission of Delacorte Press/Seymour Lawrence and Penguin Books Ltd.

Marge Piercy: "Raisin pumpernickel" and "Vegetable love" from *Available Light* (Alfred A. Knopf, 1988). Copyright © 1987 by Marge Piercy. Reprinted by permission of the Wallace & Sheil Agency. "Raisin pumpernickel" originally appeared in *Lips*; "Vegetable love" originally appeared in *Yellow Silk*.

Lily Pond: "Ovulation." Copyright © 1983 by Lily Pond. Originally appeared in *Yellow Silk*. Reprinted by permission of the author.

Anne Rampling: two excerpts from *Exit to Eden* by Anne Rampling. Copyright © 1985 by Anne Rampling. Reprinted by permission of Arbor House/William Morrow and Futura, London.

Anne Rice: from *The Vampire Lestat* by Anne Rice. Copyright © 1985 by Anne O'Brien Rice. Reprinted by permission of Alfred A. Knopf, Inc. and Futura, London.

Camille Roy: "Oct. 8" printed by permission of the author.

Miriam Sagan: "Erotica." Copyright © 1986 by Miriam Sagan. Originally appeared in *Yellow Silk*. Reprinted by permission of the author.

Leslie Scalapino: "How Can I Help Myself" from *Considering how exaggerated music is*. Copyright © 1982 by Leslie Scalapino. Selections from "Floating Series" from *way*. Copyright © 1988 by Leslie Scalapino. Reprinted by permission of the author and North Point Press.

Carolee Schneemann: "Up Is One Direction." Copyright © 1971 by Carolee Schneemann. Originally published in *Caterpillar Anthology*, edited by Clayton Eshleman (Anchor, 1971). Reprinted by permission of the author. "Daily Paradise" printed by permission of the author.

Christine Schutt: "About Her Love" printed by permission of the author.

Lynne Sharon Schwartz: from *Disturbances in the Field* by Lynne Sharon Schwartz. Copyright © 1983 by Lynne Sharon Schwartz. Reprinted by permission of Harper & Row, Publishers, Inc. and the Virginia Barber Literary Agency.

Ntozake Shange: "comin to terms" from *Midnight Birds* (Doubleday, 1980). Copyright © 1980 by Ntozake Shange. Reprinted by permission of Russell and Volkening, Inc. as agents for the author.